HOW TO DATE A DOUCHEBAG

THE LEARNING HOURS

SARA NEY

First Edition: July 2017
Library of Congress Cataloging-in-Publication Data
How to Date a Douchebag: The Learning Hours – 1st ed
ISBN-13: 978-0-9990253-3-8

Thank you, Internet, for providing the inspiration for the dating quotes at the beginning of each chapter. They're all based on *real* conversations, pick-up lines, come-ons, and texts between actual people.

For more information about Sara Ney and her books, visit:
http://www.authorsaraney.com

To Elliot,
the unlucky bastard who doesn't get his own book.

#ItsNotElliot

xoxo

Sawyer

Rex Gunderson
University of Iowa's Team Manager

R hett Rabideaux is one ugly son of a bitch.

Solid as a brick shithouse, I watch him squat over the practice mat, hands braced for balance, his stance unwavering as Zeke Daniels grapples for a hold on him.

Rabideaux is one of the few on our team that can beat Daniels at his own sport.

Raising the whistle to my lips, I ready myself to blow, to end their practice sparring round, which has turned into a pissing match.

As the new guy on the team—a transfer from Louisiana—Rabideaux is still proving himself, despite his impressive record. Nearly unbeatable, his stats are worthy of the two-time NCAA champion he is, and they're the reason he was recruited away from his university.

Iowa's coaches wanted him. Courted him.

Signed him.

I don't know what promises Coach made to the kid—tutors, more scholarship money, his mug on campus billboards—but it was attractive enough to lure him from the safety of one scholarship for another—and bring him to the lion's den of his rival.

And into my house.

Rhett Rabideaux is my new roommate.

He stands six feet tall as he shakes Daniels' hand with one swift pump. They step away from each other, backs turned, no victor—and no love lost between them, either.

I grab a few towels, holding one out for the new guy.

He snaps it out of my hand, dragging it down his perspiring face. Down the slightly crooked nose that's been broken one too many times. Over his bruised left eye. Over the stitched-up eyebrow, a gash from having his face pressed too hard into the mat at practice last week.

The dude is a mess.

A giant, sweaty mess.

Nonetheless… "New Guy, you coming out with us tonight?"

He pauses, mammoth paws still. "Where y'all goin'?"

I shrug. "I don't know—out. To the bars. Does it matter?" It's not like he knows any of the bars in town, *jeez*. He has to go where we go or he sits home on his ass, alone.

"I don't know. Maybe."

"Word of advice New Guy: when someone extends their hand, you take it."

I'm not going to beg the dude to come out with us, but occasionally, he's fun to have around, and it's nice having fresh blood around the field house.

Rhett mulls my words over. "Who's going?"

Another shrug. "I don't know, a bunch of us guys."

"A sausage-fest you mean?"

"Fuck off."

"So that's a yes?" He laughs.

"Me, Pittwell, Johnson. Maybe Daniels and Osborne." Although to be honest, *those* two are so pussy-whipped, it's not likely. They'll be home tonight, curled up on the couch watching chick flicks, their arms elbow deep inside their girlfriend's pants, or snuggling, or whatever the hell it is they do.

I keep the fact that they're probably not coming out tonight to myself.

Lucky bastards, getting laid instead.

"So, you coming or what? You can't stay holed up at the house all weekend—your dick is going to shrivel up if you don't get laid."

He arches a battered eyebrow. "Who said it's my aim to get laid?"

Aim to get laid? Who the fuck talks like that?

I hold up my hand to stop any weirder shit from coming out of his pie hole. "I'm going to pretend you didn't just say that."

"Whatever." He walks away, tossing his sweaty white towel into the linen cart as he passes it and snatching a clean one from the rack on his way into the locker room.

I trail along after him.

He stops at his locker, stripping down. He shucks his shorts, peels off his shirt, and tosses a glance over his shoulder. "If I go along tonight, are you going to lay off? You're driving me fuckin' nuts."

Wraps the terrycloth towel around his hips.

"No, I'm not going to lay off. I'm trying to show you the ropes, teach you a thing or two."

"You?" He laughs. "You've got to be kiddin' me. What the hell am I going to learn from you?"

"Well, for starters, you're way too nice. Girls always go for assholes. With a face like that, you've got to work harder to make them want your dick."

His lip curls unattractively. "Gee, thanks."

I follow him to the showers.

Zeke Daniels stands under a spray of water, steam rising around him as he washes his black hair. He scowls when he sees me, turning to face the tiled shower wall, presenting us with his massive barrier of a back.

His tattoo—a rising phoenix surrounded by geographical locations—glares moodily at me, too.

"Daniels, tell the new guy here girls like dating douchebags." The asshole ignores me, but I laugh it off—he's always joking around, that guy. "Would you at least tell him he's too nice to women?"

Silence.

"You know how girls are, they like it when you—"

Zeke finally speaks, grunting. "Gunderson, leave him the fuck alone, for fuck's sake."

4

Jesus, so moody this guy. "You going out tonight, Daniels?"

He grunts again, scrubbing his armpits. "Probably not."

"Why? You watching *The DUFF?*"

His arms are raised above his head as he scrubs his hair, and he turns slightly to give me a narrowed side-eye. "Gunderson, why don't you mind your own damn business?"

"Well, are you?"

"No, dumbass. I'm watching whatever the fuck I want to watch."

Yeah right. He's been home three weekends in a row, binging on movies with his girlfriend and playing house with the two kids they babysit.

He looks past me at Rhett and sneers. "Do yourself a favor Rabideaux, don't let this idiot lead you around. You're way too good to be associating yourself as *his* wingman."

He shuts the water off, irritably throwing another glare in my direction. "If you're not showering, Gunderson, climb down out of his ass and get the fuck out of here."

5

"They tried to dine and ditch, but the waiter jumped on the hood of their car and broke their windshield."

Rhett

"**L**et's toast to the new guy!"

Oz Osborne, a senior on the wrestling team, rises to stand at the table where the wrestling team is gathered—the *entire* team, packed into the dining room at some twenty-four-hour restaurant off campus for what they're calling a 'welcome to the team' dinner after practice.

"Here, here! A toast," someone else calls with a snicker.

Osborne raises his water glass in the air, shifting his body in my direction and speaking directly to me. "New Guy, we might question your life decisions based on your choice in roommates"—he shoots Rex Gunderson and Eric Johnson a grin—"*and* your ability to dress yourself but in true U of Iowa fashion, we officially welcome you to the team."

He lifts his water glass higher. "Some of us had our reservations about having you"—he throws a quick glance toward Zeke Daniels, who immediately glowers—"but we've got your back."

"And your front," comes a shout.

"Until you start losing," someone else adds under their breath.

Osborne chuckles and points to me. "He's right. You start losing, we kick your motherfucking ass."

More laughter. "Should we just toast to kicking his ass?"

"Everyone raise a glass to New Guy and make it quick. Daniels and I have to split—his little bro has a play at school or some shit."

The room is filled with cheers and leers from my new, overly rambunctious teammates as they enthusiastically clink water, soda, and coffee cups over the linen-topped table, liquids sloshing onto the white tablecloths. An enormous amount of food clutters the long banquet table: pasta, hamburgers, appetizers, French fries, bottles of ketchup and mustard. A few of them ordered milkshakes and specialty coffee, and there's also ice cream.

I curse under my breath; what a bunch of slobs. Look down at the ketchup near my fork and spoon. "Be right back," I mutter to Gunderson, shoving my chair back and standing. "Gotta piss."

He nods with a smirk, eyes darting around the table. "Take your time."

I make short work of taking a leak, wash my hands, and stare myself down in the mirror. I note my downturned, unsmiling face. The bruises. The hair that could use a cut. The ears that have been crushed one too many times by my headgear throughout the past few years.

Bracing my hands against the counter, I lean in.

"What the fuck are you doin' here, Rabideaux?" the reflection asks itself. "What. The. Fuck. Are. You. Doin' here?"

What the fuck possessed me to switch schools when I could have stayed in Louisiana? Finished out the season a champion, started a career instead of upsetting and disappointing my parents, uprooting myself, moving halfway across the country.

For what? More scholarship money? More expenses paid? To have a face nobody wants to see plastered on a university bill-board?

Has it been worth it?

I take another hard look at myself, disgusted, before straightening.

"Bat-shit crazy is what you are." I curse to myself one last time before tossing the paper towel in the trash.

Unlock and push through the steel bathroom door.

Head back to the table full of—

No one.

I come up short to a dining room of empty tables, save for a few surrounding booths and curious onlookers, families and other patrons eating—but no wrestlers.

The entire damn team is gone.

8

As I cautiously approach the table, our young waitress appears out of nowhere, notebook in hand, pencil stuck behind her ear, frazzled.

She grabs me by the shirtsleeve and, "Thank God you're still here! Phew! I thought you'd all left!"

"What do you mean you thought we'd all left?" I glance toward the door. "Wait, did my friends leave?"

I almost choke on the word friends, the irony of the situation not lost on me. Friends wouldn't pull this kind of shit, and I hardly know these guys.

"Yes, they ran out—I was literally about to freak out, thought for sure you guys were going to stiff me." She prattles on, oblivious to my confusion.

"So wait: what do you mean they *ran* out?" I need her to explain, in no uncertain terms.

"Well, um, I mean...yeah. They, uh, ran out."

"I know what runnin' out means, I wasn't being literal." My fingers get stabbed into my hair, and I feel it sticking up when I take them out. "*Fuck.*"

The young woman flinches.

"They seriously left me?" I clarify. "Are you sure they left?"

I refuse to believe they left me here; we're supposed to be a goddamn team. I was counting on it.

That fucker Brandon Ryder drove me in his shitty, banged-up car, and I'd bet fifty bucks it's no longer parked outside waiting to give me a lift back to the house I share with Gunderson and Eric.

The petite waitress taps me on the shoulder nervously. "Um, I hate to make the situation worse, but, um...I'm assuming since you're still here, you'll be the one paying?"

"I'm sorry—*what*?"

"Paying. For all the food."

Did she say paying for *all* the food?

My head gives an involuntary shake. "What does that mean, *all* the food?"

"They didn't pay. For, um, any of it."

"I'm sorry—*what*?"

"Are you okay, sir?" the waitress asks, taking a step back. "You keep repeating yourself. Are you having a stroke? Or like, maybe a seizure?"

"They didn't pay?" I clench my fists. "Those fuckin'…"

Assholes. Those motherfucking assholes stiffed me with the goddamn bill.

"How much is it?" I brace myself for the total, calculating it at around one hundred, maybe two—two fifty, tops.

"Four hundred and—"

"What!" I shout. I know it's loud, and the restaurant is full of people, but I don't fucking care at the moment. Outraged and pissed doesn't cover the feelings coursing through my blood right now. I want to punch something. "Why the hell would you just let them walk out of here?"

I know I'm shifting the blame, but I don't care. I don't care that this is not her fault. I need someone to blame, and she's standing right in front of me, twisting her hands and looking guilty.

"Sir, they *ran*. I…"

"*Shh*, stop talkin'. Let me think for a minute."

"I'm so nervous, sorry—we've never had anyone walk out on a bill this high before. Usually it's like, way less than this. Sometimes people even take the salt and pepper shakers."

Her eyes flicker to the stainless-steel door I assume is the kitchen, then to the cash wrap at the front of the restaurant where we waited for a table when we walked in. "I could go talk to my manager and explain the situation, but I'm worried she'll call the cops."

The cops?

Shit.

I shake my head, run another hand through my shaggy hair. "Forget it—someone has to pay or they're going to fire you." *Because you let them get up and leave without fucking paying.*

"I'm really sorry."

"So am I."

"So…" She shuffles her feet, hands me the black billfold containing the bill and a ballpoint pen. "Everything is itemized."

How convenient; of course it's itemized. "For my convenience?"

Angry, I snatch the bill out of her hand, unfold it, peer down and study it.

Shake – 5

Soda – 10

Hamburger – 4

Cheeseburger – 2

Chicken sandwich – 1

Shrimp Alfredo with extra shrimp – 1

Side salad – 4

Soup – 3

Spaghetti – 1

Wings – 5

Onion rings – 1

Mozzarella sticks – 1

Fried pickles – 1

Bread basket – 1

Ice cream – 1

Pie – 9

Steak – 6

Who the fuck orders steak at a Pancake House?

I fold the bill back in half, resisting the urge to tear it into a million, tiny, motherfucking pieces.

"Were those guys your friends?" the little waitress interrupts. "Maybe they didn't realize you were still here?"

I shoot her a look; is she couyon? *Crazy?* There's no way she believes this was an accident, and I say out loud what we're both thinking: "They're hazing me."

Shit. They are *hazing* me.

It not only violates the wrestling and athletic department's policy, but also the university's code of conduct. Actually, it also breaches several of the school policies, and there are so many things wrong with this whole scenario, it would take me all night to list them all. If our coaches found out, the team would probably be suspended.

The waitress—Stacy, her nametag says—bites her lip and stares up at me with naïve doe eyes. "It did seem strange when they all ran out of here so fast. One guy tripped on his shoelaces and fell down on the carpet."

I wonder who that could have been, the dopes.

"Yeah, well, guess it serves me right for goin' to the goddamn bathroom, huh?"

"How are you going to pay for this?" The waitress shifts uncomfortably on the balls of her feet before smoothing down her hair. "I feel so bad, but I have other tables to get to. If you don't pay, I really am probably going to get fired…"

Jesus. I cannot catch a break.

"Credit card, I guess."

I pull out my phone and unlock the credit card app, handing the device over to the waitress.

She looks at it, confused. "Do you have an *actual* credit card? I have to swipe it—I don't think I'll be able to scan this. We're pretty old-school here."

I sigh loudly, digging my wallet out of my back pocket, and slap the card in her waiting, open palm, prepared to take it up the ass—metaphorically speaking, of course.

Stacy smiles cheerfully. "Thanks! Be right back!"

Yeah, no fucking problem! I'll just wait right here because I'm not a fucking prick!

And just like that, four hundred thirty dollars and fifty-seven cents I don't have goes down the toilet—and let's not forget about my parents, who are going to kill me, especially after I fought them so hard to transfer to Iowa.

After my payment goes through and I sign for the charge, I walk outside with a receipt almost twelve inches long and try to tuck the damn thing in my back pocket.

Gratuity was included since it was such a large party.

Breathe in.

Breathe out.

Unload all my frustration in the parking lot, cursing up a motherfucking blue streak loud enough to wake my dead grand-mother and scaring the shit out of an old couple walking inside. The woman clutches her little red purse to her chest while her hus-band ushers her inside, both of them staring like I've lost my damn mind.

"Mother*fucker!*" I yell, punching the air with my fists. "Motherfucking assholes!" I kick the curb then let out another string of curses when the concrete stubs my toe. "Fuck. Fuck. *Putain de merde.* Fuck my life!"

The expletives roll off my tongue like a tidal wave but do nothing to ease the rolling storm inside me. I tally off one shitty demerit after the other: at the end of today, I will owe my parents four hundred dollars—*tick.* I'm getting hazed by my goddamn teammates—*tick.* I'm at a college in the middle of nowhere—*tick.* I don't know a single soul except for the assholes that just dicked me—*tick.*

They also left me without a ride.

Tick. Tock.

I yank the phone back out of my pocket to shoot my idiot roommates a text.

> **Me:** *Get your asses back here and pick me up.*
>
> **Gunderson:** *LOL have you calmed down yet?*
>
> **Me:** *Come back and find out.*
>
> **Gunderson:** *Not if you're going to start a fight.*
>
> **Me:** *Just tell me one thing—whose idea was it?*

Gunderson: *I'm not going to say.*

Me: *Then I can only assume it was yours.*

Gunderson: *It wasn't. Dude, trust me.*

Me: *Why don't I believe you?*

Gunderson: *Why would I pull that shit when I have to LIVE with you?*

Me: *Well you did LET THEM FUCKING LEAVE ME HERE.*

Gunderson: *Yeah, because the last thing I need is the team doing the same shit to ME.*

Me: *Thanks a lot asshole*

Gunderson: *Anytime man. Let me put my pants back on. Be there to pick you up in ten.*

Laurel

"Hey, did you see those guys?"

I'm sitting at a diner going over the syllabus for English Lit, making sure I'm not missing any bullet points for this paper I'm supposed to be writing; I can't afford to lose any gimme points.

Leaning back in the vinyl booth, I set down my highlighter and lift my head, raising a brow at my roommate, Donovan.

"What guys?"

"If you tell me you haven't noticed, I'm going to call you a liar." He laughs, spooning a chunk of waffle into his mouth. Whipped cream sticks to his bottom lip, and he licks it before taking another bite. "Lord knows I have."

"I'm not here to find a date."

"Right, but sometimes dates find *you*. Guys can't help but trip all over themselves over you." He winks, shoving more waffle into his mouth. "That is one hunky group of heterosexual males if I ever did see one."

"Aww, poor Donovan," I tease. "Drooling over a group of straight guys."

"Story of my life." He pushes a dramatic sigh out of pouty lips, twirling the straw in his cup of water. "But that's not going to stop me from ogling."

"You don't even try."

"Preach." He pauses to shove more food in his mouth. "Oh damn girl, shit is about to get real."

My head is still bent, highlighter flying in bright strokes across my syllabus. My roommate commentates like a sports broadcaster, giving a full play-by-play of the events happening on the other side of the room.

"There they go folks, ten—no, twelve strapping lads, bolting out the door. Bringing up the rear is number seven, a slow starter with impeccable thighs. Brown hair, this champ is an all-star, but can't stay on his feet."

I glance up, amused. Watch as some guy in a red shirt trips in the doorway, stumbling into the entryway. Caterwauls at the gumball machine. Slams into the parking lot.

"There they go, ladies and gentlemen, and I bet by the way they're bailing, they either owe the tax man or they didn't pay their bill. Which one could it be…"

I crane my neck, glancing across the now empty diner, out the window, to the parking lot, where the large guys—all athletes—are piling like circus clowns into three cars. They peel out, leaving nothing but dust.

My red brows rise. "Dine and dash?"

"Oh yeah, totally."

I tap the yellow highlighter cap on my chin. "I've never seen anyone actually do that."

"Really? You've never ditched out on paying a bill?"

I stare at him, disbelieving. "Are you serious? No! Have *you*?"

"Once." He laughs. "Okay, *twice*, but I was young and stupid and didn't have any money. I also stole the menu and utensils." Chuckle. "So dumb."

I can't argue with *that*, so I concentrate on my meal before it gets cold: short stack of pancakes, breakfast links, hash browns, and iced tea, extra ice.

I peel open a pat of butter wrapped in gold foil, stick it between a layer of pancakes, and wait for it to melt.

"Shit." Donovan's fork is poised above his plate. "Now what's happening?"

I twist in the booth, flipping my long russet hair over a shoulder before resting my arm against the back of the seat. Together, my roommate and I watch as a guy comes out of the bathroom at the far end of the restaurant.

Scans the room, hands on his hips.

Tall and yet somehow stalky, he stuffs his hands in the pocket of an Iowa Wrestling hoodie as he surveys the room, severe brows bent in a frown. Approaches the tables cautiously, halting when the cute little waitress approaches him with a tap to the bicep. Holds out what is obviously the bill, hands gesturing around the room. Points toward the windows and the parking lot where his friends have disappeared.

"Holy *shit*." Donovan chokes on his waffle, swallowing a difficult gulp. "Do you think those jocks left that dude with the tab?"

"Oh, it *definitely* looks like they did."

"What a bag of dicks." His eyes have a hint of sparkle, most likely at the mention of *dick*. "I'm pretty sure that was the wrestling team."

"How do you figure?"

Donovan does a quick onceover of the guy, dragging his bright blue eyes up and down the guy's built frame. His head is bent as he scrawls his signature onto a receipt and shoves it back at the waitress, scowling.

Stalks to the door and pushes through it before standing outside. Glancing around, the goliath surveys the parking lot with his hands on his hips—looks left, looks right.

"Well, for starters, almost all those dudes were wearing some form of Iowa Wrestling garb."

"*Garb*, Donovan?"

"Shhh, don't interrupt my musings."

"In that case, please don't let me stop you—proceed."

"That's it. Those were my musings."

I roll my eyes, attention shifting to the parking lot. The muted sounds of cursing tickle my ears; I strain to hear them. The words might be muffled by the double-paned windows, but from where I sit, I can read the words on his lips perfectly: "Fuck, fuck, *fuck*. Fuck. *Fuck* my life."

Amused, I chuckle to myself, hiding the smile behind a water glass. God, I am such a jerk sometimes.

The guy takes a deep breath. Balls his fists at his sides.

I watch as his wide, hulky shoulders hunch over his phone, tapping furiously on the screen. Then he shouts some more, arms flailing, fists punching the thin air. He really should calm down—the whole red-in-the-face thing is not a good look for him.

"Think we should we offer him a ride? It looks like they left him here, too."

Donovan looks so hopeful, I start laughing. "Oh my God, no! Look at how pissed off he is—there's no way I'm letting him ride in a car with us. He could be a rager."

Donovan quirks a manicured brow. "Relax. He's not going to murder us."

I cut a sliver of pancake, pop the buttery goodness into my mouth. Chew. Swallow. "Yeah, no. Not giving him a ride."

"You are such a bitch." He laughs, going back to his waffle. "You know you'd totally give that guy a ride home if he was hot."

My neck moves of its own accord, and I find myself staring at the kid through the window, at the narrow hips and out-of-style jeans riding a little too high on his waist. The baggy sweatshirt. The shaggy hair he keeps brushing out of his eyes, the angry slashes he calls eyebrows.

He's huge, gangly, and his hair is too long. His face looks beat up, and his nose is bent at the bridge.

Not cute.

Not at all.

Agitated, he bounces in his sneakers on the balls of his feet a few times before pulling that black hood up and over his head, looking like an MMA fighter *itching* for a brawl.

He's pissed off and ranting into thin air, which makes him look kind of crazy.

Donovan is right: I probably *would* give the guy a ride if he was better looking.

But he's not.

So I won't.

"I'm sure he'll figure out how to get himself home," I conclude, stuffing sausage into my mouth. "He looks industrious."

It's not far to campus; he can walk.

"No, he doesn't." Donovan laughs. "He looks like he counts with nine fingers."

Bitchy as it makes me, I join in. "He really does look dumb."

"So, no ride home then?"

I emit an unladylike snort. "Not for *him*—I mean, unless he wants to trot beside us."

No way would I ever give a guy like *that* a ride in my car.

Rhett

"Come on, Rabideaux, we do that to everyone." Gunderson scoffs. "You can't stay pissed at us the entire weekend."

He's standing next to me holding a white towel and a water bottle, extending his arm with the offerings while I do squats with three hundred pounds of weight.

I ignore him, panting from the exertion of the weights over my shoulders.

"Dude, come on. It was a prank."

Knees still bent into position, I stop, narrowing my eyes up at him. "Oh yeah?" The sarcasm is heavy. "They did it to you?"

He shifts uncomfortably, lowering his arms while I continue with my reps. "Well, no…but I'm just the team manager."

Really? That's the first time I've ever heard him phrase it so casually, like his role on the team is no big deal. Normally it's, "Show me some respect, I'm the manager," or "Team manager, but you can call me Little Coach."

Dumbass.

Lowering the bar in my hand to the ground, I set it down gently, turn toward the row of guys working the machines along the wall, and shout, "Daniels." Zeke Daniels, one of our team captains, looks up from the treadmill. "Did the team take you for dinner and stick you with the bill?"

A slow grin spreads across his face, those cold eyes rolling in my direction. Sweat covers his forehead, chest, and armpits. "Fuck no."

He's not the kind of guy you screw with.

Leaving my spot at the squatting rack, I move to the bench press, Gunderson trailing after me like a puppy dog. It's getting on my last nerve. "Gunderson, if you're not going to actually spot me, stop talkin' or get the fuck away from me and find me someone who will."

He laughs it off. "Come on man, you need to let it go. It was harmless fun."

I sit my ass on the bench, straddling it. "Harmless *fun*? That shit cost me four hundred dollars, you fuck. My parents are gonna flip their shit when they get the credit card bill."

"New Guy—"

"No. Fuck you," I grit out.

I point to Sebastian Osborne. "And fuck you."

Then to Pat Pitwell, the *one* guy on the team you can always count on to do the right thing, "And fuck you for not stopping them."

The room is silent. "Fuck all of you."

"It was a joke!" someone shouts from the back of the room. "Don't be a pussy, New Guy."

"Four hundred dollars, assholes," I repeat. "Do y'all see me laughing? I'm not laughing."

Gunderson tries to put his arm around me, but I shrug him off. "Come on, let us take you out. We'll buy you a drink to make up for it."

Is he fucking kidding me? "It's going to take more than a few drinks at the damn bar to make up for that kind of shit."

"Like what?"

I consider it for a few seconds, playing hardball. "Take it off my rent this month and I'll never bring it up again."

Gunderson's lips purse; he glances over his shoulder toward Johnson, who takes my place at the squatting bar with its three hundred pounds.

I watch him for a few heartbeats; I have way more finesse than he does with those weights.

Gunderson whines. "That's not fair. That's like me having to pay two hundred dollars of *your* rent."

Blank stare.

"That's exactly what it is."

"That's not fair."

"Are you fuckin' with me right now?" I laugh. "Are you hearing yourself? I just lost four hundred dollars—you know what, never mind. I've had it with you assholes. I'll pack up my shit and move out."

I rise, snatch the towel out of his hands, and present him with my back, wiping the perspiration off my forehead and chest.

Gunderson sighs from behind me. "Fine. I'll talk to Johnson." He pauses. "*Sooo*…you coming out with us tonight or what?"

Does this guy never let up? And why are they drinking so much during the weekend—I never did that while wrestling for Louisiana. We're only allowed to go out one night a week—one— and tonight is not that night.

I turn toward him, arching an eyebrow. "Dude, it's a *Sunday*."

"So?"

You know that saying *There's no arguing with stupid*? That's what's happening right now—I can see by the expression on his face that there is no winning this argument.

I challenge him again. "You buyin' my drinks?"

The expression on his face is priceless. "What the hell! Now I have to pay your rent *and* buy you drinks?"

My head tips back and I laugh, pulling out the heavy artillery. "It's that or I move out. Take your pick."

"Blackmail? Are you *serious*?"

"As a heart attack."

I can see the wheels churning and burning inside that thick skull of his, and I know he's waiting for me to jump up and start shouting, *just kidding!*

It ain't happening.

Seconds pass and Gunderson holds his ground.

I hold mine.

He narrows his eyes.

Flares his nostrils.

Purses his lips like a goddamn girl before relenting.
"Fine, but we're going to a house party instead."
Cheap asshole.

"My penis might be
your amusement park,
but right now,
it's closed for maintenance.
I'm sorry."

Rhett

Girls.

They're everywhere.

Pretty girls.

Unattractive girls.

Tall girls and short girls.

So fucking many of them I don't know which direction to look first. When my eyes settle on a short blonde with big boobs, I shift uncomfortably on the balls of my feet, letting my back hit the wall behind me to study her from the outskirts of the room.

When she saunters past, my thirsty eyes drink her in from head to toe; with her long wavy hair and petite frame, I appreciate the view from the top of my beer bottle. The cut of her tight shirt. The smile plastered on her heavily made-up face as she settles into her girl pack of friends, draping a bare arm over a brunette with legs a mile long and a skirt twice as short.

Coyly glances over her shoulder.

Catches my eye.

Winks.

I straighten my spine when she does a body scan slowly up and down my physique. Takes in the wide berth of my shoulders, the firm pecs beneath my tight gray shirt. My thick neck. The bridge of my nose that's been broken twice.

Bruised left eye.

Stitched-up eyebrow.

Then…

The light in her eyes dims, interest fading as quickly as it came. I don't bother smiling at her; what would be the point? Instead, I cast my gaze elsewhere before she further dismisses me by turning away.

No big deal; I'm used to it.

The fact that I'm not good-looking is hardly a secret.

It hardly matters to these girls that I'm in the best shape of my life; that I'm toned and cut. That I train relentlessly and am in peak physical condition.

That I'm a really *nice* fucking guy.

That I'm not a douchebag.

That I could fuck all night given the chance. Given the right girl.

They don't care about any of it; they want someone who looks like they just stepped off the cover of a magazine—someone like Sebastian Osborne or Zeke Daniels, two prize douchebags chicks go fucking wild over. Oz Osborne with his pretty face and perverted mouth, and Zeke Daniels with his dark, moody stare.

Stand me next to them in a lineup? I'm the last guy women notice.

The only thing remotely attractive about me is my teeth; my mom calls it my million-dollar smile because I've had so much dental work due to having so many teeth knocked out by a quick knee to the face or an errant elbow while wrestling.

Sucks to be me.

I haven't gotten laid in ages, and the last thing I want is some drunken pity fuck, a castoff from a triad or the undesirable DUFF.

Gunderson sidles up beside me, shoving another beer into my empty hand. He clinks his amber bottleneck against mine, nudging me with his shoulder. "New Guy, you getting loose tonight?"

Getting loose? What the hell does that mean?

"Please stop calling me New Guy."

"But that's your name."

"No, it's not. Knock it off."

"Well, I'm not calling you *Rabideaux*."

I laugh when he scoffs out my last name. Rex Gunderson, the team's manager and glorified water boy, is a couyon—a moron—with balls big enough to tell me *my* last name is dumb.

I bite at his bait. "Why won't you call me Rabideaux?"

"Because holy formal. It sounds like a fucking butler's name, and Rhett is worse. Makes you sound like you're auditioning for some plantation, Civil War-level bullshit."

He's right, it does. Rhett Rabideaux—the whole name is a travesty.

"Thanks for mocking my name, asshole."

"Admit it, it sounds douchey."

"I'll let Mama know you hate it next time I see her, thanks."

"I didn't say I *hated* it, just that it makes you sound like a puss." He takes a swig of beer, eyeballing a group of girls huddled nearby, one of them surreptitiously glancing over her shoulder at him. "So you gonna let loose tonight or what? We only have one night out this week; you should spend it getting laid."

Gunderson might be a fucking pain in everyone's ass, but girls seem to love him. They eat up his pickup lines like filet mignon. The cocky attitude. The stupid expressions. The arrogance and bravado. They love it.

I take a drag of beer. "We went out Friday, remember? You know we're in fuck tons of trouble if anyone posts anything online."

He rolls his eyes. "You've got to start meeting people, dude. You can't keep hanging out with just us. Put yourself out there, New Guy. Go see how friendly the girls in Iowa can be." He lifts his bottle. "Those girls right there—the ones that keep looking over here—go say hi."

I roll my eyes. "They're not lookin' at me; they're lookin' at you."

Much as I hate to admit it, Gunderson is right; I haven't put myself out there. I stay in my room all the fucking time, sticking to myself, here for one thing and one thing only:

Pin.

Win.

Graduate.

Fine, that's three things. Anyway, it helps that Iowa is nothing but corn, fields, cornfields, and highway. Makes the 'get in and get out' that much easier. No attachments. No commitments here. Nothing but all work and no play—I haven't even allowed myself friends from the wrestling team.

"New Guy." Rex nudges me back to life. "If you're going to get laid, you have to be more fucking assertive. You can't be lazy."

"Nah, I'm good standin' right where I am." Against tacky wallpaper in the back room of a crowded party.

Rex leans against it too, turning to face me. "If you're going to insist on being a little bitch every time we go out, let me give you a little word of advice: stay away from Oz and Zeke."

"Why?"

"Dude, they are *way* too good-looking. Trust me, no girl is going to give you the time of day if you're standing next to either one of them."

"I thought they had girlfriends?"

"They do. Actually, I think it only makes them more appealing to chicks."

"Why is that bad?"

"Do you want girls to bang you or them?"

"I'm not having this conversation with you right now."

"What's wrong with you? Are you gay?"

"No."

"You can tell me if you are." He holds up his palms. "No judgments."

"I don't feel comfortable hitting on women all the time, is all. No big deal."

"Why?"

"*Why?*"

"Yeah, why aren't you comfortable hitting on women? What's the deal? I know you're not shy—I've seen you have conversations with the trainers and PTs."

A few of whom are women...*attractive* women.

"I don't want to bone every woman that talks to me, Gunderson."

"*I* do."

He says it with such a straight face that I bust out laughing.

The music blasting from the speakers makes it almost impossible for me to hear him ask, "Seriously though, you want my help or not?"

"God no!" I laugh again, slapping him on the back. "The last thing I need is your brand of help. Sorry Gunderson."

"Come on man, think about it. I could be like your pimp, except without the exchange of money."

Jesus Christ, that sounds horrifying.

"Do me a favor Rex." He leans in with raised brows, interested, nice and close so he can hear me loud and clear. "Stay out of my personal business and stick to handing me clean towels."

"Fuck you," he sneers. "Besides, I don't know if I can do that. I'm too deep in it."

"Try harder."

He emits a juvenile giggle. "You said harder."

"What are you, five?"

"Sometimes."

I prod the beer in his hand. "How many beers have you had tonight?"

He holds it in the air, squinting at it with one eye closed. "I don't know, five? Six? Plus two Jägerbombs."

"What the fuck, Gunderson? We have to be in the gym at five in the morning!"

"No, *you* have to be in the gym at five in the morning. I'm just there to hand you clean towels." He holds up a palm to stop me from speaking. "Don't worry about me, *Dad*. I've got it covered; I bought a gallon of chocolate milk to help the hangover, so I should be good to go."

"Do me a favor and stay away from my room. I don't need you puking outside my door."

Again.

Rex did not make it to the weight room the next morning for practice.

I guess I could have yanked him out of bed when he failed to make an appearance in the kitchen for our morning run, but I'm still reeling from being stiffed at the restaurant—though after four, five, six beers last night, both roommates gladly agreed to split my share of the rent for the month.

The nice thing for me to do would have been to wake him up knowing he was going to miss practice and most likely, his first class.

But I didn't.

I grin, cutting across a patch of freshly mowed grass to the sidewalk that's a direct path to my study group. Bookbag slung over my left shoulder, I emit a soft, relaxed whistle, glancing into the windows of the university's student union coffee shop as I meander toward it.

Kick a stone into the freshly cut lawn.

I'm on my way to spend a few frustrating hours with two girls from my Political Strategies class who know less about fair trade agreements than I do. Best course of action and a minor consolation for this pounding headache? Chugging down a cup of the free coffee offered in the student union to clear my foggy head.

Monica and Kristy do little to get rid of the lingering aftereffects of my late night, asking question after question about foreign policy instead of searching for the answers themselves. It's two hours spent explaining and re-explaining the logistics of agreements between a manufacturer and retailer on products trademarked outside the country.

Giving them one example after another, I eventually drew Monica a damn diagram of how the whole system works.

They just weren't getting it, and I left feeling more like their tutor than their classmate.

Pulling the hood of my black Louisiana sweatshirt over my head, I sling my bag down my bicep, preparing to pull back the door to the corner coffee shop—more free caffeine before heading home because the cup I had before wasn't strong enough to cure this headache, these throbbing temples.

Not even close.

Not after the three weird texts messages I've gotten this morning, all within the past forty-five minutes that have my mind reeling.

Hey hottie. I hear you need to get laid. Call me.

You mite not be hot, but I'd do you anyway.

How do you feel about threesums? My rommates and I would pop your cherry

Two of the three are from people who can't even spell—not even with autocorrect. I delete them, wondering why the fuck they were sent to me in the first place.

My eyes cast a cursory glance at the pile of newspapers by the register, the stainless-steel garbage can in the corner as my hand tugs on the door handle.

Above that? A giant corkboard full of advertisements. Student club signups. Meetings. Tickets to on-campus attractions. Campus ministries. Roommate ads. Furniture and textbooks for sale.

In the center?

A light green sheet of paper, flopping haphazardly, held up by one staple.

I squint, zeroing in on the black and green photocopied face staring back at me.

Me.

My face.

Mine.

My fucking face, photocopied onto a dull green sheet of paper with the words *GET RETT LAID* in a dark, bold scrawl across the top.

Beneath my picture, in Rex's sloppy chicken scratch—the same sloppy writing he uses to sign his rent checks—are the words:

> *Are you the lucky lady who is going to*
> *break our roommate's cherry?*
> *Him: socially awkward man with*
> *average-sized penis*
> *looking for willing sexual partner.*
> *You: must have a pulse.*
> *He will reciprakate with oral sex.*
> *Text him at: 555-254-5551*

I read the caption, then read it four more times, eyes frantically scanning the page, barely registering what they're fucking seeing.

Socially awkward man with average-sized penis...

You: must have a pulse...

"What the actual fuc*kkk*?" I utter in a horrified whisper, grabbing it with trembling fingers and ripping it from the bulletin board.

Jesus. The idiots didn't even spell my damn name right.

"I am gonna kill those assholes," I say as I exhale harshly. "Fuckin' kill them all."

My gaze scans the perimeter of the board for more sheets of green paper, and when I don't find any, I backtrack away from the building, eyes searching for any and all within walking distance.

I stalk down the narrow sidewalk in the direction of our house, halt when I hit the corner crosswalk, smashing the walk button with a closed first.

Once.

Twice.

Again.

"Come the fuck on," I growl. "Hurry up."

After two endless seconds, I can't stand waiting anymore.

"Fuck it."

I look left, look right. Bolt into the street, jaywalking, barely dodging a gray minivan full of teenagers. Flip them the bird when they honk.

Little pricks.

Easing into a light jog, I pant in and out to control my breathing.

Calm myself.

Four minutes later, I dump my backpack on the kitchen table and storm to the living room, knowing I'm about to find them both lying casually like cockroaches on our huge couches.

I fill the doorway, clenching my fists, clenching the wadded-up sheet of green paper in my hand, staring down at them both.

"What the hell is this?" I hold up the flyer. "Have y'all gone bat-shit crazy?"

Rex yawns loudly, stretching to his full length, arms above his head. His eyes stay glued to the TV. "Dude, why didn't you wake us up? We missed conditioning this morning."

I ignore him. "First tell me what the fuck this is." I toss the ball of paper onto his chest.

Rex smirks, snuggling deeper into a black, fuzzy Iowa blanket. "Only the best idea we've ever had."

In my pocket, my phone vibrates with one notification, then another—no doubt more girls wanting to fuck me.

"When did you have time to do this?" My teeth are clenched and my jaw feels like it's about to crack.

"Last night?" He coughs then sighs. "Man, we were so shit-faced."

"Dude," Johnson agrees.

"You did this last *night*? We were together all night—when the fuck did you do this?"

"After you passed out. Remember how we got to talking about how you could use a good fuck? You've been really edgy lately."

"I didn't fuckin' say that."

"Yes you did. You were telling us it's been so long since you've gotten laid that you can't remember how a pussy feels."

"Shut up, Gunderson."

"I'm not making it up." He nuzzles the blanket. "You said you've only had sex once."

Shit. Maybe I did tell them that, 'cause how the fuck else would they know I've only done it once?

"I've only lived here for three months." I unclench my fist and point to the unfurled piece of paper in the palm of Rex's hand. "How could you have been sober enough to use a copy machine?"

"Man, it was hilarious. Johnson went all idiot savant. We went to the dorms and he bribed the RA at the desk to let us use the copier—you know the one with the big rack?"

I do.

"What time was it?"

"I don't know man, one-thirty, maybe?"

Eric rolls over on the couch to point the remote at the TV, flipping through all the goddamn channels while I stand there, outraged. He turns the volume up three octaves while prattling on with the story.

"Fucking Gunderson sits on the printer when the RA walks out and made a print of his ass. I thought the whole machine was going to bust in half. Hilarious, man. You should have seen it."

Rex yawns again. "You were the one tripping over your pants on the south lawn when you stopped to take a piss. I had to help you up."

Jesus Christ, these two.

"Did anyone see you?"

34

"No." Eric scrolls through the channels absentmindedly. "Well, yeah. Some drunk chicks saw us hanging up a black and white of Gunderson's balls and wanted a copy."

My phone vibrates in my pocket. "Unfuckingbelievable."

"It's not a big deal. He has really nice balls."

Rex nods. "I manscape."

My eyes narrow. "What were you idiots thinkin' hangin' pictures of me? Seriously, what the fuck?"

"You need to get *laid*, bro. We're trying to help."

"I'm not fucking desperate! My goddamn *face* is on those!"

Rex hiccups. "Have you seen yourself lately? You're not winning any beauty pageants, sorry to tell you."

Why am I arguing with these two idiots?

Johnson chimes in. "Dude, the only way you're getting any tail is giving it away for free."

"You need all the help you can get." Rex's voice turns soothing. "Buck up, New Guy—be glad we didn't hang all forty-five." He laughs at my horrified expression. "Johnson printed off *forty-five*! The printer just kept going and going, it was so fucking funny."

"Oh, well in that case, I feel so lucky!"

This has him scowling. "Don't get your tampon in a twist, Rabideaux. Have you checked your phone? I bet you have fifty text messages by now."

As if on command, my cell vibrates again, making my butt cheeks clench with irritation.

"Focus Gunderson. How many flyers did you hang?" I need to find them and yank them all down.

"It was only like…" Rex glances at Eric for help. "How many was it?"

Johnson squints at the ceiling, counting them on his fingers. "One, two, seven…fourteen? No, *fifteen*."

Rex laughs, throwing his hands up. "There, see? It was only fifteen. It's not like we hung *hundreds* of them."

"Where are they? How far did you go?"

"I don't know dude, who cares?"

"I fucking care!"

"We were *drunk*." He twists his body, angling for the orange juice sitting on the coffee table. "Around campus. The quad. Freshman housing. I don't freaking know, we were drunk!"

Johnson laughs. "We are so fucking brilliant—so goddamn brilliant I'm kind of jealous of ourselves."

Three more text notifications go off in my pocket. I want to take the phone out and hurl it through the fucking living room window. It spurs me into an angry tirade I didn't know was brewing inside me. "I don't believe the bullshit I'm hearin'. Why the hell would you do this? It's an invasion of my fuckin' privacy!"

"New Guy, I said chill. We thought this whole thing through—we have a plan! First, in addition to the text messages, we're going to create a SnapChat account for you. Then, we're going to—"

"Stop fuckin' calling me New Guy!" I snatch the paper out of Rex's hand and thrust it back at him, flapping it in his face. "This has my fuckin' face on it, dickhead! And you didn't even spell my name right. What the actual *fuck*?"

"Whoa. Calm your tits. If I'd have known you were going to get so upset about this, I would have gone with our earlier idea to place a Facebook status on the Campus Love Connection page."

I can't decide which is worse: having my cell phone number plastered around campus for anyone who wants to text me or having these two morons trying to find me hookups by trolling every social media platform.

Thousands of students creep the CLC page looking for missed connections and hookups, relationships and meaningless sex, crushes and shitty dates with other students at Iowa.

"This is such bullshit—I cannot believe you did this." I ball up the green sheet of paper and throw it onto the floor. "Where are they hung? Y'all are coming with me to take them down."

My roommates glance at each other.

"He said hung," Johnson whispers into the uncomfortable silence.

They both laugh.

"It's fifteen posters; why are you pissed? You need to meet people. You need to get laid, and you're not going to do it sitting around the house." He pulls his phone out from under his blanket, sliding the screen open, and clicks on a familiar app icon. "You really should check your messages. I bet you have shit tons."

"Just tell me where they are so I can go rip them down."

I should have listened when our team captain, Sebastian "Oz" Osborne, tried steering me away from living with these two: *"Rabideaux, do yourself a favor and find someone else to live with. These two are going to drive you fucking crazy."*

Everyone warned me, but I didn't know anyone before transferring—not a soul—and had a short amount of time to find a place if I didn't want to live in the dorms, figured I could stick it out.

I knew they would be annoying, I just didn't think they would be complete douchebags.

I was wrong.

My phone rattles twice before I hit the front door, letting it slam behind me. I check my rapidly growing list of messages.

I'm going to suck your dick [attachment: shot of random girl's small tits]

Hi there, I don't normally do thing like this, but you look cute…

Dude, I'm not a chick but you're a fucking god. Wanna be my wingman? You take all the new numbers from your phone and pass them on to me…

Rett COME GET LAID. Room 314, Wimbly Hall

"Judging by the bulge in his pants, I'm taking this guy home. Why wouldn't I want a dick inside me that looks like a plantation pillar?"

Laurel

"Laurel, please, please, *please* tell me you saw that poster hanging in the quad today."

My cousin Alexandra leans forward with both arms on the table, food on the tray in front of her, sly smile stretched across her dark, gothic lips. Though it's Monday and we've both just come from classes, my cousin's lips are painted crimson red, as if she's just come from a night of clubbing. Black hair flat-ironed. Brown eyes lined with black kohl. Brows defined.

We look nothing alike, she and I—not even close. So different in appearance, even though our mothers are twins. In fact, if you stood us side by side in a lineup, you'd never put us together as related.

Alexandra is tan; I am pale. Alex is short and curvy; I'm tall and willowy. She has black hair while mine is red—and not just any shade of red; my hair is dark and flaming like a brushfire, wavy and wild.

The fact that we're attending the same university and have three more semesters of these little weekly lunch dates she insists on is not lost on me. Alex takes everything I say and reports back to her mother, who then calls my mother, who then calls me.

It's so annoying, and it never fails.

I have to watch everything I say, or it gets repeated. Partying too hard, drunken nights out, guys I hook up with? Repeated.

Absentmindedly, I dig a spoon into my blueberry yogurt. Stare down into the white cream to hunt down fruit before glancing back up. Lick my spoon. "What poster?"

I may or may not have seen it.

Alex rolls her eyes; it drives me insane that she's so condescending, but arguing with her is futile.

"The green ones with some guy's picture on it. It's hill-ari-ous."

I shrug, uninterested. "No idea what you're talking about."

"Are you living under a rock? Let me show you, I ripped one down." She leans at the waist, unzips her backpack, and produces a single sheet of wrinkled green printer paper. "It's some kind of ad to get a guy laid. *Get Rett laid*, see here? Is that *not* hysterical?"

"So hysterical," I deadpan with a neutral expression.

Alex swipes back a lock of her jet-black hair. "The guy is so not cute he has to put an ad up around campus for sex."

"Just because there's a flyer up in the quad doesn't mean he can't get laid. Maybe it's a fraternity prank—has that thought oc-curred to you?"

"It's not rush season. Why would anyone do that?"

Oh my God, is she serious? Because guys are morons, that's why.

She drones on, staring at the paper in her hands. Gives her head a shake. "Not this guy, look at him—he's a real barker. You'd have to put a bag over his head to get me to fuck him."

"Jesus Alex." I shush her even though it's kind of funny. "Keep your voice down."

"Well look at him, Laurel! I wouldn't fuck him, would you?" She tilts her head and studies the sheet of paper, biting down on her lower lip. Slides it across the table, bumping the sheet into my water bottle. "Tell me I'm wrong."

My cousin's smug voice drifts across the table along with the mint green flyer.

My nimble fingers pluck it from the tabletop, smooth out the wrinkles. Blue eyes study the poorly photocopied image that was obviously fingered too soon after printing—ink is smudged in three places.

Even so, the grainy copy doesn't detract from the eyes staring back at me. My stomach flutters.

Holy crap, I know this guy.

My eyes fly over the words someone has sloppily written with black Sharpie marker: *Are you the lucky lady who is going to break our roommate's cherry? Him: socially awkward man with average-sized penis looking for willing sexual partner. You: must have a pulse. He will reciprakate with oral sex.*

Text him at: 555-254-5551

Holy shit—Get Rett Laid is Dine and Dash.

Before I can reread it, Alexandra impolitely snatches it out of my hand with a flick of the wrist. Flips her hair.

Smirks knowingly.

"*Well?*" Her question is laden with impatience only she can get away with. "Would you *do* him?"

No, I would not *do* him.

My lip curls. "Uh, hell no."

"Yes! See what I'm saying? Wouldn't it be funny though," she muses, "if one of us sent him a text and made him think we were going to screw him?"

I point my spoon in her direction, pointing out the obvious. "Do you know how many texts that guy has probably gotten? Tons. He's probably changed his number by now."

I know *I* would if my friends did that shit to me.

One of her black brows rises. "Only one way to find out."

"Alex, the last thing I want is some pissed off wrestler masturbating to my selfies."

Alex perks up—she's a total jock chaser and a sucker for athletes of any variety, cute or not. "How do you know he's a wrestler?"

I give a diminutive shrug. "I think I recognize him. I saw him this weekend, getting a prank pulled on him by his friends. They were all wearing wrestling shirts and stuff so I just assumed."

Alex leans forward, intrigued. "Pulling a prank on him? Like, how?"

"Dine and dash."

"Damn." Her pert nose screws up. "How many guys were there?"

"I don't know." I do a mental calculation. "Fifteen?"

"Oh shit." She's quiet for a few seconds. "I wonder if he's new."

"What makes you say that?"

"Dine and dash, these flyers...sounds like they're hazing him."

I nod slowly. "Yeah, that's what Donovan was thinking."

"You should definitely text him. Give him a proper welcome him to U of I." She winks.

"Ew, no. Alex, I'm not texting him." Because then he'd have my number and heaven forbid he texted me back.

"Why not! It would be funny."

"I know it would, but the last thing I want is some weirdo pervert getting my number. What if he becomes obsessed with me?" I toss my red hair. "God, can you imagine?"

My mind strays to the guy in the parking lot, big and angry and swearing at the sky. With that hoodie pulled up over his hair, he was the poster boy for psychosis.

No, thanks, I'll pass.

"Let's ask the Magic Eight Ball." My cousin giggles. "You can't say no."

It's hard not to roll my eyes, but I manage. "Please do not tell me you carry that stupid thing around in your backpack."

"Heck yeah, I have it in my bag." My cousin winks again. "For moments like this."

All right, so when we were in eighth grade, Alex was given a Magic Eight Ball for her birthday, and ever since, she uses it to make almost all major life decisions. Should I date Spencer Doyle? *All signs point to yes.* Should I go to the University of Wisconsin? *Don't count on it.* Should I go bungee jumping with six random strangers I met on spring break? *Outlook good.*

That damn eight ball has gotten us into trouble more times than I can count. It had us sneaking into an underage dance club when we were seventeen and getting busted. Borrowing our grandmother's Buick for a joyride without her permission before we had our licenses. Going skinny-dipping with that loser Tommy Martin after a field party in high school and getting caught by the farmer who owned the land.

All signs pointed to yes.

All ideas got me grounded.

"Alex, stop using the Magic Eight Ball to make life decisions for you." Us. "You're not a kid anymore." We're *young adults* now.

"But it's fun." She ignores me, digging deep into her backpack, rooting around. Produces the round black orb that's become a staple in her life. I roll my eyes when she begins stroking it like a gypsy caressing her crystal ball.

"Magic Eight Ball, should Laurel send a text message to this Rett person who so badly needs to get laid?"

She flips it over, waiting patiently for the triangle inside to settle, floating in the blue water or whatever it is they put inside that stupid thing. It floats, lilting from side to side, finally settling face up.

I lean in, curious to know my fate. "Let's see."

"Yes." Alex beams, palming it and thrusting the tiny window in my face. "Better get your phone out, loser."

"Ugh," I groan, resigned to my fate. "Fine."

I take the flyer from her a second time, run my finger along the words. Fixate on the ten-digit number at the bottom. Type it into my phone.

Glance up. "Just so you know, I'm not sleeping with some stranger."

My cousin laughs. "Have you suddenly become a born-again virgin?"

"Alex, I have some standards, and this guy…" I give him a cursory glance as I finish poking in his digits. The image, most likely pulled from the wrestling website, shows him sitting stiffly, nose in the air. Shaggy hair. Hooded eyes. Thick neck.

Not my type.

Not even close.

"This guy is so far below my standards it's not even funny." I toss my red ponytail over my shoulder. "Besides, I stopped having casual sex."

Alex scoffs. "Are you judging me 'cause I made Dylan leave his apartment to get chicken nuggets so I could have sex with his roommate, Johnathan?"

"Shut up." My brows go up. "You did that?"

"Duh. I've been trying to hook up with Johnathan forever. You knew that." If she rolls her eyes one more time, they're going to get stuck up there. "He finally caved to the power of the chicken nugget."

"Why don't you just break up with Dylan?" That seems like the easiest solution.

"Because Johnathan isn't ready for a relationship yet."

"Then why are you wasting your time hooking up with him?"

"Be*cause*, Laurel," she sneers with disdain. "Johnathan is president of his fraternity and his parents are loaded."

In case you haven't figured it out yet, Alexandra is attending college for her MRS degree, not for an education; her sole goal in life is to be a trophy wife and appear on the *Real Housewives*. For real.

"Anyway," she drones on. "We've gone completely off the rails here. You're supposed to be messaging this Rett loser. Magic Eight Ball says so."

"All right, all right, all right—but if he starts stalking me or falls in love or won't leave me alone or whatever, I'm blaming you."

"You are so full of yourself," she scoffs.

"So are you," I volley back, tapping out a quick message to this random wrestler.

Hey Rett, is it true that you need to get laid?

Hit send.
Less than thirty seconds tick by before I get a reply.

Rett*: Fuck off.*

I rear back in my seat a little, surprised. *Whoa.* Right out of the gate he's going to be a defensive asshole?
Jeez, screw you.

Me: *You don't have to be nasty.*

I say this knowing he's being put through the wringer by his teammates. I wonder what else they've done to him in the past few weeks that I couldn't possibly know about, wonder how many girls have texted him since the flyer went up.

After three minutes of waiting, Rett still has yet to offer a reply. Irritated that he's ignoring me, I send him another message.

Me: *How many texts have you gotten in the last 24 hours?*
Rett: *Did I not just tell you to fuck off?*
Me: *Is it so hard to answer a simple question?*
Rett: *Who the hell is this?*
Me: *Puh-lease, like I'm going to tell you my name.*

Yes. I type it like that.

Rett: *Then do me a favor and lose this number.*

Me: *Did it occur to you that I might have felt a connection to you when I saw your picture on that green sheet of paper?*

Rett: *Nice sarcasm bitch.*

Yikes. Someone isn't happy.

Me: *How do you know I'm female?*

Rett: *I don't, but either way, you're a giant prick. How's that? Happy now?*

Me: *Calling me a bitch wasn't necessary.*

Rett: *Neither was texting me. Get a fucking life.*

Me: *Weird, that's what I said about you.*

Rett: *Oh, I need a life?*

Me: *If you had a life, you wouldn't be hanging flyers up all over campus, begging for attention.*

I'm saying this to get a reaction from him, knowing none of it is true. A niggling twitch hits my belly—one that feels a little like guilt—and works its way into my subconscious. I know something about this guy my cousin doesn't: this boy is being hazed by his friends and probably didn't hang those horrible flyers himself.

But whatever.

It's still not necessary for him to be a jerk. If he knew what I looked like, his tone would be completely different, I'm sure of it. He'd be kissing my ass.

I give my long red ponytail an arrogant flip.

When he doesn't reply to my barb, I huff, feel my face heat, convinced it's turned an unflattering shade of pink.

"Why do you look so pissed off?" Alex glances up from her phone when I sigh. "Your face is bright red."

"'Cause this guy is being a dick."

"Asshole." Alex nods knowingly. "Figures."

Stop ignoring me, I type. *How do you know I didn't text you because I felt bad your face was hanging all over campus?*

His next comment is biting.

Rett: *I said fuck. You.*

Shit. What if he thinks I'm insulting the way he looks? I mean, I'm kind of a bitch sometimes, but I'm not purposely trying to be mean.

Me: *I didn't mean it as an insult.*

Rett: *Don't care. Whoever you are, take a fucking hike.*

Me: *Maybe I'm beginning to like boys that play hard to get.*

Rett: *Jesus Christ, take a goddamn hint.*

Me: *See now, here's the thing: if you really wanted me to go away, you would have stopped responding by now, or blocked my number.*

I know I'm right about one thing: he's interested enough to keep texting me.

Several long seconds pass and he still hasn't responded. My cousin watches intently from across the cafeteria table, arms folded, expression serene, Magic Eight Ball in the center of the table like she's a fortune-teller. Weirdo.

Impatient, I type out: *Hey Rett, what kind of text messages have you been getting?*

Rett: *Use your imagination.*

Me: *Naughty ones?*

Rett: *Yes.*

Me: *LOTS of naughty ones?*

Seriously, why the hell am I flirting with this guy?

Rett: *Yes. Obviously.*

Me: *Like what—give me an example.*

Rett: *No.*

Me: *Oh come on now, don't be a poo.*

Rett: *Do you ever take no for an answer?*

Me: *Rarely.*

Rett: *You're really annoying.*

Me: *Maybe, but am I as bad as the other girls texting you right now?*

Rett: *Yes, actually.*

Me: *WHAT?! You liar, I am not!*

Rett: *Yes, you really are. I have ten fucking chicks texting me at the same time right now and I can't shake any of you.*

Me: *Ever heard of that little thing called blocking someone?*

Rett: *A smartass, too, I see.*

Me: *A bit, and I'm impressed by your use of the correct TOO, and that you have your commas in the right spots...*

Me: *But seriously, you should be blocking these people. Have you?*

Rett: *No.*

Me: *Well you should—the last thing you need is a ton of jock chasers messaging you.*

Rett: *How do you know I'm a jock?*

Me: *I don't, just saying, in case you are.*

Rett: *If I were blocking people, you'd be the first to go. You're really annoying.*

Me: *You said that already. Besides, how am I being annoying?!*

Rett: *Are you kissing me right now?*

Me: *LOL kissing. What a fun idea, Rett.*

Rett: *Dammit. You know what I meant—you're being annoying. You keep asking stupid questions and won't leave me alone. For the record, my name is spelled RHETT. With an H.*

Me: *Then why is it spelled RETT on the posters?*

I'm not sure why I care to have it correct, but I add the H to his name in my phone.

Rhett: *My roommates are fucking idiots, that's why.*

Me: *Sounds like it. Are they the ones who put up the green flyers?*

Rhett: *Obviously. Do you honestly think I would have done that shit myself?*

Me: *Maybe. Some guys will do anything for sex.*

Rhett: *Well, not me. I would never do that. I'm in a drought, not desperate.*

Me: *Ahh, so you DO need to get laid...*

Rhett: *You're really crossing a line, do you realize that?*

Me: *Yes, but I'm protected by a cloak of anonymity*

Rhett: *What's your name?*

Me: *Can't tell you—cloak of anonymity, remember?*

Rhett: *Fine, play games. It was nice knowing you.*

I bite down on my bottom lip and give Alexandra a side-glance.

"Now what's happening? Tell me," she urges. "You look like you swallowed a dirty, smelly cock."

"He wants to know my name."

"So? What's the big deal?"

"Haven't you heard of stranger danger?"

Alex shrugs her petite shoulders. "Make one up."

"Good idea. Didn't think of that."

"You've never given a guy a fake name? Shit, I do it almost every weekend."

My name is…

Pausing, I feel a smidge guilty. This guy has been treated like absolute shit by his friends, and now I'm about to lie to him—again.

"Why are you hesitating?" Alex asks. "Throw it out there. Give him a name."

Grinning, I type in A-l-e-x, hit send.

Me: *My name is Alex.*

Rhett: *Well Alex, c'était amusant, but I have shit to do*

I sit up straighter. What the hell was that?
French?

Me: *What did that mean??? Cetait amusant or whatever.*

Rhett: *Google it.*

I sit there, staring at the words written in French, and shiver a little. Press down on the words to highlight them, copy and paste them into a translation search, hit enter: *Well Alex, it's been fun, but I have shit to do.*

I stare at that sentence.

French.

The guy speaks French.

Rhett Whateverhislastnameis speaks French.

That is…

Really kind of sexy, if I'm being honest.

I fidget in my chair, biting down the smile caused by learning this new bit of fascinating information.

"Why are you smiling? What's he saying now?"

I lift my head to meet her curious, calculating gaze. "He told me to fuck off and leave him alone."

"Jeez, what a dick."

"Yeah."

But my wheels are spinning now.

At an alarmingly rapid pace.

"I sent him a picture of my boobs
and he complimented my smile.
I'm not sure if I should be totally
offended or pleasantly surprised."

Rhett

"**D**o you assholes have any fuckin' clue how many girls have been texting me? I could punch y'all in the nuts."

"You're welcome."

"That wasn't me *thanking* you."

"But you should." Eric stretches his arm across his body, stretching his shoulder muscles. "Tell us how many chicks are after your tiny cock right now."

I plop down in a chair, tossing the cell onto the kitchen table. "My phone is blowin' up. It was funny the first ten times, but now it's getting old. They're all the same."

Eric pulls a sad face. "Poor poor baby, no one feels sorry for you."

"You wouldn't believe how perverted girls are. I feel violated in so many ways and need a hot shower."

Now he groans. "Only *you* would feel violated by women hitting on you."

"Hitting on me? They're propositionin' me—huge difference. I've gotten more offers for blow jobs in the past twenty-four hours than I can count. It's disturbin'."

"No, what's disturbing is the fact that you're bitching about it. You don't like blow jobs?"

"That's not what I fucking meant."

"Seriously man, how long has it been since your shriveled-up dick has been in someone's mouth?"

"Screw you, Johnson."

The truth is, it's been a few years. The last and only time I got laid was high school: Beth Ripley, a hometown girl who hung out with our crowd and wasn't picky about who she dated. Admittedly, she was kind of easy. Part of the agriculture club, I remember sneaking off with her during a house party, remember her fondling my dick through my jeans before sticking her hand down my boxers.

Beth was aggressive, producing a condom before I could think twice about having sex with her. Verdict: it wasn't memorable, but at least we liked each other. I came within minutes, not long after rolling the condom on.

I had a shit-ton of friends back home in Louisiana, male and female, was the two-time state wrestling champion, highly medaled, and All-American.

College is a different story. Girls want to date athletes who are pro-bound, who come with big egos and enthusiastic groupies. The quarterbacks. Team captains. Basketball players with NBA point guard potential. Fraternity guys. Preppy assholes.

Even nerds have better on campus luck than I do.

Adding to it, the guys on this fucking team have been cold-shouldering me, slow to open their tightknit circle. I'm not counting my roommates, who are outcasts themselves. Eric Johnson has the shittiest win record on the team, and Gunderson is proving to be the biggest fuckstick on planet Earth.

Regardless, pretty girls chase after these two. I regard them now from across the table, both moderately good-looking in their own way. Eric has this oddball sense of humor and pervy mannerisms that girls think are funny, and Gunderson is just an idiot.

Girls come back to the house all the damn time.

I don't get it.

My phone chooses that moment to go off like a bell for a five-alarm fire, and Johnson practically vaults himself over the table, grabbing at my phone, holding it out of my reach.

"I know you're holding out on us, dude. Let's see some of these messages."

It takes him a less than a second to access my texts, his eyes growing wide as his finger moves up and down the screen.

"Holy shit. Gunderson, listen to this one: *I'll blow you if you let me record it.*" He looks up from my phone. "Here's one that just came through—it's a crotch shot."

"Yeah, I've been getting lots of those."

His fingers scroll over my screen, eyes wide as saucers. "Dude, fuck *yeah* you have. Look at this girl's tits! They're huge!"

"Are you putting any of those in your spank bank?" Gunderson wants to know. "Please tell me you're at least yanking it to some of these."

Not that I'm going to admit it to them, but yeah, I am.

I take my phone back just as it pings again.

And again.

I look down to see a text from the same girl who's been texting me for hours.

Alex: *On a scale of one to ten, how bad do you blush when you get a new message?*

Me: *8*

Alex: *That's kind of cute.*

"Who's texting you and why the fuck are you smiling like that?" Gunderson interrupts with his loud, irritating voice and nosy questions. "It's weird."

Jesus. He's so fucking annoying.

"None of your business."

"Is it some girl you're chatting with? Come on, there has to be at least one." He's cackling. "Does this mean you're finally ready to fuck the butt-hurt out of your system?"

"No."

No.

Maybe.

My guard is coming down, so I'm not going to stand here and say the idea hasn't crossed my mind since I started texting Alex. She may have messaged me under false pretenses, but...

I feel like her intentions might be changing the more we message. She texts cute, sounds sassy. Plus, she already knows what I look like and continues to flirt with me.

Bonus.

My phone dings with a new notification and I palm it, walking away from the table, toward my room. I enter and toss myself on the bed, lying on my back, staring at the ceiling.

#DOUCHEBAG

"If he doesn't give you
the same feeling you get
when the pizza delivery
arrives at your door,
fresh and hot, he ain't worth it."

Laurel

" I have yet to meet someone who doesn't bore me to death," my roommate Lana announces, popping a pretzel in her mouth.

It's movie night at our house—Wednesday—one of the few days of the week none of us has a class, and as luck would have it, tonight, none of us have to work either.

Well, my roommates don't have to work tonight, and I don't have my job at the coffee shop anymore because as my parents put it, my new job is to *"study and get good grades with the intention of graduating in four years."*

I have no break in my academic schedule, taking four extra credits and still two classes behind my goal to graduate on time. Playing catch-up with summer classes is going to suck.

"Tell me about it," Donovan says, sticking his giant hand into the popcorn bucket perched on my lap, the three of us side by side on the couch, binging on butter popcorn, gossip, and chick flicks. All three of us are single and looking for a serious relationship.

I'm a junior now.

I'm done messing around with frat boys and one-night stands. After dating man-children who care only about two things—sex and themselves—I'm ready to find something more meaningful.

Don't get me wrong—I *love* sex, I do, and I love guys; I just haven't met one who's wanted more from me. At the end of the day, they're all just boys, really.

I'm tired of being used.

"The guys out there are nothing but fuckboys," Donovan muses with a pout, popping a kernel and chewing. "You think you girls have it rough? Girl, *please*, the gay dating struggle is real."

I snuggle deeper into his large body. "You're all the man we need, Donnie."

"Donnie." He snorts, shoving me off him. "God I hate when you call me that. It makes me sound *so* suburban."

I grin knowingly. "I know."

We hunker down for the next few minutes, quietly watching the movie, a silly romantic comedy about a girl who writes a how-to column for a magazine and spends the entire movie trying to get the guy she's fake dating to dump her.

It's old, but one of my favorites.

Lane peels her eyes from the TV. "What's that cousin of yours up to? Haven't seen her around lately."

I shrug, hug the popcorn bucket, and reach in for a buttery handful. "You know Alex."

Lana twists her torso to study my face. "Why are you saying it like that?" Narrows her eyes. "Did she do something?"

Lana, Donovan, and I met our freshman year, when Alexandra was my roommate and I hid in their dorms as a means of escape when she had guys over, or any of her ridiculously catty friends.

Over the past few years, through honest late-night life chats and plenty more drunken ones, Lana and I have formed an unbreakable bond. An only child, Donovan and I are the siblings she's always wanted, and for her part, Lana sometimes knows me better than I know myself. She knows what's best for me, and I should be listening to her more often, not my damn cousin.

"She hasn't done anything." Not technically.

"Did *you?*"

Shrug. "In a roundabout way."

"Stop vaguebooking and spit it out."

"Can you actually use that term if you're not online?" I ask skeptically, evading the subject, tapping my chin because I know it's cute.

"Stop stalling and just tell us."

I take the braid hanging over my shoulder and pick at the ends, avoiding both their curious glances. "Have either of you seen that flyer around campus? It's green and has a guy's face printed on it?"

"A guy's *face*?"

"Yeah. His face, and his phone number."

"Is this going to be a long story? Like, should I pause the movie?" Donovan asks, already pointing the remote at the television. "Tell me now or forever hold your peace."

I nod. "Okay, so, there are these athletes playing a prank on one of their teammates. They hung these horrible posters around campus—I'm not sure how many, but there's a huge caption above the photocopied face that says, *Get Rett Laid*." I cringe. "They're so bad."

Lana furrows her brow, repulsed. "It doesn't surprise me that someone would do that. People are *so* freaking rude."

I ignore the dig. "Like I said, the posters have his phone number on it..." My voice trails off, gets small. I bury my face in the blanket that's on my lap. "So I texted him."

They both stare at me. Blink.

"What did you just say?" Donovan pokes me. "You're mumbling."

"What do you mean you *texted* him?" Lana narrows her eyes. Out of the three of us, she's the only one with a strong moral compass. "Why would you do that, Laurel? It's mean."

I lift my head, continue picking at my braid.

"What was the point of the posters?"

Do I seriously have to explain it to her? "To get him laid, just like it says."

"You're not having sex with a stranger! Or did you become a prostitute overnight and didn't tell us?" Lana fires off without taking a breath. "Why would you do that, Laurel? *Why?*"

Donovan holds up his hand to stop us both from talking. "No, no, don't tell us, let us guess—Alex made you do it. Your cousin and that stupid-ass voodoo ball dared you to text the poor guy."

"Something like that." I laugh into my shoulder. They know her too well.

Lana nudges me with her pointy elbow. "So? Aren't you going to tell us what happened?"

"So I texted him and it was fun."

They look disappointed. "That's it?"

I shrug.

"Bullshit!" Lana shouts. "That is such bullshit. You can't tell me you sent some poor guy a sleazy text message and not give any details. What kind of an asshole are you?"

"Bore-ring! Boring, that's what kind of an asshole she is," Donovan adds, a singsong lilt in his voice. "That story was fucking boring, sorry."

"And a total lie—you didn't bring this up for no reason, Laurel. There's obviously more to this story, so spill, or I'm going to be horribly disappointed in you."

I pull a split end out of my red hair. "Donovan, remember that guy from the parking lot at the Pancake House?"

"Dine and dash guy?"

"Yeah." I lean forward and grab my water bottle, twist the top off and take a swig. "That's the guy. That's who I was texting."

"Are you *fucking* with me right now?" Donovan scoots forward on the couch, turning to face me. "Seriously? No bullshitting?"

I set the water back on the coffee table we all have our feet on. "Nope, no bullshit. His name is Rhett, and his friends hung the posters—the ones who stuck him with the tab."

Donovan lets out a puff of air. "Damn, I figured they were hazing him but I was hoping they weren't. Hot guys are such assholes." He sighs. "I wish I was dating one."

"No you don't," Lana scoffs. "God, listen to the two of you. When are you going to learn not to settle for the first selfish dick who pays attention to you?"

"After I've been sexed a few times." Our big gay roommate leans his head back on the couch. "I wish I was kidding."

"I don't settle." My face is scrunched up. "I can't help it if every guy I date ends up being a wanker."

Lana sighs. "I love it when you use British slang."

Sly grin. "Thanks. So do I."

The three of us rest our heads on the back of the couch, eyes focused on the ceiling.

"So what's he like?" Lana whispers without turning her head to look at me.

"Well," I begin slowly. "It's hard to tell. Obviously he's defensive about the whole thing since every skank on campus has texted him, so when I sent him a message, he told me to fuck off—but he's warmed up a little." Kind of.

"Is he cute?"

I frown. "He's slightly below average, but fun to talk to."

I can hear her eyebrows rise. "And his name is Rhett?"

"Yeah."

"That's kind of sexy." Lana's voice is wistful. "Like, *Gone with the Wind* southern plantation shit."

"Fiddle dee dee, I do declare," Donovan sits up, fanning himself and not sounding one bit like Scarlet O'Hara. "I'd like to fuck y'all on the veranda."

"Frankly my dear, you can suck my dick," Lana says in a false baritone.

Donovan scowls. "Hey, you stole my line!"

"Shut up you guys." I laugh. "You're the worst."

Lana crosses her ankles on the coffee table. "So what do the two of you talk about?"

"Well, it's only been a few times. Mostly we spent our time arguing because I wouldn't leave him alone."

"You're *such* a clingy bitch," Donovan snarks.

"Shut up, Donovan, I am not!" I smack him on the thigh, pout. "I hate being ignored, that's all."

Lana scoots forward, sucking on her diet soda with a noisy slurp. "The guy would jizz his pants if he laid eyes on you."

I do a mental hair flip but just shrug; I know I'm pretty—beautiful if we're being honest. I've been hearing it since I was young, flattery from strangers, my parents, family and friends.

And, of course, guys.

Guys love me.

My red silky hair. My slender waist and pouty lips. My fantastic boobs.

Vanity is one of my flaws, but I'm not going to pretend to be modest, either. That would be worse.

"Here's what I want to know," Lana says slowly, arm on the back of the couch, leaning into me. "Why did you text him...when you can *call?*"

I bite my lip. "You think I should call him?"

Her brows go up. "Why not?"

Why not indeed.

Rhett's phone rings four times before he answers, the rich quality of his voice reminding me of a lumberjack, a rugged outdoorsman. Masculine and heavy.

Smoky.

Far deeper and sexier than I was expecting when I dialed his number.

"Hello?"

"Rhett?"

Pause. "Who is this?"

"It's Lau—" I stop short, remembering I gave him a fake name. "It's Alex."

Silence.

"Hello?" I ask because the connection is so quiet. "Are you there?"

"Yeah, I'm here. I'm tryin' to figure out why you're callin'."

He's *southern*?

Stop it.

I don't know what I thought his voice would sound like, but I sure as heck wasn't anticipating a slow, lazy drawl with a rich tone. His deep timbre sends a startling shiver running down my spine.

Tryin'. Callin'.

"I..." I can't tell him my roommates told me to call him, or that I thought it would be fun and wanted to know what his voice sounded like. "I called on a whim."

"Why?"

"I felt like talking."

"Can I be honest with you, Alex, so we can stop wastin' each other's time? I'm sure you're really nice, but you seem a little too aggressive, and that's not really my style, so maybe you should call someone else."

Wastin' each other's tiehm...

Oh God, so southern. I wonder what state he's from and how he ended up at Iowa—and why he hasn't told me to fuck off by now. He sounds like a really nice guy, much different than the hypersensitive asshole texting me back the other day.

"What *is* your style?"

Rhett is quiet again. I hear him thinking about his next words. "Look Alex, I'm not trying to be rude, but..." He leaves the sentence open-ended, voice trailing off into dead air.

"But you don't want to talk?"

When he doesn't answer, I pull the cell away from my face to check that the call hasn't been disconnected. The timer at the top of the screen shows the seconds ticking away, so I know he's still there.

"Can you just tell me one thing?"

Reluctance. "Shoot."

"Where are you from?"

"Louisiana."

That makes me smile. "I thought I detected an accent."

The line goes quiet again, and I wonder what the hell I'm doing. This whole conversation is like pulling teeth, and the last time I forced a man into a conversation was never. Why start with him?

But then, "I was raised in Mississippi, but my parents moved back to Louisiana my sophomore year of high school."

"Near New Orleans?"

"No, Baton Rouge."

"Near all the plantations?" A low, amused chuckle greets my ears, making my girly parts get a little bit damp. *Jeez, what is wrong with me?* "What's so funny?"

"That's usually one of the first things people ask when they hear where I'm from."

"What's the second thing people ask?"

"If I've ever wrestled an alligator."

"Have you?"

Another laugh. "No ma'am."

Ma'am.

His accent is doing funny things to my lower belly, so I shift in my desk chair, rest my elbows on my desk, prop my chin in my hand. "Are you always this polite?"

A low chuckle into the receiver. "No."

"I mean, you did tell me to fuck off when I first texted you. I guess that isn't exactly polite, is it?"

"Don't feel bad. I told every single girl who texted me to fuck off." The curse rolls off his tongue, sweet and sour. *Fuck awe-ff.*

"Well that makes me feel a tad bit better," I admit.

"Did it offend you?"

"Not really."

He laughs into the phone again, and if I wasn't sitting down, my knees would be a little weak. Jesus his voice is sexy; it suddenly has me wishing he was a tad better looking.

"So, Alex, where are you from?"

A knot of guilt prickles at the mention of my cousin's name.

"Illinois. Not nearly as exciting as Baton Rouge."

"No alligators?"

"Only at the fraternity house," I joke.

The line goes quiet. "Spend a lot of time there?" he asks quietly, his voice gruff.

"Not really." Not anymore. "That place is a cesspool of bad decisions."

"So if I said, 'Alex, meet me at a frat party Saturday night,' you wouldn't go?"

"If *you* said meet me there, I'd *think* about it."

"Only think about it? Ah, I see how it is."

"What do you see?"

"I think you're tryin' to flirt with me. Am I wrong?"

I want to deny it but can't get the words off my tongue. "Are *you* flirting with *me*?"

"I'm terrible at it, but I think it would be obvious if I was. Besides, I don't even know you."

"You don't have to know someone to flirt with them, Rhett."

"I know that, but it's just not the same, is it?"

"I'm not so sure about that. For example, if I told you the sound of your voice makes my imagination run wild, what would you say to that?"

"I'd say…I'd say…" He stumbles over his words—adorable. "Shit, I don't know what I'd say."

"I can hear you smiling, so I'll take that as a good sign."

I'm smiling too—grinning actually, wide and goofy. I picked up a pen a few minutes ago and have been doodling a cartoon crocodile aimlessly on a notebook, surrounded by little black hearts.

When I look down at the paper, there are dozens of those tiny ink hearts scattered like confetti across the flat surface. "That's good, right? Smiling is good."

"It's *very* good."

"What do you look like?" I can't help asking, though I already know the answer. I want to see if he'll tell me, want to see what he'll say. "I've seen the poster, obviously, but is that really what you look like?"

"Yes." He forces out a strangled laugh.

"You *sound* hot," I blurt out, because he does. The sound of that raspy voice is doing a wild, reckless dance in my stomach, down my pelvis. "What color is your hair?"

"Brown."

"Just brown?"

"What kind of question is that?" he wants to know. "How many browns are there? Is that question a chick thing?"

"A chick thing? Yeah, I suppose it is. Are your eyes brown, too?" I wasn't close enough to see those in the parking lot of the diner, and the photocopy of his face on the flyer obviously didn't translate colors.

"Yeah. *Dark* brown."

I hum, thinking. "Do you play sports?"

"I wrestle."

"How tall are you?"

"Six one." Rhett pauses. "How tall are you?"

"Five-seven. Kind of tall for a girl, I guess."

"What color is your hair?"

"Black," I lie—again, because I can't tell him my long, straight hair is the color of flaming hot cinders. I'm a natural redhead, and he would see me on campus and know me on sight. "My hair is black."

Like Alex's.

"Black," Rhett repeats, mulling it over. "Huh."

"What's the 'huh' for?"

"You don't sound like you have black hair, that's all."

Awll.

"What color hair does it *sound* like I have?"

"I don't know, blonde? Brown? Definitely not black."

"Interesting theory. Got any other interesting thoughts?"

He stops to think for a second, and I hear him rustling around. Picture him climbing onto a bed and leaning against the wall, legs hanging over a twin-sized mattress.

"I do actually."

"Let's hear them."

"All right." Hesitation. "Since I'm never going to meet you in person, I can safely say this without anyone findin' out: I'm beginning to regret comin' to school here."

"What do you mean?"

"It's just not what I was expecting, that's all. The people I've met are..." His voice tapers off and I finish the sentence for him in my mind.

The people I've met are assholes.

The people I've met fuck me over.

The people I've met lie.

The people I've met *can go to hell.*

"The people I've met aren't who I thought they would be when I decided to enroll here. I'll leave it at that."

I don't reply because I feel like a jerk, like one of his teammates that's yanked him around, left him hanging, humiliated him publicly.

I contributed to that.

I'm doing it *right now.*

In the background, I hear banging, muffled shouting. Rhett covers the mouthpiece of his phone and demands, "Hold on *one fuckin' minute*, will you?"

He returns. "I should get goin'. Team meeting in twenty."

"This time of night?"

"Yeah."

"All right, well..." Why do I feel like I'm standing outside on a first date, waiting for my date to make a move? To ask me out again or try to kiss me? Weird.

"Thanks for callin'." That smile is back in his voice.

"You're welcome."

"Alex?"

I cringe. "Yeah?"

"Want to go to a frat party Saturday night?"

My heartbeat hitches and shockingly, I find myself a little breathless.

"I'd love to."

━━━━━━━━━━━━━━━━━━━━━━━━━━━

Me: *What are you up to?*

Rhett: *Just walked in from practice. Eating dinner with my dickhead roommates.*

Me: *How many of them are there?*

Rhett: *Two, but it might as well be ten, they're such pains in my ass.*

Me: *Who do you live with?*

Rhett: *Assholes from the wrestling team. The team manager and a senior named Eric. What about you?*

Me: *I live with my two best friends, a guy and a girl. How did you end up living with your roomies if you can't stand them?*

Rhett: *When I first transferred, I obviously didn't know anyone. Coach set it up.*

Me: *So you're a transfer...I don't think we talked about that.*

Rhett: *Yeah.*

Me: *So you don't get along with your roommates? Doesn't that make it hard being on the same team?*

Rhett: *They're total assholes. They won't stop hazing me and I'm getting tired of it. Jesus, now I sound like I'm whining.*

Me: *No you don't. Everyone knows hazing is against school policy and I'm sure it's against your athletic policies, too.*

Rhett: *Absolutely it is.*

Me: *I never understood why people—guys, especially—put up with that crap. Fraternities and sororities are the worst...*

Rhett: *Maybe, maybe not. Athletes are really bad, but no one ever hears about it.*

Me: *Should you be telling me this?*

Rhett: *Honestly? Probably not. I almost did the other day on the phone, but since I don't know you, figured it was a horrible idea.*

Rhett: *So what about you. You get along with your roommates?*

Me: *Yes. I live with a guy named Donovan, and my best friend Lana.*

Rhett: *Donovan is the guy?*

Me: *Yes, lol. Does that bother you?*

Rhett: *Why would that bother me?*

Me: *I don't know; sometimes when a girl has a male roommate, the guy she's talking to gets all weird about it.*

Rhett: *Is that what we're doing?*

Me: *I mean...I think we've slipped into the weird beginning of something. Don't you?*

Me: *Hello? Why did you go radio silent on me?*

Rhett: *Sorry. I guess I don't know what to say.*

Me: *I didn't mean anything by it.*

Rhett: *I know; I'm a fucking idiot. Ignore me.*

Me: *Impossible*

Me: *Did you have practice today?*

Rhett: *Always.*

Me: *Always? As in, every day?*

Rhett: *Some form of practice, every day, yeah. Sometimes we just work out.*

Me: *How much can you bench press?*

Rhett: *Three hundred plus, easy.*

Me: *What else can you do?*

Rhett: *What do you mean?*

Me: *What else can you DO, wink wink. LOL. Sorry. I was trying to be flirty, but I guess that didn't translate via text message.*

Rhett: *Yeah, I missed the flirting part. I was about to tell you my workout routine LOL*

Me: *Well, if I close my eyes, I can almost picture it.*

Rhett: *Speaking of which, you do know that you could have looked me up on the university's website by now for all my info, right? You know my face from the poster, and you have my name.*

Me: *How do you know I haven't already?*

Rhett: *Have you?*

Me: *No. This way is more fun, don't you think?*

Rhett: *It is.*

Me: *Are you smiling?*

Rhett: *LOL, yes. Are you?*

Me: *Of course.*

#DOUCHEBAG

"I rearranged all the furniture in my living room so I could masturbate next to the window. How is that for spring cleaning?"

Rhett

Alex: *Hey stranger.*

I roll over in my bed and yawn, eyes squinting at the bright-
ness of the phone against the dark as it buzzes, her text an unexpected surprise.

To be honest, I've been waiting all day for a message from
her; when it didn't come, I felt a stab of disappointment. Climbed
into bed and tried to forget about it. Jerked off once to some dirty
pictures on online.

Me: *Hello back. What are you doing?*

Alex: *Catching up on some homework. You?*

Me: *Lying here, deleting some of the pictures and GIFS
chicks have been sending me the last two weeks to clean up
my storage space. There are a ton.*

Alex: *Oh Lord, I can't even imagine. What's the craziest
thing a girl has texted you this past week?*

Me: *You don't want to know, trust me.*

Alex: *I DO I DO I DO!!! SHOW ME! PLEASE!*

Me: *Hold up. Give me a second and I'll show you.*

I grin as I hold the phone above my head, pressing the side
and home button. I take screenshots of the last three pictures in my
gallery.

Alex: *What's taking you so long? Now I'm getting scared—do I want to see these?*

Me: *Probably not, but if I have to see it, YOU have to see it. Please hold while I continue screenshotting for your viewing pleasure.*

Alex: *Oh God. I'm scared. Hold me.*

Me: *You should be. It's horrifying. I mean, it's naked chicks, so it's not really a hardship, but you get what I'm saying.*

I screenshot texts from three girls who sent me very pornographic pictures of their tits, their waxed pussies, bodies the likes of which I will probably never see naked in person.

I screenshot their promises of rim jobs. Heather's text bragging of her talents in bed, her pledge to get me off in various creative ways, to handcuff me to the bed and break my cherry.

Attach the photos to Alex's message. Add a few comments.

Hit send.

Watch for the delivery.

Her reply comes within seconds.

Alex: *DAMMIT RHETT, MY EYES!!! WHY WOULD YOU SEND THOSE?*

Me: *LOL, you asked!*

Alex: *You know that's not what I meant. I didn't ask to see BOOBS, and...and other things! WHAT KIND OF GIRL SENDS THOSE?*

Me: *Dude! You told me to give you the craziest shit girls have been texting me!!! Those three chicks are the craziest! Tits and ass.*

Alex: *Wait, ass?*

Me: *Yes!*

Alex: *Um...*

Me: *You wanna see those pictures, too?*

Alex: *GOD NO!!! Don't you dare send me pictures of some girl's butt. No.*

Me: *LOL. Sorry.*

Alex: *Obviously you haven't deleted any of the boob shots.*

Me: *Obviously not. That's what I'm doing right now, remember?*

Alex: *Guys are so gross.*

Me: *How am I gross because I haven't deleted a few naked selfies girls sent to a random stranger? What's up with the double standard? Come on Alex, you seem cooler than that.*

Alex: *Well what are you doing with them still on your phone?*

Me: *What do you think I'm doing with them? LOL.*

Alex: *Oh my God. I don't even want to know.*

Me: *I don't sit and jack off to them if that's what you're getting at.*

Alex: *Have you shown your friends?*

Me: *Obviously. Those girls have great bodies with some really great...boobs.*

Alex: *Do you want me to send you pictures of MY boobs?*

I pause, hesitating to reply. Do I want to see her boobs? My twitching dick certainly does.

I have no idea who this chick is, but I'd really prefer she didn't stoop to the same level as the girls who texted me have stooped. Don't want her to cheapen herself for the sake of getting some guy's attention, even if it is mine.

However, that doesn't stop me from asking, *Do you WANT to send me a picture of your boobs?*

Alex: *LOL no, but I will tell you this: they're better than those. Mine are bigger. Round. Perky.*

Shit.

I try to visualize what her tits might look like—pale and plump, maybe, in the palms of my callused hands. I'd run them down her smooth skin.

I swallow, the stirring of an erection in my pants a burgeoning distraction as I tap out a reply.

Me: *Guess I'll have to take your word for it.*

Alex: *I have to say, you're one of the toughest guys to flirt with. Why is that?*

Me: *Because I don't know you. I have to trust you first, I guess.*

Alex: *Do you have to trust me to sext me?*

I stare down at my cell, at the word sex wrapped in the promise of erotic messaging. Try not to imagine a soft hand that doesn't belong to me wrapped about my hard dick.

I squeeze my eyes shut, take a few deep breaths.

My phone pings again.

Alex: *Have you heard of sexting, Rhett? Have you done it?*

77

Me: *Of course I've heard of it. I don't live under a fucking rock.*

Alex: *But have you DONE it?*

I don't reply; I'm not going to admit to some stranger that I've never sexted—a stranger that knows what my face looks like yet still insists on flirting.

I could have passed her a hundred times on campus this week and never known it was her. It's a vulnerable place to be when I'm already feeling beaten down.

Alex: *Have you?*

Me: *No.*

There's a silence following that denial, as if we've both grown embarrassed and aren't sure how to follow it up.

I watch the three gray dots on the bottom of my cell screen appear and disappear several times as she types. Deletes. Types. Deletes. Changes her mind then starts again.

I watch those dots—watch them *hard* when they reappear.

Alex: *Are you in bed?*

Me: *Yes. Lying in the dark.*

Alex: *I just turned my light off and climbed under the covers.*

Oh shit.

Alex: *What does your bed look like?*

Me: *It's a queen. Blue quilt and pillows, green sheets. Yours?*

Alex: *Everything is white, including my pale skin, from my head down to my toes. Toenails are a pretty shade of apple green, in case you were interested.*

Me: *Alex, are you trying to...sext me?*

I hold my breath, lying still as stone on my bed. Everything is stiff, including my cock. It's rock hard, pitching a tent inside my boxer briefs, uncomfortably straining against the black fabric.

I'm dying to touch it. Stroke it. Relieve it.

Alex: *Don't you want to?*

Do I want to sext?

Me: *Is this some kind of pity fuck? I know you've seen my picture, so you obviously know I'm not good-looking, which means you're not attractive yourself, or you're trying to get the ugly guy off.*

Alex: *I thought after our phone call the other night we kind of hit it off. Was I wrong???? Tell me I'm wrong.*

Me: *You're not just jerking me around?*

Alex: *I promise you I'm not.*

Me: *You won't even show me your boobs, yet you're going to fuck me with words?*

Alex: *You're starting to sound like a prude, and it's making me feel loose, LOL. I'm not going to beg a guy to flirt with me.*

Me: *Whatever.*

This erection is making me irritable. I have to get rid of it. Want to toss the phone on the bed then toss myself with the palm of my right hand.

Alex: *I'm not kidding; all I have to do is step out of the house and guys fall at my feet. I could screw anyone I wanted, any time of day.*

Me: *Holy shit. You sound like the assholes I hang out with.*

Alex: *Well COME ON! Give me SOMETHING here. What warm-blooded male doesn't want to flirt a little??? You don't want to see my boobs any more than I want to show them to you, and you don't want to sext. Are you gay???*

Me: *I'm not gay, and I NEVER said I didn't want to see your boobs.*

Alex: *Fine then, are you human? Or does cold blood run through your veins?*

Me: *Trust me, I'm warm-blooded.*

Alex: *Oh yeah? How warm are you? Tell me, Rhett.*

Jesus, I can't take it anymore. Her nagging to get what she wants has me turned the fuck on. Throbbing, hot, stiff, hard—take your pick.

Me: *I'm hard as a fucking rock right now.*

Alex: *Is it big?*

Me: *My cock?*

Alex: *Yes.*

Me: *Yeah, I guess.*

Alex: *How big?*

Jesus Christ, I don't know if I can do this. I'm from a small town in the middle of nowhere, population two thousand twenty-nine. Graduating class of two hundred thirteen. An hour and fifteen minutes to the closest supercenter.

Seconds pass before my hand leaves the touchpad of my cell and snakes down the front of my tight boxers, rubbing the hard length between my legs through the well-worn cotton.

Squeeze.

Groan.

Fuck*kkkkkk*.

Alex: *Hello? Say something, I'm so hot right now.*

Mouth falling open, I stroke myself up and down, not giving a fuck if my dick is chafing through the material. Not taking the time to lift the waistband and stroke it properly.

Alex: *You're touching yourself, aren't you? Tell me.*

Me: *Yes.*

Alex: *Stroking it up and down?*

Me: *Yes.*

Alex: *What does it feel like?*

Me: *Hard. Good.*

Alex: *Really good?*

Me: *I mean—it's my hand, so how good could it actually feel.*

Even aroused, I attempt a joke.

Alex: *My hands are smooth and stroking my thigh, all the way up my flat belly.*

Me: *Are your legs spread, Alex?*

Alex: *Are yours?*

Me: *They are now.*

Me: *What are your fingers doing?*

Alex: *They're in the waistband of my panties.*

Me: *What color?*

Alex: *Baby blue, see-through—you can see it all through the lace.*

Me: *Fuck that sounds sexy.*

Alex: *So sexy. What color are yours?*

Me: *Black. Sometimes I don't wear any.*

Alex: *You free ball? Isn't that what guys call it?*

Me: *Yeah—how do you know that, Alex?*

Alex: *I have a brother. He's a pig.*

Me: *Would he approve of his little sister getting off with some stranger?*

Alex: *Could you do me a favor and stop calling me Alex?*

Me: *Uh, okay.*

Alex: *My brother would want to beat you up.*

Me: *He could only try to kick my ass.*

Alex: *Are you a big boy?*

Me: *Fuck yes. All fucking over.*

Jesus, is this seriously me talking right now? I've never said anything that sexual in my entire damn life.

Alex: *God I love hearing you talk like that. You sound so sexy Rhett.*

My name flashing across the screen has me digging into the elastic waistband of my underwear. Pushing down the fabric and sliding my hand inside to free my throbbing dick.

Groaning from the excruciating pain of my need, my want. *Fuck.*

Lifting my hips, I push the boxers down my thighs. Toss my phone to the comforter, spit in my palm, stroke up and down.

My phone softly pings twice and I turn my head, eyes seeking the message preview on the tiny screen. I grab the phone again and with one hand, hold the phone, letting my thumb tap out a reply while the other strokes my cock.

If I close my eyes and pretend, I can almost imagine the hand is hers.

Alex: *Say something Rhett, say something. Christ, I'm begging you. Please, this is making me feel so good.*

Me: *Jesus Alex, my balls are tight.*

Alex: *I'm so...hot for you.*

Me: *I'm gonna come.*

Alex: *Mmm, I can picture you touching yourself.*

Me: *Don't stop talking.*

Alex: *Are your boxers down around your hips?*

Me: *Are your fingers in your pussy?*

Alex: *Yessssss...*

Me: *You alone in your apartment?*

Alex: *No. Someone is in the next room.*

Me: *Are you moaning?*

Alex: *Yes, I can't help myself.*

Me: *Make it loud, let them hear you.*

Alex: *Yesss*

I rest my head against the headboard, letting my one clenched fist do all the work, working up and down the base of my cock. I close my eyes and try to visualize what Alex looks like: long black hair sweeping across her bare breasts and pale skin. Big, bare breasts with dark nipples. Legs spread. Fingers playing with her clit while she thinks about me stroking myself.

With a groan, my balls tighten painfully, pleasure starting at the base of my dick and working its way to the head. As the pre-come slickens the tip, my teeth bite down on my tongue.

I hiss.

Grip the base, jerking it hard and fast. Stroke after firm stroke until I'm coming in the palm of my hand.

My hips twitch. My dick throbs. My vision blurs.

I look down at my phone in a daze.

Alex: *Babe, did you come?*

Babe. No one has ever called me that before.

I blush at the sight of the word, knowing she wouldn't say it if she got a good, hard look at me.

Me: *Yes. All over my stomach.*

Alex: *I want to see.*

Me: *LOL. I'm not sending you a dick pic.*

Alex: *Not even if I beg for it?*

Me: *No fucking way.*

Alex: *I'm so hot for you right now, please Rhett, I'm so close to coming.*

Me: *Sorry, still no dick pic.*

Alex: *Oh shit. God, just the word dick is making me come. What would you do to me if you were here?*

Me: *I'd get on my knees and go down on you. Lick between your legs.*

Would I? Would I have a clue how to do it if I had the chance?

Alex: *Oh God, yes.*

Me: *I'd suck you off until you came on my face.*

Me: *I wouldn't even take your panties off. I'd suck right through the lace.*

Alex: *How hard would you give it to me?*

Me: *However hard you want it, baby. However hard you fucking want it...*

"I can't believe she gave her
friend the play-by-play of our
sexting conversation.
It's like being part of a threesome
I had no idea I was invited to."

Rhett

"**S**omeone remind me why we're here when we have to be checked in for curfew tonight?"

We're standing in the living room of a massive fraternity house on Greek Row, shoulder to shoulder with half the student population. The theme, it appears, is *Revenge of the Nerds* meets *Animal House*, with half the partygoers dressed like a nerd in one form or another—white collared dress shirts tied off above the belly button, black glasses with tape in the middle, short plaid skirts, thigh-high socks—and the other half in togas. Several dudes walk around with sweatshirts that say *College* in white block letters.

I'm pretty sure we were supposed to have paid at the door, but somehow we slipped through without paying the cover.

The music is deafening but the brotherhood game is strong.

And, for the first time since living with Gunderson and Eric, I'm the one who wanted to party. It didn't take much convincing—just the promise of cold beer—but they're both skeptical about the reason I suddenly wanted to go out. This isn't my scene and we all know it.

Still, neither says no the opportunity to get drunk or laid.

"Tell us again why we're at a frat party?"

"To drink free beer?"

They exchange glances. "You're the one who fights us on going out every week."

"I know, but I had a burr in my ass this morning. Maybe I'm sick of sittin' home when everyone goes out during the week."

Gunderson commiserates. "That's true. Zeke and Ozzy are out tonight. Oz's girlfriend James posted some shit on Insta about being at some wine bar, or maybe it's one of those wine tasting places."

"That's the same thing as a wine bar, idiot." Eric can't contain his disdain.

"Shut the fuck up, Johnson."

"Guys, Jesus, keep it down."

We walk farther into the room, into the party, and my room-mates immediately find people they know, girls they've fucked or fooled around with.

"This music sucks," one of my roommates complains.

"Who cares—we're not here for the music." The other one raises his beer in the air, happy to be out on a weekday. "We're here for the puss-aaaa."

Embarrassed, I deck him the arm. "Don't ever say shit like that again."

"Ow dude, that fucking hurt." Gunderson rubs his arm, grumbling. "I just want both of you fuckers to know that tonight I'm getting laid. My dick will shrivel off if I don't, so forgive me in advance for bringing some chick home."

He glances around the room, fingers steepled. "Who's the lucky girl going to be, who's it going to be..."

"You are *not* bringing anyone home tonight." I scowl. "Not tonight. No."

"Fate will decide." Gunderson throws his hands up in mock defeat. "I'm not going to beat anyone off with a stick if they want to fuck me later, that's all I'm saying."

Johnson scowls. "You're the one who wanted to come out. Do we need to start calling you New Guy *Buzz Kill?*"

"Or Boner Killer."

"Cock Blocker?" They take a liking to that one.

"Yeah, good one—I like that. Cock Blocker."

"Let's leave Cock Block to drown his sorrows in the bottle. We're wasting our time standing here in this corner—it smells like sexual repression and nocturnal admissions."

The word is emissions—nocturnal emissions.

God, what a couyon.

Johnson throws up deuces. "Later bro. Don't leave early without us."

"Don't piss me off and I won't."

They offer their knuckles before sauntering off, parting the crowd and wading through like they own the place, leaving me at the edge of the room alone.

Alone to fend for myself in a room packed full of people dressed like nerds and Greeks.

Great.

Easing farther toward the far side of the room, I plant myself against the wall, eyes scanning every face among the crowd, searching for long black hair in a sea of blonde and brown, and some neon colors like blue and pink.

Uneasy, I pick at the label on my beer bottle.

Breaking the rules to come out tonight doesn't sit right with me, and coming to meet Alex only increases the anxiety building in my stomach. I want to fucking vomit.

This was such a shitty idea; I'm not equipped to handle this. Have no idea what I'm fucking doing. What I'm going to do when I finally find her and meet her face to face.

Shit, shit, shit.

Panic sets in, my mind in overdrive, palms sweating.

I fiddle with the collar of my navy t-shirt. The logo of a popular Nantucket company sits on the left breast pocket, the only decent, clean shirt I had on the floor of my closet that wasn't wrinkled, dirty, or too dressy and didn't have a wrestling logo from the wrong college.

I feel like a fucking dope.

A bright flash of red across the room catches my eye, and whatever curse graces the tip of my tongue dies in my throat.

There she is, standing in a corner with her friends, laughing. Head thrown back, long pale neck exposed. Long red hair the color of fucking *fire*. Flawless white skin. Dark burgundy lips. Tall.

She's not Alex, but she's beautiful.

No, not beautiful.

Elle est mieux. She's better.

More.

Stunning.

Jesus, is she human? She's gorgeous and I need to shut the fuck up about it already.

I stare—of course I do—and Christ, I feel pathetic with the beer in my hand suspended halfway to my mouth, gaping foolishly from across the overcrowded party.

Black, long-sleeved polka dot midriff top with an expanse of white belly showing, she's not dressed like anyone at the party.

High-waisted shorts with two rows of silver buttons down the sides. Pale legs that go on for miles.

When she raises her eyes and scans the room, I duck my head, face flaming hot. Turn my back and chug. Chug the entire bottle of beer down for liquid courage—I need it just to be standing in the same room with her.

How messed up is that?

I don't know how long I stand facing the wall, but it's long enough that I finish off the tepid amber liquid in my bottle.

Choke it down my throat like I'm chugging warm piss.

Give the ceiling an eye roll and pivot to face the room.

Turn to find the redhead studying me.

Head tilted as her friends talk and laugh next to her, she doesn't pay them one bit of attention; all her focus is on me. She nods absently to the girl beside her, never taking that gaze off my flaming hot face.

A sly smile plays with one corner of her perfectly shaped mouth, the bold, dark lips pursing for a split second.

Honestly, she's so pretty I don't know where to look first.

Do I look directly at her? Or do I avert my eyes?

I find a nearby table and set my empty bottle there, wiping my sweaty palms down my pant legs so I can dig the phone out of my back pocket and shoot off a note to Alex.

Where is she?

She's texted me a few times since we jerked off to each other, each message short and sweet, amusing. I continue building her up in my mind, romanticizing what she could mean to me. I see her as perky, outgoing, kind of an airhead at times, but fun.

Me: *Hey. You coming out tonight?*

Alex: *I was going to, but I changed my mind. Don't think I'll make it, sorry.*

Me: *Why didn't you tell me you were going to stand me up?*

Alex: *I'm sorry! I wanted to stay home instead.*

Me: *You could have texted to let me know.*

Alex: *LOL, I didn't think I had to.*

Me: *You know, I'm only allowed to go out one night a week, and this ISN'T that night. I'm breaking the rules to meet you and you didn't bother showing up.*

Alex: *Your roommates don't seem to mind breaking the rules.*

Me: *Huh?*

Alex: *Wild guess that you're out with your roommates? Did you end up at that party?*

Me: *Yes, but I'm going to bounce. Too crowded.*

Alex: *And you don't like that?*

Me: *No, not when I should have stayed home tonight, too.*

Alex: *So you're heading home?*

Me: *Yeah.*

Alex: *K.*

K? What the fuck? Irritated, I start toward the door, pissed that Alex didn't bother telling me she was staying home then acted nonchalant about it, like it doesn't matter to her one bit that I came out.

Fucking rude and disrespectful; I should have known she was going to stand me up.

I know so little about women and the head games they play, but I should have known this was going to happen. God, I'm so fucking dumb.

Determined to leave, head bent, I push through the crowd toward the door. Stop on the porch to send Gunderson and Johnson a text, knowing they won't give a shit that I'm already leaving.

Pocket my phone and start the descent down the steps of the frat house, out the way I came in. I can't get out of here fast enough—

"Hey," a voice calls from behind me. "Where are you going?"

Pausing at the bottom of the wide porch steps, I hesitate before turning on my heel toward the house.

She's standing there, hip against the massive white column on the porch, flaming red hair and dark red lips scorching under the lights, glossy. Staring down at me, mouth curved into a sly little smile.

She can't possibly be talking to me.

With a shake of my head, I gather my senses, pivot, and keep walking.

Her voice stops me again. "I'm talking to you."

Jamming my cell into the back pocket of my jeans, I watch as the beautiful girl from the party props her elbow against the white pillar, one ankle hooked around the other casually as she stands there with a cup in her hand.

She tries again. "Not having any fun?"

I let my eyes study the length of her hips and long legs, wondering if they're as silky as they look. I examine those legs and the black cork wedges buckled at the ankle.

"I, uh, was waitin' for someone who didn't bother showing up."

"Bummer." She stares down, out into the dark yard. "Didn't feel like getting dressed up in a toga?"

"No. Didn't you?"

"Nope—that's not why I'm here."

"Why are you here?"

Those red, shiny lips curve in the moonlight. "A guy."

Obviously. Girls like her *always* have a guy.

She seems to be taking my measure; even in the dark, I can feel her eyes roaming my body. "What about you?" she asks. "Here for a hookup or just to get drunk?"

"Neither."

"Oh?"

I stuff my hands into the pockets of my jeans, the ones I washed and laid flat to dry, just for tonight. For Alex.

"Are you here for a girl then?"

My head shakes. "I shouldn't have come out tonight anyway, so I'm going home."

"Why shouldn't you have come out? Was she not worth it?"

"I thought she might be, but I was wrong."

Why the hell am I telling her all this? Like she gives a shit.

"So where is she?"

"Didn't bother comin'."

The redhead snorts, undignified. "If she couldn't bother coming, then she's probably not worth it."

"It still pisses me off though, because I wasted my time and could have gotten in trouble."

"Why's that?"

"Athletic code."

"Do you always follow the rules? Because there are athletes crawling all over the place in there." She flips her thumb in the general direction of the house behind her.

"I do when it could cost me my scholarship."

"Ahh, I see." She pauses, rich, glossy hair gleaming under the dim porch light. It's like a sheet of thick satin and looks twice as touchable.

"Are you lost or somethin'? I mean, did you follow me out here for a reason?"

Again, she regards me. "Just curious, I suppose. One second you were staring at me"—she snaps her fingers—"and the next you were gone."

I have nothing to say to that.

"Don't worry, I was staring at you, too." Her soft voice carries in the dark. "Won't your friends inside miss you?"

Not likely, but her statement gives me pause. "Why the fuck were *you* watchin' *me*?"

Yes, it's rude, but come on, both of us know it makes no fucking sense.

A soft little laugh. "Why on Earth would that surprise you?"

Noise and laughter and loud music from inside the house save me from replying. Someone begins chanting, "Chug, chug, chug," and it's quickly followed by raucous cheering. The crowd goes wild.

The front door opens, regurgitating drunk students by the half dozen. Some of them stumble down the wooden steps on unsteady feet, others to the edge of the porch to smoke or talk, make out.

The girl rises to her full height, runs those pale hands along her hips. I watch as her long legs descend the stairs, colt-like in their lithe movements. Her hand slides down the railing, index finger trailing the wood slowly, a catlike smile pulling at her lips.

She stops in front of me when she reaches the ground, our faces inches apart.

It's too dark to make out the color of her eyes, but her black lashes flutter in my direction, long and stark, a contradiction to her light skin.

She's more beautiful up close up than she is from a distance, the smell of fresh air, lemons, and spilled beer hitting my nostrils all at once.

A long finger taps her chin. "I feel like I know you."

"Trust me, you don't."

"Oh, but I think I *do*." She says it in a lazy drawl, red mouth forming each syllable.

"I would remember." I would definitely remember a girl like *this*.

I take a step backward before doing something stupid, like trying to smell her again.

Her mouth downturns into a pretty pout. "You're not leaving yet, are you?"

"I assumed we were done talkin'."

"You don't want me to keep you company?"

I swear, if my jaw wasn't locked down from my scowl, it would fall open from shock. Is this chick for real? She cannot possibly want to stand here in the dark and keep talking to *me*.

Me.

Not when there are fifty better-looking guys inside the house. Better-looking. Hot. The football quarterback. The forward for the hockey team. Preppy fraternity brothers.

What the hell could she possibly want with me?

She sighs. "You're not very chatty, are you?"

"I'm trying to figure out what's goin' on here."

"What do you mean?"

"What do you *want*?" She's way too pretty, way too far out of my league, rank, and status to be talking to me, and we both know it.

"I just wanted to see…" She swallows, her narrow shoulders moving up and down with a shrug. Every perfect line in her beautiful face is illuminated by the porch lights. The porcelain skin. The pert bow of her expertly outlined lips. "It's hard to explain."

I watch as she takes several steps backward to the banister rail at the foot of the stairs, rear end leaning against the wooden pole for support. Watching me, a strange expression crosses her face.

"I don't feel...*familiar* to you at all?"

"Uh, no."

She frowns. "You don't recognize my voice or anything?"

"Should I?"

"No, I guess not." Her sigh is long and wistful. "Aren't you going to ask my name?"

I raise my brows and tilt my head. "Sure."

"It's Laurel."

Laurel. She looks like a Laurel, delicate and beautiful and romantic. The name suits her.

I venture forward a few hesitant steps. She obviously wants to talk, so what would be the harm?

"What year are you?"

"Junior. You?"

"Same. Are you from Iowa?"

She smiles at my reply. "No. Illinois."

"I uh, have a...friend from Illinois that goes here." I slouch, shuffling my weight from one leg to another. "I'm a transfer student on the wrestling team. I was recruited from Louisiana."

"Recruited?"

"For wrestling. I'm a wrestler," I repeat dumbly, wondering abruptly if she's seen the fucking posters with my face and cell phone number hanging around campus.

Maybe she recognized me and followed me out here.

Morbid curiosity—wanted to meet the guy who needs to get laid, live and in person. She recognizes my face; I'd bet money on it.

"You can get recruited your junior year?"

"Apparently."

She doesn't respond to that, instead taking a dainty sip of beer out of the red plastic cup that clashes with her hair. "How is Iowa treating you?"

I shrug. "It's fine."

"Just fine?"

"They didn't exactly roll out the ol' welcome mat." I shift my weight, uncomfortable with the subject.

"Do you have siblings?"

"Yes, two brothers."

"Ahh," she says, relaxing against the newel post. "You look a little rough and tumble, like you've gotten into a few brawls."

Actually, besides with my brothers, I've never been in a single fight my entire life. Never decked anyone or been in a scuffle, not even close. I stay away from trouble, and with the exception of these random nights out with my teammates, I've never been a big drinker either.

That probably makes me the least exciting athlete I know, but I've got standards, and partying isn't at the top of my priority list.

"I might be big, but I'm not a brute."

Her eyes flicker up and down my body. "I can see that."

Laurel's concentrated scrutiny makes me feel awkward, like I'm ignorant and unsophisticated.

"You don't look like the kind of guy who gets off on fraternity parties."

"I'm not."

"So this girl you came to meet—you like her?"

"I was tryin' to figure that out."

"So you haven't met?"

"Not in person." Fuck this is humiliating. "I thought I'd...go outside my comfort zone for once."

"That's sweet." Her voice makes me shiver. "Really sweet."

"Is it?" Shit, do I sound too hopeful? I hope not.

"Yeah, it is. Really nice." She releases her hold on the newel post, taking a few hesitant steps toward me. "Guys just don't care anymore."

"About courtin' you mean?"

"Courtin'." She repeats it almost breathlessly, mimicking my accent, eyes sparkling.

"Shit, sorry, I forgot that's a southern thing. I meant datin'—you know."

"I know what you meant." Laurel tilts her head, studying my face. The lines around her eyes soften, red lips curve. "I like talking to you."

My only reply? Shoving my hands deeper into the pockets of my jeans and shifting on the balls of my feet.

"Can I say something else?"

"Uh, sure."

"I like your voice. It's…" Her sweet voice trails off, pauses. "It's charming."

Charming?

I must look fucking confused, because she laughs, holding her flat belly. "The look on your face right now. Oh! It's so cute. You look so confused."

"Sorry."

"Don't be. I just meant your voice is…perfect. I love your accent. I could listen to you talk all night."

She shivers, a queer expression on her face that I'm unable to decipher. It's disconcerting.

"It's kind of cold. Sure you don't want to go back inside?"

"I was thinking I'd head home if you're heading in my direction. Are you walking?"

"I came with friends, but yeah, I'm walkin' home."

"*Walkin'*," she repeats with my twang. "Would you mind the company?"

"Which way do you need to—"

Just then, there's a commotion on the porch. The heavy door flies open and two girls fall out. Laughing and loud, they giggle their way across the porch, stumbling.

Spot us in the yard, talking.

"Laurel, Laurel, there you are!" She hiccups. "What are you doing out here?" The girl is short with long black hair, and I study her. Cute. "We've been looking everywhere and every over for you!"

The girl is drunk, so drunk.

Laurel's eyes slide closed with a loud groan. "Talking to someone—I'm going to head home. You can go back inside; it's getting cold out."

The blonde girl holds a hand over her eyes, searching the yard like she's scanning the horizon. "Who are you out here with? I can't see." She huffs. "What did we tell you about going off alone? Are you trying to get roofied?"

"Or raped?" the girl with the black hair practically shouts into the yard. "No going off alone, jeez! Do you think I want to play babysitter at a dumb frat party?"

"I'm just making new friends." Laurel holds both her hands up, still facing me. She gives me a wink and a smile, like we're sharing a secret. "I'm fine, see?"

That doesn't stop her black-haired friend from trying to make out my form in the dark. She takes a few steps closer, down the steps to get a better look, squinting through heavily made-up eyes.

"Hey...do I know him?" She points an unsteady finger my direction. "Do I know you?"

"Ugh, let's just go back inside, Alex," the blonde says impatiently, obviously desperate to get back to the party. "She's fine. She's alive. You can tell your moms to chill out now."

Black hair.

Alex.

"Alex?" I ask. "You're Alex?" Wow. I don't know why, but she's much prettier than I was expecting. "You said you weren't coming."

She lied.

"Alex, can you *please* go back inside." Laurel steps in front of me, blocking my view.

Alex ignores us both. "Wait, I do know him. I mean, I don't *know him* know him, but I recognize him."

I don't know what the fuck is going on right now but the wheels are starting to spin real fuckin' fast.

"Alex, please," Laurel begs. "Go inside."

"No, it's okay." I put my hand up to stave her off. "She's who I came here to see."

Alex snaps her fingers, doing a weird little hop and clapping her hands while chanting, "Oh my God oh my God, you're him!"

Her abrupt movements send the beer in her hand dumping over the side of her red plastic cup. "You're the guy! Get Rett Laid! Oh my God, Laurel, that's the guy! Did you tell him it was you? Sexting? Were. Was." She bends at the waist, laughing hysterically. "Where is Dylan? I want sex."

"Oh my God, Alex, please just go away!" Laurel shouts, stomping her foot and pointing at the front door. "Go back inside!"

But drunk Alex only laughs, laughs and laughs and snorts, spilling beer onto the porch. The little blonde beside her gives up holding her cup too, tossing it into the yard with a hundred others.

It lands near my feet.

"Laurel," Alex screeches, drunk. "Dude, has she told you how she tricked you? That was very bad of you to tell her to fuck off, Mister Get Laid. Bad bad bad." She's shaking her finger like she's reprimanding a child.

Face flaming hot, I look back and forth between them.

Alex on the porch. Laurel alongside me.

Laurel is Alex.

I think I'm going to be sick.

I'm not an idiot, so it only takes me an instant to figure out what the fuck is actually going on here, and no way in hell am I standing around to find out the rest. Starting across the lawn, balled up fists jammed into my pockets, I stalk to the sidewalk, step onto the road to cross it as the sound of my name carries in the breeze behind me.

"Rhett, wait!"

Of *course* she knows my fucking name.

She calls it with such familiarity my gut clenches; all those questions she stood there asking me, she already knew the damn answers to.

Mon Dieu je suis bête. *God I'm an idiot.*

I keep walking. Stalking toward campus, back toward my house.

The telltale sound of her heels clicking against the asphalt urges me forward, quickens my pace to get as far away from that girl as possible.

That fucking liar.

That beautiful fucking liar—I hate her already.

God she's gorgeous.

"Rhett, wait. *Please!*" She begs as the sound of her shoes slows, unable to keep up. "Please! Please stop, just let me...ouch! Dammit! Ow. Wait!"

I hear her trip on the sidewalk and gradually slow my gait, stand on the pavement without turning around. I give her a chance to catch up, arms crossed defensively, waiting.

Because I'm a *nice* fucking guy with a conscience and can't leave her alone in the dark now that we've walked this far, not when it sounds like she's gone and sprained her damned ankle.

I hear the hard breathing, the huffs and puffs as she approaches from behind, the telltale sound of limping.

Laurel stops a meager distance behind, close enough that I can see the steam rising from her mouth as she breathes in and out, warm exhalations mingling with the cold.

We're standing in silence as she stares holes into my chest, and I can see her deciding what to say, staring at the same broad shoulders that have already carried the weight of so many burdens this year.

She tries again. "I'm sorry I lied." When I don't respond, she babbles on. "We thought it was funny."

My body stiffens. "Funny."

"I saw you and your teammates at the Pancake House the day they stuck you with the entire bill. I was there with my roommate Donovan, watching." She continues, talking a mile a minute, "Then my cousin brought one of those horrible posters to this lunch date we have every week and basically dared me to message you."

"A dare," I deadpan.

"Yes, but it sounds worse than it actually is because once you and I started talking and I realized you're actually a really nice guy, I felt terrible."

"Because I'm nice? What if I had actually been an asshole? Would you have justified it differently?"

"That's not at all what I meant."

I stare down the street, past her, into the dark. "Well, I'm glad everyone was able to have a laugh. Ha ha."

"You don't always have to be so nice to girls, you know, Rhett? Some of us don't deserve it."

"That's the dumbest fuckin' thing I've ever heard come out of anyone's mouth."

She tries again, shifting on her heels and shaking from the cold. "Some girls *like* assholes."

"Do you?"

"Yes."

"Then maybe you should walk back to the Sig house to find one and let me walk away without making me feel like *I'm* the douche here and not you."

"That's not what I'm trying to do! Why won't you just accept my apology?"

"Because you *say so*?" My snort comes out more obnoxious than I intended. "Because you're *pretty*?"

"No, because I'm sorry!"

"I don't want to accept your fucking apology, okay? It doesn't mean shit to me."

"I don't think you'd be standing here if it didn't mean anything, Rhett."

"You know *nothin'* about me," I mutter the words low and quiet.

"Maybe I want to. Has that occurred to you?"

I have nothing to say to that because I don't believe her. She's just a beautiful, spoiled girl who wants to have her way, and I can't believe I'm still standing here listening to her whine. I'm surprised she hasn't brought on the waterworks.

She seems like the type.

"*Say* something, Rhett," Laurel demands, frustrated, stomping her foot. "*Rhett*."

But I don't. My name on her lips infuriates me more, and I refuse to give this girl the satisfaction.

"It was *just* a joke," she reminds me, tipping her chin up.

"I have enough people shittin' on me right now, okay? I don't need one more."

"It wasn't my intention to mislead you."

"Those are fancy words—did you hear them at the sorority house?"

"Don't be mean. I'm not in a sorority."

"What, they didn't want you?"

Her wounded gaze focuses on me, head tilted to the side, studying my face. "It's beneath you to insult me."

I know it is, and I can't believe those words came out of my mouth. It was petty and now I feel like a fucking dick.

A car drives by, slowing down, everyone in the vehicle staring through the window as they move past, crawling along. We watch until its taillights disappear around the corner up the street.

"Laurel?" I whisper.

"Yes?" Her voice is hopeful.

"Why couldn't you just leave me alone when I told you to fuck off?"

"I'm sorry." Her voice is small.

"How about this: fuck *you*." I walk ten feet before flipping off the night air. "Fuck you, Laurel."

The first text comes just an hour later.

Laurel: *Rhett, I'm sorry. I truly am.*

Laurel: *Rhett, I know you didn't block my number. I can see the conversation dots moving at the bottom of the screen...*

Laurel: *Would you please say something? Anything at all.*

I've finally had enough. I pick up my phone and angrily pound out a reply.

Me: *Why? So YOU feel better? You're not the one who's been getting shit on week after week, are you?*

Laurel: *No.*

Me: *Right. At least we agree on something. Do me a favor: you and your bitchy little friends can leave me the fuck alone.*

Laurel: *We will. I'm sorry...*

"He took my underwear
off with his teeth then decided
he only wanted to snuggle.
Dear lord, is this the female
version of blue balls?"

Laurel

He's seated at a table in the far corner when I spot him from the door. He's not hard to miss—not with his purple Louisiana t-shirt in a sea of black and yellow, big wide shoulders, and wavy mussed hair.

He's slouching, hunched over his table.

Defeated. *Tired.*

My stomach rolls with guilt, guilt that has me rooted to the spot in the doorway, watching him.

Just watching.

For the entire four minutes I stand here, he sits immobile, studying his laptop, eyes moving along the screen, completely transfixed by whatever he's reading.

Learning.

"Just go over there," I whisper to myself, blowing out a puff of pent-up air.

I put one foot in front of the other and begin toward him, spine ramrod straight, steeling myself, prepared for another argument.

Twenty feet.

Fifteen.

Eight.

Two.

"Hi."

No reply.

"Do you mind if I sit here?" I lay my hand on the back of the wooden chair across from him, intending to pull it out.

He stiffens but doesn't lift his head. "Yes I mind."

"Would you mind if I sat at the table next to you?" I'm pushing his buttons, looking for a reaction, but he only spares me a brief glance.

Shrugs. "Free country."

I bite my lip to hide a smile, glad he didn't tell me to take a hike. "I guess I deserve that rebuff."

Up goes one eyebrow. "Rebuff?"

"Yes, that's when you—"

He snorts but still doesn't look at me. "I know what a rebuff is, Laurel. I'm just surprised *you* do."

Shit. I get that he's pissed, but does he have to be such a jerk? I huff, loudly. "You don't have to be mean."

"Oh, I'm so sorry. I didn't realize you, of all people, were so sensitive. Guess you're not a fan of being on the receivin' end of a *joke*."

My fingers grip the chair across from him tighter. "I get what you're doing."

"Jokes are supposed to be funny, right? Ha ha."

"I guess I deserve that," I allow, shifting on the balls of my feet, transferring the weight of my backpack from one shoulder to the other. It's getting heavy and I don't know how long I want to stand here holding it. "So, can I sit here?"

"I don't know why you'd *want* to."

"Because I..." I can't finish the sentence because I don't know what to say.

"You want to sit here because you feel bad? You feel guilty? You want to apologize again?" He's rattling off questions, rapid-fire, but still not looking at me. "Trust me, whatever you have to say, you can stop worrying about it. I'm over it."

What a liar.

"Rhett, please, I'm trying here."

He grumbles under his breath in a language I can't understand. "Oui en effet."

"Why won't you at least *look* at me?"

This time his hands pause above his laptop keys. He lifts his face and narrows his eyes—his dark brown eyes.

"You're a real bitch, do you know that?"

"I-I…" My mouth falls open. "No need to be so harsh."

"You honestly thought all that shit was cute, didn't you? Texting and sexting me then showing your fucking cousin."

"No. That's not how it was."

"Do you think you can pull that shit because you're pretty? Think you can do whatever you want?"

"*No.*" I mean, *sometimes*, yes.

"God, I'm such a fucking idiot. I should have known."

"I didn't show my cousin the texts, I swear. I just told her about them because she kept asking."

"What's the difference? Telling and showing are still invading my privacy."

I roll my eyes. "Only if you're going to be literal."

"She knew you texted me as a joke."

"Yes."

"And she knew about the sexting."

I blush. "Yes."

"Sex isn't a big deal to you, huh?"

"I didn't say that."

"But you don't believe in privacy?"

I groan. Why is he being so stubborn? "The only thing I lied about was my name. Fine, *and* my hair color. It's not like I did anything terrible. I'm *sorry*. How many times are you going to make me say it?"

Those wide shoulders lift nonchalantly. "You're the one who walked over here. I told you to leave me alone."

True, but this is going to drive me nuts. "You're wrong about me, you know—sex *is* a big deal, and so is my privacy," I say in a defeated voice, bravado gone.

"Whatever." Rhett takes a pair of ear buds off the table, stuffs them in his ears. Lowers his head.

My bag is heavy and I hoist it, unsure.

I know he doesn't want anything to do with me, and I respect and understand why, I just…

Can't let it go.

Can't.

And yet, I don't know what else there is to say to him. What can I do to make it better? Nothing.

There's nothing.

Just as I'm about to give up and walk away, "Laurel, either sit *down* or walk away." He shoves the chair I'm gripping out with his foot.

Thank *God.*

I hurry to set my bag down in the extra seat before he changes his mind, pulling mine the rest of the way out so I can join him. To study.

Study *him.*

I take another good, hard look while he's pretending to ignore me.

He's certainly not what I'd call cute, or good-looking, or handsome by any stretch of the imagination—and I presume he already knows it.

However…

There *is* something drawing me to him, and I wish I knew what it was so I could make it stop, make this weird fascination I have with him go away.

Maybe it's the fact that he wants *nothing* to do with me. Maybe it's the challenge he presents. Maybe it's his broad shoulders and corded, athletic neck.

The shaggy brown hair hiding his eyes.

The scowl that crosses his face every time he turns his hurt eyes on me.

And, of course, let's not forget this small fact: his friends are determined to get him laid. Plastered his face and number around campus. If that means what I think it means, Rhett is hard up.

Or maybe his friends are just giant assholes.

Total douchebags.

Either way, I love a good challenge, and he's giving me one

whether he intends to or not.

The idea thrills me.

Plopping down across the table, I spread out my supplies, making myself at home as if I have every right to be here. Flip open a textbook, crack open my laptop.

Proceed to ignore the fact that Rhett is resolute in his determination to ignore me.

Get to work on my homework, determined to word vomit enough characters to constitute an entire English Lit paper on *the importance of strong female protagonists.* It's just riveting enough I might actually pull off near perfect points.

Satisfied with what I've written after forty-five minutes of actual working, I hit save then go to save it to an external drive. As I'm about to do that—

"How long are you going to sit there pretending you're not dying to say something?" His low timbre sounds both irritated and resigned.

I raise my head and smile in his direction, pleased he's finally paying me some attention. "Long enough. I was waiting you out, hoping you'd be the first to speak, and you were."

I give him a wide grin, biting down on my lower lip, feigning bashfulness.

He blinks.

Blushes.

Runs a big hand through his hair and blows out a puff of air, like an angry dragon.

I hone in on the fingers in his hair, those rough man hands. The hair on his forearms. The big palms flattening over his unkempt locks.

Okay, so maybe he's not *horrible* looking after all. He's not Quasimodo, the Hunchback of Notre Dame horrible, he's just not...

Cute, or pretty, like some guys are. He's not hot.

At least, not in the conventional way.

Everything about him is *too* something. Too rugged. Too unpolished. Nose too broken. Eyes too serious. Hair too disheveled. Forehead too scarred. Ears too bent.

Ears too bent? God I sound like an asshole.

But I like that he is kind and charming and southerly sweet. A gentleman.

And he definitely seems to need friends—new ones, not the guys who keep shitting on him and leaving him hanging out to dry. Those guys are nothing but trouble.

I've dated guys like that, obviously, the athletes who think they're the kings of campus. They train hard, party harder, and seem to only want one thing.

Sex.

Uncomplicated sex. No-strings-attached sex. No commitments. No emotions.

Just sex.

I wonder if Rhett is the same way, but it's highly doubtful—not with the way he rejected my advances. Didn't bite when I was flirting. Seemed embarrassed by my attention.

Although…he did get off by our sexting because he told me he came all over his stomach. I know he came because I did too.

My cheeks flush, remembering the conversation that's saved on my phone. I may or may not have peeked a few times since, just because. No harm in that, right?

"So you might as well tell me what you're workin' on," Rhett finally says. "Since you're determined to stay sittin' here."

Sittin' here.

"An English paper."

"How's that going?"

I beam. It's nice that he's asking. "Almost done."

He grins then, and I stare, struck by how nice his smile is. How it lights up his face. How straight his teeth are, how white. He actually has really nice, beautifully shaped lips.

A small divot in his chin beneath his five o'clock shadow.

Hmm.

I grab hold of my pen to keep my hands busy and tap it a few times against the tabletop. "What about you? What are you working on?"

"Correcting French midterm papers."

"*French?*" What! "Correcting French papers? What are you, a professor?" I tease.

A soft chuckle escapes his mouth. "I'm a TA for the French Immersion class." He shrugs like it's no big deal.

"Wait, *what?*" Aren't immersion classes the ones where you speak zero English?

"I'm a TA for the—"

I put my hand up to stop him. "No, no, I heard you fine the first time. How are you fluent enough to correct *midterm* papers?"

"It's my second language; my grandmother lived with us growing up and she's old school. She's from the Louisiana bayou, and Creole French was her first language."

"So French is your major?"

"International studies. It felt like a natural fit." He shrugs.

"Wow. International studies? That's...wow. That's unexpected."

"*Oui.*" He laughs, my eyes following the corded muscles in his strong neck. "Mai je suis fort en ce sujet."

My eyes widen, because sweet baby Jesus that was sexy.

Whatever it was he just said, I want to hear more.

It was hot.

I lean in. "What did you just say?"

"You said, 'That's unexpected,' and I said, 'Yes, but I'm good at it.'"

I swallow, shifting my gaze. "So French was the language you used in our text messages."

"Oui. Parfois je ne peux pas m'en empêcher." He laughs, spreads his big hands flat on the table and leans back in his chair. Props his hands behind his head.

I track his movements, eyes raking the hard planes of his pecs beneath the purple tee, the smooth pale skin of his biceps.

Oh jeez Laurel, get a grip.

"What did you just say?"

"I said, sometimes I can't help myself." Another pleasant laugh and the butterflies in my stomach awaken. "It just comes out. I don't know I'm doing it half the time."

"Wow. Did you only speak French growing up?"

A quick nod and his arms come down. "When my Nanan lived with us. We stopped when she died a few years ago, right when I started high school."

"Nanan is your…?"

"Sorry. That's what I called my grandma."

Cawled. "I'm sorry."

His left shoulder lifts. "She was old."

"Yeah, but still. My grandparents were from Poland and I never hear them speak a lick of Polish, just gesundheit when we sneezed."

Rhett wrinkles his forehead, confused. "Gesundheit is German."

I sigh. "I know."

Rhett laughs, low and rich and deep, his neck bent, smiling down at the table, not meeting my eyes. Bites down and drags his teeth across his bottom lip. Back. Forth.

I tear my eyes away, blushing.

"So." I open a new file on my computer to appear busy, shooting a cursory glance over my laptop screen. "A wrestler, huh?"

"All my life."

Obviously. He still has his hands behind his head, so my eyes take another jog along the lines of body, down his toned arms and torso—the results of a lifetime of being physically fit.

He has *really* amazing arms.

"Laurel?"

I snap to attention. "Huh?"

"I asked if you've ever watched wrestling."

"Uh, no." *Not yet.* I make a mental note to Google it later. "Do you love it?"

Rhett shrugs modestly. "I'm good at it."

He's lying again. They don't recruit juniors in college and steal them from other Division I universities if they're just *good*.

"I bet you're not just good. I bet you're *phenomenal.*" I lean forward, watch his eyes dart to the neckline of my plunging V-neck shirt then fly to my face. I smile wickedly. "How do you feel about those little speedos they make you wear?"

This time when he laughs, he throws his neck back, the Adam's apple in his throat moving from the motion. He hasn't shaved today; the coarse stubble covering his neck makes him look harsh and slightly sloppy, like he rolled out of bed and didn't care.

His hair though? It's wavy and looks like he might have actually brushed it. Thick and silky, even if a tad long, just *begging* to have a set of hands running through it.

"Those speedos are called singlets."

"I know that, but it's fun to tease you."

Rhett blushes deep, scarlet red, from the collar of his shirt to the tips of his ears.

"Million-dollar question: does the lack of material ever make you uncomfortable?"

Another laugh. "No. I'm used to it."

"Never?"

"No."

"Does the fabric ever, you know…get stuck in places it shouldn't?"

He wheezes, surprised by my inappropriate question, coughing into his elbow, chuckling. "Sometimes."

"Rhett?" I say it quietly, switching gears.

"Yeah?"

"I know it's not my place to say this, especially since we're just getting to know each other, but you know…" I take a deep breath. "You know your friends are *jerks*, right?"

It's the last thing he expects me to say. "Yeah, I know."

"I've seen some real douchebags in my life, but those guys take top prize. What a bunch of assholes."

"Not much I can do. I'm stuck here for the next two years."

"Stuck?"

"Yup. There's no turnin' back."

"That's right—you transferred all the way from Louisiana."

"Correct, and my parents were super pissed about it, so there's no transferring back." He picks at a sheet of white notebook paper on the table.

"And you're living with those guys? The dine-and-dash crew?"

"Two of them, yeah."

My smile is sad. "You seem like a decent guy. You don't deserve to be treated like crap."

He grimaces. "I know. Trust me, I know."

"Can you tell me about all the hazing that's been goin' on?"

Rhett crosses his arms, the bulk of his biceps flexing beneath the sleeves of his shirt, the fabric straining and stretching across his broad chest.

Nice.

"I guess." His sigh is weighty but he gives in. "Obviously I'm new to the team, right? A few of them have been callin' me New Guy since day one, which drives me bat-shit crazy. My roommates can't stand my last name."

"Which is…"

"Rabideaux."

"Rabideaux," I repeat. *Rab-ee-doe.*

Rhett Rabideaux. I turn the name around in my head, romanticizing it.

Kind of sexy, really.

So *French.*

"What about you? What's your last name?"

"Bishop."

"Laurel Bishop." It slides off his tongue slowly, quietly, like he's saying it to himself and not to me. I see it rolling around in his brain, see him trying it out.

"*Oui*," I whisper.

His eyes crinkle at the corner when I throw out the one French word I've picked up over the years, his dark chocolate irises softening as we regard each other across the library study table.

Those soulful eyes of Rhett's land on the big, messy bun perched and piled atop my head. Fly to my hairline. Eyebrows. Lips.

I smile.

He clears his throat.

"Can we talk about the dine and dash for a second? You know I was there with my friend Donovan." I hedge carefully, knowing it's rude to ask. "How much did that cost you?"

"Four hundred bucks."

"What!" I come out of my seat, indignantly shouting in the library. "Four hundred? Are you *shitting* me? Sorry, I shouldn't swear, but are you *shitting* me right now? That's horrible!"

"Shh, Jesus Laurel, calm down. Sit back down." He leans over, those long fingers yanking on the hem of my shirt, tugging me down into my chair. "I'm still trying to decide how to tell my parents before the credit card statement does the tellin' for me."

I plop back down but, sympathetic, reach across the table and squeeze his forearm...his warm, solid, strong forearm. I'm tempted to wrap my palm around it for good measure. "I am so sorry. That sucks."

He pulls his arm back, drags it under the table and out of my reach.

"Why are you sorry? It's not like you did anything wrong."

"No, but I *did* text you after they put those flyers up, and that probably didn't help."

God, I'm as big a douchebag as those assholes he hangs out with.

9

#DOUCHEBAG

"She's the kind of girl
who misses her mouth
when she eats cereal;
do you honestly think
she's coordinated enough to
screw you wearing high heels?"

Rhett

Laurel's wide eyes are the oddest shade of blue I've ever seen up close. Dark, with a little bit of brown around the edges.

Blue with a heavy liner running the ridge on top, sweeping out at the corner. Her skin is clean and clear, unblemished.

A ginger with no freckles, cheeks a bright pink, lips full and glossy.

Beautiful doesn't begin to describe Laurel Bishop.

She fiddles with her notebook, picking at the end of the metal spiral, lithe fingers fidgeting, bright blue nail polish shining.

"I feel really bad." Her voice is a whisper. "I didn't mean to hurt your feelings."

"You didn't. It's fine."

"Please don't act like it's fine."

I consider this. She's right; I shouldn't act like what she did was fine when it's clearly not. She didn't hurt my feelings, but I can't lie—it was fucking humiliating.

What she did was shallow and thoughtless and shitty.

"All right, fair enough. I won't."

She nods with authority, bun flopping atop her head, the massive nest of red hair lolling to one side. Fucking adorable.

"Good."

My mouth forms a lopsided grin. "Good."

Laurel's blue gaze drifts down my face, staring at my mouth, then the cleft in my chin, before averting her eyes. Her cheeks turn a delicate shade of pink.

What's that about?

My stomach chooses that moment to growl, a reminder that I haven't eaten in—I check my phone for the time—two hours. Considering I'm on a nutrition schedule that has me eating every forty-five minutes to two hours, I'm due for a snack—and by snack, I mean carbs, maybe some protein so I'm not hungry again later.

"Was that your stomach?" Laurel giggles.

"Yeah, sorry. I'm gettin' kind of hungry."

Laurel sets her pen down. "Then let's go get something to eat."

Let's? As in, *together*? Is she serious?

"Pretty sure the sandwich shop in the union closed at ten."

Which was an hour ago.

Laurel rolls her eyes. "I know. I meant pizza or something. I think Luigi's is open until one." She checks the time. "We have tons of time."

"You want to get pizza?" *With me?*

"Unless you're not that hungry? I think I have a granola bar stashed in my bag somewhere if you want it." Laurel leans, making a show of unzipping her floral backpack and sticking her hand inside. "Or maybe an apple?"

"I could do pizza," I say it slowly, weighing my words.

I'm going to regret it later because binging on pizza is a terrible idea with a weigh-in looming; I have to make my weight class or I'm fucked, but if this girl had suggested we eat a steaming pile of dog shit, I'd have gone along and eaten it without protest.

Fuck it. I'll eat the goddamn pizza.

Her eyes light up. "Really?"

"Yeah. Let's go."

When she stands, arching her back to slide into her jacket, there's no stopping my eyes from straying to the thin fabric of her shirt, roaming across her breasts. They linger on the nipples showing through her bra.

My throat tightens and I swallow, glancing away guiltily. Pack up my shit alongside her, hoist my backpack. Instinctively place my hand near the small of her back, guiding her toward the heavy set of exit doors.

"My car is outside if you'd rather drive?" I point in the direction of my vehicle—the black Jeep Wrangler I've had since I turned sixteen, the one that's seen even less action than me.

"Want to walk?" Laurel stalls on the sidewalk. "It's so nice out."

Walking feels intimate, especially in the dark, so I waver. "Uh, *sure*."

"Let's at least put our bags in your car though—I don't feel like hauling my backpack four blocks. I'm not nearly strong as you."

She smiles serenely over her shoulder, and I wonder what it would be like to have a pretty girl like her smiling at me like that for real, like she meant it.

Like she was attracted to me, even for a short time.

"Good idea." I walk around her, reach for the handle of my Jeep, unlock it with the key. "Here, let me get the door. Hand me your bag."

"Thank you."

Our fingers brush when she hands me her backpack by the shoulder straps. I ignore the spark, tossing her bag in the front seat, followed closely by mine. I grab a baseball cap off the dashboard, fitting it to my head backward.

We start through campus, our destination straight on the other side, four blocks away.

It's dark and dimly lit despite all the prospective student information bullshit they give you about blue panic lights and security. It's not entirely safe—not if you're female. The wide center quad is hazy, a grassy knoll dissected by four merging sidewalks, fountain in the center.

Laurel stays close, hands at her sides, shifting as we walk, hips swaying, occasionally bumping into me, so close I can smell her.

We walk in companionable silence, mostly because I have no fucking clue what to say to her. None at all. Do I talk about the damn weather? I don't want to bring up my friends—or hers, for that matter, because they seem like little bitches. School? Hobbies?

Shit.

"So what do you do besides wrestle?" Her soft question breaks the silence as we cut across the lawn, hanging a left at the poli-sci building that's been under construction all semester.

"Good question. I..." I pause.

I almost tell her there *isn't* anything besides wrestling, but I stop myself. Think. Rack my brain, trying to come up with other shit I enjoy doing so I won't sound like a pathetic loser who does nothing but go to the gym every day with nothing else to fill my time. Workout. Watch every fat calorie and carb that hits my lips so it doesn't impact my weight class.

I can't tell her I sit home on the weekends because it's too expensive to fly or drive home to visit my family. I don't go out and party often because I don't drink much—too many wasted calories.

"Do you like movies?" she supplies, glancing over in the dark. The sound of leaves crunching under our shoes accompanies us on our walk.

We have two blocks to go.

I can already see Luigi's lit-up sign glowing in the night; my stomach senses it, too, because it growls.

"Yeah, I like movies. What about you?"

"I *love* movies. I love *going* to the movies." Laurel clears her throat. "It's been forever since I've been to one."

More silence as she waits out my reply, but I don't know what she wants me to say, or if she's hinting at something.

I feel like a freaking idiot.

"What's the last book you read?" I finally ask when we hit a crosswalk, looking both ways before stepping down into the road, crossing to the next city block.

"A romance novel. It took me two weeks because, well, studying and stuff got in the way." She hops down beside me, keeping stride, her elbow brushing my arm. "What about you? Do you like to read?"

"The last book I read was a mystery. I..."

I hesitate, not wanting to sound lame.

"You what?"

"I, uh, spend a lot of time at the public library."

"The public library?"

"You know, the city library, where they have more fiction than at school. I study there, too. Mostly on the weekends."

Laurel makes a little humming sound. "I never thought of studying there—maybe I should come with you next time, if you don't mind the company." She's teasing me again, giving me a little bump with her hip.

Mine singes from the contact.

"It's quiet. I can hear myself think."

"Do you miss your friends from Louisiana?"

I shrug. "I don't think it's the same for guys as it is for girls. Most of my friends were teammates, and they were pissed I left the team. Haven't talked to most of them in a while."

"I bet."

We arrive at Luigi's. I get the door, hold it open so she can enter first.

When Laurel brushes past me, I catch another whiff of her. Whatever she's sprayed on herself or in her hair, it smells fucking fantastic.

She steps up, over the threshold, shooting me a look over her slim shoulder.

"Should we sit there, by the window so we can people watch?"

"Sure. We can watch the drunks heading to the bars."

"That'll be fun. I'll sit while you grab a menu?"

I grab one, head back to the table.

Her eyes rake me up and down, crinkled at the corners, watching. Always smiling at me like she has a naughty little secret, looking me up and down as I move across the room. I fight my initial instinct to look away.

Chin in her hands, Laurel's intense gaze starts at the tips of my black tennis shoes. Lands and holds steady on my crotch. Roams up my chest, my shoulders, the pleasant smile never leaving her face.

Mischievous.

Playful.

Sexy, even with her flaming red hair piled on top of her head like a rat's nest. She has a cute silver headband in her hair, too.

I join her at the table and watch as she reveals a tube of strawberry lip balm, coats her top lip, then her bottom. Smacks them both together, puckering before tucking the tube away, satisfied.

Rubs them together again as she watches me.

When I clear my throat, her eyes flicker to my neck.

"What are you in the mood for?" I ask.

Laurel hums, a little smile playing at her lips as she picks at the corner of the menu. "What *am* I in the mood for? Good question." Pauses. "Extra cheese? And whatever else you want?" Her smile, by all accounts, is perfectly innocent. "I love pizza—I could eat it every day."

She hands the menu back across the table.

I unfold it, pretending to study the damn thing but mentally calculating the money inside my wallet. I think there's a twenty tucked away somewhere, possibly a ten and a few singles to cover a large?

One thing is for sure: I cannot charge this meal on my credit card, although it's possible dinner with a pretty girl would constitute an emergency charge, at least to my mother.

"Let's do a large supreme? With everything?"

"Don't forget the extra cheese." Laurel beams, her straight white teeth twinkling at me.

Jesus. I've never been in such close proximity to anyone so fucking *beautiful* in my entire, depressing life—it's so unsettling that I shake my head to stop from gawking at her.

A waiter comes over to take our order: large pie with everything, extra cheese, two waters. He takes our menu before walking off, shooting a double-take over his shoulder in Laurel's direction, bumping into a table on his way back to the kitchen.

He returns with our waters a few seconds later.

"When is your next wrestling meet?" She sips her water through the straw, pink lips puckered.

"Weigh-in is early Friday morning."

"Weigh-in, does that mean you have a meet soon?"

"Day after next."

Those clear eyes widen. "When do you leave?"

"Bus pulls out first thing tomorrow morning."

"Where are you going?"

"Ohio State."

"Ohio State," she repeats, an awestruck lilt to her tone. "Wow. How many times have you played them? Is that the right word? Played? I have no idea what they call it in wrestling." She's kind of babbling, her laugh light and playful.

"I get what you're askin'. Yeah, I've had matches against them before."

"Wait, if you weigh-in on Friday, isn't eating pizza right now a bad idea?"

Yeah, it really fucking is—it's horrible, as a matter of fact, but I don't say the words out loud because I don't want her to feel bad for bringing me here. Instead, I go with a non-committal shrug.

"Hey!" Laurel perks up. "How do you say pizza in French?"

"Pizza."

"Oh." She looks adorably disappointed. "What about this?" She's holding up a fork.

"Fourchette."

125

"How do you say…" Her eyes scan the room looking for more objects for me to translate. Cup. Table. Bathroom.

"Tell me how to say, 'I hate this red hair.'"

"Tes cheveux roux sont beau." *Your red hair is beautiful,* I say with a straight face. "Tu es belle." *You're beautiful.*

Laurel squints her weirdly hued blue eyes at me. "That was an awful lot of words for 'I hate this red hair.'"

I laugh. Shrug. "I don't make the rules."

When she crosses her arms, her breasts push up. "Were you making fun of me? Be honest."

"Are you for real? No, I wasn't makin' fun of you. Why would I do that?"

"Hmmm." She eyeballs me. "Just making sure."

"Are all girls like this?"

"Like what?"

"Suspicious."

Her laugh is a gentle lilt across the table. "Probably. I'll try not to sound so needy."

The pizza arrives—steaming cheese and toppings set in the center of our table on a metal rack. Cheese oozes off the top when I lift off a piece, and I can't help but mentally tabulate the calories I'm going to have to jog off from each slice.

Probably a few laps around the block tonight, and a few miles at first light, just in case.

Fuck.

Each bite goes down easy, warm and cheesy, and I close my eyes, moaning. Chew. Swallow.

"God this is good." I emit a long groan, cracking my lids. "Christ Almighty, it's been so long."

Laurel gapes blankly at me from across the table, lips parted, eyes wide, entire face flushed. She croaks, "Has it?"

Why is she staring at me like that?

"Shit, yeah. It's been forever since I've had pizza. Definitely not during the season."

"Right." Slowly, she lifts her own slice, nipping off one bite then another, chewing thoughtfully. "How long will it take to burn that off?"

I bite down again. Moan. Swallow. "You don't want to know."

"Are you going home to do sit-ups?" she teases.

"No. I'll probably go for a run."

Her pizza halts halfway to her mouth. "Seriously? But it's dark outside."

"Is it?" I tease.

Her brows scowl. "That's not exactly safe."

She really is fucking adorable.

"No one is goin' to jump me if that's what you're worried about." I laugh. "I run at night all the time."

Her blue eyes start an appraisal of my upper torso, raking up and down and across my chest. My shoulders. Land on my biceps.

Stay there. "That's probably true—I know I wouldn't want to mess with you."

"Have you ever taken self-defense classes?"

"No."

"Do you have mace? Pepper spray?"

"No." She nips at her pizza with a smile, amused.

"You really should, especially if you're going to be walkin' around at night by yourself."

"Could *you* teach me self-defense?"

"Wrestling isn't the same as self-defense, but I could probably teach you a few tricks."

"Oh *really?*"

I gulp down some water. "Yeah, but you and your friends should probably take a class. They're usually free or really cheap at most rec departments."

"Hmm, what if I just call you to be my escort instead?" She wiggles her eyebrows, blue eyes sparkling, alive with interest.

I lean against the wooden chair back, crossing my arms with a firm nod. "You should take a class."

Laurel

Rhett's arms are crossed and my brain automatically does that *thing* it naturally wants to do: checks out his muscles. His dense, smooth biceps and strong arms are overlapping, thumbs tucked under his pits.

He's huge.

My mouth goes dry, the urge to lick my lips strong. I reach for my glass and take a drink of water instead, swallowing down the first real stirring of lust.

Jeez he has a great body.

I snuck peeks at it our entire walk to Luigi's. Rhett's height has him standing over me by a good six inches, and there's no doubt he's packing a serious physique under all those clothes. Hat twisted, brim to the back, his brown hair sticks out from beneath the cap in wispy curls. Broad shoulders, each straining muscle visible under that stretched purple shirt.

Rhett's neck cords with each swallow of hot, gooey pizza.

His dark brown eyes regard me, not a single flash of desire reflected there, although they *do* keep flickering to the mop of flaming red hair piled atop my head, to my lips.

I toy with a piece of cheese dangling from my next slice. "You're probably right. I think it would be smart to take a class. It's something I've wanted to do forever."

I can't help letting my mind wander to what it would be like if *he* gave me a lesson or two—that big, strapping body flipping me to the ground, hovering over me, panting.

I shiver.

Guh.

Down hormones. *Down* girls.

Yes, I've dated insanely attractive guys, guys that are hotter than even *I* am, with amazing bodies and better stamina. Athletes with pedigree, gorgeous faces, and...no personality.

Those guys didn't give a shit about my safety, and they certainly weren't trying to talk me into taking self-defense classes with my girlfriends.

Now, I'm sitting here with Rhett, a nice guy who hasn't objectified me once—not even when we were sexting the other night, no matter how hard I tried to make him take the bait.

I wonder about his track record with women. When's the last time he had sex? What turns him on? Physically, what's his type?

I stifle the thoughts when the bill comes, pull some cash out of my back pocket, slip a ten onto the table.

"I've got it." Rhett shakes his head, pushing the money back toward me in protest. *I've gawt it.*

My chest swells.

He's so polite.

"Rhett, you just had to charge four hundred dollars on your credit card. You don't have to pay for the pizza," I argue feebly. Something about the set of his jaw has me hesitating to push the issue.

He shakes his head. "It'll be fine; my parents will understand the reasons behind it."

"When are you going to tell them?"

"I plan to do it after I win at Penn. They'll watch it on TV, and then I'll call while my old man is high off my victory."

I return the money to my pocket. Stand. Shrug into my jacket.

Rhett waits by the door, holding it open for me like a gentleman so I can step out into the dark night. We walk in silence for the first block while I wrack my brain for something to say, growing more aware of his body heat the farther into the dark we stroll.

"Sorry you have to go jogging tonight."

"Don't worry about it—I'm used to it."

"Want me to come with you?"

He stops in his tracks. "You're a runner?"

I'm thankful for the dim streetlights when my face heats up. "Well...*no.*"

"Oh." He starts walking again, stuffing his hands inside his pockets. "I keep a brisk pace that would probably kill you." He shoots me a sidelong glance. "Do you play any sports?"

"I do. I played volleyball here freshman and sophomore year."

"Why'd you quit?"

Shrugging, I kick at the pavement beneath my feet. "I hate to call it quitting—I'd rather call it burnout. I had no life and got sick of it. Plus, the drama from my teammates and practicing non-stop was exhausting. So one day I just..."

I risk a glance in his direction, wondering if I'll see disappointment etched across his expression.

Athletes don't usually identify with quitters, and if I'm being honest, I fall into that category.

"What did your parents say?" he asks into the night.

"They were relieved. I think they were sick of getting crying phone calls from me every week. Plus, I was a walk-on, not a scholarship athlete, so there was no free ride for tuition. My grades were suffering, and I can't afford to be here five years."

Unlike Rhett, who was courted and recruited by not one, but multiple top-tier universities. I wonder how good he actually is, making a mental note to Google his stats when I get home.

We walk the remaining three blocks, hands brushing a few times in the dark, neither of us choosing to break the distance by stepping away.

We arrive at his Jeep.

"Need a lift home?" His deep voice is a rumble in the night.

My eyes flicker briefly to my SUV parked three spaces down. I clamp my lips shut.

"Sure. That would be great."

Rhett hits his key fob, unlocking the doors. Pulls the passenger side open and holds it. "Hop in."

I get all melty at his chivalry, brush against him when I scoot past to scramble inside, settling into the cab of his Jeep with a sigh. Setting my backpack in my lap, I glance around curiously while he jogs around the front.

He waves to someone coming down the sidewalk from the library. Throws them a smile.

Yanks open his door and climbs up.

"Which way we headed?"

"I'm three blocks in the other direction, over near Kinsey. Know where that is?"

"Huh," he says, putting the Jeep in reverse. "That's where I'm at."

"On Kinsey?"

"Yeah."

"I'm one over—technically I'm at the crossroad, McClintock, but everyone knows Kinsey so I just say that."

"Got it."

I study his profile, the bump in his nose. The strong set of his jaw. The stubble on his neck and chin. The reflection from the rearview mirror like a mask across his dark brown eyes.

Surprisingly, the cab of the Jeep smells clean but masculine. Musky, like cologne, and not old gym socks.

I'm tempted to scoot closer for a covert whiff of him but think better of it because, *Jesus*, I must be losing my damn mind. I can't be attracted to him.

Can I?

Shit, what if I am?

It takes a measly three minutes to reach my street, the glowing windows of our little college rental a small beacon at the end of the road, ramshackle but quaint.

"I'm that one." I point to the tiny white house on the corner, the one with dilapidated siding and a broken screen door. Our landlord hasn't cut the grass or fixed the cracked window above our kitchen sink, but you can't see any of those imperfections in the dark.

Donovan and Lana's cars are both gone.

They must be at work.

Still, the little light above our stove glows, dim but warm.

"This one?" Rhett slows to a stop in front of my house, shifting the Jeep into park. His arm goes across the seat back, body arching to look out the windshield behind us. "See that house over there? The blue one?"

I crane my neck, cheek brushing his hand. "Where?"

I'm such a damn liar—I can totally see which house is his, the blue one with black trim. When his hand inadvertently brushes against the back of my neck, tickling the loose hairs...

I shiver.

"That one there. It's..." He counts the houses between his house and mine. "Nine houses over." He tips his chin down so he's looking into my eyes. "What are the odds?"

"What are the odds?" I repeat, whispering into the dark, staring at his profile when he glances out the driver-side window. I stare at his full *lips*.

Rhett pulls away. "Where's your car?"

"Uh...my roommate has it. She must be working."

"You goin' to be okay by yourself?"

"I'm here alone all the time," I remind him, in no rush to climb out.

"Duh. Right." He nods. Clears his throat. "Right."

Rhyt.

"Thanks for the ride."

"No problem." When he smiles, *jeez*, it changes his whole face. His straight white teeth shining in the dim light, the small cleft visible in the center of his chin. I want to press my finger there just to see his reaction.

"Good night, Rhett."

"À la prochaine, Laurel," his mouth whispers, and holy *mother* my ovaries can't take it. My crotch actually tingles.

"Um, maybe don't do that."

"Don't what?"

"Speak French. Around me, specifically."

One brow rises. "All right...I won't?"

"Good." My hand reaches reluctantly for the door handle. Grips it. "Okay. I should go inside, I guess."

"Night."

"See you around."

"Au revoir."

I narrow my eyes; he did that on purpose. "*Bye.*"

"Laurel, do you need help getting out?"

"No, I'm good." I heft my backpack. "On second thought, this backpack is really heavy."

The poor boy looks so confused. "You need me to carry it?"

"Would you?"

"Uh...*sure.*"

I wait for him to come around to the passenger side, open the door, remove the backpack from my very capable hands.

Then I stand next to the Jeep, imagination getting the best of me, wanting him to try to kiss me against the cold, steel door of his car. Wanting him to put his hands on my body, slide them under my jacket. Drop my bag and press his lean hips into mine. Run his *giant* wrestler hands up my ribcage, under my shirt.

I imagine all this while he stands waiting for me, imagine what it would be like if he touched me.

He doesn't.

Of *course* he wouldn't—why would he?

He's a freaking gentleman.

I sigh, following him to my door.

I'm quickly learning that Rhett Rabideaux isn't most guys.

Tres inconvenient.

Rhett

Laurel: *I know I already mentioned it, but thank you for dinner tonight*

Me: *You're welcome.*

Laurel: *And thanks for bringing me home. It wasn't necessary.*

Me: *No problem.*

Laurel: *You're a really nice guy, do you know that?*

Me: *So I've been told.*

Laurel: *What do you have going on this weekend?*

Me: *Meet Friday. Back Saturday.*

Laurel: *Oh that's right, Ohio State. Do you think you'll go out this weekend when you get back?*

Me: *Probably not. I usually spend the weekend after a meet icing my body.*

Laurel: *Do tell.*

Me: *Ha ha.*

Laurel: *Sigh. You are a tough crowd, Rhett Rabideaux.*

Me: *Hey, can I ask you something?*

Laurel: *Sure!*

Me: *I was telling my roommates I drove you home tonight, and after I mentioned where you live and pointed out your house, one of them said they always see three cars parked in front of your house?*

Laurel: *Ummmm.*

Me: *Did your roommate borrow your car, or did something happen to it? Or…*

Laurel: *No.*

Me: *You can tell me if something happened to it, Laurel.*

Laurel: *Promise you won't get mad?*

Me: *Sure?*

Laurel: *My car is… God, I don't know how to tell you this without sounding like a horrible person.*

Me: *Jeez, just tell me where your car is. Did it get towed?*

Laurel: *My car is parked in front of the library.*

Me: *What do you mean?*

Laurel: *I mean, my car was three spots down from your Jeep. It's still sitting on campus—is that what you want me to say?*

Me: *I don't get it.*

Laurel: *What don't you get?*

Me: *Why would you accept a ride home when your car was literally RIGHT there? Now you have to go back and get it.*

Laurel: *Why don't I let you figure that one out for yourself? Or if you really can't figure it out, ask one of your more experienced roommates.*

The last text comes through and I shake my head, baffled. Why would she have had me take her home if her car was parked *right* there?

It makes no goddamn sense.

Fresh from the shower, I toss the towel I used to dry my hair onto the bathroom floor then walk into the front room. My roommates are both spread out on the couch, watching some dude on a home improvement show saw a piece of wood in half and nail it to a wall.

I clear my throat. "Hey. Question."

"Shoot." Neither takes their eyes off the giant screen.

"So, remember how I told y'all I drove Laurel home, and then you said you always see three cars in her driveway? I messaged her about it."

"Yeah?" Gunderson's ears perk up at the mention of a girl's name, his eyes fastened to the TV.

"She had her car at the library."

Eric points the remote at the TV, hits pause. "Your cars were both at the library?"

"Right."

"But she had you give her a ride home."

"Yeah."

He points the remote, hits play. "Uh, yeah—she wants to bone you."

I laugh, crossing my arms.

Johnson shakes his head, disgusted, and sneers. "The chick obviously wanted you to give her a ride home, fuckwit, and there's only one reason why. How goddamn dumb are you?"

"Fuck you, Johnson."

"No, fuck *you*, Rabideaux. That chick wants you to fuck her."

I stand there, holding my towel closed.

"Honestly New Guy, if you can't figure out what it means when a chick tries to be alone with you, your chances of getting laid at this point are slim to none."

"Agreed," Gunderson chimes in. "She either has horribly bad taste in guys or is mentally unstable. Are you sure she's hot?"

"Yes."

"Can I interject again?" Eric interjects. "Members of the jury, I'd like to point out that this chick has been *dick*ing you around for days, and you're letting her lead you around by the balls. You need to either fuck her already or tell her to stop messaging you."

"Yes! Thank you!" Gunderson shouts, banging on the coffee table. "Exhibit A: first she lies to you about who she is. Exhibit B: she lied about her car and faked needing a ride."

My roommates are on a roll now. "New Guy, I don't give a shit *how* hot this chick is, you need to dump her."

Gunderson nods enthusiastically "You cannot let bitches treat you that way, dude."

I listen to them rambling on and on as if I'm not standing here, wondering what the fuck is *wrong* with these two? Seriously, they're so fucking ridiculous. And the way they talk about women? Not cool.

No wonder they're both single.

Not that I have any room to talk, but still…

"Can you not refer to her that way, please? Laurel isn't a bitch."

"Maybe not, but she sounds calculating."

"Well, it's your fault I'm in this mess to begin with, isn't it? The whole thing with those damn flyers is the reason she and I are talking in the first place."

"But you admit she's been lying from the beginning."

"Are you pre-law and didn't tell anyone about it?" I ask him, narrowing my eyes at his cross-examination.

He ignores me, ticking off Laurel's offenses on his fingers. "And she's a cock tease."

"How is she a cock tease?" These guys really are aggravating. "I'm not trying to sleep with her."

"Fine. I'll give you that one concession—she's not the cock tease, *you* are. Look, all we know is that this chick likes you for some ungodly fucking reason—she must to be panting around after you like this."

I sigh. Why did I bother asking these two for their opinion?

"That is not what's happenin' here, not at all. We're friends—she wouldn't date a guy like me."

"That's probably true—you are pretty ugly."

"Fuck you, Gunderson."

10

#DOUCHEBAG

"I don't want sex or anything;
I just really want someone to
tell me how pretty my hair is."

Laurel

I've been up every night this week.

Night after night, fitful, lying in bed, flat on my back, staring at the ceiling, unable to sleep. After hours of restless tossing and turning, I finally gave up and let my mind wander. I could not get that boy out of my head, and for the life of me, couldn't figure out *why*.

Maybe deep down inside, I still harbor guilt over the whole texting thing, the lying, or maybe I feel sorry for the shitty way his friends treat him—they really are dicks. Watching him be the brunt of jokes isn't funny now that I've actually met and spent time with him.

Rhett Rabideaux might not be Prince Charming, but he's something else entirely: he's real. He is who he is, and makes no apologies. He's polite and sincere and…

And this morning, I'm paying for the fact that I lay in bed awake until nearly one AM thinking about him.

His body, his voice, his face.

What is my problem?

Yawning, I stride toward campus, long legs stepping over every crack in the sidewalk, the heels of my black boots hitting the concrete with a *tap tap tap*.

I look both ways when I approach a curb before stepping down.

"Laurel, wait up."

At the sound of my name and the tread of tennis shoes hitting the pavement in a light jog, I stop dead in my tracks. Whip around to see who's behind me, my heart skipping a beat.

Be still, my silly, racing heart.

Stop it.

Maybe it's the cold weather, but my cheeks flush at the sight of Rhett jogging toward me: gray athletic pants hanging low on his hips, dark navy sweatshirt, backward baseball cap, black backpack slung over his broad shoulder.

His gait is easy as he hits a stride, slowing to a walk once he nears, a crooked smile playing on his friendly mouth.

"Hey." He's not even panting. "Mornin'."

Mornin'.

"Hi." I bite back a smile at his sweet southern drawl, lowering my head to the sidewalk so he can't see my stupid grin. "Headed my way?"

"Looks like it." His eyes rake up and down my body, my cool weather outfit. The apple green sweater that sets off my fiery red hair to perfection. The knit cap pulled down over it. The skinny jeans tucked into tall boots.

Together, we head toward campus, walking side by side. Squirrels dash out of our way and I squint at one in the middle of the sidewalk up ahead.

"I swear these squirrels are out to get us. I don't trust the way that one is staring at us."

Beside me, Rhett laughs. "I hadn't noticed."

I pause. "You haven't noticed all the squirrels? They're everywhere! I'm convinced they're trying to take over the world—in fact, I'd bet my life on it."

We near the gray fox squirrel, his shaggy tail pointed in the air, balancing him as he rises on his haunches, nose sniffing the air.

"He's checking for bad nuts," Rhett quips.

"Well if he's sniffing at *you*, I doubt he'll find them." I can't help the words when they slip out of my mouth. Rhett is a good guy, and I find myself wanting him to know that's how I feel, what I think about him.

He's one of the good ones.

"Did you just imply that I'm a good nut?"

"Yes, is that corny?"

We laugh again, the crisp morning air filling my lungs with satisfying contentment. It feels *good* to be walking next to Rhett, his large body taking up the entire right side of the sidewalk.

"This whole morning has been...good." Off to a great start and getting better by the second.

I shiver inside my fuzzy sweater, but not from the cold. When the light changes to walk at the corner, we hustle across the street, step up onto the curb. Enter the edge of campus, heading for the commons.

"What class you headed to?" My curiosity gets the best of me.

"Nonverbal Communication. What about you?"

"English. Nothing groundbreaking or cool, like French class."

"Cois-moi, ce n'est pas si intéressant " He chuckles. "Trust me, it's not that exciting."

It's way too early in the morning to be getting turned on by his mastery of the French language. *Way* too early.

Nonetheless, my girl parts give a quiver.

"Do you do that on purpose?"

"Do what?"

Since I've decided to start being honest with him, I might as well confess. "Do you speak French knowing it drives me mad?"

His face scrunches up. "It makes you mad?"

"No. It *drives* me mad." I shoot him a coy, sidelong glance. "There's a huge difference."

"Oh." He falters on the sidewalk, perplexed. "There is?"

I laugh, despite myself. "Yeah Rhett, there is." *That shit is sexy as all hell.* But I'm not about to fill in the blanks or point out what they are. He's a big boy; he can figure those out for himself.

We pass the union and the art building. Pass the large fountain in the middle of the square. It's time for me to head left and Rhett to head right, but for whatever reason, we both delay parting.

"Well, I guess this is where we go our separate ways." This is also more awkward than the uncertainty of standing on my front porch in the dark; part of me wants to reach a hand out and touch him, the sleeve of his hoodie, or the lock of hair sticking out from under his ball cap. "Will I see you around at any parties?"

"No, we're leavin' for another match. They're usually every week during the season."

"I didn't know that." I should, because I've dated athletes before, but something about this guy is making me a little nutty.

"How soon do you leave?"

"Early."

"Does that mean an early night, too?"

"Usually, yeah."

"Well good luck this weekend."

"Thanks." He shuffles his feet uncomfortably, stuffing those large hands inside the pocket of his hoodie, as if he doesn't quite know what to do with them.

It's on the tip of my tongue to ask him if he wants to do something for dinner—I mean, everyone has to eat, right, so what would be the harm in grabbing food?—but I'm unable to do so. A commotion in the quad distracts me, voices growing louder behind us.

Rhett's eyes get wide, head tips back. My gaze strays to the column of his throat as he moans. His muttered curse is followed by new voices.

"New Dude!"

I crane my neck and gawk as two huge guys approach, tall and big and crazy good-looking. Kind of pretty, ripped from head to toe, the two of them couldn't be more dissimilar: one jovial and friendly, the other sullen and broody. I recognize them both from the billboards gracing the entire façade of the track and field house.

Wrestlers.

Wrestlers I don't remember seeing at the dine and dash, though I'd bet money they were probably there.

I narrow my eyes.

"New Dude, hold up. Don't try to hide from us, we've already seen you." The guy's smile is cheeky—he's clearly entertained—

as he runs a thorough body scan of me from head to toe, checking me out despite the fact that I'm with Rhett. "Your friend here is hard to miss."

He's flirting with me and I don't like it.

True, I'm not *with* Rhett, but they don't know that. For all they know, I'm his girlfriend.

The chatty one skids to a stop in front of us, gives me another body scan, not missing a single detail of my person.

Rhett

"**D**ude, aren't you going to introduce us?" Oz Osborne's smile resembles the Big Bad Wolf, arrogant and bold and confident.

I knew Oz was obnoxious, but I didn't think he was this big of an ass. I watch as he visibly gives Laurel a onceover, eyes trolling along her body, up and down then up again, not three feet in front of my face.

When we'd originally met and he warned me away from Gunderson and Eric, I assumed he was a decent guy that was looking out for his new teammate, assumed he wanted to be friends and not dick me around like everyone. Not only that, Oz has a girlfriend. I've seen her at a few home matches, a pretty, conservative girl that likes to hang out at the library where Zeke's girlfriend works.

I know, because I've seen them all there studying together.

So why is he standing here eye-fucking Laurel?

Not that she and I are a thing, cause we're not. Obviously we're not—anyone with a set of eyes can see that—but still.

Fucking rude.

Dickhead.

Laurel sticks her hand in Oz's direction, shaking it. "Hi, I'm Laurel." She holds her hand out for Zeke, who stares down at it with a scowl until she pulls it back.

Douchebag.

"Laurel, nice to meet you." Oz turns his blue gaze on me, something like respect shining behind his eyes. "New Guy, you headed to the gym or what?"

"Class."

"Damn. I was hoping you'd show me how you slipped Gehring into that hold last week." He rubs his chin. "When you gonna be around?"

I rock on the balls of my feet. "Why don't I just show you tomorrow?"

"Where? On the damn *bus*?"

Good point.

Zeke Daniels scoffs, arms crossing over his massive chest. "*I* can show you how he did it."

Oz rolls his eyes, turning to level our teammate with a stare. "I haven't seen you use that move *once* this entire year."

"That doesn't mean I can't fucking do it."

"Whatever dude, I'm going straight to the source." Oz clamps his hand on my shoulder, speaks to Laurel. "This guy is one of the best fucking wrestlers we've ever had. Have him show you his Penetration Step." He winks at her. "He can take that move straight into the Spiral Ride."

Seriously, what the fuck is he doing?

Is he trying to make me look good in front of Laurel? Match-making? Does he honestly think a girl that looks like *her* is going to date a guy who looks like *me*?

For her part, Laurel gives me a glance, her gaze trailing down my body, shining and alive with interest, cheeks flushed from the brisk fall weather. "I'll take that into consideration." She flirts back coyly, touching my sleeve as she says, "I've been trying to convince him to show me some self-defense moves."

She has?

I stare down at her fingers resting on my forearm. Her nails are a bright green, same as her sweater, which looks soft and snug-gly and touchable.

Just like her.

Zeke Daniels uncrosses his arms with a grunt. "Self defense— that's what I've been doing with my girlfriend, Violet." He curtly nods his approval. "She's so tiny."

"Does she work at the library?" Laurel asks.

"Yeah. She's a tutor."

"I've seen her. Blonde? *So* cute."

Zeke grunts, nods. "That's her."

Laurel's eyes catch sight of someone in the distance, fingers giving my arm another little tap. "Oh! There's my cousin. I'm going to run and catch up to her." Her hand leaves my sleeve, glossy pink lips curved into a pretty smile. "I have to give her a message from her mom."

"Sure."

"Bye Rhett. Talk to you later?"

"Uh yeah, sure."

"Good." She turns and takes a few steps, glancing over her shoulder once, probably at Oz and Zeke, her fingers giving a little wave. "Bye Rhett."

She said that already.

"Thanks for walking me to class."

I blink in her direction.

The three of us watch her walk off, hips swaying, red hair sweeping back and forth across her back, sashaying all the way over to her cousin.

None of us speak.

Until, "*Dude*. Who. The. Fuck. Was. *That*?" Oz asks in fragments. He socks me in the arm, right in the fucking deltoid.

"That was Laurel," I stupidly reply, rubbing the sting out of my upper arm. Motherfucker hits hard.

"Are you screwing her?" Oz asks. Beside him, Zeke grimaces at his crude question. "Please say yes."

I laugh bitterly. "Sorry to disappoint y'all."

"Why the hell not? Fire Crotch is fucking hot."

Fire Crotch? Jesus, what is wrong with this guy? He's worse than Gunderson and Eric combined.

"Did you seriously just ask if I'm having sex with her? Look at her." *Then look at me.*

We crane our heads to look again. Laurel strides down the sidewalk in the center of campus, bright hair a beacon in the distance, color set off by the hue of her sweater. Links her arm with Alex. Guides her toward the philosophy building, where her English class is held.

"Oh I'm looking at her alright." If I didn't know the guy had a girlfriend, I wouldn't know the guy had a girlfriend. "You sure you're not dating her?"

Now Zeke is rolling his eyes. "Of course they're not dating, he just said it twice. Why don't you ever fucking listen?"

"We hardly know the guy," Oz argues. "Maybe he just doesn't want to tell us."

"Know how we know?" Zeke smacks him in the stomach. "Because Rabideaux doesn't have the balls to date a chick like that. He wouldn't have a clue what to do with her."

They study me for a few awkward beats, both of them nodding slowly like they have the goddamn answers to everything. Much as I hate to admit it, they're right; I wouldn't have a clue what to do with a girl like Laurel.

Osborne narrows his eyes in my direction. "Please tell me he's wrong. Please tell me you're at least hooking up."

I sigh, hefting my backpack. "I'm not dating her."

"Hooking up?"

"No."

Oz throws his hands up, frustrated. "Dude, why not? Did you see the way she was checking you out?"

"She wasn't checkin' me out; she was looking at you idiots."

Whack. "Are you fucking blind? That chick is into you, trust me."

But he's wrong, so wrong.

He must be.

"He didn't call me beautiful,
but he came in less than
three minutes, so that's basically
the same thing, right?"

Laurel

My knuckles rise to knock, rap on the wooden front door twice before releasing the screen and drawing back.

I take a step back, smoothing back long red hair with the palm of my free hand, smile plastered on my face, butterflies multiplying one by one in the pit of my stomach.

It takes three long minutes for the door to swing open and Rhett's face to appear, shrouded in the darkness of the house.

Shoot, why is it dark inside the house? Was he already sleeping?

It's only eight thirty.

"Laurel?" Rhett presses his hand to the screen, pushing it open a few feet. "Is everything okay?"

He's wearing a cutoff t-shirt.

I stare, dumbfounded, brain processing the visuals hitting me hard, one at a time: Rhett wearing a cutoff shirt...the bulge of his sunless arms. My eyes do a quick scan along his smooth clavicle, visible from the scoop neckline of the shirt, a smattering of light hair in the center of his chest.

I stare some more, the plate of cookies in my hands forgotten. My gaze drops to his biceps, rakes along his deltoids and triceps, solid and lean. I want to skim my palms over it all.

"Is everything okay?" he repeats, pushing the door open farther. "Laurel?"

"Everything is fine," I murmur, reluctantly dragging my gaze off his upper torso.

"Then why..." Are you here?

The unfinished question hangs between us.

"Why am I here?" The weight of the plate in my hands is a gentle reminder. "Oh jeez! Duh! Here." I thrust the cookies in his direction. "I hope you like chocolate chip."

Because they were all I could afford to make after running to the grocery store for the ingredients I didn't have, which was most of them: flour, butter, and chocolate chips. Fortunately, it was a simple recipe—easy to make in a short amount of time.

They're still warm, fresh from the oven.

Rhett stares down at the paper plate. "You brought us cookies?"

Us? Like him and his roommates?

"No, I brought *you* cookies." I nibble my bottom lip, worried he's going to think I'm clingy, but his crooked smile is warm. It gets me warm, too. "Are you allowed to eat these?"

His smile gets wider. "Yeah, I can eat your cookies."

I can eat your cookies.

I search his face for traces of sexual innuendo, find none.

Bummer.

"They're for the bus ride tomorrow."

"You brought me cookies for the bus ride." He stares hard at the plate. At the cookies. Up at my face, confused.

Please don't ask me why, I silently beg, *because I don't even know the answer to that myself.* If I said I had just wanted to do something nice for him, I'd be lying. Cookies are the last thing on my mind as I stand on this stoop.

We stand awkwardly at the threshold of his house, me on the tiny front porch, him in the entryway holding the screen door ajar. The wind picks up, sending a cold breeze across the steps.

It lifts the hair off my shoulders and sends a tingle down my spine.

"Wanna come inside for a minute?"

Uh, do basic white girls drink pumpkin spice lattes? Yes I want to go inside! I school my expression so I don't come off as over-enthused or desperate. That might freak him out.

"Sure."

Still holding my plate of baked goods, I step up into the house when Rhett pushes the door all the way open, offering entry. I purposely brush against his hard, athletic body like a cat—it can't be helped! He barely left me any room to enter; obviously I had to touch him.

Giving him my most innocent smile, I enter the living room, eyes scanning the perimeter. Brown couch. Brown love seat. Tan coffee table. Giant TV. Cords everywhere.

Typical bachelor pad.

It's too quiet and too dark.

"Are your roommates home?"

Rhett closes the door behind us. "No. They're both at the field house. Rex is the team manager, so he has to make sure everything gets put on the bus. He's probably counting equipment. Eric is with the trainer getting his ankle checked out."

"Want me to set these on the counter?"

"Sure. Wait, no. Maybe I should put them in a baggie and shove them in my duffle so the guys don't eat them all."

I preen, standing a little taller—he doesn't want to share my cookies.

"Good idea."

Rhett finds a plastic baggie after opening four drawers in the kitchen and we put the cookies inside, two at a time, him stealing one before I slide the baggie closed. He pops it in his mouth, biting down, his straight, white teeth pulling it apart.

Chewing.

The tendons in his neck work and I watch him swallow, eyes drawn to his throat.

"Now I want milk." His lips tease.

"Want me to get you a glass?"

"Nah, I got this water." He picks up the glass from the counter, washing down his chocolate chip cookie with a few gulps. "That was awesome. Thank you."

His hip hits the counter, eyes casting a wary glint over my shoulder, out the window behind me. "Dammit."

"What?"

"My roommates are already back." He pauses, the silence almost deafening. A set of headlights shines into the dimly lit kitchen, casting shadows against the walls. "Uh, want to go to my room?"

Not really—I kind of want to meet these assholes in person, but knowing he doesn't want me to, I nod my head. "Sure. We can do that."

He grabs the cookies off the counter and we set off down the dark hallway to the bedrooms. Behind the second door on the right is his room; painted beige, it's much tidier than I was expecting—and clean, especially considering this was a drop-by. His bed isn't made, but the covers aren't thrown everywhere, either. It's kind of sparse—at least, compared to what I'm used to.

Desk in the corner. Dresser against the far wall. Queen-sized bed. Navy bedding.

Green plaid pillows.

Interesting.

"Where are all your trophies?" I mean, don't guys hang stuff like that up for bragging rights? My ex-boyfriends always did. "I'm assuming you have a bunch of those, right?"

"Packed up in my parents' basement."

He must not have wanted to haul them all the way to Iowa from Louisiana.

"Do you have a lot of them?"

Rhett shuffles to the closet, barefoot, and slides the door closed. I watch the muscles in his back flex when he shrugs, facing away from me. "I guess."

"So you're just okay? They recruited you out of the goodness of their hearts?"

This makes him chuckle. "I'm tryin' not to sound like a conceited asshole."

From the living room, we hear the sound of the front door open, close. Two loud voices bantering back and forth in the kitchen, cabinet doors opening and closing like the place is being ransacked.

Whoever his roommates are, they're loud.

Ignoring the sound of them rifling through the cupboards for food, I stray to Rhett's desk, fiddling with his pens, poke one around the surface with my green fingernail.

Unlike my laptop, Rhett's is void of decals and stickers. Unlike my notebooks, his are plain and have no doodles scribbled on the cardboard covers.

I glance at him over my shoulder.

He goes to stuff his hands in his pockets; discovering his navy pants have none, he runs both hands through his hair, blowing out a puff of air.

"What's wrong?" I ask.

"Nothing."

All right, Rhett, I get it—you don't know how to tell me you think it's weird that I'm in your room. That it's making you uncomfortable and you don't know how to act. What to do with yourself, or your hands.

I get it.

It's cute.

Different, without a doubt.

I stroll to the bed, slide down the front of it to the floor. Lean my head against the mattress and shoot him a friendly smile as I run my palms down the length of my legs, down my black leggings, plucking at the fabric.

He bites back a smile, sauntering the few feet it takes to reach me, squatting on his haunches then joining me on the floor.

We both stare at the closet.

"Do you ever get nervous going into a match? Or meet? I still don't remember what you call them." I laugh.

"The whole thing is a meet. The part where I wrestle an opponent is a match. And no, I don't get nervous. Not usually."

"Because you're so good?"

"Maybe, or because I've been doin' it so long it's second nature. My body is on autopilot, you know?"

I do know. "That's how it was with volleyball. My parents started me when I was eight, and I never had a break." I pause. "I couldn't do it anymore. I admire you for sticking with it, though. I know it's hard."

"It can be."

He can't fool me; I know what the life of a D1 athlete is like, and his sport is far more intense and backbreaking than volleyball ever was.

"Does your family visit?"

"They used to come to every single home meet."

"But they haven't since you've been in Iowa?"

"Nope. Too far."

"Have you gone home?"

"Nah. It's a long drive—I'd rather not make it alone."

He steeples his fingers on his knees, and I study his hands, learning the lines of his veins and the bend of his fingers, his large, masculine hands.

I bet they're rough.

I bet they're capable.

I bet...

I sigh.

His room smells good and *he* smells great, and he's sitting less than an inch away. His thigh is touching my thigh, his hips touching my hips. It's not on purpose, obviously—this is Rhett we're talking about here.

But he's close enough that the nerves in my body are sending electric jolts to places I'd rather they didn't, especially since it's apparent this guy isn't interested. I'm a fool for pushing the issue simply because I'm curious.

Calling him. Texting him. Bringing him freaking cookies— Jesus, what the hell have I been thinking?

This little playground crush I seem to be developing on him is going to end up with me getting hurt—or worse, looking like a complete fool. I can picture it now: poor, clueless Rhett, avoiding me like the plague because I scared the crap out of him with my assertive nature.

Maybe *this* is why I date guys who aren't emotionally available. Getting him comfortable with me is proving to be a challenge when most guys have been easy—the breaks are always clean and easy, too. No one gets hurt because no one actually cares, nothing invested but physical gratification.

He turns his head when I exhale; up close, I can see the different hues of his irises. How long his lashes are. The scar in his left eyebrow. The small, discolored skin along the bridge of his nose where a bruise is healing.

Rhett's eyes stray to my lips.

Mine stray to the hardwood floors beneath us, taking in the square footage. "You know something? I think there's plenty of room in here to give me those self-defense pointers."

"Now?" He looks dubious.

"Do you have any better ideas?"

Like making out, just to see what it feels like? Rolling around naked on the bed, perhaps?

Rhett bites the inside of his cheek. "Let me think of an easy one for you to do. Most of them wouldn't work as self-defense."

The room is quiet while he deliberates, and I watch his facial expressions change, the wheels of his brain turning. "Okay," he says at last. "I think I have one. We're both goin' to have to stand up."

He rises to a full stand in one fluid motion.

Rhett leans down, offering both hands to help me off the ground. When he holds them out, palms up, I slowly slide my skin across his. Flesh to flesh.

My pulse quickens at the contact.

Our eyes connect; I know he feels it too.

He must, or I'll go crazy trying to convince myself there's something building between us even if *he's* convinced himself there *isn't.*

"Thank you," I murmur, my body still humming from his touch.

"You ready?"

My blue eyes glide over the smooth skin of his exposed collarbone, the hard valley between his pecs.

Am I ready? Oh yeah—*so* ready. "Yes."

"All right, so, uh." He wipes his palms on his pants. "I guess we'll go with the double takedown. So you're going to have to widen your legs and squat, like this."

Rhett spreads his legs, squatting, hands up with his palms facing me, waiting for me to mimic his stance.

"Like this?" I purposely prop one foot out, uneven, hip jutted out.

"No, like this." He stands, breaking position. "Here, let me show you."

He moves into my personal space, large hands gripping my hips, shifting my body to the right. Palms skim my thigh, tapping the inside of my sensitive flesh until my legs are spread—it's like he's tapping a lifeless slap of meat. Clinically. Mechanically.

Rhett is clearly in his element when it comes to wrestling.

"Now bend them a little bit more, and put your hands out, like this." He manhandles me until I'm positioned the way he wants me. "Good. Now when you come at me, you're going to put your hands around my hips and move them around to my backside, head down toward my stomach." His mammoth hand pats the area below his sternum. "Try to aim here."

"What?" My head gives a shake. "No way! I'm not doing that!"

He frowns, sighs. "Fine. I'll do it to you, then you can try it on me afterward."

I smile innocently, the thought of his hands sliding down my ass a thrilling prospect. Bonus points if he squeezes it.

"All right. I'm totally okay with that."

"Raise your hands a little higher, like this," he instructs, demonstrating.

Rhett is all business. His eyes don't so much as flicker down my body—not once, not even when I stick my boobs out to test his resolve.

"When my head hits your stomach, my hands are gonna get up underneath and pull you down, and you're going to hit the floor." He pauses. "Just FYI."

"Got it."

"I'll try to lower you gently."

Oh jeez. My girly parts tingle.

"Normally this is done from more of a run and the—"

"Just do it!" I laugh. "The anticipation is killing me."

"Sorry. I've never done this on a girl before."

"Rhett, just—oh my God!" I gasp when his head hits my tummy and I'm lifted off my feet, on my back within seconds, air whooshing out of my lungs with an excited breath, breath catching when his face appears in my line of vision.

Hovers over me, shaggy hair in his eyes. "You okay?"

My lips part, exhilarated. "*Yes.*" I'm more than okay, especially when his face moves in, eyes roaming my face. "Are you checking me for a concussion? Because I'm fine—my head didn't even hit the ground."

He had a hold on me the entire time he was leveraging me to the floor, quick, agile, and completely in control of his movements. Stealthy. Steady. Strong.

Gentle.

"I can't believe you just did that," I murmur, relishing how near he is, the hands now circled around my biceps.

"Shit, I'm so sorry."

"Don't be. That's *not* what I meant."

"Oh." He tosses his head, jerking the hair out of his brown eyes. "What did you mean?"

"That was amazing." My breath hitches, gaze skimming his bare shoulders. "It took no effort."

"Lots of practice," his lips say.

"Practice makes perfect," mine reply, mind wandering to what else would be perfect with a little bit of practice, mentally ticking off a list: wrestling...kisses...*sex*.

I'm willing to bet he could give me an orgasm or two with a swivel of those muscular hips. My body aches to arch, pelvis wriggling under the length of him, inches from what I know is inside his navy pants.

"You know..." I begin. "You can't seriously expect anyone to actually use that for self-defense, especially not a girl."

"I panicked," Rhett admits with a cute, crooked grin, teeth raking along his bottom lip. His low laugh is deep inside his chest. "You came over unannounced, askin' about self-defense."

My fingers find their way to his wavy hair, brushing aside the stray locks so they're out of his eyes. "No, I came over to bring you cookies."

Rhett seems to bask in my touch, briefly tilting his cheek into my palm, resting it there. My thumb traces the skin along his jaw, across his lower lip.

"Laurel?"

His face inches closer.

I suck in a breath.

This is it—he's going to kiss me. "Yes?"

"Est-ce que je peux t'embrasser?"

"I don't know what that means," I say in a breathy whisper.

"What are you hopin' it means?" Our mouths are a sigh apart, the air between us tickling my lips. His powerful chest brushes my breasts and this time, he doesn't move away.

"Say it again."

"Est-ce que je peux t'embrasser?" His mouth is hot, near my ear, warm breath sending a spark up my middle, dampening my underwear. "Dis oui, s'il te plait."

Est-ce que je peux t'embrasser; dear Lord, I hope it means he wants to kiss me. I hope it means—

Rhett's bedroom door busts open, hitting the wall behind it, just as Rhett's soft lips lightly sweep mine, tentative.

"Holy fuck." There's a skinny guy with blond hair filling the doorway, legs spread, folded sweatshirt in his hands. "Did I just interrupt something? Please say yes."

Rhett is off me lightning fast, quicker than he flipped me on my back, and the loss of his heat leaves me cold. He turns to help me from the floor, my hands gripping his.

"What the hell, Gunderson. Learn to knock."

"We just got home—I wasn't expecting you to have anyone in here, dude. It's not my fault."

"It's still my room."

Gunderson shakes his index finger in the air like he's making a point. "Technically this month it's partly mine since I had to pay some of your rent."

Rhett's sigh of exasperation is loud. "Gunderson, get the fuck out."

"Whoa, whoa, whoa, let's not be so hasty." He throws his hand out toward me, tucking the sweatshirt under his armpit so he can greet me properly. "I'm Rex, team manager. And you are..."

"Gunderson, this is Laurel."

I peek out from around Rhett's imposing form and give his roommate a little wave, despite the fact that he's five feet away. "Hi."

"Laurel." Gunderson's face is nothing but an idiot grin, all teeth and stupidity. "Dude, you're Laurel? You're so fucking...*wow*. I'm almost tempted to tell him to forget everything I said about you."

When the rude bastard narrows his beady eyes at me, I narrow my blue eyes back. Then the jerk has the balls to ask, "What are your intentions with our buddy Rabideaux here?"

"Jesus, Gunderson." Rhett groans. "Get out of my room."

"It's a legit question, dude! I'm doing you a favor."

Rhett gives his roommate a delicate shove through the threshold of his bedroom, his mammoth-sized hand reaching around. It goes to the small of my back, just above my ass, that one spot heating my entire body.

His thumb inadvertently settles near my ass crack.

I'm tempted to wiggle my butt.

"This is why you can't get laid, you know that, right," the jerk mutters when he's ushered into the hallway. "You can't even joke about sex."

Rhett's hand lingers on my rear, slides up my spine when his roommate disappears from sight. Reaches for a sweatshirt off the hook by his door, tank top rising when he lifts his arm, smooth expanse of midsection exposed from the motion.

I ogle his body.

Washboard abs. Flat stomach. The telltale sign of a happy trail leading from his belly button, disappearing into the waistband of athletic pants so thin, I can see the outline of his dick.

He slides the sweatshirt over his head. When he comes up for air, tugging the hem down over his pants, he says, "I should get you home."

Instinctively, I want to pout. Stomp my foot. Demand he lay me down on the floor and put his hands back on my body where they belong.

"Okay."

We walk in peaceful silence past the nine houses that separate us. I wordlessly count them as we go, trying to enjoy Rhett's company, to shift the focus so I'm not fixating on that almost kiss in his bedroom.

He was going to kiss me, I know it.

It's a short jaunt to my house and a shorter walk up the sidewalk.

"I have to be up early, so…" Rhett lingers, kicking at an invisible pebble on the concrete slab that is my entryway. "Thanks for the cookies."

"Good luck tomorrow." I want to go up on my tiptoes and wrap my arms around him, kiss his cheek.

Something.

*Any*thing.

"Thanks."

"Let me know how it goes?"

"I will." Rhett runs a hand through his shaggy locks, stepping back down onto the path in front of my house. "Night."

"Good night."

Rhett: *Hey.*

Me: *Hey yourself! How did it go today?*

Rhett: *Great. Won both my matches.*

Me: *Are you on your way home?*

Rhett: *Not yet. We're staying the night then head out in the morning.*

Rhett: *It's fucking loud in the hallway—the groupies for this school are everywhere.*

Me: *Groupies?*

Rhett: *Yeah, you know…*

Me: *They seriously hang out at the hotel?*

Rhett: *Yeah. The guys usually tell them where we're staying and they follow the bus back to the hotel, for hotel sex I guess.*

Me: *Can I ask you a personal question that's none of my business? You don't have to answer.*

Rhett: *Sure.*

Me: *Are there any groupies in your room right now?*

Rhett: *LOL, no.*

Me: *Why is that funny?*

Rhett: *You really think I'm the type groupies latch on to? They usually hang on the other guys, thank God.*

Me: *Okay. Good.*

Rhett: *It was a good day. I'm freaking tired—I can't believe these guys are going to be up all night.*

Me: *I really wish I could have seen you in action.*

Rhett: *Well, I mean, you can—if they're not being aired live, they're usually on one of the sports networks or YouTube. Just Google it.*

Me: *Really???*

Rhett: *Yeah. The matches are all televised.*

Me: *Well then excuse me while I go find vids of you wrestling...*

"I would probably bang him
given the chance,
but how awkward would
Bible study be after that?"

Laurel

I totally Googled him.

I couldn't stop myself—didn't want to.

An image gallery of Rhett fills the screen of my computer, almost every small thumbnail a photograph of him in a wrestling singlet. Pictures of a younger, high school-aged Rhett. Three state championships wins, I note with pride. Arm raised after each sweaty victory, sometimes held up by a coach or ref.

Him in a purple and yellow singlet from Louisiana. A few team composites. Surrounded by teammates in a practice gym.

Bent over in what the caption calls a "guardian stance".

There are so many photos and articles of him, I could sit clicking on them for hours.

My face burns hot from the images of Rhett in his wrestling singlet, from the sight of his sinewy, sweaty muscles, growing more defined with each year that passed.

The mouth and ear guards.

His thighs.

Oh my God, his thighs.

His dick beneath the spandex material.

I stare at that spot between his legs, pulling my monitor in close, studying the screen like a pervert, like a horny teenage boy.

I assumed he had a great body, but the actual sight of it half naked?

Jesus, it's making my panties damp.

I zoom in on an image of Rhett with his hands behind his head, catching his breath, perspiration on his chest gleaming under the bright stadium lights. His brawny biceps inflated, flexed. The veins pronounced from the increased adrenaline.

The tight black spandex that leaves so little to the imagination.

The sensitive nub between my thighs throbs and I squeeze my legs together to alleviate the pressure building there.

This creeper session is seriously better than porn.

The only difference is, this boy? He's real, not unattainable, and lives only nine houses away.

I imagine all the sneaking around we could do on our roommates. I imagine him crawling through my window, waking me up with his face between my legs. His hands running along my skin, up under my sleep shirt, sliding into my white eyelet shorts.

Imagine myself running my hands under the straps of that black singlet, sliding them down his brawny biceps, hands dragging down his damp, sweat-covered chest.

"Uh, what are you doing?" My roommate stands in my doorway, hand braced against the doorjamb, brows arched.

"Oh my God Donovan, Jesus Christ!"

"Scared you, did I? What are you doing in here?"

"Nothing! Jesus." Shit, did I say that already? "You scared the crap out of me. Don't you ever knock?"

I slam my laptop closed with a thwack, heart rate accelerating at an alarming pace.

He laughs. "What were you looking at? You look weird." Donovan narrows his eyes. "Your face is as red as your damn hair."

"*Nothing*, God Donovan!"

"You look guilty as all hell. Just tell me what you were looking at and I'll leave you alone."

"No you won't."

"You're right, I won't. So just tell me." His manicured eyebrows rise and the nosy asshole laughs, wriggling his fingers. "I want to see. Learn to share, Bishop."

"No." I hug my laptop. "Mine."

"Tell me what it is!" he whines, entering the room, his big body filling my personal space. Ugh, he is so annoying sometimes.

"Get out!" I sound like a little kid telling her pesky brother to get out of her room. "Seriously, I'm not kidding."

"You never act like this." He sits on the edge of my bed instead, resting his chin on my footboard. "Truth: were you looking at porn?"

"Truth? No!" *It was something better.* My panties are so damp, I might as well have been.

"If it's not porn—not that I'm judging—why the hell are you bright red? Tell me." He holds up two fingers like a Boy Scout. "No judgment. I jerk off at least twice a day."

Gross. "I did *not* need to know that."

"Would you just freaking tell me before I wrestle you to the ground?"

Wrestle me to the ground? My red face gets warmer, imagination getting the best of me as it produces visuals of *Rhett* wrestling me to the ground.

I almost tremble with delight.

"Fine, you win—I was looking at pictures of Rhett. He's the guy I've been, you know…" The inflection of my voice conveys my meaning, and Donovan nods.

"The guy Alexandra had you text that you're *not* hooking up with?"

"Right."

"Let's see him in action, come on, come on." He bounces on the bed, impatient. "You know I can't resist men in tights."

I crack the laptop. Enter my password with nimble, eager fingers.

He looks over my shoulder. "You totally want to text him right now, don't you?"

"Oh my God, yes." I click on the browser window. "So bad."

"Where's he at this weekend?"

"On his way home I think, from Penn State."

"Penn State? Woo, fancy."

Donovan slides my laptop to his lap, scans the screen with perceptive eyes, raking over the images of Rhett emblazoned there.

One photograph after the other. Clicks on one, zooms. Studies it. Clicks another, then another, all without saying a word.

"Well." My roommate sighs. "He's certainly no Thad Stanwyck."

"Thad?" I huff indignantly. "Seriously Donovan? Why the hell would you bring him up? Ugh."

Thad was a guy I dated last year for four long, exhausting months. As gorgeous as he is vain, Thad is a stereotypical carbon copy of your tan, arrogant, privileged student athlete with a revolving door of bed partners.

I don't know what the hell I was thinking hopping on the carousel; being his girlfriend was emotionally draining.

The sex was robotic and routine.

Dick? Average.

Dates? Nonexistent.

Communication? Worse.

To compare Rhett to Thad isn't fair, despite their obvious physical differences.

"He's nothing like Thad." *He's better.*

He's amusing, and charming, and refreshingly oblivious.

Clueless. Obtuse. Naïve. Take your pick.

"What are you going to do about it?"

"I don't know." I chew on my thumbnail. "Think I should text him?"

Donovan nods, handing me back the laptop. "No, I meant—what are you going to *do* with him?"

Guh! "I honestly don't know yet."

"Do you like him?"

"I think so, yeah. I mean, yes. I'm starting to."

"Like with feelings and bullshit?"

I smack him then shove him off the bed. "Donovan!"

He stands, heading for the doorway. "I'll let you have your privacy but you better pony up the details next time. No games with him. Guys hate that shit."

"Okay, promise."

Palming my phone, I thumb through our last chain of messages.

Tap out a quick text.

Hey there…

Rhett

"Who were you talking to?" Gunderson asks, throwing his lanky body into the seat behind me. He invades my personal space, resting his knobby elbows on my headrest, peering over the seat and into my space. "You look all dreamy-eyed and shit."

We're on a bus on our way back from Pennsylvania after one of Iowa's biggest overall victories of the season: defeating top-seeded Penn State.

I'd just ended a call with my dad when Gunderson plopped down—the call where I broke the news of the four-hundred-dollar Pancake House tab to my parents.

"Were you talking to Laurel? Are you seeing her tonight?"

It's on the tip of my tongue to tell him to stay out of my business, but instead, I say, "No. It was my dad." I crane my neck so I can look him in the eye. "I had to explain about the four-hundred-dollar credit card charge."

"Oops, my bad." My roommate cringes. "How'd that go?"

"Terrible."

"Does he not give a shit that you just beat Penn? I mean, it's Penn fucking *State*."

"Not really, not when it comes to money he doesn't have." I narrow my eyes into slits. "The whole conversation was fuckin' shitty."

Shitty is an understatement. My parents—my father in particular—were so fucking pissed, the entire call was mostly him sputtering with anger. He's mad, understandably so.

"I wondered when you were going to call," my dad said by way of greeting when I called them after my win.

"You saw it already?"

"Yes Rhett," he said sarcastically. "I saw it already. We check your credit card statement and your brothers' a few times a week. I've been waitin' several days for you to call and enlighten me."

There was a dead silence on the line as I found the words to explain myself. "There were fifteen of us and we went to eat as a team and—"

"They stuck you with the bill," he interrupted, not a hint of amusement in his tone.

"Yeah."

My old man snorted into the receiver of his phone. "This wouldn't have happened if—"

"If I hadn't transferred? Yeah, I know." Because my parents never miss an opportunity to remind me about their disappointment that I'm at Iowa.

"You'll be workin' it off this summer I'm going to assume."

"I won't have to. My roommates are splittin' my half of the rent to make up for the money."

"That isn't the goddamn point, Rhett."

"But Dad—"

"And I'm callin' your coach. This is hazing and it's bullshit, do you realize that? Your mother is beside herself with worry. What else have they done to you?"

I slouched into my seat on the bus, lowering my voice. "Dad—"

"What kind of operation are they running over there?" he demanded, raising his voice.

"Dad—"

"Don't Dad me, Rhett. I'm callin' your coach. This kind of bullshit would never have been tolerated at LSU."

Nothing I say will change his mind because I left a great school to be part of the hailed NCAA championship wrestling team for better opportunities, more exposure, and more scholarship money—and my parents are never going to let me live it down.

I try to wipe the entire conversation from my mind, attempt to ignore the sound of my father's fuming, disappointed voice in my head.

Gunderson stares down at me over the seat.

"Let me put it this way: it's a good thing I'm so far away and can't go home for break. My dad would kill me."

"Look, that sucks. I get it." Gunderson hesitates a beat, leans farther over into my seat, eyes darting around the bus like he's trying to be sly. "But switching gears, some of the guys have been talking…"

Jesus Christ, here we go.

I wait him out.

"We've been talking about all your girl problems and want to help."

"My girl problems?" I don't have girl problems…do I? "I don't have girl problems—the only problems I have are you butting into my business."

"Just hear us out before you get premenstrual, okay? We have a few things to say—wrote them down, matter of fact."

I glance around, catch several of the guys casually watching with interest, quickly averting their gazes when they notice me scanning the bus.

I narrow my eyes.

"So you're the village idiot they've nominated to relay the message?"

He grins, satisfied I understand. "*Exactly*. As the team manager, I might be the messenger, but I didn't come up with this awesome shit on my own."

A sheet of paper appears in my line of vision, Gunderson smoothing out the wrinkles on the headrest, clearing his throat and giving someone toward the back of the bus a quick nod. He receives his signal to begin.

His voice goes up an octave and clears his throat as if he's about to deliver an inaugural address. "*We* have a few rules *we* think will help get you laid. Since you brought Whatsherface home the other night, you've been kind of bitchy." He looks down at the paper, then back at me, grinning. "That part was improsized."

"You mean improvised?"

Gunderson rolls his eyes. "That's what I said."

You can't argue with stupid, so I keep my trap shut.

"First off, you're too nice. Not a single one of us has ever heard you insult a member of this team, or insinuate that you're sleeping with someone's mother or sister. That's not normal."

In the background, one of the guys coughs out, "Pussy."

"I don't know if you've noticed, but girls are attracted to ass-holes. Just look at Daniels and Osborne if you don't believe me— two of the biggest pricks dating two of the loveliest girls. Coinci-dence? I think not."

"Did you just call James and Violet lovely?" comes a shout from the back of the bus.

"Shut up Pitwell, I'm handling this." Gunderson cups a hand around his mouth like a megaphone, bellowing down the center aisle of the bus. "I have the floor here—you all had your chance." The paper in his hands gets raised to his face. He clears his throat dramatically.

"As I was *saying*, try insulting us more to be funny, especially around women, and brag." He catches someone's eye and winks. "You have stats better than Daniels, why don't you talk about it?"

"Yeah dude, what the fuck?"

I eyeball Gunderson skeptically. "Are you purposely trying to turn me into a douchebag?"

"Yes. You're way too fucking nice. Maybe it *is* time to douche that shit up a bit."

"Wow. You guys must think I'm really fucking dumb, huh?"

Behind me, someone huffs. "New Guy, stop acting butt hurt and listen to what he's saying."

Gunderson rolls his eyes, irritated at continually being inter-rupted. "Thanks Davis, but I can handle this."

He returns his attention back to me—unfortunately. "Which brings me to the point: your nickname."

"I don't have a nickname."

"Exactly. That's why you need one. New Guy is only going to cut it first semester, then you won't be new anymore. It'll just sound idiotic."

"Uh…"

"Ozzy. Zeke. Boner. Pit. See? We all have nicknames, so don't be a little bitch about it. We voted, and we think you should be called Quasimodo because you're so damn ugly."

I throw him two hard middle fingers. "Fuck. You."

"When you come up with a better idea, let us know. Until then, you're Quasimodo. Also, we noticed you don't wear enough cologne. No one has suggested you stink, but—"

"That's ee-fucking-nough," I growl. "Get the fuck away from me." Fuming, I push the ear buds back into my ears, hoping he'll take the hint and leave me the fuck alone.

A sheet of paper flutters into my lap not two seconds later, and I grab it. Fist it into a ball. Toss it to the floor. It sits there an entire twenty-three seconds before I sigh, bending at the waste and scooping it back up.

I hate litter.

The list is entitled *How to Be a Bigger Douchebag*, and I scan it, disgusted.

1. Insult your friends more to be funny. No one likes someone who's too nice, especially women.
2. Brag.
3. Give yourself a nickname.
4. Text other women during your dates. This will make you look desirable to the opposite sex.
5. Wear more cologne.
6. When asking a girl out, don't just ask—tell her she's going out with you.
7. Wait at least three hours before texting her back.

The list is one dumbass suggestion after the next, and I have to seriously wonder if they think I'm a fucking moron. Honestly, is that their impression of me, or are they genuinely just a fuckful of douchebags?

I shove the wadded-up list into my backpack as we pull into the stadium parking lot, the weight of this whole transfer pushing down on my shoulders. They may be wide, but they can only carry so much, and this month has been a shit storm I can't find my way out of.

My phone pings.

Hey there...

Laurel.

I smile, replying before I have to stand to collect my things.

Hey. What's up?

It's basic and impersonal, but I still haven't figured out why this girl insists on befriending me. Why she's still texting, why she flirts with me. Why she brought me warm cookies I'm almost positive she baked herself.

I'm genuinely confused.

Confused as fuck.

She could have dropped the pretense of liking me the second I put two and two together at that party and realized who she was.

Laurel: *You up for going out tonight? A few of us are downtown, somewhere nice. Want to meet us out and swap beer for wine?*

Wine instead of beer? Who is this chick?

Me: *I should probably stay in.*

Laurel: *Tired?*

Me: *Something like that.*

Laurel: *Well, if you change your mind, you know where to find me.*

Me: *Thanks for the invitation.*

Laurel: *:)*

"*Now* who were you on the phone with?" My other irritating roommate is on his tiptoes, trying to see over my shoulder as we make our way to the exit. I wish he'd climb down out of my ass already.

"Laurel." Like it's even any of his business.

Eric nudges me in the spine with his elbow. "Dude, for real?"

I glower. "Yeah, for real."

He shuffles behind me, lugging his duffle.

We walk in succession, each of us with our head down, tired, filing off the bus single file like we do week after week during the season.

"I have to see this chick—Gunderson said she's smoking hot." He's riding my tail, bag literally bumping into my thighs. "Is that true?"

"Uh..." I hesitate. "I guess."

"Gunderson said she has red hair—how red we talking here?"

"I don't fucking know, Eric. Red."

"So, you're dating a fire crotch?"

Jesus Christ, for the fifth time, "I'm not datin' her... and don't call her fuckin' fire crotch."

He scoffs. "If you put a little effort into it, you could be slicing that pie. He said you're giving her blue balls."

"Should I bathe in cheap cologne, act like a dick, and give myself a pet name to lure her in?"

"*Nick*name—there's a difference." He bangs into me again with his bag.

"Would you shut up?"

We're still bickering when a firm hand grasps my forearm.

"Rabideaux."

That voice. The use of just my last name.

Shit.

I turn to see Coach, grimace when he pulls at the brim of his Iowa wrestling ball cap, hard eyes focused, mouth set into a firm line. "You have a minute?"

"Uh…" *Fuck.* "Yeah, of course."

He sees the glance I shoot Gunderson and Eric, leveling my roommates with a narrowed stare.

"Meeting in my office. Twenty minutes."

"Yes sir."

We watch as Coach walks off, head bent, talking with the director of wrestling operations and our strength and conditioning coach, heading back toward the stadium, where their offices are housed.

"Dude, what's that about?" Gunderson asks.

"No idea."

But I have an inkling.

A hard knot forms in the pit of my stomach, squeezing from the inside, tightening with every step I take toward the building, every step I take that's farther in the opposite direction of my Jeep.

I guesstimate it takes eight minutes to reach Coach's office. Twelve more for him to flag me inside. Another to close the door, settle into a seat, and wait for him to speak.

"So." He begins, leaning back and steepling his fingers in front of him. "Tell me how it's going."

He drops his hands to the desktop, plucking a sticky note off the surface, pinning it between his fingers, bright yellow with something scrawled on it that I can't read. Coach flicks it with his middle finger, tapping the yellow square back and forth, back and forth.

I stare at that small sheet of paper, trying to read the words written there in marker, the bold, black letters across the middle. It's a name and a phone number, I discern that much.

"It's going great," I lie.

"Is that so?" He leans back, adopting a contemplative expression. "Want to tell me why we would have gotten a call from your father if everything is so goddamn *great*, Rabideaux?"

He leans forward and the wooden chair beneath him protests with a loud, creaking squeak.

"I don't know what my dad would have said to y'all, but I can promise you I'm handlin' it, sir."

We sit in uncomfortable silence while he contemplates his next words.

"You know, son, we as a coaching staff, along with the university, have a strict zero tolerance policy against hazing, so I'm going to need a few names."

My lips purse. "You know I'm not gonna do that sir, with all due respect."

"I figured as much." He eyes me with a frown. "You kids and your misplaced sense of loyalty never cease to fucking amaze me." Pause. "Tell you what I'm going to do: I'll be talking to your team captains about our little problem before it escalates."

"It's not a problem, sir."

He chuckles sardonically. "How much was the bill you had to pay?"

My lips press together. *Fuck.*

I don't know why he's asking the question; I'm sure my dad already gave him the answer. "Four hundred and change."

"And that's not a problem for you? You running a charity for hungry, malnourished wrestlers we didn't know about?"

"No sir."

"Your father is not pleased, Rabideaux. He's fucking pissed, and I personally do not enjoy getting my ass chewed out by angry parents. I have a duty to your families to prevent this sort of bullshit."

"I'm aware of that, sir."

"You're also aware that you, along with your teammates, signed an honor code?"

"Yes sir."

"Can't do much without specific names." He pauses again. "Course, I could just suspend everyone."

Fuck.

"Sir…"

"Let me give this problem some thought."

"I understand."

"I'll be watching, Rabideaux."

I nod.

"Now get the fuck out of my office, and close the door behind you."

He doesn't have to tell me twice.

Laurel

We don't go to a wine bar.

Not even close.

I'm out with Alexandra and her two best friends, Gretchen and Kari, and we most certainly aren't anywhere classy; in fact, the place is a dive.

It also happens to be the home of a fraternity fundraiser—a bar and a frat party all in one place, imagine that.

For the third time tonight, I give Alex a nudge, tugging on her sleeve and leaning in, peering into her plastic beer cup. It must be bottomless since it never seems to be empty.

"Come on, Alex, it's getting late. You said we weren't going to stay long."

"I know, but Johnathan's been behind the bar for an hour, and he's almost done with his shift. I want to see him before we go."

John is the president of the Sigs, one of the university's largest fraternities. The biggest partiers. The deepest pockets.

The worst reputations.

My cousin has been fucking him behind her boyfriend's back for weeks. "Alex, I'm sure John won't know if you leave a bit early. He will live—you both will."

"I'm his ride home." She flips that long black hair over a bare shoulder. "Sober driver."

"What! You promised him a ride *home?*"

"That's not all I promised him." Her laugh is flirty and borderline obnoxious.

"Are you shitting me right now? What does Dylan think of that?"

Her bottom lip juts out. "Who cares? And why do *you* care? I'm sorry Laurel, I'm not leaving. If you want to go, go."

"It's freezing outside!"

The temperature is glacial and I'm already freezing my ass off in tight black capri leggings and a mid-drift top, no jacket, half-boot heels.

What the hell was I thinking coming out dressed like this?

Oh, that's right—I was hoping Rhett would change his mind and come out once the team rolled back into town.

My cousin rakes her stony eyes up and down my outfit. The tight black top might be long-sleeved, but it's paper thin and flimsy.

"Laurel," she scoffs, irritated. "It's not *my* fault you didn't bring a jacket." When she crosses her arms, I know we're done with the discussion, so I can do one of three things: stay, walk home, or call someone to come get me.

I rack my brain—Donovan is on a date with some new guy he met last weekend at a student senate retreat, and Lana picked up an extra shift at the banquet hall she waitresses at. There's a wedding tonight and she didn't want to pass up the tips.

"Well?"

I wave her off. "Don't worry about me. I'll figure it out."

This isn't the first time she's chosen a guy over her friends, and it won't be the last; Alex makes a habit of putting beaus before bows.

Despite the date rape talk we always have before stepping out for a party—or any night where there's alcohol being served—no one leaves alone. We come together, we leave together.

That is, unless *she* wants to hook up.

Then? All bets are off.

I narrow my eyes. "Whatever. I'll figure it out."

Her smile is satisfied, the spoiled brat. "Text me when you get home so I know you got there safe."

"Because if I'm not, you're going to come riding to my rescue?"

She scrunches her face up, insulted. "Of course I would!"

"Then why are you letting me leave here? Alone?"

"God Laurel, then stay. Don't be such a bitch about it."

I throw my hands up. "I'm done. I'm going." Giving my head an exasperated shake, I walk away dreaming up a thousand snarky tidbits I'm going to tell my mother in the morning when I call home.

"Okay. Be safe!" she calls out. "And text me when you get home!"

Right. Like that's going to happen.

Outside, I find a corner, brace myself against the brick wall. Unlock my phone and scroll through the contacts, trying not to fool myself.

There is only one person I want picking me up, and he's at home, probably in bed, unwilling to come out and spend some time getting to know me.

I nibble on the inside of my cheek, uncertain. What if he doesn't answer?

But what if he does?

"Screw it." The words rise on a puff of breath, the weather so cold my bravado turns to steam.

Rhett's name lights up my screen, the counter ticking at the top.

One second.

Three.

Eight.

"Hello?"

"Rhett?" I hear rustling, like he's in bed and unwrapping himself from a mess of sheets. For a brief second, I imagine he must be shirtless, barefoot, and only wearing boxer briefs, his hard body tangled in nothing but blankets—

"Hello?"

Does he recognize my voice? "Hey. It's Laurel."

"Hey, what's up?" He yawns.

"I hope I'm not interrupting anything." I roll my eyes; how stupid do I sound? It's obvious he's in bed or something.

Shit. What if he's not alone?

Pfft.

Duh, this is Rhett we're talking about—of course he's alone.

"No, you're not interrupting anything." He pauses. "I thought you were going out tonight?"

"I was. I *am*—out, I mean." I continue babbling. "We're out—my cousin and I, and her friends."

I clamp my lips shut.

"Are you drunk dialing me?" he asks slowly, cautiously.

I laugh uneasily, shaking slightly from a combination of cold and nerves. I wrap myself in a hug, wishing I had coat, or even a sweatshirt—anything to ward off the chill.

"No, I'm sober. One hundred percent sober." Okay, more like ninety-six percent, but who's counting? "It's freezing out, and I'm standing against a brick building. It's so loud inside."

"Are you okay?"

"Yeah, I'm fine. Just a teensy bit stranded."

Silence. "Uh…"

"Is there any way you can you come get me?"

More silence.

I can hear him squinting, narrowing his brown eyes. "You sure you're sober?"

"Positive."

More rustling. It definitely sounds like he's in motion. "Where are you?"

I press myself against the stone and smile. "Duffy's."

"Duffy's, Duffy's…" He's trying to place the coordinates of the bar. "Okay. Give me ten."

"All right."

"Go back inside to stay warm. I'll text you when I'm a block away."

"Okay, I will." I bite back a grin. "And thank you."

Rhett grunts. I imagine he's stepping into athletic pants, sliding them up his lean hips. "Be right there."

And he is—right here I mean. I spot him within eight minutes, his familiar black Jeep pulling up to the curb in front of the run-down bar.

I push through the door, take the steps and eleven paces to the curb, purse hanging from a chain over my right shoulder.

Rhett has already hopped out of the car, jogging around to my side, beating me to the passenger door, his eyes giving my body a quick, barely perceivable scan.

I shiver again, but not from the cold.

"Hey." He smiles down at me, giving me wide berth so I can hop in.

I pause before climbing in, giving him a breathy, "Hey," and my own perusal of his figure: gray athletic pants hang low on his hips. Dark gray Iowa t-shirt pulls tight over his broad shoulders. Brown leather flip-flops despite the cold temperatures.

His toes stick out over the ends. Cute.

I brush against him, grabbing the door to steady myself, leaning in unnecessarily close; Rhett smells freshly showered.

Clean.

Masculine.

Like cologne and soap and fresh air.

Or maybe it's just the fresh air…

I can't tell if his eyes are glued to my ass as I climb in, but just in case they are, I give my hips a slow swivel. Inch my way unhurriedly onto the seat. Buckle up. Watch as he makes the jog back to the driver side.

Bite back a smile when he checks for traffic before pulling open his door.

Run a palm down the stray strands of my long, wavy hair. It falls over one shoulder, smooth and silky, down over the curve of my breasts.

"Thank you for picking me up."

"No problem."

"I can't *thank* you enough." Shit, did that sound sleazy? Suggestive? Like I was offering to pay him for my ride in blow jobs?

Why would my mind go there? Jesus, Laurel, why are you thinking about what's inside his pants?

Guh!

The radio begins a slow love song that after tonight, I won't hear without thinking of Rhett. He reaches forward, twisting the volume button to the left. Turns it down so all we have for company is the sound of his purring engine.

Under the streetlights, I study his profile, butterflies wakening in the pit of my stomach. They rise, stretching, wings beginning to flutter at the silhouette of his bottom lip and curve of his Grecian nose.

Rhett clears his throat. "So."

He's so awkward and cute. I want to climb into his lap, but I'm pretty sure he'd freak out, slam on the brakes, and crash into a pole, injuring us both.

Can't have that, can we?

The smell of him makes me squirm in my seat in the best possible way.

I swallow, trying to focus on the road.

"What did you end up doing tonight?" I croak out, fiddling with the buckle on my purse.

He shifts in his seat. "Not much. Showered when I got back. Graded some papers."

Graded papers—ugh, he's so smart.

God I love that.

He gives me a sidelong glance, eyes darting to my legs in the cloak of darkness. My boobs. My hair. "What about you?"

"I thought my cousin and I were going to have a quiet night with a few friends, right? At a wine bar or something, but we ended up at Duffy's instead. She has the hots for one of the Sigs, and they were doing a mixer there tonight."

"Don't your friends have that pact about not letting each other leave alone? Who's driving the rest of them?"

I stare at him in disbelief; was he listening the night Alex and I were arguing on the front porch of that party about never letting each other leave alone?

I think he was. *He was actually listening.*

"I think Alex is planning on bringing this guy John back to her place, to, uh, you know." *To have dirty, meaningless sex.* "So she couldn't care less about me, especially when she's been drinking."

"Not cool."

"Trust me, we had words about her letting me leave."

"Words?"

"A talk. She was pissed I wanted to go while she's trying to cheat on her boyfriend—who was there too, by the way."

"Oh. Right." I swear I can *hear* him blushing.

"And since it's so cold—"

"No way should you be walking home alone." He bobs, affirming my thought. Grips the wheel tighter. "Horrible idea."

"I'm glad you were home."

"Yup, that's me—old reliable," he quips. "Always home."

"You were the first person I thought to call."

Because if there is one thing I'm learning about Rhett Rabideaux, it's that I can count on him. He's steady and strong and dependable; I know it from the bottom of my soul. He has qualities I'm coming to realize are more valuable than blatant sexual appeal.

It doesn't take us long to reach our block, hanging a right then a left until I can see both our houses.

"You can just park at your house if you want. I can walk the rest of the way."

"No way. It's colder than a witch's ti—"

"Sorry? A witch's what?"

"Nothing."

Tit? Was he going to say *tit*? There's no way. Not Rhett.

Heat finds my cheeks. "Anyway, thanks for the rescue."

"No problem."

I touch his forearm. "Seriously. Thanks for coming to get me."

"You're welcome. You weren't interruptin' anything important."

Interruptin'.

"Still, I appreciate it."

"I would do it for any one of my friends."

"Friends." *Right.*

I clear my throat, adjusting the purse on my lap, my little house at the end of the street in full view. Rhett slows down, pulling up along the curb.

We sit in the dark before he cuts the engine and opens his door. Makes that walk to the passenger side door. Opens it like a gentleman so I can step down, his gaze finding the pale sliver of bare midriff before pulling away longingly.

It was brief, but I caught it.

I step down onto the street, one long leg after the next. Let him walk me to the front door, keys jingling in one hand, purse clutched in the other.

I skim his torso with my hungry eyes; I cannot help it. I haven't seen him in over twenty-four hours, and now that I've seen pictures of Rhett online in a wrestling singlet, well…

There's no stopping my body now.

It gives a little shake, back hitting the front door. I regard him under the dim light of the single bulb lamp on my porch, through the cool fall air.

"Thanks again."

"No problem."

"Would you like to come in?"

He shuffles on the balls of his feet, both hands stuffed into the pockets of his gray pants, unintentionally pulling the fabric taut over the front of his crotch. I try not to gawp at the telltale sign of his bulge, but it's—

"I better not."

My shoulders sag. Better not? What on earth does *that* mean?

"All right then. I guess this is good night?"

God, I can't help thinking that's totally something I would say if this were a first date.

"Bonne soirée, Laurel." It's hard to read his expression in the dark, with his hooded eyes shadowed by the overhang on the porch, but I can read enough of his mouth to glean a hint of doubt.

The hesitation. The insecurity.

"Does bonne soirée mean good night?" I whisper, eyes trained on his mouth.

"Oui." His eyes smile against the backdrop of the dark chocolate brown, warm and endearing. Unassuming and sweet.

I have to know what his lips feel like, the little voice inside my heart whispers.

I have to know what they feel like pressed against mine. Have to know what the freshly shaven skin of his neck feels like against my cheek. How it smells.

If I don't find out soon, it might be the end of me.

So I let my purse fall to the ground beside my shoes. Step closer, lean in, closing the distance between us with my mouth, with my body.

When my breasts brush his chest and I close in the space to inhale his aftershave, the breath whooshes out of my lungs. Cologne, deodorant—whatever he's wearing, it's divine.

Eyelids flutter closed when the tip of my nose brushes the smooth side of his neck, inhaling his skin.

"Laurel," he croaks cautiously, spine ramrod straight. "Are you *drunk*?"

His breath smells like minty toothpaste.

I'm fairly confident I want to lick him.

I press closer still, the heat radiating from his hard, male physique more dangerously intoxicating than any sensation I've felt in ages.

"No." I've never been soberer in my entire life. "I'm not drunk…not on alcohol."

Rising on my toes, I need only another inch to reach his mouth. Breasts pressing into his chest, my lips graze his, the barest trace. Rhett's body freezes, rooted to the porch, the breath leaving his body so fast I feel his heart beat in time to mine.

I kiss him once, letting my pucker linger on the indentation at the corner of his mouth. Kiss him again, basking in his full bottom lip. The bow in the top. Silky. *Soft.*

My hands find a straight path up his firm pecs, over his stiff nipples. Slowly discover their way to his jaw. Land on his biceps and rest there, resisting the urge to squeeze the muscles under my fingertips.

Rhett lowers his forehead to mine with a shaky countenance, but it's not what I want. Does nothing to satisfy my newly insatiable curiosity, this longing I've felt since first meeting him face to face.

I want him to kiss me.

I *need* him to kiss me.

I need to know if this connection building between us is *real.*

Painfully slowly, his lips part the barest of a fraction— *barely*—meeting the next brush of my mouth. He receives it tentatively, unsure.

Then another and another, the soft whisper of our kisses in the dark.

Our lips.

When I raise my lids, I discover his are closed, long lashes brushing his high cheekbones. Nostrils flared, controlled breaths in and out. Nowhere near satisfied, my eyes scan his scar-marred face before sweeping my mouth once more across his.

I want to sob when his mouth finally opens, tongue touching mine, low groan escaping his chest; it's long and loud and *primal*. Almost a whimper. Painful.

He's shaking.

My hands fall limply to my sides, weightless, body and nerves losing all center of gravity, knees wobbling when his mouth hovers over mine and his delicious tongue agrees to get acquainted. Our heads slant for a better angle.

God, I want to run my fingers through his shaggy hair. Kiss his face, his eyebrows, his broken nose.

He leans into me, too, my breasts swollen and his chest rubbing, pecs so mouthwateringly hard I can feel his nipples through my shirt. Through my bra.

Rhett kisses me like he means it, hard but gentle. Lazy but controlled. Firm and soft and then, "Tu sens merveilleuse."

His raspy French murmur sends a tingle shooting straight down my spine, down to my toes. Whatever the words are he's whispering, they send a ripple of desire through my core, getting me—*oh God*—so hot.

I want to curl up inside those words. Get naked in them.

Everything with Rhett and me started off so wrong in the worst ways, and now being with him just...

It's right.

I like him.

Really like him.

I find the strength in my arms to raise my hands. Slide them heatedly up his abs. Sternum. Collarbone. Poise to cup the back of his neck and pull him in.

"Laurel..." he whispers, forehead falling back down onto mine. "Laurel."

"Yes?"

"You..." He swallows. "Should go inside."

"I should?"

He nods. "I should go."

"You should?" But why?

Face flaming hot from embarrassment, I forget about the biting cold when I step back feebly, butt hitting the door. Turn to unlock it, fumbling with the key, body trembling. Tears tingling the bridge of my nose in between my eyes.

I refuse to turn around and look at him, so I tell the door, "Good night."

I sense Rhett hesitating behind me. "Good night."

It's not until I'm inside, body slack in the entry hall, catching my breath, do I realize: not *once* did Rhett's hands leave his pockets.

Rhett

I can't go into my house.

So I sit in my Jeep, parked in front of it with the engine still running, hands still gripping the steering wheel.

What the *fuck* was that all about?

What the fuck was *that*?

What *was* that?

Someone needs to spell it out because I'm confused as fuck.

Laurel kissed me.

I replay it over and over in my head, head tipped back, hitting the headrest. Stare unblinking at the ceiling of my Jeep, at the wide expanse of tan fabric, breathing hard, fighting for control over my accelerated heart rate.

Take my pulse: 140.

Jesus.

Are my roommates right? Does she *like* me?

There's no freaking way. Not possible.

With a trembling hand, I skim the front of my gray pants, across the length of my hard cock, pressing down but not stroking. I saw her blatantly checking me out on the porch but dismissed it as curiosity. I'm not completely clueless; I know I have a great body. I train hard for it, day after grueling day.

It's my face that isn't winning any beauty contests.

Never would I have thought a girl like that would look twice in my direction.

Now? I'm not so sure.

"He was smart enough to bring
condoms to our study date,
so I'm sure he'll do just
fine on the exam."

Rhett

I haven't been able to think of anything but that kiss. Can't step outside without shooting furtive glances at the small white house sitting at the end of my block, watching for her to come out.

Watching for any sign of her, really.

That kiss happened three days ago and I haven't seen or heard from her since—not that I expected to. It's not like we're dating; it's not like she's obligated to.

Still…

One part of me is really fucking disappointed I haven't heard from her, while the other part of me wonders if she's been waiting for *me* to message *her*.

Shit.

I sit, deliberating, unable to concentrate on the papers stacked in front of me. My friends would have no problem figuring this shit out; they'd message her without hesitating, probably would have the minute they walked off her porch the other night.

I stare at the essays blankly, composing a text to Laurel in my mind before typing one out, hoping like hell she welcomes the random message.

Me: *Hey there.*

Laurel: *Hey stranger! I was wondering where you'd gone.*

Dammit, I was right—she's been waiting for me to message her first. Sometimes I'm such an asshole.

Me: *Correcting papers and studying at the library.*

Laurel: *Which one?*

Me: *Public. Over off Broadway*

Laurel: *You're not hiding are you?*

Me: *LOL, no.*

Maybe.

Laurel: *How would you feel about some company?*

My chest expands, constricts, heart racing.

Hell yeah I want her company—I fucking miss her beautiful face. Her bright red hair and flirtatious smiles. The way she touches my arm with the tips of her fingers.

Me: *You should probably get your ass over here.*

Laurel: *Be careful—it sounds suspiciously like you're flirting...*

Me: *I'm doing my best.*

Laurel: *That was a good start—I'll be there in twenty. Walking.*

Me: *Want me to come get you?*

Laurel: *No worries, I'll manage ;)*

Shit. If she's walking, that means she's going to need a ride home, and we know how that ended last time—with me pussing out on her front porch.

I clear room on the table, stack the sparse number of school supplies I have on top of a notebook, and straighten the chairs. Reach up and run both hands through my hair, finger-combing that shit. I glance down, giving my plaid flannel a cursory onceover for stains.

Roll the sleeves to my elbows.

Stand to smooth down the front of my jeans, realizing too late I'm primping like a fucking girl.

For a girl.

I sit my ass back down, stare at the entrance. Check the time stamp of Laurel's text and glance at the clock.

It's been eight minutes.

Eleven.

Fifteen.

At nineteen minutes, I sit up straight when the doors at the entrance breeze open, followed by a cool gust of wind I feel from my spot in the corner.

Laurel pauses in the doorway, backpack draped over one shoulder, scanning the perimeter, seeking me out.

I use the time to check her out.

Skinny jeans. Brown half boots. Green plaid shirt, navy vest. Flaming red hair down in loose waves—wavy enough that even I know it didn't happen naturally.

She spots me. Begins weaving her way in my direction, eyes focused on my table.

On me.

Beams down at me when she reaches the table.

"Hey."

Bites her pink bottom lip. "Hi."

Okay, what now?

"We match," I blurt out dumbly—we're both wearing plaid.

The corners of her eyes crinkle, delighted. "We do."

"I saved you a seat." I laugh, and Laurel's eyes scan the nearly empty library.

"Not exactly a hub of activity, is it?"

"Nope. That's what I like about it."

"I don't blame you. This is nice." With her backpack rested on the chair, she unzips it, pulling out her laptop. Notebook. Pen. "Can you believe I've never been here?"

"Did you find the place okay?"

"Yeah. That's what GPS is for." She winks flirtatiously, removing her vest and hanging it on the back of her chair.

"You used your GPS to get here?"

"Haven't you ever used the walking guide?"

"Uh, no?"

"Oh man, my friends and I do it all the time. It's the only way we can get anywhere around here." Laurel hesitates. Brushes an errant strand behind her ear, gathering her hair and pulling it over her right shoulder in a red waterfall.

So fucking pretty.

She sits, clearing her throat. "What are you working on? Grading papers?"

My head shakes. "I was, but now I'm editing my paper for European Union and Foreign Politics."

"Wow. That sounds... It sounds..."

"Borin' as fuck?"

"That isn't what I was going to say—at all." She laughs, covering her mouth with the palm of her hand to stifle the sound. "Are you ever able to do homework on your bus rides?"

"I could, if my teammates would leave me in peace."

"What do you mean?"

"Well." I set down my pen. "When we came home this past weekend, they spent half the trip riding my ass, handing out dating tips and shit."

Her brows furrow, pinched attractively at the bridge of her adorable nose. "Dating tips? Like what?"

"The shittiest, worst kind of advice. Probably thinkin' I'd actually take it and look like a dumb fuck in front of you." Her eyes widen. "Sorry, pardon my French."

She smacks my arm at my pun. "Cute."

I lean in. "Get this: they told me when I'm around a girl, I should insult my friends to be funny."

"Uh..."

"How would you feel if you were on a date and the guy spent the entire time textin' other people?"

"I'd hate it." Her head tilts. "Did they tell you to do that?"

"Yeah—so my date would think I was important."

"That's...wow. I don't even know what to say. That is *really* shitty advice."

"I know."

"They didn't..." Her voice trails off. "Um, they didn't tell you how to ask a girl on a date, did they?"

"No." I snort. "Thank God."

"Why? You don't think you need it?"

When I finally take the time to study her reaction, she's watching me attentively, blue eyes shining, mouth set in a determined line. Waiting.

"I didn't say that."

"You know," she says slowly. "If you want to practice...you could always pretend to ask *me* out."

Her shoulders give a casual shrug, nonchalant, but the high color of her flushed cheeks and blazing, sparking eyes tell another story.

"I wouldn't know what to say." Which is true, I wouldn't—not to her, or any other female, especially when I'm being put on the spot.

"Try it," she urges with a gentle smile. "I won't bite."

"Uh..." I look to the ceiling for answers. At the bookshelves. Across the library at the circulation desk.

Laurel emits an amused chuckle. "Wow. Maybe you do need help." Pause. "Go on, *ask.*"

"You just want me to pretend?"

There is a long pause. "Sure. Pretend ask me."

"*Pretend.*"

Curt nod. "Mmmhmmm."

I lean back in my chair to study her, the slight downward tilt of her pink mouth. The unflinching eyes that are a tad too wide. The blush creeping up her lovely neck to her smooth cheeks.

"You wanna go out with me sometime?"

"There, was that so hard?" she whispers.

"I guess not."

Laurel's lips part, smile feebly. "Easy."

"So then what happens?"

She sits up straighter in her chair. Flips her hair. "Well, then I'd lean in like this." She leans in, arms crossed on the table. Whispers, "I'd be breathless and my heart would be pounding, and I'd say something like, 'I would *love* that.'"

Jesus.

A few silent moments pass, the only sound the ticking clock on the wall. Our breathing. The sound of my heart pounding in my ears.

The shuffling of papers from the front desk.

"Rhett?" Her voice is just loud enough that I can hear it, barely a sigh.

"Laurel," I say teasingly.

"Why *haven't* you asked me out?"

More tension-filled silence stretches between us, the question weighing down the air.

She can't even look at me when she says it.

My head gives a shake. "It's just—that *cannot* be what you meant."

"Why not?"

I shift in my seat uncomfortably, not sure what to say. I mean, it's not like I'm going to start spouting off the million ways she's out of my league. How she's gorgeous and I'm not. How as a set, we don't match. How I'd have to be a fucking dumbass to ask a girl like *her* out on a date—a delusional fucking dumbass.

I look at her from across the table. Rosy cheeks, inky lashes. Clear skin and perfect nose. Creamy complexion. Gleaming satin hair. Great boobs and slim waist.

Jesus, she's...

She's like nothing I've ever seen.

And for whatever fucking reason, she seems to think I'm *some*thing. Wants to spend time with me. Get to know me.

It's...

Unsettling.

Unreal.

"You're serious?"

"Why wouldn't I be?"

Because. Because our whole friendship began as a joke, a stupid fucking prank my idiot roommate and *her* cousin railroaded us into. Laurel wouldn't have texted me. Would never have flirted, sexted. Would never have come up to me during that party otherwise.

Shit, I cannot stop warring with myself on this. Cannot wrap my brain around it.

If I'm so horrible, then why did she kiss me on my porch?

She kissed *me*.

That shit just doesn't happen to guys like me. Ever. I know it, and so does everyone else. It's a universal law, and who am I to throw off the gravitational pull?

I'm not blind, and I'm certainly not dumb.

I raise my eyes. "You really want to know why haven't I asked you out?"

Laurel looks down at the table top, avoiding my eyes, feigning sudden interest in her English paper, in her pen cap, ticking it open and closed. Even with her head bent, I can see her cheeks are flushed, clearly mystified.

"Why haven't I asked you out?" God, what the hell is wrong with me? Why do I keep fucking repeating myself? I'm worse than a goddamn parrot.

"Please just stop saying that," she beseeches, turning a darker, unflattering shade of pink.

"I just don't know...what's...going on?" Seriously, why am I being such a spaz? It's like I've stepped into a parallel universe, some fucked-up episode of *The Twilight Zone*.

I watch her lips twitch. Clearly flustered by my lackluster reply, Laurel avoids eye contact. "Never mind, Rhett. Just let it go."

"Laurel—"

"Please stop talking about it. Forget I said anything."

I clamp my lips together. Then, "I didn't realize you *wanted* me to ask you out."

"Well you do *now*." She looks up at me, confused. Her pretty brows bend. "I've been flirting and messaging you for *weeks*. I brought you cookies. I called you to pick me up from a bar in the middle of the night. Kissed you on my porch."

She's breathing harder now, getting upset. Narrows her blue eyes at me. "What did you think I was *doing* all this time?"

"I don't fucking know, Laurel. Friendzonin' me?" How stupid do I sound? I throw my hands up. "I thought we were studyin'. What did *you* think we were doin'?"

"But I *kissed* you."

True. But, untrusting, I ask, "Was it because of some dare?"

"How can you ask me that? What kind of girl do you think I am?"

"Laurel..." My tone holds a warning.

"I thought you were waiting to ask me out until the time was right," she blurts out, cheeks red as her hair. "I can't believe I said that. I don't ask guys out—I've never asked a guy out *in my life*, and I'm not starting with you."

"I'm not tryin' to upset you, I'm just so damn confused."

"Confused? *Awesome*." The laugh that comes out of her throat is almost maniacal. Now she's throwing her hands in the air, defeated. "That is just awesome. Can we forget this whole humiliating conversation took place?"

Uh, not likely. Not ever.

This shit is going to be burned into my brain forever.

"I don't think so." My head shakes, a reminder that I should probably get a haircut before I can't see. It's already too long for Iowa's wrestling uniform code. "Can we talk about it?"

Jesus Christ, what am I saying?

Except she's the one shaking her head. Picking up her things. Stacking her books and closing her laptop.

"No." Laurel hastily shoves everything into her black backpack, zipping it with a resounding *whirrrr*. Angry. Self-conscious. Upset.

"I'm so embarrassed." She stands abruptly. "I'm leaving."

Shrugs into her vest.

Hefts that book bag onto her slender shoulders and gives me a nod, chin trembling, on the verge of tears. Hightails it away from my table, bumping into bookshelves and periodicals along the way.

Go after her idiot! the logical part of my brain screams. *Go after her.*

But I've never been quick on the uptake, and I've never made a girl cry—not in my entire fucking life. So, I sit on my ass in shock, the loud library clock ticking through second after unbearable second.

She's all the way to the entrance of the library before my brain catches up to my common sense and has me rising to follow her, leaving all my shit on the table. Racing to the door, busting through the entryway.

I shove through the heavy glass doors, step out into the cold night air, look left, look right.

Watch as she marches down the center of the sidewalk, toward campus, heeled boots clicking on the pavement. Head bent. Shoulders slouched.

Shit.

"Laurel!" I call her name through the crisp air, the words a cloud of steam. "Shit. Laurel, stop!"

She pauses to turn, her flaming hair catching fire under the glowing street lamps. "Leave me alone, Rhett. Please."

"Goddammit, stop!" My long stride takes the steps two at a time until I'm halfway down the sidewalk myself. "Where the hell do you think you're going?"

"Why bother following me? What could you possibly say right now that's going to make me feel like less of an asshole?"

My hands go up, beseeching. "Jesus Laurel, help a guy out. Tell me what's goin' on here. Please."

"Fine! You want me to spell it out? I *like* you, okay? Just so we're clear on *what's goin' on here*."

I rear back. "You *like* me?"

"Yes, you idiot!" Her head shakes. "Yes. I like you—how can you not have figured it out by now?"

I open my mouth. Close it.

I think I'm going to be sick. I'm going to barf right here on the sidewalk in front of City Hall and the library. I've never asked a girl on a date—ever—and I don't know if I can start now.

Not one like *this*. Not one that *looks* like this.

I've been doing my best not to judge her based on appearance alone, but why the fuck is a girl like her taking an interest in me? I have no fucking idea. Not a clue.

The wane smile she shoots me is sad; my reaction to it wells deep inside my chest, heart thumping so powerfully I can feel it in the pit of my stomach.

Holy shit—Laurel fucking Bishop likes me.

Yet...

"Do you mean that, or are you saying that because you feel sorry for me?"

"Feel sorry for you?" Laurel walks back toward me, beautiful hair shaking and catching in the lamplights above. Christ, she's pretty, so sweet and funny and so fucking out of my league. "Why would I feel sorry for you?"

She takes one step, then another, until I'm looking down at her, the top of her head meeting the bottom of my chin. Warm light glows through the windows, illuminating her alabaster skin when she tips her face up.

Hesitantly, I raise my hands, unsure of where to put them—where she'll *let* me put them.

I settle on her arms, my palms large enough to encircle her biceps, the flannel fabric of her shirt soft under my rough skin. I watch as her nostrils flare and her pupils dilate, eyes sparkling.

"I'm sorry I'm such a fucking moron.'"

She demurs under my touch. "It's okay. I get it."

"Come back inside," I murmur, catching an end of her silky hair and rubbing it between my fingers. "Let's get my stuff and take you home."

"All right."

One step up and she's beside me, reaching between us, sliding her petite hand into mine. It feels delicate and small, a contradiction to mine. I glance down at those clasped hands, knowing I must look fucking shocked, because when she sees my face, she draws her hand back.

"Sorry."

"No—it's okay. I'm just not…"

"Not used to it?"

That's the understatement of the goddamn century. "That's one way of puttin' it."

"I don't want to force myself on you." Laurel's brow furrows. "I want you to like me back, not be browbeaten into it."

We're in the lobby of the building now, between the main doors and the entrance. It's old and dark and faintly lit. Gray tiled floor. Black marble walls. Heavy steel doors encasing the entire space.

I glance down again at our hands. Over at the steel entrance doors.

Hesitate.

"Rhett?"

I don't know what comes over me, but suddenly I'm releasing her hand and guiding her by the hips toward the cold marble. She doesn't protest. Doesn't question my actions.

Under the Community Library sign—on which every library director's name dating back fifty years is listed in shiny, gold letters—I back beautiful Laurel Bishop against the wall.

She's breathing hard before I even dip my head to inhale the tender spot beneath her ear, nudging her hair aside. It's silken and glossy and smells fucking fantastic.

I flick her earlobe with the tip of my tongue, wondering where this bravado came from.

As she tips her head back, a gasp escapes Laurel's lips.

I lay my lips on her neck, desperately wanting to suck. Grip her hips with my fingertips and murmur into her ear. "Tu me rends fou pour quelques semaines." *You've been driving me crazy for weeks.*

"What are you saying?" she asks with a sigh, tilting her head, giving me access to the pale column of her neck.

"J'ai peur de t'aimer." *I'm afraid to let myself like you.* Behind a cloak of ambiguity, knowing she couldn't possibly understand, I whisper the words I'd only reserved for myself. "Je te veux tellement." *I want you so bad.*

My hands run up her hips, pinning her to the cold black wall, the dark my ally. The last thing I want her to see is the lovesick expression on my face. The puppy dog eyes and the pleading.

The truth is: I want her so fucking bad.

I want her to *like* me in ways that have nothing to do with friendship.

I want...

I want to kiss her and touch her and *God* do I want to have sex with her.

I tell her with my mouth, inside the marble vestibule, with the slow roll of my tongue against hers. The slight roll of my pelvis. I bend my knees so she doesn't have to tiptoe, reach under her with my hands and scoop her ass into my palms, easily dragging her up.

When her feet leave the ground, I press her back flat against the wall for support, stifling her gasp of surprise with my mouth. Her legs go around my waist to hold on, but there's nothing urgent about our kisses. They're lazy and slow and tentative. Soft.

I pepper her jaw with my lips.

This is nothing like that awkward kiss on her front porch; it might be tame, but it's life-altering.

Laurel runs her nose along my jaw. Brings a hand to my cheek and strokes my face. "Making out in the library feels sacrilegious."

"How so?"

"I don't know, it just does." She laughs. I set her on her feet, separating our bodies reluctantly.

"Come on." She takes my hand. "Let's get out of here."

***

Me: *What time do you have class tomorrow?*

Laurel: *Ten fifteen. You?*

Me: *I have to be on campus around then. Want me to come get you in the morning and we can walk together?*

Laurel: *Sure, I'd love that. Want to meet outside on the first block? Intersection of Dorset and Winona?*

Me: *No. I'll come get you at your house. 9:45?*

Laurel: *That sounds perfect.*

14

"His face is what I call 'sittable.'"

Laurel

I check my hair at least a half-dozen times, once more running a palm down the loose waves to smooth them, tossing them over my shoulder when I'm done. Tilt my head this way and that in the mirror, the light catching on my large gold hoop earrings.

Add another coat of black mascara. Lip gloss.

My navy-blue t-shirt is long-sleeved, and I throw a vest over the top. Black leggings. Tall black boots.

I want to look cute, but not like I'm trying too hard since Rhett isn't judging me by my appearance. I've noticed that about him—he's focused on *me*. Not my hair, or my face, or my boobs.

Still, I want to look cute—for *him*.

Satisfied with my reflection, I hit the light on my way out of the bathroom, gathering up my backpack, phone, and sunglasses.

Unbutton my vest so my boobs show.

Button it.

Catch my reflection in the mirror by the door, give my hair another fluff.

Rhett is sauntering down the street when I come out of the house, bag slung over his broad shoulder, holding the strap with one hand, the other shoved into the pocket of his dark, slouchy jeans.

He's got a blue ball cap covering his unruly hair, and I can see the curly ends sticking out of the bottom from my spot on the porch. His Henley sweater is gray, layered over a white t-shirt, the stark white peeking out from beneath his collar.

Man, this guy is growing on me like a weed.

"Mornin'." His voice is a deep baritone, the kind of deep from having just woken up, the sexy deep that makes your insides quiver, shakes your shoulders.

"Hello to you." I hold up my offering. "Hungry?"

Two vanilla protein shakes.

Rhett takes one, surprised. "Thank you."

"I have water bottles in my backpack, too."

His brows go up. "Really?"

"One for you, one for me."

We start off under the brisk morning clouds, overcast skies above, an impending rain forecast looming. I sidle a few inches to my left, closer to Rhett's imposing form.

Brush my elbow against his arm. Once. Twice.

I watch as he bites the inside of his cheek to stop from grinning. To occupy himself, he opens up the protein shake and takes a long pull, Adam's apple bobbing as he swallows, smiling around the bottle. "What class do you have this morning?"

"Astronomy."

"A*stron*omy?"

I laugh, taking a swig of my shake. "Yeah. I had a science gen-ed to fulfill. I dragged my feet freshman year, so I have to take it now." I shoot him a sidelong glance, eyeing his ball cap, the hair looping around his ears. "What about you?"

We arrive at the crosswalk, stopping to check traffic.

"Global Environmental Policy and Negotiation."

"Did my eyes just bug out?" I laugh. "Because that sounds intense."

"It is."

"How do you manage?"

Those hefty shoulders lift into a shrug. "I just do."

A cool breeze blows across the commons, and I step closer still, my body aching for physical contact.

"You cold?" he asks, brows drawn. "Do you want to go back for a jacket?"

"No. I'll be fine once I get inside." It's my fault I wanted to look cute and not *puffy* from a thick coat.

"You sure?"

"Yeah." I shiver.

In my imagination, Rhett's hand moves up and down my back, doing that thing you do when you're trying to keep someone warm. I'd snuggle into him, settle under his armpit. Bask in his warmth.

Sigh contently.

Instead, we march onto campus in the direction of the science building in a comfortable silence. It feels good being next to him, and when we get closer to my building, I'm tempted to rise to my tiptoes and show him just how—

"Hey Rhett!" A female voice interrupts from behind.

Together, we turn.

A pretty little brunette stands about ten feet away, sheepishly clutching a stack of books in her hands. She's short, perky, and eyeing him up and down.

"Hey Monica."

Ah, so he does know her.

She spares me a brief glance but shoots him an eager, blinding smile.

"Are you going to be coming to study group this week?"

"I'm not sure. I'm caught up with all my notes, so..." Rhett's voice trails off. "I don't know, maybe."

"If you can't make it, maybe we can change it?" She blushes, shrinking down into her winter coat. "I'm sure the others would be glad to see you there."

And by others, she means herself.

She's so hopeful.

Something in the pit of my stomach curls, wraps itself around my heart and squeezes.

Monica has a crush on Rhett.

Crap.

Monica has a crush on Rhett, and she's in his study group for the entire semester.

Ugh.

Not going to lie, insecurity wells up in the form of jealousy, and in a move I'll later classify as blatantly territorial, I loop my arm through his, relaxing my hand on his bicep. The muscles flex instinctively beneath my palm.

Monica's eyes slide to that hand, landing and resting there. When her mouth forms a little O of understanding, my inner bitch does a fist pump, throws a parade, and waves at the onlookers.

Yes, that's right—he's *mine*.

"Oh. Okay, well…okay." Monica's dull brown ponytail blows in the breeze. "Guess I'll see you in class."

Rhett nods, clueless. "Yup."

"Bye." She scurries off, and we both watch as she hastily disappears into the university union. I'm holding Rhett by the arm, right next to his warm, heated body.

My hand gives his muscles one solid squeeze before releasing him, stepping away. "Thanks for the company."

"No problem." He looks down at the ground then up at me, hair in his eyes. "Have a good day."

"You too." I smile up at him. "What are you doing later?"

"Practice. We have a home meet this week."

My brows shoot up into my hairline. "You do?"

"Yeah." He pauses. "It's at the arena."

The arena is huge.

"Isn't that where they have basketball games?"

"That's the one."

"Wow. That many people show up?"

Rhett laughs, snaking his fingers under his baseball cap and readjusting it. Plays with the bill, squeezing it tighter over his forehead. "Yeah. That many people show up."

"How would you find me in the crowd if I showed up?" I playfully tease.

"I have a feeling you'd be hard to miss." He dips his head, embarrassed.

So freaking adorable.

"I'd love to come see you wrestle. What time does it start?"

"Six. I can…" He trails off. Clears his throat. "I can make sure you have tickets at will call."

I take that moment to lean in, the front of my vest brushing against his sweater, getting up nice and close. "I would love that."

I'm not trying to invade his personal space, but I do it anyway. He smells freshly showered and incredible, clean and strong and male. "You smell good."

His white teeth play peekaboo with his lips. "So do you."

We stand outside the brick science building, grinning at each other until a girl from my class walks by, staring openly. Curiously. Wiggles her brows as she passes. I don't know her name, but I recognize her; she sits in the back row, too.

I'll have to introduce myself.

"I guess I should go inside."

"Right. I should…" He throws a thumb over his shoulder.

I don't want him to go. I want to skip class and spend the day with him, doing nothing together. Get to know him better. Find out what makes him laugh. What pisses him off. How he's settling in with the rest of his team now that the dust on the dine and dash has settled.

"See ya." I don't even try to hide my idiotic grin.

Neither does he. "Bye."

Then I'm rising up on the toes of my black boots, stretching to reach his strong jaw. I kiss the underside of it, stubble pricking my lips in the most delectable way.

His breath stops, lips part.

"Message me later?"

He nods. "I will."

"Bye."

God, this is as bad as when I was in high school, flirting on the phone with my teenage boyfriend: *You hang up. No, you hang up! I'll hang up when you hang up…*

I peel away from him, stepping backward toward the building before I turn and finally commit to going to class.

Sigh.

━━━━━━━━━━━━━━━━━━━━━━━━━

"So what's going on with you and that guy?"

I'm having lunch with Alex—the first time since that day she brought the *Get Rett Laid* poster—and she's just switched gears on me after giving me the entire rundown on her boyfriend/sidepiece saga.

Juggling two guys is going to catch up with her, but who am I to judge? Alexandra is going to do what she wants to do, whether it's wrong or right.

"What's going on with *what* guy?" I play dumb.

"You know, the ugly guy from the flyer—the dude from the party."

My nostrils flare. "Okay, first of all, he's not ugly. Secondly, his name is Rhett, and he's a really nice guy."

My cousin rolls her eyes. "*Right.*" She clearly doesn't care. "He's nice because he has to be."

"You think it's fair that people judge me without getting to know me first because I'm attractive?"

"So you agree? You think you're really pretty?"

"Stop quoting *Mean Girls*, I'm being serious." I pick up one of the French fries on my tray and pop it in my mouth. Chew. Swallow. "I'm not going to do that to Rhett—he's such a good guy."

"So?"

"So what I'm saying is, he and I have gotten close in the past few weeks."

"How close?"

"I don't know…like, I'm waiting for him to ask me on a date, close."

Alexandra leans back in her chair, stunned. "Seriously?"

"Yes, seriously."

"Wow. You really do like him."

"Yeah. He's great." I lean forward. "He speaks French and it's so freaking hot."

"Shut up."

"Ugh. Every once in a while he says something I can't understand and I pretend he's telling me to take my clothes off and strip down naked."

"That escalated quickly."

"I can't help it. He grew on me really quickly. We haven't had any deep, meaningful conversations, but I feel this weird connection that's more than physical—although I totally want to have sex with him too. His body is crazy hot."

Alex stares. "You should hear yourself."

My shoulders move up and down. "No apologies."

"Is this a guy you want to bring home to Aunt Karen and Uncle David?"

"My parents? Yeah, I think they'd love him."

"Well shit. I don't know what to do with this information."

"That's because your situation is fucked up. Pick a guy and date him. Stop fucking your boyfriend's roommate. There, I said it."

"You wouldn't understand what it's like being average."

"Why? Because I have bright red hair and big boobs and guys think I'm nice to look at? How does that make my life easier? All guys do is use me. That's no fun either." I pick up another fry, but my stomach is in knots and I can't bring myself to put it in my mouth. "All I'm saying is, Dylan likes you. Either break up with him or stop seeing Johnathan. The shit is going to hit the fan and you're going to be standing under it without an umbrella when it does."

"You think I don't know that?"

"Do you *care*?"

She picks at the food on her tray. "Honestly? Not really."

"Well then, I'll worry about my guy problems, and you can worry about yours." The water I chug goes down smooth, but it feels shitty that my cousin can be such an asshole.

"I 'liked' his in a relationship status to show him I know he's in a relationship with someone not as pretty as me."

Laurel

"Those outfits are like the speedos of the athletic world, but better." Donovan pokes me in the ribs with his forefinger to get my attention. "Do you see that guy from Ohio? I wonder if he's single."

"Or straight?" Lana teases, stealing the licorice from his hands and sticking it in her mouth.

"Would you two knock it off," I plead. "I'm nervous enough as it is."

"I would be, too," Lana says, ripping off another bite of red vine. "The groupie game is strong in here tonight."

We're seated in the third row from the floor with the tickets Rhett had dropped at will call—three rows from the mats, sweat, and strapping male wrestlers.

So far, my roommates and I are enjoying the view.

"There are so many balls here I don't know where to look first," Donovan mutters excitedly. "And here I thought baseball pants were where it's at. Compared to these singlets, they might as well be wearing diapers out there. I've slipped into my fantasy."

"Would you please stop?" I laugh. "Stop staring at everyone's balls."

"I can't help it." He holds his hand out as if he's presenting someone with a platter. "They're literally right there. See? Balls."

"And those groupies are on that shit hard," Lana points out. Again.

She's right though; the arena seems to be full of girls holding signs meant to draw attention to themselves, to attract attention from the players—wrestlers? Some of them wear next to nothing.

Fortunately, we're not seated in the student section, not part of the throng. Unfortunately, we have to stare at that section from across the arena. When my eyes scan the crowd, they hit a sea of signs along the way.

WE WANT 2 HAVE YOUR BAE-BIES, OZ

OPEN FOR PITWELL, 24 HOURS!

RETT WE WANNA LAY YOU! CALL ME

Glitter, rhinestones, and markers. Sorority letters and tight t-shirts. Awkward and uncomfortable, I have to sit here and stare at the signs begging to lay Rhett Rabideaux.

WILLING WITH A PULSE #GETRETTLAID. CALL ME!!

Over my dead body.

If anyone is having sex with him, it's going to be *me*.

Our boys earn themselves victory after victory, and the moment Rhett steps out onto the mats, I know I'm about to get educated on just how damn good a wrestler he is.

Why Iowa courted him so hard to bring him across the country, to our team.

He's amazing.

Tall and lean, he is nothing but muscle. Firm contours of sweaty, sinewy brawn. His thighs online and in photographs are nothing compared to his thighs in person, live and in color.

Jesus.

"Are you imagining yourself fucking him?" Donovan asks, nudging me.

"Yes," I whisper, staring.

"So am I." My roommate laughs.

"Shut up, Donovan!" I shove him, eyes never leaving the center ring, the blue mat under the spotlight where Rhett takes a guardian stance, eyeing the Ohio wrestler he's about to combat for the win.

For the pin.

Every cell in my body is aware of him, knees bent, arms out for centered gravity. Head goes down as he grapples with his opponent from Ohio, grabbing hold by the back of his neck. Pulling him down.

Rhett's head hits the guy's stomach, hands snake beneath his crotch, lifting. Ohio, as I've come to call him, flounders as his feet are suspended above the mats, Rhett flipping him onto his back.

Oh my God—that's the double takedown!

He's doing the move he did on me.

Seeing it done on someone else—with more force but just as much control—has me clasping my hands, lifting them to my mouth. Squealing when Rhett and Ohio are flat on the mats, twisting and flipping and rolling around on the floor.

Flipping and rolling: that's how it looks to me.

"Damn!" Lana shouts. "Holy shit, look at him!"

Rhett has Ohio on the mat in less than a minute, pinned by the neck in a chokehold or whatever they call it, the rest of his body a brick wall of force intended to keep his opponent down.

The ref counts the match.

One.

Two.

Three.

Rhett stands, sweating, the referee holding up his arm, declaring him the winner. His roommate runs to him with a white towel and a water bottle as his coach slaps him on the ass—his firm, tight ass, the muscles constricting with every step he takes to the sideline.

I find him easily afterward; he's alone in the hall, black duffle slung over his left shoulder. Head bent, tired. Lonely?

Watching him approach, I recline against the cinderblock wall of the basement tunnel that leads to the locker rooms, hands flattened against the cold partition behind me.

I'm wearing a tight black Iowa wrestling t-shirt I bought especially for the occasion, skinny jeans, and black half boots. My red hair falls in a straight curtain, and I feel my cheeks flush as he gets closer.

"Hey." He looks up when I greet him, disbelief in his eyes at the sight of me. Pleasure.

He's pleased.

"Hey. You came." His white teeth wink at me. "And you waited for me."

"Of course." My heart begins a steady beat inside my chest. "You're amazing. That was incredible, Rhett." I blurt out the words, not nearly as eloquent as they sounded in my head while I waited for him to emerge.

"Thanks." His brown eyes drag up and down my body, penetrating. Unless my imagination is playing a cruel trick on me, Rhett is throwing heat he's never thrown my way before. "I'm glad you're here."

"Did you see me in the stands?"

Affirmative. "I knew just where to look, and that hair of yours is hard to miss." He moves in closer, fingers flexing at his sides. Open, closed. "Man, you're a sight for sore eyes."

His voice is low. *Intense.*

"I am?" My heart races. Nerve endings practically tingle with anticipation.

"Yeah." He clenches and unclenches his fists. "I am so full of adrenaline right now."

I glance down at his hands. "Looks like it."

"I could run ten miles."

I've heard of these adrenaline highs, the rush athletes have after a game, the blood still raging through their strong, fit bodies. I've heard stories from other girls about sex marathons after a game. Sex for hours and *hours.*

I can see the tension in his eyes, the high color in his cheeks and face and neck.

He's turned on.

221

Rhett approaches. Drops his duffle to the ground and stands in front of me, chest heaving up and down inside his tight compression shirt. Pecs firm. Nipples hard.

I want to run my palms up his torso.

"Je vais t'embrasser." His mouth is moving, speaking words I don't understand, inching closer.

I nod. "Okay."

Those rough, callused hands cup my jaw, thumbs stroking my smooth skin.

"Je suis content que te es ici, Laurel." His lips brush the skin beneath my ear. "I'm really glad you're here."

He's so gentle. So tender.

My eyes slide closed and I bite my lip, bite back a moan.

"Putain, tu es jolie," he murmurs into my ear. "You're so fuckin' pretty."

"Merci." It's the only other French word I know, and it slips out on a whisper as I tilt my neck so he can plant a kiss there. His warm hands slide to the back of my neck, lips dragging along my jawline. To the corner of my mouth.

I part my lips as his full mouth glides over mine, the tips of our tongues meeting. Rhett tastes like spearmint toothpaste, hard work, and good decisions. A *sure* thing.

Commitment.

It doesn't take long for us to get carried away, and soon, we're making out in the empty tunnel as if our lives depend on it. Rhett has me pinned to the wall, years of repressed sexual energy and adrenaline bubbling over, and before I know it, his chaffed hand is sliding down my spine.

Across my waist. Up the front of my shirt, thumb brushing along the undersides of my breasts.

My capable hands rake up his chest, around his neck. Tangle into the hair that could use a trim.

It's all so fucking good.

I'm pinned to the wall, his pelvis—his hard dick—pressed into the apex of my thighs, and I do the only thing I'm capable of doing at the moment: I moan.

We're just getting to the good stuff when the sound of my moan mingles with the sound of voices echoing out of the locker room door. We're not alone.

"Shit." Rhett breaks contact, muttering. Lips hit my temple, land a kiss along the collar of my shirt. "Come with me. Let's get the fuck out here."

I nod. *I'd follow him anywhere.*

I grasp his hand as he swipes his bag from the ground, the two of us breaking into a light jog in the hall, desperate to get to his car.

Desperate to be alone.

I'm being pulled behind him, his hand clutching mine as he guides me down the tunnel toward the exit that leads to the parking lot.

"We'll come back and get your car later."

This side of him thrills me, the bossy, in-control side—the side that only took minutes to pin a two-hundred-pound man onto a blue wrestling mat.

I let him lead me down the hall, out the door, to the dark parking lot.

"Where are you parked?" My eyes do a quick scan for his Jeep, the only car parked at the far end...

"It's right over—" He stops in his tracks. "What the fuck? What. The. *Fuck.*"

He drops my hand, pointing to the Jeep at the far side, wrapped in...

I hate asking out loud, but, "Is that plastic wrap?"

He stalks in the direction of his car, grinding out an angry, "Yes."

The Jeep is indeed tightly wrapped in plastic, a clear coat of something sticky beneath it, like someone smeared Vaseline then swathed the Jeep with an industrial-size roll of saran wrap.

"I can't go home. It will just end up in a fight." His hands go behind his head, pacing. "Those fuckin' assholes."

"Who would have done this? We weren't inside long enough for someone to have done it while you were in the locker room, were we?"

"No. Someone else could have easily done it, but I doubt it." He picks at the plastic, peeling back a layer. Shoulders slouch, defeated. "Fuck. This is going to take all night to get clean."

I lay a gentle hand on his firm tricep. "Come with me now and I promise we'll come back in the morning and figure this out together."

"Yeah." He hefts his bag. Nods. "All right."

I take his hand, tugging him toward my car, my father's late-model SUV. I used to hate it because it's so big, but man, I can fit so much shit in the back.

Once, in high school, I had twelve of my friends piled in. Not safe, I know, but…we were stupid back then, and irresponsible.

It's big, safe, and outdated—and it's all mine.

"This is your car?"

"Yes." I laugh, hitting the locks. "Hop in."

His large body hits the seat, collapsing into it. Buckles himself in. Sags, head hitting the headrest.

Poor guy.

I pat his thigh.

Start the ignition, pull out of the parking lot with Rhett beside me, staring out into the dark night.

I feel so bad. "Where should we go?"

I'm not ready to take us home.

"Anywhere." He turns his head to look at me. "Somewhere quiet."

I rack my brain for possibilities, the only spot that's coming to mind a lookout point off campus, high in some bluffs. It's secluded and remote and no one will bother us there.

Slowly, I wind my SUV up the narrow road toward the highest point in the county, just a two-mile ride out of town. The road twists up and around, a short ten-minute drive.

It's a popular spot, high in the hills, the sight panoramic, crossing twenty miles into the distance—and when it's dark, nothing beats the span of glowing city lights below. *Nothing.*

We're lucky tonight—when we pull in, there are only two other cars present, and my guess is that they're empty. The reason people come up is for the view, and the view from the overlook is a hot spot for photo ops; I never pass up a chance to bring my parents here when they visit.

I find a spot, cut the engine.

Unbuckle and turn to face him. "Do you want to talk about it?"

"Not really."

I nod in the dark.

It's pitch black up here, save for one poor excuse for a flood light. This is not a place I'd want to be alone with someone I just met, and probably shouldn't be here with a guy I'm just getting to know.

But my instincts are screaming that Rhett's one of the good guys.

"Have you ever lost a match?"

I hear him shrug in the dark. "Sure."

"Like, how many?"

His soft chuckle comes out of the dark, warming my insides like warm, gooey caramel. *Mmm.*

I poke his bicep with the tip of my finger, teasing. "Come on, tell me. You obviously know the exact number, don't be modest."

"Five."

225

"Five this year?" When did their season start, and how long does it last? "That's not…terrible." *Is it?*

"No, five since I was a freshman."

"Five?" Holy shit, that's *it?*

"Yeah, that's it."

My face turns red, and I'm grateful for the dark. "I said that out loud?"

"Yeah, you said that out loud."

"Jesus, Rhett, that's…I mean, I know nothing about wrestling but I know a little about stats, and that…wow. Five."

"Thanks."

There's a console in the center of the front seats, separating us by about ten inches, and his big hand is rested on top of it. I can see it even in the dark, his skin illuminated just enough.

"The more I learn about you, the more I like you."

I lay my hand on the console next to his, breathlessly waiting to see if he'll take it.

It takes several heartbeats, but he does, sliding his rough palm over my knuckles. Stroking the silky skin I meticulously maintain with expensive lotions and sea salt scrubs.

The callused pads of his fingers against my smooth skin are a delightful contrast, reminding me of how different we are, how strong and virile and hardworking Rhett is.

Our fingers entwine.

"This is nice."

"It is." His gravelly voice is a low murmur, barely above a whisper. "I needed this."

"Honestly?" I give his hand a squeeze. "Me too."

We study each other in the dark, hands clasped. Lean in at the same time, separated only by the console, lips meeting under the dull flicker of light. My eyes flutter closed when his mouth presses against mine and I sigh, accepting each and every kiss.

Blissfully, I sigh again, loud and long into his mouth when his tongue touches mine. Stroking.

He's a damn good kisser.

I hum. "*Mmm.*"

His long fingers bury themselves in my hair, pulling me closer, grasping the back of my neck. Our lips suction together, needy.

I've never been this hot for anyone before; my body is on fire, a blazing inferno. Ignited, I want to touch him, not just kiss him.

"Mon Dieu tu sens merveilleuse," he croaks out, fingers still buried in my hair. "You feel good."

Crap. I am *so* screwed with this guy.

"Back seat, Rhett, back seat." I pry my lips off him, instantly mourning the connection. "Back seat, now."

I hit the unlock button on the door and we unbuckle our seatbelts, frantically scrambling out our doors and into the back. Rhett folds inside, parking himself center on the seat. Legs spread, I immediately climb on top, straddling him, craving the connection.

Flick the hat off his head.

My fingers plow through his shaggy locks, lips graze the column of his throat. Jawline. Temple.

I lean into him, breasts squished against that solid wall of a chest, rubbing over him like a cat against a scratching post. I groan when his mouth finds my lips, his hands skimming up and down my backside. Palms grabbing hold of my ass and squeezing.

My palms find his biceps, caressing. Run up and down his arms, across his shoulders, exploring. He's so warm and firm and strong. Ridiculously strong.

I marvel at his body, wishing there was more light, wanting to see the expression on his face when I kiss the bump on the bridge of his nose. The scar on his eyebrow.

He reads my mind.

One of those brawny arms rises, swiping at the light switch in the ceiling. When it goes on, he leans back to study me. I return the favor, learning the contours of his face, just *looking*, my gaze tracing the arch of his brow. Cheekbones. The lines in his forehead.

He really is pretty darn cute.

I lean in to kiss him again, sweet, passionate open-mouth kisses that light a fire inside my soul—inside my panties—and fog up the windows. I arch so he can see my face.

A tentative finger traces along my jaw, down my neck, down the center of my sternum. I suck in a ragged breath when that finger hits my belly button, fiddling with the hem of my shirt. Taking his hands in mine, I guide them to my waist, under my shirt. Break any invisible boundaries he may have created in his mind, *needing* to feel his hands on my bare skin.

They skim up my ribcage, slowly, gliding their way to the tender undersides of my breasts.

Feather light, driving me in*sane*.

I sink deeper onto his lap, lining up my pussy with his stiff cock, rotating my hips like a stripper in a nightclub giving a lap dance, head rolling back as his tip finds that sweet spot down below.

His pants are mesh polyester, thin.

My leggings are cotton, *thinner*.

Our guttural, simultaneous moans fill the cab of my car.

Rhett grips my hips, working me back and forth over his erection; I can feel everything through the threadbare fabric of my pants. Underwear. His pants.

My hands grapple at his waist. Haul his gray compression shirt up and over his head. He gives his hair a shake as I toss the shirt to the side. My hands—my *lucky* hands—roam his upper torso, greedy for his warm skin.

"Your body is insane. Unbelievable." I could eat him up.

Rhett's head sags against the seat when my mouth sucks on the space where his shoulder and neck meet, my tongue gliding. His flesh is smooth. Tight.

Hot.

So hot.

I circle his dusky nipple with the tip of my finger. Pluck it just to hear him gasp.

His paws are back on my body, skimming the sensitive skin near the waistband of my pants. He strokes my flesh but holds back, gripping my ribcage but not touching my boobs.

I bit my lip, debating.

Watch his face as he momentarily closes his eyes, lips parting, lost in the sensation of the gyrating motions in his lap. Over his erection.

Unable to stand it, I grip the hem of my Iowa t-shirt, pulling it off so I'm on his lap in nothing but a wireless bra.

I know what he sees, what my body looks like—he's not the only one who works out, and my breasts are pretty damn fantastic.

"Shit," he mutters at the sight of me, gripping my hips tighter.

"Like what you see?"

He swallows, hips rocking beneath me. "Yeah."

Then look your fill, Rhett Rabideaux.

Rhett

I don't know where to put my hands after Laurel peels her shirt off and tosses it aside, but I sure as shit know where to *look*.

I can't not stare; it's impossible. Laurel's perky tits are right fucking there, in my face, an erotic wet dream come to life.

She trails her fingertips along the straps of her lacy, see-through bra, up and down and back again, slowly tracing the edges near her nipples. Wiggles her ass on my lap.

Leans forward, long red hair brushing my chest.

My nerves are going fucking haywire, exploding, every touch shooting off a sensitive spark. My chest, her hair, skin, thighs.

My cock is ready to detonate.

I'm so fucking hard it's like I can feel the blood draining from my brain and rushing to my throbbing dick.

At the sensation of her fantastic boobs rubbing against my pecs, back and forth and up and down, I swear I almost jizz my fucking pants.

"Touch me," she whispers near my ear, licking the outer shell. Guides my hands back up her bare torso.

Wordlessly, my palms cover her breasts, over the pale lace, languidly tracing the delicate scraps her hands were covering, the pads of my trembling fingers running up the straps of her bra.

Yeah, that's right—I'm goddamn *trembling*.

Dragging both straps down, I incline, and when I kiss the swell of her plump flesh, goose bumps form on her skin. Her hair falls over one shoulder, and I move it aside to kiss her neck. Kiss her throat, dragging my lips across her bare shoulder, two bra straps limping lifelessly down her triceps.

Until they fall down her arms.

I tenderly palm her boob, thumbs slowly brushing back and forth across her stiff nipples. Around and around her areola. Her head goes back, a strangled moan escaping her throat, filling the void in the car.

Laurel rotates her hips, grinding down on my dick while I cup her boobs. I can feel the slit inside her black leggings, the head of my dick seeking the heat I know must be primed as fuck. Slick.

"You're going to make me come—God, you found my clit," she says as she pants, her words drawn out like a whine. "I'm so close."

Come. Clit. Close. Those three words, a heady aphrodisiac.

"Fuck, so am I."

"*I want you so bad.*" I don't know if she says it or if I do.

When I suck her tits into my mouth, one stiff nipple at a time, she grabs a fistful of my hair. Tugs. Bears down on my lap, dry humping the shit out of me.

My hands grab her ass cheeks, instinctively dragging her down harder. It feels *so fucking good* it's almost agonizing. My brows furrow as if in pain as my arms wrap around her, holding her tight.

Our mouths fuse, one breath.

My balls tighten; her boobs feel like heaven in my mouth and against my bare chest and I want to fuck her, fuck the fucking shit right out of her, so bad my mouth waters at the thought.

Laurel sucks my earlobe when I tip my head back against the headrest, her labored breath fueling me on, hips thrusting upward, wanting to be inside her.

"Oh! Yes, yes, keep doing that…" comes her frantic whisper.

Another set of headlights eases up the rise, but we're consumed with each other, one thing on our minds—coming.

"Mmm," she groans into my mouth, riding my lap, mimicking sex I've only seen in Tumblr porn. Grabbing my hands and planting them back on her tits. "Mmm, *yes*." Laurel hisses through her teeth. "Don't stop touching me or I'll die."

It's more than I can take.

The slow build inside my balls grows.

"Shit," I growl. "Shit, shit." I'm going to come in my shorts, something I've never done in my entire fucking life, because I've never had a hot girl grind on me, never even been alone in the same room with a hot girl before Laurel.

Ever.

"Are you coming?" she whimpers.

"Are you?"

"Yes, yes, don't you dare stop."

I couldn't even if I wanted to, not for a million fuckin' bucks, despite the imminent chafing happening inside my boxer briefs.

When we come, we shudder together, her arms sliding around my neck, warm lips finding the pulse in my throat. She nuzzles my shoulder, mouth resting below my ear.

"I like you." Her fingers reach up, toying with a curl at the back of my head. "A lot."

"Je vous aussi," I murmur into her hair, stroking it with my palm, hand gliding down the smooth skin of her back. *I like you, too.*

And it scares the shit out of me.

16

#DOUCHEBAG

"This morning confirmed it—
it's definitely Maybelline."

Rhett

"**W**ake up, fuck stick. Coach called an emergency meeting."

Jesus Christ, does it ever end with this guy?

I crack an eyelid, rolling toward the voice of my roommate, feeling for my phone, wanting to check the time. "How did you get in here? I thought I locked the door."

"It was easy." He yanks back my covers. "Get up. We have to hustle."

"Why?" My bare feet hit the floor. Legs stand.

"I don't know, but we have to be at the field house in fifteen minutes. Get your shit on and let's go. Johnson's driving."

A pair of pants and hoodie get tossed on the bed, the sweatshirt nearly hitting my face.

He's exiting the room when I call him back.

"Hey."

He turns, hand grabbing the doorframe. "Yeah?"

"Who did it?"

"Did what?"

"Don't play dumb—who fucking vandalized my car."

My roommate shuffles on the hardwood floor, eyes trained on the beige wall behind me. "I don't know."

"Would you cut the crap?" I pull the black sweatshirt down over my head. Yank on the athletic shorts. "Who fucking was it?"

"I'm telling you, man, I don't know!"

"You've got the balls to stand there and lie to my face? Nice."

I gather up my bag, stuffing in an extra pair of shorts.

"This is just a meeting—you won't have to work out," he's quick to point out.

I ignore him, throwing a jock strap, tank, and socks in my duffle.

"Yeah, well, I didn't take the NCAA championship twice by pissing away my days, did I, Gunderson?" I glance at him hovering in the doorway. "Get the fuck out if you're not going to give me any information."

He hesitates. "It was some sorority girls."

I straighten. "What?"

Gunderson shrugs his scrawny shoulders. "It was some sorority girls. Someone thought if would be funny if you came outside and your Jeep was wrapped in, uh, plastic wrap."

"Who's banging sorority girls?"

"I don't know, everybody?"

I toss a new pair of tennis shoes in with my clothes. "That really narrows it down, doesn't it?"

"If I knew, I would tell you."

I laugh cynically. "Yeah right."

"Look, man, I'll help you get your Jeep home, okay? We'll do it after the meeting."

"Don't fucking bother."

"I come to the stadium this morning and what the hell do you think I see in the parking lot? Any of you ladies know the answer I'm looking for?"

Crickets.

"No one has anything to say this morning?"

We all stare dumbly at Coach, who looks like he's about to pop the straining blood vessel in the center of his forehead. He is fucking *pissed*.

"I saw Rhett Rabideaux's Jeep wrapped in fucking plastic. Who here thinks that shit was funny? Who here thinks it was safe? Show of hands."

His question is met with stillness, silence, so he powers on.

"What the fuck is wrong with you guys?" He paces to the side of the room normally reserved for reviewing tapes, slamming a clipboard onto the table he uses for transcripts.

Coach rakes a weathered hand through his graying hair, hands behind his head, staring at the wall. "I don't know what I'm supposed to do here. I have to hold someone accountable. If no one speaks up, you're all suspended until we figure it out."

Still, no one utters a word.

Until, "Coach, I don't think it's fair to suspend everyone because of a stupid prank."

Coach doesn't even turn around. "Shut the fuck up, Tennyson. Unless you can supply me with a name, consider yourself on probation."

Someone coughs.

"Come on Coach," Brandon Tennyson argues. "I'm sure whoever did this"—he glances around the room, eyes narrowed into dangerous slits—"*who*ever did this was just trying to be *funny*."

"I assure you, ladies, the staff didn't get the joke." Coach turns toward Iowa's coaching team, gesturing toward the support staff. "We've been here for hours, discussing our options. The way we see it, there aren't many alternatives. We cannot have a team full of little pricks who think hazing a new teammate is tolerated. You are adults. It's time to take your punishment like grown men."

One of the freshman redshirts raises his hand. "But Coach, won't we have to forfeit the season if you suspend us?"

"BINGO!"

Throughout the room, a ripple of countless murmurs, profanity. Complaining from a few braver souls.

Sebastian Osborne clears his thick throat, speaking up, humor infusing his deep voice. "Coach, come on, isn't there something we can do so we're not fucking up the rest of our season? Some of us depend on the scholarship money."

One of those someones being him.

Coach studies his cuticles. "You boys should have thought of that when you left Rabideaux stranded in the parking lot last night."

Osborne isn't giving up. "Isn't there something we can do? There has to be."

"Funny you should ask. As a matter of fact, there is." He motions for Roger Danvers, our conditioning coach, to join him in front. Danvers ambles forward with a scowl, tossing a pair of keys at Coach, who holds them up, jingles them. "See these keys? These are your ticket to freedom."

Confused glances around the room.

"Danvers is going to list off our suspects. Those people are going to take Rabideaux and these goddamn keys and head up to my lake house for a little team bonding, and I don't want to see any of your fucking faces back in this room until you figure this shit out. The next little asshole to pull a prank gets suspended from the team, and expelled from school." His beady eyes scan the room. "Are we clear?"

A collective nods waves through the group.

"I didn't hear you: are we clear?"

"Yes."

"Not one goddamn prank or I will make sure your time at Iowa is over."

Silence.

"Gunderson. Johnson. Ryder. Tennyson…" Coach rattles off the ten names he suspects of guilt. "That's it. Now get the fuck out. You have one hour to hightail it out of here and get your asses to the cottage before I have them in a sling." He raises his voice a notch, pointing to the team captains. "Zeke and Oz? Congratulations, you're playing chaperone. My office, now."

Well *shit*.

Laurel

The last person I expect to bump into at the campus coffee shop is Rex Gunderson, the wrestling team's manager and Rhett's roommate. He spots Alex and me in a corner booth, smiles wide, ambles over when I catch his eye.

"Mind if I sit for a second?" He takes the seat next to Alex without waiting for a reply.

"Uh, sure." My cousin rolls her eyes. "Be my guest."

"Thanks." He wastes no time eyeing up my blueberry muffin. "Mind if I..."

No manners, I swear. "Yes, I kind of mind."

Rhett's roommate ignores me, splits the top off my muffin, breaks in it half, and shoves my fluffy, berry-filled pastry down his gullet. Swallows. Eats the other half. "You talk to Rhett yet?"

"Not today." I swear this guy always has an agenda. "Why?"

"Just wondering."

When he moves for the bottom half of my muffin, I slap his hand away, irritated.

"Not to be rude, but want to tell us what you want?" Leave it to Alexandra to cut to the chase. For once, I'm grateful for her rude demeanor. "We were in the *middle* of a conversation."

This doesn't seem to faze Rex Gunderson. "So we had an emergency team meeting this morning. I don't know if Rabideaux told you about it, but since I walked in and here you were, I might as well give you the good news."

"What news? Is he getting an award for something?"

"Uh, no. A few members of the team are being sent on a retreat this weekend."

My brows rise. "Oh?"

"It's at a cabin in Big Bear. Hour from here, know where that is? Google it."

I peel the paper liner off my muffin. "Uh huh."

"You wanna come?"

I raise my eyebrows again. "Me?"

"Yeah. All the girlfriends are going along. I figured Rhett would want you along too, but he's such a damn pussy."

"You really think he'd want me to go?" It's still early in the day; surely he'll mention it if he wants me there.

"Of course. You're hot." I do a mental hair flip. "Plus, don't you think he'd feel like an asshole if he was the only guy there without his girlfriend?"

That's the second time Rex has used the word girlfriend, and I wonder if he's daring me to contradict him.

I don't.

"I don't know Rex, I think that's something he should ask me himself."

He laughs. "We both know he doesn't have the guts."

True. Rhett is a tad insecure about our budding relationship; the last thing he'd want is to leave himself open to rejection.

Still. "Are you sure it would be okay? Other girls are coming?"

"Oh yeah, I'm totally sure. You can even ride with me and surprise him when you get there. He will *piss* himself."

I nibble my lip. "I know, but I really don't want to have any secrets from him." Not after lying to him in the past. "You understand that, right?"

"I get that, and I respect that." When he goes to pat me on the hand, I pull it away. "But! Don't you think surprising him will be *way* more fun?"

He has a point: surprising Rhett at the wrestling retreat *would* be fun. Spending the night with him in a secluded cabin in the woods? With possible naked body parts? *Yes please.* Who knows what would happen between us in that kind of secluded setting…

Although, the thought of keeping the secret from him already plants a small seed of guilt inside my belly, given the rocky way we started our relationship. Lie after lie.

Would not telling him be a betrayal?

Rex stands, grabbing the last bite of muffin off my plate. "Just think about it. Take my number and text me if you change your mind."

He rattles off his cell, and I program it into mine—just in case.

"Okay, I will. Thanks."

Alexandra leans forward when he finally struts off. "Dude, you totally have to go."

"I know, and I'm going to, I just can't decide if I should do it without telling him. I don't want to freak him out or add more pressure. Those guys are such assholes."

"Maybe he'll tell you about it later. It's only like, one o'clock."

"Maybe."

"Do you trust his roommate?"

"I don't know—*Rhett* doesn't trust him, so no, not really."

Alex takes a bite of celery stick, crunching as she chews. "Know what I think? I think you're being paranoid."

"About what?"

"About what would happen if you went. He's not going to be mad, Laurel. He's *a guy*, and guys think with their dicks."

Shrug. "Maybe."

But maybe not.

"You always overthink everything. Seriously, what's the worst thing that could happen if you go? You finally get laid? The other girlfriends are going—do you really want him to leave him there stag? Some of those WAGS are bitches."

"I do not overthink everything. I'm using my common sense and trusting my better judgment instead of being impulsive."

"But think about it this way: this is your chance to get him alone in the middle of nowhere. You'll probably be sharing a room." My cousin's black eyebrows wiggle. "Or you can sneak away for some alone time, maybe go skinny-dipping."

"Are you out of your mind? It's cold out."

"True, and there is that problem of shrinkage." Alex dangles a limp straw wrapper over her tea mug. "I know you want to go. Stop pretending you're not going to."

She's right.

I do want to go.

If Rhett is going to be stuck in a cabin with all those dicks for the weekend, he needs a friend, an ally.

And that person is me.

Rhett: *We had a meeting this morning. Just wanted to let you know I won't be around this weekend, you know, in case you wanted to hang out.*

Me: *What's going on?*

Rhett: *Coach is making us do a team retreat at some cottage in the woods? Won't be back until Sunday but I'll have my phone.*

Me: *I'll miss you. Have fun…*

"You know it's a good night when you find your torn-up underwear in your purse and a Nerf dart falls out of your jeans."

Rhett

The sound of tires gradually moving over solid ground fills the air, my roommate's black car slowly creeping up the wide, rocky driveway in the woods.

We're gathered on the deck of Coach's lake house, a huge log cabin with tons of windows and a wraparound porch, isolated in the middle of nowhere. Fire pit. Two piers. Jet skis, speedboat, and pontoon. It's more than enough to keep us occupied while we're stuck here for twenty-four hours.

No one has dared touch anything in the house for fear of breaking something or messing shit up.

Coach would kill us.

The place is meticulously maintained and obviously worth a shit ton of money.

Beer cans popped, we're gathered on the wooden deck, taking up every chair we could find in the storage shed, waiting for a few stragglers. Gunderson, Pitwell, and three others haven't arrived yet.

"The look on your face when you walked into the practice gym the next day after those dicks stiffed you with that bill." Oz Osborne laughs in my direction. "Priceless."

Zeke Daniels—notoriously quiet—chuckles into his beer can, lips twisted into a smirk. "I wish I would have seen your expression when you saw your Jeep."

"Fuck you, assholes." I laugh. "I'm lucky I wasn't alone—those fuckers just left me there."

"*Yeah* they did." Oz laughs, high-fiving Tennyson. "Do you know how long it took to find some girls to wrap your Jeep like that? Like an en*tire* five minutes."

They laugh again, the noise echoing in the woods. It's taken a full three hours with these guys to finally laugh everything off;

their good-humored ribbing feels like an opening for a place in their tight inner circle.

"I have to ask, why did y'all keep doing that shit to me?"

"Because you say things like *y'all*." Daniels snorts and rolls his eyes. "We've never had a new guy join the team so late, seemed reasonable to make you earn our respect."

"By wiping my Jeep down with Vaseline?"

Oz takes a drink of beer. "Huh, is that what they used? I thought they'd use cooking grease or some shit like that." He's impressed. "Vaseline is way better."

"Haha fuckers."

"What the hell is taking every else so long to get here?" Brandon asks, craning his neck toward the driveway, trying to conjure up the stragglers. He's seated next to Ryker, the asshole who gave me a ride to the Pancake House but left me stranded there.

"Don't know." Osborne checks his cell phone, casting a glance around the group, making eye contact with several of the guys. They glance at each other, Oz's brows rising when Johnson's eyes flick to the cell phone in Oz's palm.

His brows rise, too.

Weird.

If I hadn't been staring straight at him, I would have missed it. A queasy feeling settles in the pit of my stomach. They're planning something; I would bet money on it.

There are three of us on the deck now, the rest methodically disappearing one by one as cell phones start pinging with notifications.

"Where the hell is everyone going?" I wonder out loud, wanting to keep track now that my radar has gone up. "Are we doing a bonfire or what?"

"Um." Oz doesn't meet my eyes. "Changing into swimsuits."

"Y'all brought suits?" My eyes narrow. "It's not even sixty degrees."

The shore down by the water is lined with three kayaks, two canoes, and a rowboat; Coach's kids must use that shit when they're here. If the weather would cooperate, thirteen athletes stranded in bumblefuck with no gym for miles would be having a field day with those water toys.

But, it's fifty-four fucking degrees and windy with a storm approaching from the west. No one is getting in the water, not without freezing their balls off.

"You afraid of a little shrinkage, New Guy?" Ryker jokes.

Hardly.

I've seen these douches naked in the shower and have nothing to be ashamed of.

In the driveway, Gunderson's car door opens. Slams.

Then another slam echoes, causing everyone to turn.

My throat drops to the pit of my stomach when that bright familiar hair is tossed, the russet waves popping against the green leaves of the trees. She bends, ass in the air, to retrieve something from the front seat, and I stare, dumbstruck.

What the hell is Laurel doing here.

"Well looky who it is, New Guy, your two favorite people: Gunderson and Fire Crotch," Johnson says as he ogles her.

I take a shot, rising out of my seat and landing a fist in his rib-cage. "Don't call her that, dickhead."

"Sorry, but her hair is red." The idiot says it like I'm the ass-hole here. "That makes her a fire crotch."

Ryker sniffs. "Do her curtains match the drapes?"

Johnson laughs, rolling his dull brown irises. "Like he would know."

What the hell *is she doing here?*

Laurel is gorgeous, a delicate juxtaposition against the rustic landscape. Fiery red hair in a high, flirty ponytail, her tight white tee is smoothed over her set of fantastic breasts, black leggings showing off her sexy, incredible figure. White Converse crunch the loose gravel beneath her feet as she takes a few tentative steps toward me.

Wiggles her fingers in greeting. "Surprise?"

That is a fucking understatement.

"Was it a mistake coming here?" She raises a hand to her hair, fingering her ponytail. "You don't look as excited as I thought you'd be."

"I…"

Her blue eyes scan the shore down by the lake. The deck. Peer into the house through the panoramic windows.

"Um, where are all the girls?"

"Girls?"

"Yeah, the girls. Rex said there would be a bunch of girls here? He said…" Her voice trails off. "Well *shit*."

I stuff my hands into the pockets of my jeans. "I don't know how to tell you this, so I'll just say it: this is a mandatory team buildin' weekend. There are no girls here."

"Oh my God." Laurel's skin burns as bright as her flaming hair, fists clenched into balls at her hips. "Gunderson, that jerk! Now I'm stuck here with a bunch of *guys*?"

"It's fine, we'll manage. Let's grab your stuff and stash it in my room until we figure this shit out."

"I'm going to *kill* that roommate of yours. I knew I shouldn't have trusted him. God, I feel like such an ass."

"Don't worry about it." My hand goes to the indent of her waist as we make our way to Gunderson's car to grab her stuff. "To be honest, you're a sight for sore eyes. It's nice having a friendly face show up."

A beautiful, sexy, smiling face.

Her scowl is adorable. "I'm still going to kill Gunderson."

Yeah. I am too—the whole lot of those dickheads.

I grab her bag out of the trunk—a large, quilted, floral duffle bag with a cross-body strap—hike it over my shoulder, and lead her back toward the house.

She trails along behind me, small hand slipping into mine.

I stare down at our clasped hands as we step up onto the cedar deck, smile down at her, helping her up onto the raised porch.

In the short time I was at the car gathering Laurel's things, the guys were evidently busying themselves picking up the beer bottles and cans from the patio. Daniels holds a black trash bag open while everyone tosses the garbage inside.

He gives Laurel a nod, his weird, piercing gray eyes checking her out skeptically. "What's up?"

She blushes under his scrutiny. "Hi."

"Laurel, you remember Zeke Daniels? Don't mind his pissed-off expression, he has resting dick face."

"Okay." She laughs as we pass him, allowing me to lead her into the house. Inside the log cabin is more wood, split logs from floor to ceiling, a massive fieldstone fireplace standing eighteen feet tall.

With the impending cold weather, someone had the foresight to light a fire.

Facing it, a leather sectional and an ottoman covered in cow print fabric. Plaid pillows and fuzzy throw blankets.

"Wow. This is incredible." Her mouth tips down at the corners. "It's a shame I won't be staying."

There's a bunkroom above the garage, but we drew straws and I ended up in one of the guest rooms overlooking the lake, so that's where we head.

I lead her to the stairs, lugging her heavy bag.

"What the heck is in here?" I grunt, readjusting the strap digging its way into the muscle of my right tricep.

"I didn't know what the weather was going to be like, and I wanted to have options...sorry."

"I'm just teasin'."

Her arm reaches around, turns the handle, and gives it a shove so I can walk through and dump her duffle on the king-sized bed.

"Do you have a bathroom in here?"

"Yeah, through that door."

"Okay. Give me a second?"

"Take all the time you need."

Laurel is halfway through the bathroom door when she turns, resting her hand on the doorjamb, biting her bottom lip and studying me where I stand in the center of the room. "I'm so sorry I just showed up like this. I really did think there would be other women here."

"It's okay. Don't worry about it."

"I know, it's just…I don't want to make this any harder for you than it's been with your team." She palms the doorknob. "The look on your face…you looked shocked."

"I was, but that's just because I…" Was happy to see her. Relieved, even. Fuck yes I was glad to see her when she stepped out of that car. "Anyway, take your time. Then we'll go see if any of the guys want to start the grill; I'm starving."

"Perfect." She gives me a warm smile. "I'll be right out."

"I'll wait."

Laurel

My hand lifts to the ponytail in my hair and I ease the rubber band out. Slide it over my red locks, dragging it until it's all the way out. Give my head a shake, letting the whole mess cascade around my face.

Fluff it.

Run a hand down the front of my shirt, smoothing the hem over the top of my black cotton leggings. Turn this way and that to check out my profile in the mirror.

Stomach is flat. No underwear lines.

Boobs look great.

Bending, I untie both my shoes, kicking them off. Pull off my socks, ball them up, shove them inside my Chucks. Grab a washcloth, dampen it under the faucet, and wipe my stinky sneaker feet with a little soap and water.

Blow out a breath before pulling the door to the bedroom open.

Rhett is seated at the foot of the big bed, legs spread, arms braced on the mattress behind him, backward baseball cap making him look young and carefree with his ears sticking out under the edge.

His crooked smile gives me pause, and before he can rise, I step into his open legs. Lean in, hands sliding to his shoulders, lips pressing against his.

If he's surprised by my physical attention, he recovers quickly, mouth widening, meeting my kiss with a solid peck of his own. Arms go around me, hands firmly cupping my ass cheeks and squeezing, tongue exploring my mouth.

"*Mmm.*" I press in closer, bending to press a kiss to his temple. "We can't get carried away or they're going to think we're fooling around in here."

"Trust me, they don't have that much faith in me."

"Then they're idiots," I whisper. Rhett's giant hands span my waist, fingers fanned out, thumbs nearly touching. "Because I…because…"

I like you.

Think you're wonderful.

Want to be more than friends.

Only I can't get the words out; they're lodged in my throat.

"You can't stay." His head hits my belly and I take the opportunity to run my fingers along the column of his strong neck.

"I know." But I'm here now.

He lifts his head. Tips his chin so he can look me in the eye. "During dinner we'll figure out how to get you home. Maybe Gunderson will let you take his car, and he can ride home with someone else—it's his fault he put you in this position."

Us, I silently correct him. Gunderson put *us* in this position.

"That works."

"All right. Let's go find something to eat."

Rhett stands before I can back away, our bodies smashed together, the rigid length of him distinctly noticeable against my thigh. He lifts an arm, hand sliding to the back of my neck. I rise to my tiptoes, meeting his lips for another kiss.

Sigh.

The house is eerily quiet when we finally crack the bedroom door, emerging into the lofted overlook above the cavernous living room.

The empty living room.

The empty living room with the perfect view of an empty deck and an empty beach.

"Where the hell is everyone?"

"Maybe they went out on the boat?"

I lag behind him, peer over the guardrail of the loft. Stare down into the empty, silent kitchen. No way are twelve wrestlers this quiet.

"Do you suppose…" I can't even finish the sentence, certain I know the answer. "They left us here?"

"Let's check their rooms for luggage."

We find nothing as we hit room after room, not a trace of anyone except us.

"I should have fucking known they were going to pull something like this." He gets out his phone. Pounds out a message.

His cell dings within seconds and he proceeds to go angrily back and forth several times before I can't stand it any longer and ask, "What did he say?"

Rhett slaps his phone in my open palm and my eyes scan the messages in the group chat.

Rhett: *Where the hell are you assholes? Did you run to town or something?*

Gunderson: *Gone like a freight train, gone like yesterday.*

Rhett: *What the hell are you on about? Are you here or not?*

Gunderson: *No dipshit.*

Rhett: *So y'all didn't run out to pick up dinner or what?*

Johnson: *No dumbass. Like, gone. For the night.*

Gunderson: *We went home.*

Rhett: *ALL of you?*

Johnson: *Yeah. All of us.*

Rhett: *You fucking left us here? Stranded?*

Johnson: *Yah, calm down—it's only an hour away. Thought you'd want to be alone with Fire Crotch.*

Gunderson: *We like to think we're doing you a favor.*

Rhett: *HOW is stranding us an hour from home doing us a favor?*

Gunderson: *Tonight when you're banging the ginger, you're going to be THANKING us. I accept cash and gift cards in any denomination.*

Ryker: *Don't worry your pretty little heads—we'll be back in the morning to fetch you.*

Gunderson: *And dude, lighten up. Have fun before she wises up and figures out how boring you are.*

"They left us here?"

Not going to lie, I'm not broken up about it—not even a little. In fact, quite the opposite.

Instead of anger, a bubble of excitement wells up inside me and I tamp down the happy dance my feet want to do across the hardwood floors.

"So we're here…alone?"

"Looks like it."

"For the entire night?"

"Yeah. Jesus Laurel, I am so sorry." Rhett blows out a puff of frustrated air, hand gripping the back of his neck. "It's one thing for them to fuck with me, but another for them to involve you."

I can't very well say, *I'm glad the idiots are gone, let's cuddle,* can I? Not when he feels so guilty that I'm stuck here.

So I go with, "Let's make the best of the situation. What do we have for food? I really am starving."

Together we head to the large kitchen, noting a heavily stocked fridge with relief. Water bottles, juice boxes, chocolate milk. Eggs. Vegetables and fruit. Hot dogs and chicken breasts. It looks like someone went to a deli and bought pasta salads.

In the freezer, several frozen pizzas. Popsicles. A container of vanilla bean ice cream. Frozen broccoli and scallops.

"It's not the burgers I thought we were going to have, but want to toss in a pizza?"

"Or two?"

"Or two." Rhett smiles, grabbing the pies. "Supreme and a cheese?"

"Works for me. I'll preheat the oven."

We set to work in the kitchen together, doing a little dance at the stove, skirting around each other—the one couples do, accidentally-on-purpose brushing against each other when reaching for something, when opening a drawer or cabinet. When we brush hips as I stand lining a cookie sheet with aluminum foil, my whole body heats from the contact.

Outside, the sun is setting against the horizon, the silhouette of several boats on the water lending a picturesque backdrop to the already scenic view. An orange, lavender, and blue horizon touches the tree line above. It's beautiful.

Tranquil. Peaceful.

Just the thing Rhett needed.

I pluck two cups from the cupboard. "So when the guys come back tomorrow, do you think you'll actually get any team bonding in?"

He opens a few drawers before locating a pizza cutter. Shrugs. "I don't know. I thought we already had."

I lean my hip against the cabinet behind me, hands braced on the granite countertop. "Are you really that bent out of shape at the thought of shacking up with me for the next sixteen hours? Or are you just mad they won't grow up and act like adults?"

"I'm pissed that they're morons."

My brow goes up. I want him to admit he wants to be stuck here with me. "So you're not mad you're here with me?"

"No, I'm not mad about that."

"Good. Because I'm not exactly hating it."

Rhett looks down at the floor, a crimson blush creeping above the collar of his plaid button-down, coloring his cheeks. His shaggy hair is wavy today, and I catch whiffs of fresh air when he moves past me to grab a hot pad.

Lays everything by the stove so it's ready when we need it.

We load the pizzas into the oven one at a time, closing the door. Set a timer for twenty minutes.

"So what should we do while they're cooking?" He can't meet my eye.

What should we do? *Boy do I have a few ideas...*

"I'll fill these glasses with water, then you wanna sit on the deck while we wait?"

"Sounds good."

Outside, I shift a few chairs around, dragging two so they're side by side, facing the water. Facing the sunset. The glowing horizon, sun fading into night, a few stars peeking through the dusk.

The sliding door opens and closes. "I'll keep the lights off so we don't attract the bugs."

He joins me in the green Adirondack chairs, hands me my glass, spreads his legs, and stares into the distance. We're quiet a few blissful moments. "This is nice."

My head falls back against the wooden chair. "I could definitely get used to this." The lake water hitting the break wall along the shore. The fresh, pine-filled air. The rustling of the trees. The crackling remains from embers of the abandoned stone fire pit.

Sitting out here, next to Rhett.

A deep sigh escapes my lungs. Eyes close, lashes rest on my cheekbones.

"Do you suppose they're jealous of you?" The question—which hadn't occurred to me until this second—leaves my lips before I can give it a second thought.

"Who?"

I peel my eyes open, turning my head to meet his brown gaze. "Your teammates."

"Jealous? Of *me*?"

I laugh quietly. "Why is that such a foreign concept?"

"What do they have to be jealous of?"

I sit up, twisting to face him in the chair. "Because you're the best wrestler on the team. You came from out of *nowhere* as a transfer and you're putting their personal stats to shame—or am I wrong about that?"

Rhett's shaggy hair lobs back and forth when he shakes his head.

"You're a nice guy—that probably drives them nuts, too. *Plus*, you're dating me."

He snorts. "Out of all the people you could be dating, you expect people to believe you choose me?"

"I mean, don't you want to? To try?"

"That's *not* what I mean."

"What do you mean?"

"You want to date me?" His left brow is lifted. "I have no experience with…"

Is he trying to tell me he's a *virgin*? I school my expression so my eyes don't bug out of my skull. "You mean you've never…"

I make a motion near my crotch with my hand, hoping he understands I mean *sex*.

"Shit, no. I'm not a virgin. I meant I'm not boning a new chick every weekend like *some* people." Rhett's face turns red. "I meant I have no experience with someone like you."

My heart falls into the hollow in my stomach. "What does that mean?"

"I'm not…"

Like one of his hot teammates. Like Thad, who has more in the looks department than actual God-given talent. Like the overconfident fraternity boys always hitting on me. Like every stereotypical athlete you read about, creating unrealistic expectations for women—and, apparently, men.

We get quiet again, the sound of a motorboat in the background, zooming across the water, reverberating in the dark.

"Maybe that's what I like about you." I take a long sip of water, jiggling the ice. "I find it very hard to believe no woman has ever wanted to be your girlfriend. Maybe you just haven't given anyone the chance."

My mind strays to Monica and I scowl.

He laughs, the sound echoing in the woods. "Trust me, it's not like I haven't wanted to, especially those years when my hormones were raging."

I lean forward, interested. "Are they raging now?"

"Oh yeah." He laughs again, relaxed. "So hard."

Man, he's cute when he smiles.

Sexy.

The timer on his phone goes off, the notification annoying, coupled with a vibrating tone. We stand. Head into the house, the smell of pizza greeting us.

My stomach growls.

"Want to watch a movie while we eat?"

"Sure."

"You set up while I do the pizza?"

He nods. "Yeah, I think I can figure that shit out. What are you in the mood for?"

Something that requires us to turn off the lights and sit close. "Um, whatever. You pick."

I putz around in the kitchen, removing both pizzas from the oven, laying them on the granite to cool. Cut them both, loading two plates with slices of both, surreptitiously watching him fuss with the remote control in the living room.

Turns the TV on. Turns it off.

Bends over to fiddle with the cable box.

I stifle a smile, waiting until he locates the movies on demand and begins scrolling through our options, pausing on a few to read their descriptions and ratings. Stops on a chick flick I've seen no less than twenty times, but would watch again. A French docu-series about the king.

He looks at me over his shoulder, pausing on an old comedy. "How about this one?"

"You want to watch *Superbad*?"

"Only if you want to watch *Superbad*."

I know my grin is huge, teeth flashing. "I love that stupid movie."

"Cool. So do I."

It's so freaking dumb and hilarious. I haven't seen it in years.

I bring the pizza into the living room with a few napkins, eye-balling the couch, strategically trying to locate the best spot. I set the two plates on the coffee table. Pull it a little closer so we can put our feet on it, too.

"I feel guilty eating in someone else's living room—my mother would kill me." I laugh. "I'm going to hope and pray I don't get sauce on any of these pillows."

Rhett commiserates. "We weren't allowed to eat anywhere but the table, unless we had friends over—but then again, I have two brothers, so."

I plop down on the couch, cross-legged. "Your poor mom."

"My mom is fucking awesome." He laughs, tearing off a hunk of pizza with his teeth. It rips in half, the gooey cheese stringing off of it—and for whatever reason, I find the whole thing crazy erotic. Especially when his tongue darts out to catch an errant blob of sauce. Licks his lip clean.

"I have to stop feeding you this garbage. It's not good for you."

He tilts his head in thought. "Why is it you only feed me pizza? Are you trying to make me slow to start during my matches? I have to make weight, you know."

His chocolate eyes sparkle.

Guh!

My gaze roams his torso; I bet there's not an ounce of fat on the guy, and I sincerely hope I get to see him without a shirt later. "I doubt you have a problem staying in shape."

He tears another hunk off his slice. Chews. "Only because I work out constantly."

"What's the most commonly asked question when people find out you wrestle?"

"That's an easy one: if I enjoy rolling around on the floor with other guys."

Yeah, even I've heard that one, and I know almost nothing about wrestling. "What do you say to that?"

His shoulders move up and down indifferently. "It's not a big fuckin' deal."

"I have another question for you: are you going to stand there all night or sit next to me and watch the movie?"

"Shit. Scoot over."

I move to one end of the couch, leaning against the armrest, facing Rhett, legs sprawled out in front of me, toes wiggling.

He emulates my position.

I bend my knees, match up the pads of our feet, and give a little push. "Now we can play footsies."

"Is that what that is?" He stares at our joined feet.

"Basically. You don't have any foot phobias, do you?"

"No."

"I lived with Alex my freshman year—she has a foot phobia. I'd climb down off our bunk and one morning, I accidentally stepped on her pillow." I take a bite of pizza. "She freaked."

"Jesus."

"It always worked in my favor, because I began to exploit her weakness, right? So if I needed her awake for whatever reason, I would threaten to put my feet on her quilt and she'd bolt out of bed."

"That sounds...ruthless."

"So ruthless. I fight dirty."

"I'll remember that."

The movie we started half an hour ago plays in the background, long forgotten. Dim lights, warm quilts, and nothing but quiet for company, we hunker down on the couch.

I pull back my right leg, hook the bottom of his pants, open the leg hole with my big toe. Wedge it inside, rub back and forth along his calf, grateful I thought to freshen up my nail polish with a bright melon color aptly named *Lazy Dayz*.

Because that's what this has been: a lazy day. Driving up with Rex, who chattered non-stop the entire way. Spending the rest of the time here doing nothing, really—nothing but adding to the list of reasons Rhett Rabideaux is slowly becoming the best thing that's ever happened to me.

Being here with him is right where I want to be.

No pressure.

Mutual respect.

All the delicious sexual tension…

My brain undresses him from my spot across the couch, wanting to peel back his soft flannel to see what's hidden beneath. Run my hands under his tee. Down his jeans. Over his erect—

"Laurel?"

"Huh?"

"You wanna keep watchin' the movie, or…" He clears his throat. "Go to, uh, bed?"

Bed, bed, bed. "Your choice. I could go either way."

Say you want to go to bed.

The napkin in his lap gets folded in half. "I mean, we're not really watching it, so…"

There's nothing casual about the way I shrug. My fake yawn. "I'm tired."

My feet hit the floor at the same time his do. I rise to stand. Rhett reaches for my plate and napkin. I take the water glasses.

"I'll put our plates in the garbage. You want to take a shower before bed, or…"

"I took one this morning, so I'm good." My long hair is shiny and still smells like honey and almonds. "What about you?"

"I didn't." Rhett lifts his pit, sniffing. "I'll jump in real quick if you want to get into, uh…get in your, uh, pajamas or whatever."

That *or whatever* holds, lingering in the air.

Rhett clears his throat. "I know you were probably expectin' to room with one of the girls tonight, so I can sleep in a different room."

Over my dead body.

"So I'll just go jump in the shower and then we can figure it out..."

The only thing we have to figure out is which side of the bed I'm sleeping on.

My mind almost immediately goes to that place—you know the one, the space in my brain where I envision him naked in the bathroom, dripping under the warm spray of the shower. Lathering himself with woodsy body wash in all those sweaty, delectable places.

"I'll be up in a second to change into PJs." I let my eyes linger on the front of his button-down shirt. Flannel. Comfortable, like a hug.

"Give me ten."

"Take your time." Another fake smile.

Ugh. He has the best ass.

Rhett ambles out of the room with a backward glance while I get busy tidying the living room, tossing the pizza crusts he didn't eat into the garbage can and wiping off the counters. Rinse our glasses and refresh the water with more ice.

Flip the lights off in the living room and turn one on above the window over the sink. It's pitch black outside—if it weren't for the bright light of the moon, there would be zero visibility. A small green light shines in the middle of the lake, slowly gliding along in the dark, surely a fisherman making his way home.

From upstairs, I hear the shower running, head in its direction, determined to ignore the longing in my heart. What is my problem? Why am I so desperate for Rhett's attention? I've never been this aggressive with a guy before—never!

What is it about him that has me starting now?

Why do I find him so damn irresistible?

I push through the bedroom door, listen to the water hitting the tile as it sluices off his slick, damp body.

Note his jeans and shirt thrown at the foot of the large bed. The white gym socks on the floor. His baseball cap.

I pick it up from the quilt, walking to the mirror. Smooth down my hair and fit the hat to my head. Bend the bill, gazing at myself in the glass.

My hair is a solid sheet falling over my shoulders; the dark purple, tired cap is tearing in several places, Louisiana patch faded.

It's too big for my head, but I look cute, and I secretly conspire to steal it from him every now and again. Maybe if I'm wearing it when he comes out of the bathroom, lying in the center of the bed, sprawled out naked...

Oh, who am I trying to kid? That would probably scare the shit out of him.

I sigh, remove it. Set it on the dresser.

My overnight bag sits in the corner, so I retrieve it and plop it on the bed. Unzip. Spread it open, peering inside at the cute clothes I packed when I thought there were going to be other girls here.

The pink plaid pajama set? Flannel. Baggy.

Modest.

I hadn't wanted to prance around in a room full of people I barely knew with my boobs hanging out, so into the overnight bag they went.

I sift through the contents for a tank top. Snatch out the clean pair of underwear I tossed in. Stand in the center of the room, debating my choices: flannel pajamas, sexy tank top and underwear.

Flannel pajamas, *sexy tank top and underwear...*

I bite my lip, apprehensive.

On one hand, I don't want to give him the wrong idea about me. On the other, I want him to make a damn move, touch me in all the wrong places.

I want him to touch me *so* bad—touch me without asking for permission, not hesitantly, like he's afraid this is another cruel joke being played on him.

At this point, he knows I like him. I've literally come out and said the words; it's no secret, so what is he always *waiting* for?

Screw it.

I'm going for it.

I'm going to make him so hard he'll be cross-eyed.

Shoving the plaid pajamas down into the depths of my bag, I pull out the tank top. It's white and threadbare. The panties? Sheer and practically see-through.

Score.

I smile at my evil feminine wiles, goose bumps covering my flesh when the water shuts off, at the sound of the shower curtain rings being slid aside.

Slip the black leggings down my legs. Step out of my navy cotton underwear and into the nude ones. Remove the white long-sleeved shirt and my bra. Glance at my bare breasts in the mirror above the dresser, arching my back long enough to admire their lift and fullness.

Run my hands over my nipples so they stiffen.

I affix my gaze on the door to the bathroom, my imagination projecting the image of Rhett dressing in conservative layers: boxers, sleep pants, sweatshirt.

So lost in thought, it barely registers when the door flies open, catching me off guard, steam rising out from behind him. Rhett's large physique is framed in the door, sinewy upper torso still damp. Smooth chest, broad shoulders.

Sleep pants. No shirt.

His eyes widen at my semi-nudity, attach to my boobs. "Shit."

I'm not wearing a shirt. My palms fly to cover my bare chest.

"Jesus Laurel, I'm so sorry."

My heart thumps at a thousand beats per minute. "It's nothing you haven't seen before, remember?" I ask, gently reminding him about the dry humping we did in my car.

I cover myself with one arm while I pluck the tank top up off the bed, turn my back on him, and yank it on over my head.

I'm tall, but not nearly as tall as Rhett, and feel slightly vulnerable standing before him in just a tank and panties, the half-dressed state a reminder of the precarious status of our relationship.

He crosses his toned arms, eyes falling on the front of my thin shirt. I know he can see my nipples through the fabric.

I run a hand through my hair, letting his gaze run the length of my body.

"Mind if I brush my teeth?"

"Oh shit, yeah. I have to do that, too."

We stand, side by side at the sink, sharing toothpaste and real estate in the bathroom. Every cell in my nervous system aware of the heat he's throwing off. Eyes focused on every one of the flexed muscles in his reflection in the mirror as he works the toothbrush around his mouth.

Brush. Spit. Brush.

I run the water, rinsing. Brush. Spit.

It's weird doing this with him, intimate somehow.

Plus, I'm in my underwear, trying to drive him wild with lust, furtively watching him brush his teeth—his white, straight, beautiful teeth that I want nipping my bare skin.

God, listen to me.

I stroke my purple toothbrush a few more times, liberally swiping my tongue and gums. Spit. Wash my brush off, setting it on the porcelain sink. Run a hand behind my neck, sweeping my bright red hair over one shoulder.

Meet his brown eyes in the mirror.

He stands, toothbrush suspended in his clenched hand, staring at my reflection, eyes scanning my face, softening at the corners.

"You know, when I first saw you with…you know, no clothes on, I thought you'd be covered in freckles."

"You did?"

"Yeah. I thought all redheads had freckles."

"Nope." I eyeball myself in the glass, raising an arm for inspection. "Probably the only ginger I know without them."

"Where do you get it from?"

"My mom has red hair."

"Sister?"

"Oh, totally."

"Huh." He sets his toothbrush on the edge of the sink.

His hair is already beginning to dry, curling up at the ends. It's so gosh darn cute brushed off to the side, unlike its usual scruffy mop.

Sigh.

Rhett

I can barely take my eyes off Laurel, though I'm doing my fucking best not to ogle her. In that see-through tank top and those panties? It's damn near impossible.

She might as well be naked.

I hit the light when we're done in the bathroom, padding across the hardwood floor on bare feet, conscious she's watching my every move. Take my dirty clothes from the foot of the bed, stash them on a chair in the corner so they're out of the way.

"I put your hat on the dresser for you," she softly supplies. "I tried it on."

My face flushes. "You did, huh?"

"Yeah. I looked cute."

I bet she did.

I bet if I kissed her, she'd kiss me back.

Eyes on her face, not on her boobs, eyes on her face, not on her boobs.

I feel the waistband of my pants for pockets, desperate to occupy my hands. I've turned into a ball of nervous fucking energy. "So, obviously this bed is free—and the one next door. Where do you want to sleep?"

"Honestly? I want to sleep wherever you sleep."

"You want to sleep in the same bed?" *Shut the fuck up, idiot!* I sound like I'm arguing with her—what fucking moron argues about sharing a bed with a pretty girl? Me.

"I mean, won't you be lonely in here all by yourself?"

"I'll probably pass out as soon as my head hits the pillow."

Why am I still talking?

Her face falls, and Jesus, why did I say that? I've turned into my damn roommate, who never says the right fucking things.

265

"Okay, well...I guess I'll take the room next door." When she turns for the door, slowly, like she's walking to her untimely death, I let my gaze wander to her slim back. Let it travel down the curve of her spine. The curve of her tight ass, round globes of pale skin playing peekaboo with the delicate panties up her ass crack.

She pauses at the threshold, hand resting on the wood. "Good night."

I swallow. "Good night."

"Tonight was..."

"Nice?"

"Yeah."

Fuck, why can't I ask her to stay? Climb into the bed and wrap us both up in the blankets, pull her on top of me and kiss her senseless?

Because I have no game.

I am *not* my friends.

"Bonne nuit, Laurel," I murmur.

Her breath hitches and she narrows her blue eyes in my direction. "I said don't do that."

"Do what?"

"Speak to me in French."

"You don't like it?"

"You know I do." She nods. "I do like it."

"Je ne comprends pas..." *I don't understand.* I don't understand anything about girls, or relationships, or what I'm supposed to be doing right fucking now.

I'm floundering.

She turns to face me, making her way across the room. Stands in front of me.

"Say, I think it sounds beautiful." She's whispering, our bodies inches apart.

"Je pense que tu es belle," I whisper back. *I think you're beautiful.*

"Now say, I don't want you in the next room."

"Je ne te veux pas dans l' autre chambre," I repeat. "Restez avec moi." *Stay with me.*

Her breasts brush my chest, the pad of her index finger tracing the contour of my upper lip.

"You have a beautiful mouth."

"Toi aussi." *So do you.*

I feel my neck bow. Head bent down. Shoulders sag, body relaxed.

"Je te veux plus que n'importe quoi que j'avais voulu dans ma vie." *I want you more than anything I've wanted in my entire fucking life.*

"Yes." Laurel's whisper hits me in the groin at the same time my mouth lowers, lips parting breathlessly. I'm already panting. Anxious. Excited.

Aroused.

Our foreheads touch.

Fingers entwine.

With my head bowed, I have a clear shot down her shirt, straight into her cleavage. The tips of her nipples, hard, rubbing against her white tank.

I blow out a breath, squeeze her hands.

Controlled.

When she moves closer into my space, breasts brushing my hard pecs, I can barely stand it. Lose all brain function when she rubs those gorgeous tits against me, lifting her chin.

Nudges me with her nose until we're eye to eye.

"Rhett." She speaks breathlessly. "Kiss me good night."

We're both shaking, my entire body invested in this moment. I know hers is too by the way her shoulders give a tiny quake when I rest my lips on hers.

Press them there, undemanding.

Her mouth is pliant, lips full and pouty.

Tongue softly touching mine.

I release her hands and raise mine to her face. Cup that beautiful jawline of hers in my huge hands, planting a kiss on her so fully I feel it all the way to my fucking toes. Pull back so I can study her face.

Her blue eyes blaze back at me, bright as her hair.

"Stay with me." *Restez avec moi.*

Please.

Laurel nods once, decisive.

When I take my hands off her body, she drags me to the left side of the bed. Peels back the covers and slides in, hair fanned out across the forest green sheets, practically glowing.

I stare down at her. "I have no idea what I'm fucking doing."

"It's okay, neither do I."

Her eyes get wide when I climb under the covers, sliding in as casually as I possibly can, heart beating wildly out of control. She closes the gap, scooting closer, legs and hips and thighs pressed to mine.

"You're so huge." Her arm reaches out, palm pressing against my chest, hand roaming down my sternum. My shoulders quake from the feather-light touch, all the blood in my body flowing to the nether region. "You're so warm."

My body is a hotbox, a burning, raging inferno of sexual repression. I imagine that soon I'll have sweat dripping down my forehead from the tension.

God, I'm so hard. So fucking *hard*. If she gets near my dick—touches it—I swear I will come right off this fucking bed.

With an unsteady hand, I skim her hip. Thigh. Marvel at the silky expanse of pale flesh against the rough skin of my callused palm. Bury my fingers in the hem of her white tank top, skimming up her torso.

I'm dying to see her naked breasts again.

Count to three, building courage.

I go for it.

With my other hand, I pull back the fabric of her thin shirt, tugging it down, exposing the pink flesh of her nipples. They're damn near perfect considering they're the only ones I've ever seen nude. The only ones I've touched.

The one girl I ever made out and had sex with was back in high school—when we were both seventeen and hardly developed. Some making out, very little foreplay. We definitely didn't undress.

Cupping Laurel's round breast, I gently stroke the underside with my thumb.

"Oh jeezuz!" She gasps, head tipping back. "*Finally.*"

My lips graze Laurel's throat, rough whiskers from my stubble marking her porcelain neck. Kiss the exposed white flesh of her cleavage as I gently caress her boob.

"You feel so good," comes her quiet murmur as she tussles my hair. Gasps when my tongue darts out to dampen the skin under her ear. "Take my shirt off."

She's a bossy, assertive little thing, and for that I am grateful. "I want to feel you against me."

We work her shirt off and my eyes, damn them, are mystified by her boobs. Round. Full, with dark pink areolas, they're better than any tits I've seen in any porn.

"I don't know why I even put that stupid shirt on in the first place. Who was I kidding," she grumbles when I toss it to the ground. Laurel arches her back, fans her hair out on the pillow, rests her hands behind her head, watching me watch her, eyes glowing.

Jesus.

A smile tips her lips. "It's okay to touch me. I want you to."

When I hesitate, her arm reaches out. Finger traces the flannel covering my dense thigh.

"Your skin is sexy."

"You think so?"

"Oh yes, so sexy Rhett. I have daydreams about you."

I pull back, surprised. "You do?"

"All the time. Sometimes I Google you and watch your wrestling meets." She pauses. "Not in a creepy way, I swear."

Do girls consider that creepy? I sure as hell don't.

"Are you a fan of mine?"

"Number one."

We're lying here half naked and I remember she wants me to touch her. I start with the flat of her stomach, emboldened when she bites down on her bottom lip. Nostrils flare.

Sliding my hand up, we both watch when it cups her breast. Laurel's lips part, pupils dilate.

She's reacting to *my* touch—and it's fucking amazing watching her face glow as she gets turned on. Intoxicating.

Her eyes track my hand, watch as my thumb brushes her nipple, head dipping to lick it.

"Out of curiosity," she gasps. "How's your stamina?"

Why is she asking me this *now*? "I don't know, good? I can run for miles without breaking a sweat."

She giggles out a groan. "That's *not* what I meant."

When I was younger, I used to imagine that when I finally started fucking someone on the regular, I'd be able to hold out coming for a long time, that I'd fuck for hours. Now that it seems like a definite possibility, I wonder if I'll be able to last five minutes.

Three.

"I've heard wrestlers...that they have great stamina."

"Oh yeah?" Bold now, I suck her nipple. "Where'd you hear that from?"

Her head tips back. "Wrestlers and hockey players. It's all in the hips."

"Are you..." Shit, how do I put this without sounding eager? "Are you saying you want to find out?"

"*Yes* I want to find out. I wanted it to be now." Her little moan is breathy as I continue sucking. "But…maybe we should wait—not rush it."

I'd be lying if I said I wasn't disappointed; me and my stiff dick shrivel a little.

"Right. Totally."

Her fingers dig into my scalp. "*God* that feels good." One breathier moan then, "Stop. I want you on your back."

"Yes ma'am," I croak out because honestly, who am I to argue?

She rolls toward me, propping herself up on her elbow. Hand gliding across the mattress toward me, fingers climbing up my abs, tracing my belly button. Index finger tracing my happy trail, skimming the waistband of my flannel bottoms.

Our eyes are fastened together. My breath hitches when her palm glides down the front of my pants, fingers brushing the pubes above my dick. Eyebrows shoot up into her bright red hairline.

"No underwear?"

"No."

Smirk. "Good."

My leg twitches when Laurel unties the string on the waistband. Gives the band a gentle tug, yanking the hem down my hips.

"Help me out?"

I raise my hips, shoving down my pants, the cool air of the cabin hitting my painfully sensitive nuts. Kick them off under the covers. Damn near shout when Laurel pushes back the bedspread, hand breezing over my pelvis, gripping the base of my cock. Slowly pumping up and down.

"God I've been wondering what this looked like," she's saying. "I can't wait to feel you inside me, Rhett. I'm wet just thinking about it. It's going to feel so good."

Oh my *fucking* God.

Her free hand floats along my inner thigh muscle, squeezing. "Baby, your thigh muscles are insane."

She's talking, but the only word I hear is *baby*.

My cock jerks involuntarily, head hits the pillow. Fists clench the bedspread. "Oh fuck."

A soft chuckle. "I'd say you've earned this."

This?

Oh fuck, is she going to suck me off? Is that what this is? *Please God, please say yes.*

Shifting closer, her hand moves up and down on my shaft. "Do you like that?"

I can't do anything but part my lips and give a jerky nod.

"I've, you know, fooled around before, but haven't given anyone a blow job. I want to do that with you."

Do what? She wants to do what with me? What is she saying? What's my name?

All I feel is her hand on my cock, the pressure. The pleasure. When she lets go and straddles me, pressing her mouth to mine, our lips and tongues are a tangle, a messy tangle. Hot. Open mouths. Frantic.

Our teeth knock together, hands grappling everywhere. Skin, tits, ass.

"God, you drive me crazy." Her mouth gives my neck a lick. Collarbone. Nipple. Eases slowly down my torso, kissing and licking her way down my happy trail. Grips my dick with one hand, balls in the other. Index finger pressing on my—

"Oh J-Jesus Ch-Christ!"

Her mouth is slick heat, wet, tongue teasing the head. The sensitive tip. Sucking.

And sucking and sucking until I barely remember to breathe. "Goddammit, oh *sh-shit. Shit.*"

Please God, I pray, don't let me come. Make it last.

Suddenly it's clear to me why the guys on the team are constantly making blow job jokes, the stupid assholes—it feels so motherfucking incredible.

I moan, head tipped back, hands clenching the comforter so I'm not tempted to bury them in her hair and tug. Bite down, dragging my teeth across my lower lip. "Uhhh…yeah…"

Laurel's head bobs up and down on my cock; my vision blurs, trying to focus on her face. It's impossible.

"Fuc*k* Laurel," I groan loudly. My eyes give in, rolling to the back of my head, stars flashing behind my eyelids. "Fu…*k*."

When she hums from the back of her throat, I lose it. Lose my shit, thrusting into her mouth, once, twice. Balls tighten, cock twitching. Nerves sending spasms throughout my lower body when I come.

Tiny jolts of pleasure.

Nothing has ever felt so good in my entire fucking life.

Laurel

When Rhett comes, he makes the most amazing sounds. Euphoric, sexy, dragged-out moaning, his hands bearing down on the sheets. White-knuckling.

God it's sexy, this power. This control.

I run my hands along the smooth skin of his thighs, the white flesh sprinkled with dark hair. Masculine and musky, his dick still hard.

It's an incredible dick, slightly larger than average, blunt and ribbed in all the right spots, I know it's going to be orgasmic when we finally have sex. *I bet he can make me come twice with glute muscles like this*, I muse, sliding my palms around to his firm ass, imagining it pumping into me over and over, missionary, the thought getting me hot.

I flop down on the bed next to him, letting my hand land on his stomach. He takes hold, tracing my palm with his index finger, breathing labored.

Rolls to face me, lowering his head to my breast. Flicks my nipple with his tongue. Sucks until it's good and swollen, pulling back and blowing cool air over the tip.

I love it. I love how Rhett makes me feel.

How the smallest little things he does send waves of longing through me.

Waves of desire.

Joy.

Rises to his haunches, that big body hovering. Studying. Brown eyes learning every one of my soft curves, from the smooth expanse of my clavicle down to my knees. Up and back again until those eyes land on my underwear.

Comes back down on all fours, mouth playing near my ear. Day-old stubble tickling my neck.

"Do you want me to…" He swallows, hesitating.

I wait, wanting to hear him *ask* before I start begging. Wiggle my hips, wanting him to get me off.

God I've been so horny since I met him.

"Say it." I turn my head a fraction, lips brushing his ear. "Ask me."

"Veux-tu que je te fasse un cunni?" His husky whisper hits the shell of my ear, vibrating in my core. "Do you want me to go down on you?"

"When you put it like that? God yes."

"I've never, uh, done it before."

Why does this not surprise me? "Really?"

"No." He crawls down my body in the same unhurried way I crawled down his, fingers hooking the elastic of my sheer panties but not pulling them down. "These are sexy."

His *voice* is sexy. Intoxicating.

His warm breath doesn't just melt my girl parts; it makes them squirm. Huge hands part my legs, the rough patches on the pads of his fingers a tingling contrast on my skin.

He hasn't even put his mouth on me yet.

I crane my head to see what he's doing, why he's stopped. "Babe, what are you doing?"

Trying to drive me insane?

"Lookin'."

Lookin'. Oh jeez, that accent.

"You're so fucking sexy." Lips kiss my inner thigh. Pelvis. Nose runs up and down my underwear, causing a loud gasp to escape my throat. "You already smell like sex."

Elbows bumping my knees apart, he slides his face home. Gets comfortable near the foot of the bed. Fingers pull the fabric on my underwear aside, tongue drags up the middle of my slit without preamble.

Instinctively, I grab a fistful of his hair, spread legs already shaking from the ministrations of his tongue. Incapable of speech as he goes to town down under, my mouth falls open.

No sound comes out.

For the next few minutes or seconds or decades, I lay shaking on the bed as Rhett makes me come with his tongue, mouth, and fingers, his palms gripping my ass. Forearms keeping my legs open.

My head thrashes, shoulders coming off the bed.

"*Rhett.*" I want him to stop—stop and climb up my body and give it to me good with that hard dick of his. "I w-want…"

His reply? Sucking harder on my clit.

I immediately come. "Oh *shhh*…it…oh*hhh*…"

Pound the mattress, trying to get a grip on my uncontrolled hormones. My quivering body feels like it's hooked up to an out-let, hundreds of electrical bolts surging through it. Every nerve ending fires at once, and I lie here, shuddering. Tingling.

When Rhett comes up for air, he wipes his hand across his mouth, creeping up my body. Lies on top, planting a kiss on my lips. Open-mouthed, I grip the back of his neck, pulling him in, tongues fusing.

The weight of his body is like a drug, his dick sliding into the space between my legs but not inside me.

Not yet, anyway.

His lips kiss my temple. "Did I do that right?"

"I think I just died." My breasts are crushed against his chest and it's kind of turning me on—again. I writhe beneath him. "This is me talking to you from the afterlife."

"I thought it would take you longer to come," he admits.

"Me too, jeez. That was embarrassing." I sigh. Kiss his chin. "I was hoping it would last longer." Brush the hair out of his eyes. "How did you learn how to do that if you've never done it before?"

"Uh…"

I narrow my eyes. "Do you watch porn?"

His laugh is deep, amused. Guilty. "Sometimes, yeah."

"Good. So do I."

Rhett's grin is so damn cute, my stomach knots. "We should get some sleep, huh?"

"Yeah. I'll go wash up and then we should hit the sack. The guys will be back in the morning."

"Ugh, don't remind me."

When I roll away, he plants his palm in the center of my ass, smacking it. "Do we, uh, want to put our clothes back on?"

I raise a brow. "Do you?"

"Not really. I've always wanted to sleep naked with someone."

My brows go up. "This is a real night of firsts for you, isn't it?"

"You makin' fun of me?"

"No. If you want to be naked with me, then I want to be naked with you."

"All right. No puttin' our clothes back on." He helps me out of bed and I pad behind him into the bathroom, admiring his round ass, the muscles constricting in his hamstrings and quads.

"Clothes would be a travesty at this point."

We go through the motions of brushing our teeth again. I leave so he can pee in privacy. Return to bed, slide to the far side, drag the covers up past my boobs.

Fall into a blissful sleep.

"He and I tag each other
in memes and speak in
GIFS all day long.
I guess you could say
it's getting pretty serious…"

Laurel

"God. I think I'm actually, you know…" I wave a hand in the air, unable to find the words.

My cousin rolls her eyes. "No. I *don't* know."

Is she really going to make me say it? Ugh.

"I think I'm falling in *you know what* with Rhett."

"In love?"

"Shh, yes." At least, I think that's what this is.

He's all I can think about; everything about the guy makes me so freaking happy I can't even stand myself lately.

"Instalove is *so* tacky, Laurel."

"I'm not saying that's what this is. I'm just saying…I really like him. God, I cannot wait to see him, and when I do, I want to barf from all the nerves."

Alex stares. "You're making it sound like you're pregnant."

Why do I keep torturing myself by having these lunches with her? She's not a nice person.

I should be having this conversation with Lana or Donovan— or both.

"Would you be serious for a second? And keep your voice down—this is how rumors get started."

"Why should I keep my voice down? You're fucking a solid five on a scale of ten. I have a right to be upset."

I reel back, shocked. "*What* did you just say?"

Her chin tips up. "You can do a whole lot better than the *Get Laid* poster guy."

I narrow my eyes. "He is the top wrestler at *two* D1 schools— that hardly makes him a charity case."

Why am I defending him to her? She's being a petty bitch.

Still, she's my cousin; if we fight, it's likely to get back to my parents, and I don't want any phone calls from my mother.

"You're having sex with him. Doesn't his face bother you?"

I don't correct her, just stand, gathering up my things. "What is your *problem* today?"

"I don't have a problem, but *you*? You need to get your eyes examined." She bites down on a carrot stick, casually crunching down on it. "You're slumming."

"I'm not going to sit and listen to you cut down who I chose to date. Rhett is amazing. I like him."

"Whatever." Her carrot gets dipped in ranch dressing. "Are you and your boyfriend going to be at the football season opener party this weekend? Rhett is allowed out on the weekends, isn't he?"

"We'll see." I scowl down at her, fists clenched at my sides. "I might not be in the mood."

"Look at you, all in a snit."

"Do you blame me? You're being foul."

"Whatever—I can't help it that your boyfriend isn't hot. That's your problem, not mine."

"I'm leaving." Take a few steps back. "Have a nice lunch." *Don't choke on your unsolicited opinions*, I silently add.

She scoffs. "I will."

Outside, my back hits the brick wall when I pull my phone out, checking for messages.

Rhett: *Hey.*

I light up when I see his name, all the catty drama from my cousin fading fast, his ability to cheer me in an instant unfailing. My heartbeat quickens.

Me: *Hey yourself*

Rhett: *You still on campus? I'm near the union, heading home if you're heading that way anytime soon.*

Me: *Perfect. Give me five—I was just having lunch with my cousin. Meet me by the main entrance?*

Rhett: *Yup.*

I all but skip over, the sight of him leaning against the brick building, one leg propped against the wall making me giddy. Thumb moving over the screen of his phone, his head is bent, a button-down shirt over a plain t-shirt and jeans a departure from his usual hoodie. Backward cap, this one from Iowa.

It looks new.

He looks nice.

Cute.

I speed walk that way, happy to see him. Rise on my toes, plant a kiss right on his lips. It takes him a full three seconds to respond, hand sliding around my waist, pulling me in. Pressing his lips to mine.

PDA—it's about damn time.

We start off, his arm still slung around my middle, and I hunker down under his armpit. It's cold and I'm not wearing a jacket, but Rhett's kicking off more heat than a radiator—not to mention, I love being glued to his side.

"You smell good," I blurt out, the raging hormones inside me needing to chill the fuck out already.

I preen when he kisses the top of my head, pleased he's starting to get the hang of this dating thing.

"What's going on this week?"

"I have a meet, remember? It's home, but it's a big one, so I won't be able to see you much. We have to eat together and study together this week. Coach is still pissed about all the hazing shit."

"What did he say about the cabin?"

"He hasn't said anything directly to me yet, but I know he's pulled Osborne and Daniels into his office a few times." He

281

laughs. "Those assholes never even came back to the cabin Sunday morning."

"Thank God everyone else did."

"Yeah."

"So how does your coach know everything got resolved?"

"Pretty sure a few of the guys made up some kumbaya bullshit about bonfires and trust falls."

"And he bought it?"

Rhett shrugs. "Guess so. He hasn't suspended anyone."

Six of the twelve wrestlers had returned the following morning, just in time for breakfast, wielding three dozen donuts and bottled waters and making a serious effort to put all the bullshit behind them. Then, after spending some time down by the pier, fishing, and hanging out, we all caravanned home. Spent the rest of the night cleaning the grease off my car.

Ambling leisurely all the way back to my house, we reach the concrete walkway, taking each concrete step one at a time. It's a tiny porch with little room for multiple people, so I'm leaning against the screen door.

"You want to come in for a little bit?"

He worries his bottom lip. "No, I should get home. I only have twenty minutes to eat, change, and head to the gym. Practice until ten."

I scrunch my face up. "When is your meet? I'll probably bring Lana and Donovan if they're not working—I hate the thought of sitting by myself." And no freaking way am I sitting alone in the student section, not after seeing all those signs, all those girls.

"Saturday mornin', early. Matches start at nine. We have to be there at five."

I rack my brain, mulling over my schedule. "I have a study group at ten, but I'll skip it."

"Don't skip a study group to come see me; there are still a few home meets you can catch."

"I know, but I want to. I'll make it work." I pause. "So curfew tomorrow night, yeah?"

"'Fraid so." He's pressing into me now, smiling down at me with those pretty white teeth. "I have to be home by nine and stay there."

"So we'll just have to do something at your place? That's allowed, right?"

"Yeah, it's allowed." Nuzzles my neck. "What should we do?"

"It's supposed to rain—we can watch movies?"

"Netflix and chill?"

"Yes." One hundred percent yes to the fooling around during the movie.

"Damn." He grins. "I've always wanted to Netflix and chill."

"Are people still calling it that?" I tap my chin, feigning indecision.

"I doubt it. I was never cool to begin with so I have no idea what people are doing." His pelvis meets mine, the hard-on in his jeans pressing into my stomach. I'm tempted to run my hand along the denim fabric, drive him a little bit crazy before he has to leave. "I should leave."

My chin tips up, lips straining toward his face. "You sure you don't want to come in?"

"Can't." He swallows. "I'm already runnin' behind."

"Then get going—don't make me the reason you're late."

The last thing I want is him in trouble with his coaching staff because he stood on my front porch flirting. "Go. Get."

"All right." His head bows the barest of a fraction. "Tu me manques."

"Same." With every rush of wind, Rhett's hair wisps around his goofy ears.

He laughs against the crown of my head. "You don't even know what I just said."

"It doesn't matter."

Kisses my hair. "You are really something, do you know that?"

"I try." I'm really trying to be the kind of woman Rhett deserves, someone honest who loves him for who he is.

"I should go."

"Kiss me before you do?" Asking gets easier and easier, and he's happy to oblige. "How do you say it in French?"

"Embrasse moi."

"Embrasse moi," I echo, parroting his inflection down to the syllable.

"Very good. You're a natural."

"Embrasse moi."

He does.

He kisses me and kisses me good, like he means it, right in the middle of my porch, in the middle of the day, like he's not going to see me for the rest of the year.

My toes curl inside my boots, all the tingles, tongue curling around his. Open-mouthed making out, neighbors be damned.

When he pulls away, we're breathless, steam rising from the cold. "See you tomorrow night?"

"Yes please."

I watch his firm ass swagger down the sidewalk with a few long strides, backpack slung over his shoulder. Watch as he stops and turns.

"Laurel?"

Jeez, why is my heart pounding so hard? I can hear it in my ears.

"Before, when you couldn't understand what I was saying?"

"Yeah?"

"I said I missed you."

My teeth bite my lower lip. Grin like a fool. "I missed you too."

Rhett: *What did you end up doing tonight?*

Me: *A paper—the one I was going to study group for on Saturday. Trying to make up for the lost time.*

Rhett: *I'm really okay if you skip it.*

Me: *Is it weird to admit that I might have been Googling you to watch your old matches?*

Me: *Once...or twice.*

Rhett: *Really? When?*

Me: *After I found out your last name. I watched your matches on the internet, then I looked up pictures of you.*

Does that weird you out?

Rhett: *That you took an interest in what I was doing? No, not at all. I'm flattered.*

Me: *You're incredible. It's no wonder they wanted you to come to Iowa. I imagine Louisiana was pissed when they lost you.*

Rhett: *Yeah, basically. It was rough. It was a shit show when I told everyone I was transferring.*

Me: *I'm sorry :(I know if must have been a hard choice.*

Rhett: *I still can't believe I transferred.*

Me: *Are you happy you did?*

Rhett: *I am now.*

Me: *I can't wait to see you tomorrow.*

Rhett: *Me either. 6:00? Too early?*

Me: *No, perfect! I'm dying to see you. See you tomorrow <3*

19

#DOUCHEBAG

"He just used a semicolon
in the middle of a sext—
could this guy
be any more perfect?"

Laurel

I've been anticipating this moment all day—maybe longer. Nerves have me fiddling with the hem of my gray shirt, tugging it down over the waistband of my jeans though it's cropped.

Half boots.

Cute.

Self-consciously, I wonder if I should have worn yoga pants. After all, we did say we were going to watch movies, and I don't plan on doing that particular activity in the living room where his roommates can bother us.

I've had just about as much Rex Gunderson as a girl can take.

I ring Rhett's doorbell, stuff my hands in the pockets of my khaki green jacket. Paste a smile on my face when the door cracks open and Eric Johnson's mug peers down at me through the screen.

"Sup Fire Crotch."

My eyes narrow. "Fire Crotch? Really? You're taking it there, huh? Right to my face?"

He shrugs, pushing the door open, letting me enter. "Why not?"

"Most people wait a few weeks—you know, until they get to know me better."

"Guess I have bigger balls than most people."

I doubt that. "Guess so." Glance around. "Rhett's home, right?"

He closes the door behind us, pointing. "Bedroom."

"Thanks."

"Make good choices," he says at my back when I hit the hallway. "Or don't."

Rhett's door is ajar, and I give two soft taps to the frame. "Knock, knock."

He's at his desk, shoulders hunched. Head bent. Looks up, startled. "Hey! Shit." Stands, shoveling a stack of papers before pushing back from the table. "I must have lost track of time."

"Grading papers?"

"Oui."

I practically purr, already excited to be in his bedroom. Drop my purse and meet him halfway so he can drop a kiss on my lips. Scan the bedroom, eyes hitting the bed first, of course.

He's tidied up.

Rearranged the room, bed pushed against the far wall. Dresser opposite, television perched on top. Moved the desk next to the closet.

My jacket comes off and I hang it on his desk chair, plopping down to remove my shoes. Without them, I'm an entire three inches shorter.

"Did you eat?" he asks. "Don't say pizza."

"Haha. Yes, I had some chicken bake Donovan threw in a crock pot this morning before class with white rice and canned veggies." I pull a face. "Did you eat?"

"Shit tons of water." He laughs. "Bagel, peanut butter, fruit. I'll probably get up to pee a lot and should eat again before bed."

I crawl on the bed, flopping down on his pillows. Lean over and take a whiff, wanting to bury myself in the smell of him.

My shirt drifts up when I roll to my back, baring my flat stomach; his brown eyes fall onto my pale, smooth skin. I smile. Cross my arms behind my head, letting him look.

I'm nice like that.

"Aren't you exhausted?" I wriggle my toes, elongating my body on the bed, raising my arms into a stretch. "Let's watch a movie. Come lie down by me, your pacing is making me nervous."

It's not; I just want him to lie down so I can touch him. Get this whole pretense of watching television over with so we can fool around.

He moves to the door, turning the lock. Removes his ball cap before sitting on the right side of the bed, shaking out his hair and presenting me with his back. Grabs the remote.

Scoots back until his rear hits me, lying on his side facing the TV.

His broad back blocks my view, but I don't even care. I didn't come here to watch a movie; I came here to spend time with him, get to know him better.

Weasel my way into his heart.

"What do you want to watch?" he rumbles, already flipping through Netflix.

"How about *New Girl*. Have you ever seen that?"

He clicks it. Hits enter so we're starting season one, episode one. Tosses the remote to the foot of the bed. "I don't watch a lot of TV to tell you the truth. Mostly just have it on as background noise."

When he flops onto his back, I seize the opportunity and roll toward him, snuggling up into his side. Lay my hand on his stomach, cheek on his chest. His abs constrict from the contact. Dick twitches beneath his mesh gym shorts.

I bite back a smile.

His arm comes down around me, pulling me close. On the television in front of us, Jess and the gang meet for the first time, and I giggle against Rhett's chest at the on-screen antics.

Run my hand under the fabric of his shirt, sliding it north, over his rippled abdomen. Up his sternum, palm skimming his nipple.

For the next ten minutes, we lie together silently, motionlessly except for our breathing.

Then, "Do you ever lie in bed the night before a meet and think about it?"

"Sometimes."

"Do you know who your match is against tomorrow?"

"Sure do—name is Eli Nelson. Five ten. One hundred ninety-eight pounds. Seventeen percent body fat. Record is thirty and four, from Spokane, Washington."

"Anything else?"

"His girlfriend's name is Candace, and she's a Scorpio."

"You're making that up."

"Yeah, I made that up." He laughs.

"Nervous?"

"No. I've wrestled him before."

"Did you win or lose?"

His brow quirks. "Do you even have to ask?"

I blush. "Want me to rub your back?"

Rhett hesitates, glancing down at me. "Sure."

"Want to take off your shirt?"

"Is removing my shirt part of the standard massage package?"

"Yes, sir."

"Guess I'm taking off my shirt, then."

I fight the urge to rub my hands together, the anticipation of his incredible physique palpitating my heart. He uses his rock-hard core to rise, raises his arms above his head, drags off his shirt. Lies down on the bed, on his side, presenting me with his powerful back.

The muscles are taut, firm. Skin is surprisingly smooth. I explore first, palm grazing his warm flesh, running it along his deltoid. Down his dorsi. Up his spine and across his shoulders.

Marvel at the strength in these shoulders, the power in his obliques. Explore the tops of his glutes, wanting to pull back the waistband of his shorts and dip my hand inside.

He shivers. Skin prickles with goose bumps.

"Is this massage supposed to tickle?" he mutters.

"Shh, relax," I croon into his neck. "It's the new butterfly technique. They only teach this in French massage parlors."

"Ah, well, that makes sense I guess."

I lean in. "I promise it comes with a happy ending."

I simply *cannot* stop my hands from wandering; he feels too, too good under my insatiable hands.

My fingers play with the ends of his hair, trail down his thick bicep, down his forearm. Over his hip, over his ass. Both palms run parallel up his spine, thumbs kneading on their climb up.

I knead his neck, squeeze his shoulders, thumbs doing all the work. The sound of his contented sigh is *agony*.

So much so, I can't stand having clothes on anymore. Pull away to remove my own shirt. Unclasp my bra. Brush my long hair out of the way so there's no barrier between us when my hard nipples brush the flesh of his back.

God, the skin-on-skin contact is intoxicating.

He groans when I kiss between his shoulder blades, breasts brushing his back. Delicate kisses on the back of his neck. Warm, wet kisses. Soft. Gentle.

Sexy.

I scoot closer so I can kiss the spot behind his ear. Lick his lobe. Slide my hand around his middle, covering his pec with my palm. Caress it.

His huge bear paw finds my hip, pulling at me from behind, hauling me closer, stroking my thigh as I pepper his body with my mouth in a most unmassagelike way.

"Shit, Laurel. Move back, let me roll over."

I roll back. He shifts toward me.

Our mouths fuse together, tongues mate. Those large, capable hands rake up my ribcage. Cup my breasts and stay there, kneading.

"Your hands feel so good." I encourage him with a breathy moan into his mouth, my fingers finding the curls at the base of his neck. Playing with them. Kissing him senseless.

He breaks away. "My hands aren't too rough?"

"No. No, they're amazing. Put them back."

The truth is, I *can* feel every coarse callus on the pads of each finger, each and every one a souvenir of the sacrifices he makes to win. For his team. To be the best. Reminding me how damn resilient he is. How fit and virile and masculine.

Those magic hands splay over my collarbone, sliding down my shoulders and arms like liquid. Lose themselves in the waterfall of my wavy hair. Play with the ends, brushing it to the side.

My chest is heaving from my beating heart when Rhett pulls back, studying my pale torso wordlessly, several torturous seconds, reluctance written clearly in his questioning gaze.

Hesitantly, his hand reaches out, fingertip finding my dusky areola. Silently, his brown eyes linger on my breasts, fixated. Remain there, tracking the movements of his own thumb when it brushes over my puckered nipple.

Then the other.

Raging hormones cause my breasts to swell. Heavy. Begging for relief.

Still, he slowly learns my curves, the cool air of his bedroom hardening the already stiff peaks. God, it's so terrible.

"What are you thinking?" I whisper, arching my back into his cupped hand.

"I'm thinkin' 'bout everything." Finger goes lazily round and round my nipple. Plucks at it lightly.

It's begging for attention.

Mmm. My teeth rake across my lip. "Wrestling?"

He licks his lips. "Definitely *not* wrestlin'."

"What then?" I exhale the words, almost out of breath.

"I'm thinkin' that these are the prettiest breasts I've ever seen." Fingertip skims the tender flesh of my side boob. "I can't believe I'm touching these."

He can do more than touch them—and I want him to put his mouth on me so desperately I'm practically panting.

Just then, a loud bang hits the bedroom door—two hard thuds with the flat of someone's fist, a high-pitched male voice calling out, "Special delivery, motherfuckers!"

More thumping has Rhett's hand going still, shifting, flattening on my ribcage. Pressing another finger to his lips. "*Shh.*"

Then he yells, "WHAT? *Jesus.*" Cranes his neck toward the banging. "What do you *want!*"

Brief pause. "Ginger, you in there? Make sure our man packages his meat!"

I raise my head to the sound of scraping across the hardwood floor: a long, gold strip of condoms being shoved under the door. Laughter in the hall, followed by the distant sound of the front door slamming.

Two sets of intense gazes fixate on those gold foil packages.

His.

Mine.

Sex, sex, sex, the condom packets broadcast to the room. *Orgasm, orgasm, orgasm.*

I know Rhett is thinking it too, and I can't even be sorry for the interruption because I didn't think to buy any, and if I know Rhett, he doesn't have any either. If we were going to have sex, he wouldn't have premeditated it, would have had to get up, walk down the hall, and ask his roommate for one.

The sight of them seems to fuel us both into a passion-induced haze, and he positions himself on top of me, bracing up on his elbows, hovering. Rotating his hips. I can feel his long, rigid erection through his gym shorts, through my jeans.

He strokes the loose hair fanned around my head. Runs a finger along my jawline. Down my neck, to the spot behind my ear that has the ability to drive me crazy with lust.

Takes his time before placing a chaste kiss on my temple. The corner of my eye. Mouth. Chin.

He lets out his breath. "Laurel?"

Mine catches. "Yes?"

"Do you…" When he pauses, I arch my entire body, closing the gap between us, tips of my breasts brushing his pecs.

Wiggle.

"Do I what?" Nuzzle his neck. Lick. "You can ask me anything."

Our mouths fuse again before he responds, swallowing his question, four hands suddenly *everywhere*. Frantic. He rolls again, taking me along with him; I'm on top, straddling his hips.

Gazing down while he gazes up, I position myself over his erection. Undo the metal button on my jeans while he watches, transfixed. Pull down the zipper as his hands roam parallel up my obliques. Skim the underside of my breasts.

Toy with the waistband of my pants.

I lean in so my breasts brush against his bare skin. "Do you like that?" I ask, nose trailing along the shell of his ear. "I love your skin. You're so warm."

His hands run the length of my spine, bury themselves in the back of my pants. I lift myself when he gently pushes the denim down over my hips. Thumbs hook inside my underwear.

"I'm desperate for you," I moan in between kisses. *"Desperate."*

God, I like him so much. Drown in his goodness. His kind spirit and pure heart. The romance of his second language. Sweet brown eyes and beautiful smile.

"You are?"

"Yes Rhett, I am."

"Do you want me to…" His gulp is labored, Adam's apple bobbing. Stares up at my breasts, then at the door. At the floor. "Do you want me to…pick those up off the floor?"

I kiss his jaw, sucking on his lower lip. "I think we're ready to take the next step, don't you?"

His giant paw cups my jaw, eyes searching mine. "I know I am, but I don't want to pressure you."

"That's funny—I was thinking the same thing about you."

We laugh, nerves sending my giggle into small fits. My lower half shakes, body void when he dumps me on the bed to leave my side, stealing across the room, snapping up the condoms off the floor. Tosses them on the bedspread so they're nearby. Shucks his shorts, pushing them down his powerful thighs. Stands in nothing but his boxer briefs, flushed, climbing back into the center of the bed.

Pulls me flush against his big, strong body and kisses the stuffing out of me, hands spread on my back, on my glutes, squeezing, a ripple of pleasure already building inside my core.

God I love it when he squeezes my ass.

"I'm glad we got the sex talk out of the way." I laugh when his mouth moves to my collarbone, gasp when he licks the valley between my boobs. Bumps my nipple with the tip of his nose before drawing it into his mouth and sucking. Flicking it with his tongue. "S-So glad."

"Looks like someone brought me more cookies," he whispers against my bare flesh.

"Are you hungry?"

"Starving."

We're obviously not talking about cookies; we're talking about sex, and I like it. I like this sexy but cautious side of him. He's taking risks with me that he's not entirely comfortable with, and I admire him for it.

I'm so outside his comfort zone, it's laughable.

Yet, here we are.

"Is that going to be our code word for sex? Cookies?" I lift my hips when he dips his hands into the waistband of my pants, drags them down my hips.

He's grinning from ear to ear. Kisses my belly button. "You think we're going to have enough sex to need a code word?"

"God I hope so." I groan when my pants get thrown to the floor. Then, "But I wasn't thinking about sex when I baked those cookies for you, so get that out of your head."

"I might be clueless about some things, Laurel, but I know what it means when a girl drops by my place with baked goods."

I roll my eyes playfully. "Fine, I'm busted—I did want you eating my cookies."

"They were good. Melted in my mouth." His lips graze my throat. Clavicle.

"Sweet?"

Laps at my nipple. "So sweet."

Ugh, this boy. Those words. *That tongue.*

"You're sweet." I brush the hair out of his eyes so I can get a good look at him. "I find you irresistible."

He studies me, braced on his arms. "Yeah?"

His voice is a deep timbre that gives me the chills, brown eyes mesmerizing.

"I wouldn't be here otherwise." I run my hands down his muscles, his rock-solid biceps. Ugh, these arms. "Embrasse moi." *Kiss me.* "Then let's get under these sheets."

He pulls down the corner of his quilt so we can scurry beneath it. When we do, I slide off my panties, dropping them beside the bed.

"There, naked."

He swallows. "I don't know if I'm going to last—it's been a few years. I don't want to embarrass myself…or disappoint you."

"Disappoint me? Not possible."

I wonder if I should suck him off, get him to come quick so when we finally get to the business of having sex, he lasts longer. I'm selfish like that.

Throwing back the covers we climbed beneath, I drag my breasts down his bulky frame, hands looping the elastic waistband of his navy underwear. Drag them down, mouth on his thick, erect—

"Oh shit," he groans when I suck. "What are you doing?"

"Foreplay." I hum, finger immediately seeking the hot button under his cock. Press down in tiny circles just like I read once in a magazine. His hips twitch, legs start to shake.

I smile around his dick.

"Shit Laurel, if you keep doing that I'm going to come."

That's the whole point of this pre-sex blow job.

I suck hard and long, palming his balls. Hum onto his cock, the tip hitting the back of my throat. Feel the telltale signs of pulsing—a good sign. Too easy.

"Stop, oh *fuck*...I'm gonna come." He's panting after only a few minutes.

Suck, suck, suck.

Rhett's head tips back, glorious throat constricting. Hands grip my shoulders. "Fuck, *oh fuck*, fuck yeah."

Small tremors. Thighs quiver.

Rhett comes in my mouth and I suck, swallowing. Remove my mouth, wiping it with the back of my hand. Admire his body as he lies there, spent, the aftershock of the quickie 'gasm wearing off.

I lean over toward the bedside table and grab the water bottle, twisting off the top. Chug. Gurgle. Replace the cap and slip under the covers, pulling them up around us.

Lie facing him, watching as he comes down off his climax, eyes hooded. Lips set in a content line, I spread out beside him, hip against his cock.

One kiss. Two.

One to my brow. Tip of my nose.

Bow of my lips.

I open for him, legs spreading when his hand drags along my inner thigh. Tongues touch lazily. Unhurried. Dreamy. My tender breasts full.

Aching.

Rhett's rough, callused fingers splay, gripping the sensitive skin between my thighs. "You're beautiful."

I've heard it a thousand times before, but this feels like the first. Coming from him? It's significant.

I'm not just a pretty face to Rhett. Not just arm candy or a trophy to be won and flaunted among his pompous friends. If anything, he wants to keep me for himself.

"Tu es belle." He kisses my temple.

Tu es belle—it sounds familiar. He's said it to me before, I know he has, but I don't have time to wonder what it means as I allow myself to get lost in his touch.

Rhett

"Tu es belle." I kiss her temple as my fingers explore between her legs. She is beautiful, hair spread out on my pillow, blue eyes sparkling ardently. Lips swollen from my kisses, pale skin red, marred from my beard stubble.

When Laurel stretches like a cat, arms above her head, my body begins responding in kind to the sight of her naked flesh. Her round breasts and flat stomach. The shaved valley between her slender thighs.

She tips her head, arches her back as my fingers part her slit. I run one up and down, tiny circles against her pussy. Laurel bites her bottom lip, nostrils flaring.

Lips part the barest of a fraction. Eyes roll.

Reaching out, her fingers rake through my hair, watching me as I finger her. Shit, I don't know if I'm even doing it right—but her face is flushed and she's squirming a lot, which I take as a good sign.

"You're getting hard again." She wiggles her hips.

Impatiently? Excited.

I *am* getting hard again—thank Christ. Eyes scan the bed for the condoms I threw down earlier. They're near the foot of the bed, close to the edge, but not so far I won't be able to reach them when I need to slip one on.

Condoms.

I've only ever worn them twice—for the same fuck. The first time I tried putting one on, it snapped when I rolled it, breaking. The second attempt went marginally better, the actual sex act lasting only as long as it had taken to put the damn thing on in the first place. Beth, my first partner, wasn't a virgin, didn't come when we fucked, and whined about it the entire drive home.

We stayed friends—because we're from such a small town—but it was always awkward after that. Just awesome.

Laurel is wet, my fingers slick. Thumb caressing the swollen nub hidden there. She moans. Thrashes her head.

Whines.

Gazes at me with eyes so glazed over with a looming orgasm it makes the throbbing between my own legs increase tenfold.

"I want you i-inside me when I...oh God..."

"Should I get the..." Condoms?

"*Yes*," she hisses. Her legs squeeze closed when I fly to the foot of the bed, snatching up the strip of condoms and tearing one off. Rip the package open with my teeth like a savage, roll it on like I've done it a hundred times.

When I rise to climb over the body personifying every sexual fantasy I've ever had, I take a second to appreciate the view: Laurel's legs spread wide, inviting me to slide inside that smooth pussy. Long, wavy red hair. Amazing rack. Hands white-knuckling the bedspread.

Impatient. "I can't stand it anymore. *Hurry*."

Trembling, I reach down, grabbing my cock, guiding it into her heat, hoping like fuck I stick it in the right hole.

Then?

A collective moan when my dick slides in, inch by glorious inch, guided by the white light behind my eyelids. Vision a blur. Loud, passionate groans our only soundtrack.

I push into her gently, elbows braced on either side of her gorgeous face, bending to kiss her. Her mouth opens, tongue plunging into mine. Starving, sexy.

Over and over.

I can't believe I'm having sex with Laurel Bishop, my brain screams, momentarily distracting me from all the sliding in and out I know I should be doing.

God she feels good. Hot.

Fuck she feels good. Slick.

Jesus she feels good. Tight.

I thrust into her, pleasure coursing through my blood, veins. Head. Feet. Legs. Balls. Dick.

"Rhett," she whimpers, tapping my bicep. "I knew you would feel good."

"You've thought about it?"

"Only a hundred times a day."

Her fingers dig into my hips, nudging me off her. Shoves me to my back, legs swinging into a straddle. Eases down around me, sinking onto my dick. Undulates her hips, back and forth, in a slow, intoxicating rhythm.

And this is the part where I fucking die and go to heaven…

Holy Christ. Holy shit.

Oh fuck.

I use the swivel in my hips to thrust up, her hands planted behind her head, deliberate…mind-blowing…rolls of her narrow hips …

"God, Rhett, yes…right there, yeah yeah," comes her plea, her chant. "Keep doing that with your hips, don't stop, don't stop."

Her tits bounce as we fuck, hair falling in a shocking red wave, the entire visual more than I can even fucking handle. I can't take my eyes off her—couldn't if I tried.

Laurel's hands skim my pelvis, nails dragging along the skin there. Head tipped back, she moans as we move together, bodies in synch, her tight—

"You should see yourself," she whispers on a whimper. "You're gorgeous."

And in this moment, I believe her.

I have to.

Because there's something in her eyes when she looks down at me, an expression I can't place. Words waiting on her lips, words she wants to say. Adoration in the bend of her brow and the depths of her pretty blue eyes.

Yearning? Maybe.

Desire? Yes.

Affection. Devotion.

Shit, if I didn't know any better, I'd think she was in love with me.

I know sex can make you say and do some pretty fucked-up shit, but I don't think I'm wrong here. Feel a shift when she breaks the contact, leaning forward, palms grabbing the wooden headboard behind me. Rocks her hips—

"Harder. Grab my ass," she demands. "Feels so...*mmm*."

Bends her head, hair falling in a cascade, so long it hits my chest. When she leans down to kiss me, I push it out of her face, cradling her jawline as she screws me on top.

Christ, shit, fuck...

"*Rhett.*" My name, said like *that*, on her lips, silently spilling into my mouth. "God, baby, oh *Goddd*."

"Laurel," I chant back, lost in the feel of her tight pussy. Her tongue.

The look in her eyes.

"*Baby.*"

When we come, it's together—mouths falling open, two sets of wide eyes bonded, intense—something I assumed was only reserved for movies. For cheesy romance novel bullshit. For my dipshit friends and their relationships.

Not for me.

Laurel takes her hands off the headboard, placing them on the pillow beneath my head. Rests her cheek on my sternum, listens to the erratically beating heart within my chest.

I stroke her hair. Back.

She kisses my shoulder.

"Rhett?"

"Hmm?"

There's a long stretch of calm, her fingertip tracing along the veins in my forearm.

"I..."

"You what?"

"Nothing."

———

"Did you hear that?"

"Hear what?"

Laurel sits up, yanking a sheet over her pale breasts. "Doesn't it sound like there are a bunch of voices in the living room?"

Insatiable, I drag her back down to the mattress, throwing back the sheet, mouth latching on to her nipple. Suckling. "No."

"Rhett, stop!" She makes no move to smack me away, letting me taste her skin. "I'm *serious*," she all but moans. "Listen for a second."

I pause. Listen.

She's right—there are voices coming from the front of the house. Voices I don't recognize.

"You don't think your roommates are having a party, do you?"

When I shrug, hand creeping below the covers, back between her legs, she spreads them for me. "Who knows. I don't trust those two."

"But you trust me," she boasts, hands cupping her bare breasts. "You want more of these?"

My dick twitches. Hardens. "Fuck yes."

"You want my cookie?"

"Fuck ye—"

Footfalls in the hallway give me pause. A loud banging at my door.

"New guy!"

"WHAT!" I shout, horny and immediately irritated. Laurel kisses my back when I twist my torso toward the door, eyes searching the room for my boxers.

"Dude." Gunderson laughs through the door. "I hate to break up the party, but you have company."

A warm mouth drags down the back of my neck. "Tell them to piss off."

"No can do."

Petite hands snake around my middle, wrapping around my—

"Godfuckingdammit Gunderson, I said piss off!"

"Afraid that's going to be impossible amigo." His annoying laugh drifts through the door.

Laurel's soft hands slowly pump up and down my cock. *"Why the fuck not?"*

Jesus Christ, did I just grunt that entire sentence out?

"What'cha doin' in there, buddy?" More laughter. "Better finish up and come out here—I know how much you love surprises."

"Jesus Christ, Gunderson."

"Just put some pants on and throw a shirt on your ginger—you'll thank me later."

The doorknob jiggles. Another knock, this one different—seven short raps in a pattern.

Delicate.

Familiar...

Fed up, I throw back the covers, slip a pair of boxers over my raging boner, perturbed.

Unlock and yank open my bedroom door. "What the hell did I tell you assholes about—"

Holy shit.

"Mom?"

"Surprise!" My mother reaches forward, pulling me in for a hug. Squeezes me tight. Backs away, looking me up and down. "Sweetie, where are your clothes?"

Behind me, in a heap on the floor—because I kicked them off before climbing into bed to fuck Laurel for the last two hours.

The corner of my eye catches the distinct shape of three gold discarded condom wrappers, and I kick the remaining ones away with my toe, out of sight. They skid across the floor, sliding under my dresser.

"My clothes? Uh…"

"Do you need me to do your laundry?" She pushes forward, jamming the door with her hip. I push back, stopping it with mine. Her brow furrows. "Why are you blocking the door? Let me in—I'll grab your dirties."

Dirties? Shoot me now.

"Mom, it's fine."

"We're just so excited! We wanted to come see you for your birthday." Her hands grasp my face. "You look so good, sweetie!" She wraps her arms around me again. "Your father and I—"

I know the moment her eyes catch sight of Laurel over my shoulder, through the crack in the door, will never forget her stunned silence as long as I live. It's *palpable*, followed by a dramatic gasp. "Who—I mean, oh my! I…goodness!"

I've never seen my mother at a loss for words, and right now? She has no fucking clue what to say. Averts her wide eyes, face flushed.

I crane my neck, catch Laurel's grimace, sheets pulled up to her neck, brilliant red hair in a tangle, cascading over one bare shoulder. It's obvious she's naked, embarrassed, and thoroughly fucked.

Her words are strangled. "Oh my God Mrs. Rabideaux, hi. I … we … oh my God." She disappears beneath the sheets.

"I am so sorry! The boys didn't tell us you had company." My mother peeks over my broad shoulder one more time; she's curious, interested now that the shock seems to have worn off. "I am so sorry!"

Laurel emits another groan.

"Mom, can you give us five minutes, to uh, you know … change."

"Of course! Yes. Goodness." In two seconds, she's going to start spinning in circles. "I'll just...y'all get changed. I'll go wait in the living room with your father."

"Jesus. Anyone else come with you?"

"Your brothers. My baby turned twenty-one, of course we drove up!" She does a small squeal then chokes down another one. "Y'all have a big meet this weekend and your dad thought it was time to check up on you after all the..." She lowers her voice to a whisper. "All the trouble with the team."

I lean against the doorjamb, continue blocking her view into the bedroom. "She knows about the drama, Ma. You don't have to whisper."

"She's so pretty!" my mother gushes in a staged whisper. "What's her name? Is that your girlfriend? Are you a *couple*?"

"Mom, please, just—"

Her hands go up. "I'm going, I'm going."

I blow out a frustrated puff of air. "Five minutes."

"I'll stall your father." She kisses me on the nose. Pats my cheek. "You look great. Put some pants on and throw those condom wrappers in the garbage."

Slowly, I close my bedroom door. Stand in stunned silence, staring holes into the dark wood

I turn. "So...my parents are here."

"How am I supposed to go out there, Rhett? Your mom practically saw me naked."

"Pretty sure my mom knows we were in here having sex."

Her head pops out from its hiding spot. "At least she knew you were seeing someone though, right?"

I fidget.

"Rhett, please tell me she knew you were seeing me so I can shrug this off as embarrassing, but not hopelessly unfortunate."

Shit. "She didn't know. I-I mean, we...I... Shit."

Laurel slides out of the bed, magnificently nude. "You can tell your mom I'm your girlfriend if you want, all right? I don't want your parents thinking I'm some random girl you picked up down-town for the night."

"Trust me, that thought won't cross their minds."

"I know, but still. It would make me feel better. Less..." She waves a hand around. "You know, like I do this sort of thing all the time. Her opinion of me matters, Rhett. This is not the impression I wanted to make when I met your parents for the first time."

She was planning to meet my parents?

When?

She prattles on. "My mother would die right now if she saw me. Die. Then she'd kill me." Laurel bends at the knees, scooping up her bra, glancing over her shoulder as she fastens it. "Can you imagine what my dad would say?"

Her body shivers.

Retrieving her underwear, she pads over to where I stand, bolted to the floor. Kisses me on the lips. "I knew you would have great stamina."

"Babe, don't touch me. The last thing I need is another fuckin' hard-on."

Her gaze is wicked. Delighted. "Your parents are out there."

"Yup."

"You poor thing." Her hand comes around, slapping me firm-ly on the ass. "Better not leave them sitting with your roommates too long. No good can come from that."

Laurel

Rhett's mother rises from the sofa, her shoulder-length brown hair cut into fashionable layers, her lithe frame a ball of energy. I swear, she's positively about to burst at the sight of me. His two meddling roommates loiter in the kitchen, leaning against the counter, listening to the whole exchange. Brothers flank either end of the couch.

I shuffle into the living room, embarrassed, just my purse dangling from my hands as I do the walk of shame through Rhett's living room, hair mussed, lipstick kissed off, mouth stained.

He moves to introduce us, face flushed, but Gunderson beats him to it, calling out from the kitchen. "Have none of you met Ginger, Rhett's girlfriend?"

His mother's brows go up, gaze trained on my flaming red hair. "Your name is Ginger?"

Ugh, why are his roommates such idiots?

My face heats up. "No ma'am, it's Laurel."

"It's good to meet you. I wish we'd known…"

Again, the peanut gallery chimes in. "Tsk, tsk, Rabideaux—you didn't tell your parents you had a girlfriend?"

I wish he would stop talking. He's embarrassing Rhett and making a mess of everything.

"Girlfriend?"

"Uh…"

"That's your girlfriend?" one of Rhett's brothers practically shouts. "Holy shit. You're *hot.*"

"Austin!" His mother gasps. "Manners!"

"We're, uh, datin', I guess," Rhett says by way of explanation, hands shoved into the pockets of his Louisiana hoodie.

"Your mother and I thought we'd drive fifteen hours so we could wait in your living room while you threw some clothes on."

"Charles!" his mother scolds. Turns to me. "This is what we get for comin' unannounced. We were plannin' on maybe doin' dinner, but it's so late now and Rhett has check-in and can't leave so I think I'll pack the boys up and head to the hotel."

I smooth down my hair self-consciously, sure it looks like I've been rolling around in bed all night having sweaty, hot sex...which I have. "And I should get going. I, um...it was *so* nice meeting you."

I need to get out of this house; I'm so embarrassed.

"Will you be at the meet tomorrow, Laurel?"

"Yes! I would love to sit with you if that would be okay?"

Mrs. Rabideaux beams. "We would love that."

Rhett

"**R**hett Clayton Rabideaux." My mom starts in as soon as I set foot back inside the house after walking Laurel home. "How could you not tell us you have a girlfriend?"

"It never came up." Not with all the bullshit I've been dealing with lately. "Besides, she's not really my girlfriend."

Mom's face falls. "Oh."

"If I could interject here." Gunderson clears his throat, interjecting from the kitchen. "That's a lie, Mrs. R—your boy here is full of shit. They're definitely an item."

Fucking Gunderson.

My parents both raise their brows. Turn back to me.

"I guess we're kind of...talking."

Fuck. Laurel would be so pissed I'm explaining it this way. She's the type of girl that demands respect, and here I am, being cavalier, butchering the explanation like she means nothing.

"Are you using protection?" my dad inquires, pointing the remote at the TV, eyes locked on the screen. "Your mother and I are done raising little kids."

Oh my fucking God. "Yes."

"No worries, Mr. R, we hooked young Rhett up with the world's finest prophylactics. No STDs in this house—not on my watch."

"That's disgusting," my brother Beau chimes in.

"What's an STD?" the other one wants to know.

My mother ignores them both.

"Laurel is so beautiful," Mom enthuses. "Even her name is pretty, sounds like a flower."

I know.

"How the hell did the two of you meet?" Beau rudely asks.

I glance up. Catch my roommate's eyes across the kitchen as he pretends to be busy making himself dinner.

Gunderson shrugs.

Oh, *now* he has nothing to fucking add to the conversation?

"We met at a party."

Gunderson snorts.

"Where did you take her on your first date?"

Jesus, what is this, the Spanish Inquisition?

"We, uh, haven't gone on a date yet."

"You're screwing her and you haven't taken her on a date?" my dad deadpans from the couch, setting down the remote and suddenly paying rapt attention.

"Charles!" Mom reprimands him while turning a raised brow on me. "Is this the kind of gentleman I've raised? One that doesn't take his girlfriend out on dates?"

"I never have time, Mom!"

Why am I defending myself? Jesus.

"Well what is it you *do*?" she presses.

"I don't know—we study. Hold hands. Walk to school together. She comes to my meets. I don't know what else to do with her!"

"*Oh* boy," Gunderson deadpans from the kitchen, chewing on a carrot.

"That's your idea of dating?" My youngest brother snorts. "Taking her to watch you wrestle? You sure are full of yourself." He turns to my roommate. "What do they call that?"

"Egomaniac," Gunderson supplies.

"Shut up, Beau, you're not helping."

He shrugs, thumbing through the fitness magazine he swiped from the coffee table, looking for female models.

"Trust me, she doesn't care that we just hang out," I counter.

My mother crosses her arms. Glaring.

Disappointed.

"I've never met a young woman who didn't want to be properly courted."

I have a flashback to our conversation in the library, the one where she asked why I'd never asked her on a date.

"Forget I said anything," she said after bringing it up. Too late, I clamped my lips together, confused as fuck.

"I didn't realize you wanted *me to ask you out."*

She looked up at me then, pretty brows bent. "I've been flirting and messaging you for weeks. *I brought you cookies. I called you to pick me up from a bar in the middle of the night. Kissed you on my porch. What did you think I was* doing *all this time?"*

"I don't fucking know, Laurel. Friendzonin' me? I thought we were studyin'. What did you *think we were doing?"*

"I thought you were waiting to ask me out until the time was right," she blurted out, cheeks red as her hair. "I can't believe I said that. I don't ask guys out—I've never asked a guy out in my life, *and I'm not starting with you."*

Shit.

I'm an ass.

———————————

Me: *Sorry about that whole thing with my parents.*

Laurel: *It's okay, I survived. Only a mild heart attack. Lana charged me back to life with sushi.*

Me: *I apologize in advance for anything my family says tomorrow.*

Laurel: *I'm so nervous. I hope they don't think I'm...you know, sleazy or whatever.*

Me: *They don't think you're sleazy. They spent the entire past hour grilling me about you.*

Laurel: *I guess I can use tomorrow as an opportunity to redeem myself from the walk of shame I did in front of them tonight.*

Me: *Tu me manques déjà*

Laurel: *Does that mean what I think it means?*

Me: *What do you think it means?*

Laurel: *You miss me terribly?*

Me: *Uh, that's kind of exactly what it means. LOL*

Laurel: *You are the sweetest. Honestly. I miss you so much. Do I sound clingy saying that?*

Me: *No, because I just said it.*

Me: *My parents just left.*

Laurel: *And?*

Me: *And I'm thinking you should get your sweet little ass back over here.*

Laurel: *God, now all I can think about is you touching me.*

Me: *Then what are you waiting for?*

Laurel

"So what did your parents say after I left?" We're lying on our stomachs in the middle of his bed, feet dangling off the other side. I switched into yoga pants before coming back over, but I don't expect them to stay on long.

"My mom only wanted to talk about you, and my dad kept tryin' to talk about wrestling."

"What did she want to know about me?" My stomach can't help but leap at this news.

Those broad shoulders of Rhett's move up and down in a shrug. "You know, the usual."

Oh God, if he's going to be vague, I'm going to have a stroke. "Like what?"

"Rex would not shut up about you being my girlfriend." He laughs it off, but I detect an undertone in his voice that has my ears perking up. "And my mom kept pryin' for details."

Pryin'.

I swear, my heartbeat quickens. "What did you say to the girlfriend thing?"

"I didn't want her to get all excited, you know? My mom's the type that would start plannin' a weddin' and shit—she has three boys—so, you know, I told her the truth, that we were talking."

I pull back. Talking?

I mean, I get it; he doesn't know where we stand, and neither did I until just now. I try to laugh, swallow down the disappointment. Downplay how that word makes me feel.

Talking.

What does that even mean?

"Talking."

His laugh sounds strangled. Nervous. "You know—hanging out."

Stomach in knots, I turn to face him, body twisting. "Is that what you want? To hang out?"

"What do you mean?"

"Don't you want, you know…more?" With me. Specifically.

"What do *you* want?"

"Rhett, I'm asking *you*." I'm curt, but need to know I'm not wasting my time with someone who doesn't want me back—that his heart, like mine, is invested.

If even just a little.

It hasn't occurred to me before this moment that he might be using me for sex, using my body, like the guys that have come before him—but hearing him hesitate like this? It just might break my heart.

My eyes squeeze closed; I can't look at him. "I'm not trying to push you into anything Rhett, I swear I'm not. I can handle the truth, I just need to know if you want what I want." *Before I fall completely and madly in love with you.*

I'm more than halfway there already.

Feeling decidedly Alex-like, I realize I'm an utter asshole for bringing this up. It's unfair to him, I know this; he has never been in a relationship before, so how would he know how he felt about me after only a few weeks? The last thing I want to do is railroad the poor guy into a relationship by being pushy. For all I know, he hasn't had a girlfriend for a reason.

What if he doesn't *want* one? Just wants to sow his wild oats? Catch up from his lifelong dry spell?

I like him far too much to stay silent.

I have to know.

"Are you askin' if *I* want a girlfriend?"

I roll to my side, studying his expression. "I guess I am."

He mulls it over, rolling to his back, arms behind his head, staring at the ceiling. "*Any* girlfriend, or someone specific?"

I narrow my eyes; who knew he'd be this cheeky? Bite my bottom lip to stop myself from smiling.

"Don't be coy," I scold, impatient. Sulking.

"Oh, *I'm* the coy one, huh?" his deep voice teases. "So what I'm gettin' from that cute pout of yours is you wouldn't mind, you know, being, uh…committed."

My ears perk up.

Commitment. I almost breathe the word out loud. *Yes.*

"So, no sleeping with other people while we're sleeping with each other," he muses.

"*Right.*"

"That won't be a problem for me." When he laughs, I want to smack him for joking around and not giving me a straight answer. Ugh.

Ten minutes later, he still hasn't answered my question.

Ten minutes later, I reach to pull on my Chucks, crouching at the foot of the bed. Slip one shoe on, moving to zip the soft leather up its side.

A warm hand touches my spine, caressing my back, up and down. Kisses my neck from behind. "Goin' somewhere?"

"Home." I glance at him over my shoulder.

Rhett furrows his brow. "But I thought…"

I shoot him a sharp look, trying to control my out-of-control emotions. "You thought *what?*"

I know I'm being hypersensitive, but I'm in uncharted territory here, completely out of my element, and don't know quite what to do with myself. Normally I'm the one calling the shots in my relationships, the one being chased after, showered with compliments, and getting gifts.

Rhett has shown me none of those things, and yet…

Here I am, dreaming about him every day and every night. Falling asleep with a smile on my face, waking up thinking about him, with his name on my lips.

"I-I don't know what I thought," he stammers, hands splayed helplessly. "Help me out here, Laurel. I don't know what I did to piss you off."

"Truthfully?" My shoulders slouch, fingers releasing their hold on my shoe, letting it drop to the ground. I sit up straight, ashamed. "I don't know why I'm leaving."

What a liar.

I don't have a clue what we're doing and can't handle not knowing. I guess that makes me a control freak, doesn't it? I can't push the subject with him because if I do, I run the risk of pushing him away.

Rhett simply isn't equipped to deal with a girl like me.

It's depressing.

As it is, I practice every ounce of self-control I have, doing my best not to eat him alive. It's *hard*; he's so freaking irresistible.

"For what it's worth, I want you to stay." He leans in again, brushing my long hair out of the way, kissing the back of my neck. "Stay."

My body gives in, falling back down onto the mattress. He hovers above me now, shaggy hair falling into his concerned brown eyes.

"All right." I trace his jawline with the tip of my finger. "You're right."

"I have to be up really fucking early, but you'll have the house to yourself in the morning. The guys and I have to be out the door by five."

"Five?" I wrinkle my nose. "Is it even light out that early?"

"Barely."

"Rhett?"

He gazes down adoringly.

"I'm sorry."

"For what?"

"For being such a...girl."

He rears back, grinning. "What does that mean?"

"It means…" I worry my bottom lip with a sigh. "That I'm letting my insecurities get the best of me."

"Uh, okay." Translation: *I have no fucking clue what you're talking about.*

"You know what would make me feel better?"

His brows rise.

I raise one of mine.

Two seconds later, he's on his haunches, peeling off his shirt.

He's hot and horny, wanting to have sex constantly, the condoms we had almost entirely gone once we rescued them from under the dresser.

"Laurel?" The gentle whisper comes from somewhere above my head. A light caress touches my back. "Laurel, I've gotta go."

I roll to my back, his hand taking the short journey across my flesh when I turn. Stretch, sheet sliding down my pale skin.

Groggy but not blind, I catch when his eyes roam my naked upper body. Give him a tired little smirk and let him ogle my amazing breasts.

"Mmm, morning baby." I can't help calling him that; it feels so right.

"Sorry to wake you, I just wanted to say goodbye."

When his hand settles on the flat of my stomach, I reach for it. Drag it up my ribcage, resting it on my breast. His thumb immediately begins a tender stroke over the crest.

"You have to leave right this second?" I whisper, hand reaching out to stroke along the visible outline of his dick beneath black mesh gym shorts. I wonder if he's ever had morning sex, or at least thought about it, about having it with me. Probably not since he's standing next to the bed, completely dressed, showered, and ready to leave. "Once more before you go, *please* babe."

"Once more *what* before I go?"

Is he serious? "A quickie."

Rhett wars with himself, debating, and I wonder if it has more to do with my hand on his junk, his hand on my boob, or my use of the word babe.

His cock, at eye level, twitches. Grows.

My arms stretch above my head lazily. Breasts tempting, hair fanned on his pillow, I know I'm an alluring sight, unfurled like a cat in the sun. Irresistible to his hormonal, raging body.

I know it's wrong to make him choose, but I want slow, orgasmic, morning sex, and I want it *now*.

"Make love to me real quick," I whisper, hips rolling beneath the sheets, already damp between my legs. "*Please*, baby."

Baby: I know with that one word, I've got him by the balls.

Duffle dropping like a lead weight to the floor, Rhett hurriedly yanks his shirt up over his head. Shucks his shorts, shoving them down his muscular thighs. Crawls under the covers between my spread my legs, palm running up my calf, leg, cupping my breast. Squeezes gently. Sucks a nipple.

He's a fantasy come to life, hard as a rock and warm and smelling like peppermint. Shampoo and woodsy soap. Feels like heaven in the dusky morning light barely filtering through the sheer curtains.

"Gotta make this quick." Hesitates before pushing in. Long and hot, he's already learned what makes my body purr. "S*hhh*it, Laurel."

Wide awake and full of raw power, his hips thrust, doing all the work for both of us, face buried in the crook of my neck, mouth on my skin. Hips rolling slowly at first, his stiff cock hitting my sweet spot almost immediately.

Ah, the beauty of morning sex—or maybe I'm just so turned on by him I was already halfway there.

When Rhett's large hands grip my ass, sinking in as deep as he can go and pumping into me wildly, I whimper, clinging to him, orgasm imminent.

Horny, adrenaline-fueled Rhett feels…is…

"*Perfect. So* perfect."

We make no sounds when we come, no grunts, no moans.

Just the sound of our heavy breathing in the first light of day, bodies pressed so closely together there's no room between us, not even for a whisper.

His kiss hits my lips when he pulls out; rising to clean himself up, he gathers his clothes to pull them on. I watch him dress, sated, chin propped on my elbow.

His body is chiseled perfection. His heart? Sweet and a bit naïve.

Mine flutters, observing him hustle around his room; he deserves this wave of love I suddenly feel for him.

We both do.

"Breakfast in the fridge." He swoops in again to kiss the pulse in my neck, lips lingering. "My parents will be in section three, right where you sat last time. My mom will be watching for you."

I roll up in his covers. "Kay."

"Bye." Long pause. "Babe."

My heart races when he tests the endearment for the first time, leaving me just a little bit breathless. Jeez, I miss him, and he hasn't walked out the door yet.

Get a grip, Laurel. "See you later, baby. Good luck."

One more sweet kiss to my collarbone and he's gone.

I flop down on his pillow, burying my face in the space he recently occupied. Give it a sniff, sighing all over again. Roll onto his sleeping spot and slip into blissful, satisfied slumber.

#DOUCHEBAG

"My birth control app
just woke me from a horrible
dream where I woke up pregnant.
It took me a solid three minutes
to realize it wasn't real,
thank God."

Laurel

"Laurel sweetie, over here!" An enthusiastic hand goes up in the third row, waving furiously. I don't know how I manage to spot her in the massive crowd, but the arm is attached to Mrs. Rabideaux; she beams at me as I make my way down the bleachers, down the stadium steps.

I shuffle my way toward Rhett's family, cheeks flaming hot, already embarrassed. The last time I saw his mother, I was leaving her son's house, post-coital, ratty sex hair and all.

But, I suck it up; if he and I are going to be long-term, then I have to get this whole awkward situation over with and move past it.

Pasting on a smile, I weave my way through the third row, toward the empty spot next to Rhett's mother. Her smile is so big, arms welcoming, some of the anxiety melts away. When I finally reach them, her arms embrace me. Squeeze.

"I'm so glad you're here!" Mrs. Rabideaux enthuses. "Normally it's always just me at these things with all these men."

"Thank you for letting me sit with you, Mrs. Rabideaux." I have to raise my voice so she can hear me. "Honestly, I've only been to one of these, and I brought my roommates so I didn't have to come alone."

"Please, call me Wendy."

I blush. "Thank you, Wendy."

"Sit, sit. Here, I brought seat cushions. This promises to be a long match—they're getting ready for qualifiers."

I plop down beside her on the Iowa stadium seat. "Qualifiers for what?"

"The NCAA championships. They're coming up soon—next month."

"Oh!" I didn't know that. "Has Rhett ever won anything like that?" Could I *be* any more clueless?

"Twice," she boasts, puffing out her chest with pride.

"*Twice!*" My heart races. "Wow. I mean, I knew he was good, but…*twice?*" I scan the mats in front of us for that face I've grown to adore. Find him pacing, decked out in black pants, track jacket. Black shoes with white stripes slashed through the side.

"Why aren't they wearing headgear?"

"It's optional at this level. Some wrestlers choose not to wear it because it gets in the way." She drones on. "In high school—not that it matters anymore—he was All-American, sweetie. Didn't you know that?"

All-American? "What does that mean?"

"It means he was one of the best high school wrestlers in the nation, along with near perfect grades."

Wendy's eyes catch me ogling her son, and she shoots me a sidelong glance before joining my perusal. "How is he doing? Honestly."

I take my eyes off Rhett long enough to give her a reassuring smile. "Better now, I think?"

She analyzes my expression closely. "You *are* referring to the four-hundred-dollar restaurant bill?"

Shit. How much has he told her about that? About all the other incidents?

The look on my face—and my hesitation—has Wendy studying me closely. "If there was more, you'd tell me?"

I nod slowly. "There have been a few other little things."

I can't lie. Can't.

This is his *mother*.

"Like what?"

"They, um…vandalized his car."

"What do you mean vandalized his car?"

"They, uh…" I clear my throat, itching to stretch out my collar. "Covered it in grease and wrapped it in, um, plastic wrap."

"Who is *they*?" Wendy's eyes are dangerous slits, sliding to the other men warming up beside Rhett.

"We don't know. Some sorority girls, I think? I was with him so he didn't have to drive the Jeep home, but…he was really upset about it."

Her lips press into a thin line. "What did Coach Donnelly do about it?"

I swallow. "He, uh, made them do a team-building exercise at a cabin in the woods. It's been much better since."

"Hmm." She pulls her brown gaze off her son. "He seems happy. I'm disappointed he felt like he couldn't tell us."

I don't know what else to say but, "You know how guys are."

"Well, he's always been stubborn." Her head dips. "It's hard having him so far away. I worry. A mother should know her son is being taken care of."

My arms slide around her shoulders and pull her in. "I'm taking care of him. He has me."

"I can't get over the fact that my baby has a girlfriend. He's never had one." She pauses. "He wouldn't want me tellin' you that."

"I don't think he considers me his girlfriend yet, but…I think we might be moving in that direction—I mean, I hope we are." Shut up, Laurel. Stop talking. "I really like him."

Her eyes soften with my words, eyes scanning for him again. Her gaze roams up, over the student section, and I know the instant her eyes land on a poster board sign that says: DOES RETT STILL NEED 2 GET LAID?

And another: RETT ANSWER MY TEXTS & I'LL BLOW YOU & UR "MIND"

If I thought Wendy's eyes were narrowed before, they're nothing compared to the daggers she's shooting across the gym floor now. "Are girls always this forward? Why would a young woman offer to have sex with my son?"

My lips clamp shut.

"Do you see that?" She's pointing now, jabbing her husband in the arm. "Charlie, are you seein' this? Look." Jabs him again. "Look."

Mr. Rabideaux squints, glancing briefly around the stadium seating. Goes back to ignoring us, leaning forward, hands braced on his knees to better take in the action.

And that face Rhett is making now, as he waits to start his match? It's the same look he makes when he's concentrating on something I'm saying—or when he's putting his big hands on my body. He's making that same intense face now, under the bright lights of the center mat.

Stretching on the balls of his feet, working his hamstrings.

Stalwart focused.

Beside me, "What is wrong with those girls?" She nudges me, truly worked up. "Is it always like this?"

I answer as honestly as I can without ratting myself out. "Well, I've only been to one other match, and there were signs like that, yes."

"Why would they do that? 'Get Rett Laid'? Of all the things."

She huffs, agitated, crossing her arms. "Doesn't that bother you?"

I shift in my seat, uncomfortable. Squirming.

"Yes."

"Does it bother *him*?"

"I don't know if he notices. He hasn't said anything, and I haven't asked."

"Honestly." Huff. "Where do these girls get the nerve? How are they allowed in with those signs?"

If my face isn't flaming as hot as my hair, I would be shocked. It must be; the blush burning me up from head to toe has the temperature in my body skyrocketing. "I don't know ma'am."

I gulp. Guilty.

Sweating.

It's horrible.

I can't outwardly admit *I was one of those girls*. A girl that called her kindhearted son out of the blue, because of a poster hanging on campus, to mock him. To tease him because I thought he wasn't that good-looking.

Granted, I didn't show up in public waving a sign promising blow jobs and sex, but I did text him, proposition him in a roundabout way.

Nagged until he relented, talked, and flirted with me.

I'm a terrible person, with no better morals than those young women, or my cousin Alex.

My eyes shift to Rhett, who removes his warm-up clothes one article at a time. Watch as he pulls the pants down his hips, steps out of them, the word Iowa in bold yellow emblazoned on his dense left thigh.

God, how could I have ever thought he wasn't attractive when now, he's the most handsome guy I've ever seen? It breaks my vain heart knowing how I acted—like an asshole.

I'm not out of his league; he's out of mine.

I swallow the hard lump of emotions in my throat, adapting a forward pose, just like his father, waiting for Rhett to step center ring, under the lights, his pale skin already glistening from perspiration.

He reaches to adjust the spandex of his singlet, tugging the fabric out of his crotch, fiddling with the leg holes. Shakes one leg then the other. Each arm. Pivots head from side to side.

His opponent is a big guy, virtually identical in stature down to the serious expression, neither acknowledging the crowd when the announcer broadcasts their names, their stats.

Rhett Rabideaux, transfer from LSU. Winningest wrestler in the past three years at both Louisiana and Iowa. All-American. Two-time NCAA champion in his weight class. Six foot. One ninety. Hometown: Bossier City, Louisiana. Proud parents, Wendy and Charlie Rabideaux.

I suck in a breath when the wrestlers take their positions, anxious.

Rhett and I have known each other only a matter of weeks and the amount of pride I'm feeling at this moment is insurmountable. Indescribable.

I want to puke I'm so nervous.

His mom notices my bouncing knee, grips my hand, squeezing. "Exciting, isn't it?"

"He's *amazing*." I sound breathy and wistful, even to my own ears, captivated by her half-naked son.

I feel her stare a few long heartbeats as she takes my measure. Gauges my sincerity.

Smiles. We hold hands when the ref blows the whistle, signaling the start. Wendy clutches my forearm as Rhett and Eli Nelson grapple, bent at the waist, heads lowered, both wrestlers dipping low.

"You want to stay low when you're wrestling someone who can shoot hard doubles from their knees," his mom says by way of explanation, as if I have a clue.

I obviously have *no* idea what she's talking about.

The boys are quick, fast on their feet. Rhett's head drops, pushing into his opponent's midsection until they're both barreling toward the white outer circle. Eli fights it, but slides out of bounds.

"That's called a push-out," Wendy says. "Rhett gets one point."

"One? That's it? He should get five for that!"

Rhett and Eli immediately enter more grappling, pulling on each other's heads. "I don't know how I feel about this," I admit. "He's not going to get hurt, is he?"

"Not likely. He hasn't really had any major injuries in the past few years besides cuts."

The whistle blows, and both guys stand, walking to their respective corners for coaching, water.

Then just like that, the whistle blows and they're at it again, Rhett with three points, Nelson with one. It's fast, much quicker than I thought matches were going to be, both men determined to get the upper hand. Agile and swift. Legs hooked, Rhett has his around Eli's waist, shoulders pressed into the mats, near the white, out of bounds.

Reset, and Nelson is down on his knees.

Just like he had me last night.

I tune out Wendy, the announcer calling out the points earned. Watch, riveted, as both men take to their knees, Rhett positioning himself behind Eli, cupping his elbow, arm sliding around his waist. I know it shouldn't remind me of sex, but it does, and my wanton girly parts come to life.

God, he is so damn hot.

The muscles flexing in his arms. Thighs.

Ass.

All of it so, so hot.

Maybe we should play wrestling tonight? Would he be into role playing?

I squirm in my seat, leg bouncing impatiently, hormones in overdrive. "We're not allowed to go down to see them afterward, right?"

"No sweetie, not until the event is over." Wendy pats my hand. "And they usually head straight to the locker rooms." She gives me a sidelong glance. "What are you kids doin' tonight?"

"Are you not staying?"

"No, it's a long drive and the boys have school Monday." Her eyes are glued on her son. "We're going to stop at a hotel tonight so we're not so tired getting home tomorrow. My husband has some work calls to make on Sundays so he wants the whole day." Her smile is secretive. "That gives you free time. Alone."

I knew I liked his mother for a reason.

"We haven't talked about plans for tonight. Maybe he'll want to go out with his friends? But, um…I didn't know it was his birthday before yesterday, so I just went and bought him a cake today. I thought I'd surprise him if he's not too tired to hang out."

Her brows go up. She takes her eyes off the mat and turns her entire body toward me, the crooked smile on her mouth looking so much like Rhett's.

"Birthday cake?"

"What? Can he not eat cake?" *Ugh, I am such a thoughtless idiot. Duh, the calories!* "Crap, I'm sorry—I didn't think about him weighing in."

Although, I can think of a few other things to do with the frosting instead of eating it.

"No, honey, he can have cake. I'm sure he'll love it." She pats my thigh the way only a mother can, so knowingly. "He's going to love it."

Rhett

I'm so fucking tired.

Drained.

Ass dragging, I meet my family in the tunnel by the locker room, Laurel's bright red hair the first thing I see when I lug my duffle of dirty clothes into the hall.

Tight black Iowa t-shirt. Skinny jeans. Black boots. Sexy as hell, and here for *me*.

I want to fist pump, slap myself on the goddamn back for my good fortune. I peel my eyes off her just long enough to greet my parents.

My mom steps forward, arms spread wide. "Congratulations honey. Great match."

"Thanks," I mumble into her shoulder as she crushes me to her body. My mom is tiny compared to me, small in stature but not in attitude—not with three sons.

My dad might wear the pants, but Mom controls the zipper.

She stands on her tiptoes, whispering into my ear. "Dad and I are taking the boys. We're going to head out of town."

It's only Saturday; it makes no sense to have driven all this way only to turn back around the next afternoon—none.

"Why?"

She's still whispering in my ear. "I didn't realize... We want to give you your space. I'm sure you have better things to do than hang out with your parents." Her arms go around my waist, hugging me. "Laurel couldn't take her eyes off you tonight—she really likes you. I hope you realize that."

Pulls back, straightening the collar of my shirt. Grabs my cheeks and kisses the bridge of my nose.

"So handsome."

I roll my eyes. "*Mom.*"

"What? Can't a mother tell her son he's handsome?"

Jesus. "Stop."

"Quit arguing and go say goodbye to your brothers. Hug Dad," she instructs, nudging me toward my siblings, smacking my rear.

I ruffle the hair on top of Beau's head. He whacks my hand away.

Austin lets me give him knuckles.

My dad grips me by the shoulders, pulling me in. Slaps my back twice. "Have to get home for my Sunday phone calls. Plus, your mother seems to think you want time alone with your new girlfriend."

My face was red from adrenaline; now it heats from total fucking embarrassment.

"Wear a condom. Don't be a jackass."

I open my mouth to protest, but he cuts me off. "I spoke to your coach and he assures me you boys are on the right track after your stay in the woods or whatever the hell that was, but I want you to call us if anything happens." He shoots a glance at Laurel, who stands laughing with my brothers. "I'm going to assume with that red hair, she's a little spitfire. Maybe she'll be good for you."

She will be.

She *is*.

"But use your damn head—this one." He taps my skull. "Don't get her pregnant."

Jesus Christ, Dad.

"All right. We're going to head out. Proud of you."

"Thanks." I mean, what else is there to say?

"Walk us out." Another smack on the back, hand clamping down on my shoulder, guiding me back to my mother. Brothers. Laurel.

She's blushing when I sidle up, shooting shy glances at my parents, the concrete floor below our feet, back at my parents. "Hey."

"Hey."

The tension surrounding us is palpable; the last time we stood in this hallway at the end of a meet, after a match I'd just won, I pressed her against the wall and stuck my tongue halfway down her throat.

Instead, my hands hang at my side, right arm shouldering the weight of my duffle.

Side by side, we follow my parents down that long corridor, walking so closely together our fingers brush. Laurel wiggles her index finger, brushing it over the flat of my hand.

My mom catches me biting back a stupid grin when she glances over her shoulder, raising her brows, watching us both. Pushes my brothers along in front of her because they insist on dawdling.

We reach the heavy steel doors, shoving through to the stadium parking lot, trailing the group to my mom's black suburban— the same SUV that drove me from practice to matches to meets and home again for years, until I could drive.

We stand next to it, my brothers not giving a shit about saying goodbye and immediately hopping into the back seat.

"Bye sweetie." Mom's lower lip has a slight quiver. "So grown up."

I want to groan out loud, but pull her in for a hug instead. "Bye Mom. Love you."

She sniffles into my neck. "You look so happy."

"Then why are you cryin'?"

"Because my baby is falling in love."

I glance around to see who's watching, patting her head. "Jeez, Mom."

"A mother knows these things."

"Mom—"

She scowls, tearing up. Sniffles. "Let me say what I have to say."

"Here?" Now? *Jesus.*

Laurel and my dad look on, awkwardly standing next to the car, not knowing what to do with themselves while we stand having a sidebar. Dad shoots a taut smile.

"You work too hard. I want you to have some fun."

"I am."

"But you don't, not really. You hole up in your room and keep to yourself, and I know you've had a tough time." Her hands fiddle with the buttons on my shirt. "But now you have Laurel, and I think…she has your back. She's a good friend."

Friend.

Mom squints at me. "Don't give me that look, you know what I mean."

I have no idea what *look* she's talking about, so I jerk my head with an acquiescent nod to make it stop. "Fine." Okay. Whatever.

"Okay then, I guess we're going." Kisses my cheek. "Home for Thanksgiving. We'll pay for the gas."

I rock on the balls of my feet. "Okay."

Her eyes dart to Laurel. "You can bring a guest home this year if you'd like."

"*Mom.*"

Her hands go up. "What?! I'm just sayin'."

"We'll see." I smile down at her. "Love you guys. Thanks for comin'."

Her lip quivers again. "We love you." She turns, taking the few steps to Laurel, wrapping her arms around her, too. "Bye sweetie. It was good meetin' you."

"Bye Mrs. Rabideaux." Those blue eyes find mine over my mother's shoulder, sparkling with mischief. "Drive safe."

"Everyone in the car!" my dad bellows, having long passed his patience threshold, pounding the hood of the car with his fist. "Boys, buckle up."

We watch as my parents get in the car. Dad starts the engine, puts the car in drive, and heads across the parking lot toward the massive stadium entrance.

Before I can think about what I'm going to say next, Laurel flings herself into my body, arms folding behind my head. My heavy bag falls to the pavement and I haul her against me, mouth melting onto hers. Tongues mingling with no preamble, adrenaline still coursing through my body.

"I love watching you wrestle. It's such a turn-on."

"Yeah?" I could get used to this, having her to greet me after coming down off a win—or loss. Telling me how amazing I am after every match, boosting my ego. Sticking her tongue down my throat and rubbing her tits against my chest.

Laurel pulls at my hips, and I guide her back until her ass hits the driver side door of my Jeep, not giving a damn that my parents are probably still on the street adjacent to the parking lot and can most likely see us making out.

"Aren't you tired?" The palms of her hands sneak beneath my shirt, running across my abs. Belly button. Toy with the waistband of my pants.

"No." Not only am I not tired, I've never been this horny in my whole goddamn life.

"Are you too tired to do something tonight?"

Too tired to hang out with *her*? Not likely. "Like what?"

"Your mom mentioned it was your birthday last week. Why didn't you say anything?"

"I'm a guy. We don't usually give a shit about our birthdays."

"*I* give a shit about your birthday because I give a shit about *you*." She plants a kiss on the tip of my nose. "I might have a treat for you."

This piques my interest. "Oh yeah? What kind of treat?"

"Don't get too excited—it's nothing big. Just something small because I didn't get to celebrate with you on your actual day."

"All right." We part so I can open the passenger side door. She hops up. "Your place or mine?"

"Mine, if that's okay? I cleared it out—Lana went home, and Donovan is spending the weekend with the new guy he's dating."

Her roommate is gay? Huh.

How did I not know this?

When we make it back to her place and I sidle up to the curb, she unbuckles, twisting her fantastic body, leaning across the center console for a kiss, breath minty from peppermint gum.

We make out for a good ten minutes, tongues rolling, hands roaming, until I'm painfully hard and ready to bang Laurel in the back seat of my Jeep.

I want her that fucking bad.

Instead, she pulls back, chest heaving. Eyes sparkling. "Give me twenty minutes and come back?"

Shit.

Adjusting the raging hard-on in my track pants with a groan, I nod, raking one of my large palms through my mop of hair. I went twenty-one years with (basically) no sex; I can wait another twenty minutes.

"Yup."

"Eek!" Another hasty kiss pressed to my mouth and she's gone, fleeing to the front porch of the house. Gives a little wave before she and her flaming red hair disappear into the house.

Would it be weird if I sat here and finished myself off? Jerked off in her driveway? I sit with my hand hovering about my cock, the stiff erection straining for release.

Cover it with my palm, one of the *worst* fucking ideas I've ever had, because it twitches, triggered.

Glancing at the house again, groaning when I give in and slide a trembling hand into my pants, fisting my shaft with one hand, the Jeep's grip bar above my window with the other. Slide my hand up and down, building speed, head tipped back when my balls tighten. Stroke and stroke, Laurel's red hair dominating my fantasy. Her creamy, pale breasts. The well-manicured landing strip between her spread thighs.

Shit, yes. Yes, oh fuck—fuck, I'm whacking off in front of a girl's house like a complete goddamn pervert. My pace quickens out of desperation and fear of being discovered, but it feels so fucking good I can't stop.

#DOUCHEBAG

"We got to my house,
snuggled while watching
Sixteen Candles, then fucked
during the repeat airing."

Laurel

The birthday cake sits dead center in the dining room, a round, red velvet confection covered in white cream cheese frosting. Twenty-one candles are sunk into the saccharine center, the lights in my small dining room dim. Normally, we use this waste of a space for piling our shit on the table, but tonight, the room is clean, paper and clutter stacked neatly on the sideboard our landlord kept with the house.

Fussing with my dress, I button and unbutton the top twice, examining myself this way and that, smooth legs, cleavage, hair. My dress is flirty, black, and hardly appropriate for the cold weather we've been having, but we're inside where it's warm, and it's sexy, so there is no way I'm changing out of it now.

The doorbells rings; fluffing my hair in the mirror, I plump my cleavage. Swipe on more lip stain. Smooth down the pleats in my black, flouncy skirt.

My breath hitches when I slowly drag open the door.

Rhett stands on the porch holding a small bouquet of flowers. Black polo shirt and dark jeans, he fidgets a little under my scrutiny.

"Jolies fleurs pour une jolie fille." He hands them to me once I stop gaping and shove open the door. "Pretty flowers for a pretty girl."

I press my nose to the delicate pink buds. Inhale. "You're not supposed to be bringing me gifts—this is your night."

"You are...stunning." He steps into the entryway, pressing me against the door. Pressing a heated kiss on my gasping mouth. "Étourdissant."

"These are beautiful." I exhale. "Thank you."

Usher him inside, turn the lock on the door. Pad barefoot into the room, dragging him along by the hand. The house is dim, save

338

the flickering candles in the center of the dining room table. Twenty-one glowing wishes, dancing in the shadows.

"Let me find a vase and some water for these." I plant another kiss on his cheek. "Take off your shoes and get comfortable."

Better yet, take off your shirt, pants, and anything else you've got on while you're getting undressed. Save us the time later. Ha ha.

His shoes get set by the door as his sharp brown eyes scan the room. Take in our beige sectional and the framed grouping of roommate photographs on the wall above it.

It's a good kind of strange having him in my house; he's huge, much bigger than Donovan, and an imposing figure, broad shoulders, and narrow waist.

I watch him from the corner of my eye as I cut the ends of the flowers, run the stems under water, and place them in a large mason jar.

So pretty.

I join him in the dining room, where he stands staring down at the cake, a beacon in the darkened room.

"Babe, there are no chairs in here."

Babe.

"I know, I know," I fuss. "But I thought it would be romantic to sit on top. You know that scene in the movie *Sixteen Candles*, where Jake Ryan finally gets Samantha in his house? And then they finally…"

Well, actually, they do *nothing*, because the damn movie fades to black before they get to the good part before they start to make out or have hot, passionate, cake sex.

Er…

Or maybe not.

Rhett bends at the waist, giving the underside of the table a cursory onceover before pressing on the surface, both palms splayed on the top. "I think it will hold us."

His slow hands skim my hips when he approaches from behind, trailing up the silky fabric of my skirt. Spanning across my
waist, they haul me up and onto the table as if I were light as a
feather.

He crosses the room in three strides. Removes his socks, tossing them to the carpet. Sits on the edge of the table, pivoting his
legs to the center. Crosses his legs.

Flicks his hair.

The cake blazes before us, candles down to within an inch,
outdated chandelier above us at a dim glow.

"Happy birthday," I whisper. "And congratulations on today.
I'm glad I was there."

Our eyes meet across the table. "Me too. Knowing you were
there was...different."

Tempted by the sweet icing, I dip my finger in the frosting
and lick it clean. "Different? How?"

"Sensing your presence. I've never had someone I care about
come watch me before besides my family."

"Oh, I was watching you all right—all the parts of you." I
wiggle my manicured brows. "Speaking of watching you, your
mom was really bothered by the signs."

"What signs?"

"The ones people bring to cheer you on. I didn't think those
were allowed at wrestling meets."

"I mean, they're allowed, but most people don't bring them.
It's not a sport like football where people are screamin' in the
stands."

"Well your mom wasn't a fan. She was horrified. She kept
asking how girls could proposition a guy like that. It was terrible...I felt so guilty."

"You're nothin' like those girls."

I groan out of frustration, run a hand through my long hair.
Flip it over my bare shoulder. "I felt so guilty about the whole fly-

er thing, I almost told her." Move in closer. "It was on the tip of my tongue."

His eyes get wide, the glint unmistakable. "Is that so?"

"So close."

He leans forward a few inches. "Dodged that bullet then, didn't we? She would have flipped the fuck out."

"Wendy? Uh, yeah. She was glaring daggers at those mat chasers."

Our noses touch. "She's always been overprotective."

"I don't blame her." I will be, too, if I have sons.

"Why?"

I reach down, swipe a finger full of frosting, tongue swirls over it. Sucks. "Because you're *mine*."

We lean into each other, over the blazing cake, lips unyielding. My tongue goes right into his mouth, dragging along his, our moans a delicious chorus.

"You taste so fucking good," he says, sucking the frosting off my bottom lip.

I shiver. "So do you."

The candles, pretty as they are, are hot. Burning brightly beneath us, singeing the bodice of my dress. I pull back, grinning. "You better blow out your candles and make a wish before we burn this place down."

Rhett studies me intently, our eyes meet and hold. "I wish—"

"No!" I chastise. "You don't say it out loud or it won't come true."

"It won't?"

"No." Do guys know nothing? Ugh.

"I wouldn't be so sure about that." His body bends, shoulders hunch so he's within reach. He inhales a deep breath and blows and blows until all twenty-one candles are extinguished, gray smoke rising from the wicks.

We watch as it dissipates into thin air.

"Want some birthday cake?" I whisper.

"Yeah." He grins. "Is it as sweet as your cookies?"

"Sweeter."

"Got a knife?"

"No."

"Forks?"

I shake my head. Mouth the word *no.*

"No forks. No knife." He feigns a search for cutlery. "No plates. How do you suggest we eat this?"

"We'll have to be creative. Are you creative, Rhett?"

He rolls his eyes. "No."

I laugh at his honesty. Laugh at how darn cute he is, finger dipping into the top of his cake one more time. Break off a small chunk and raise it to his lips, feeding it to him.

His mouth opens, takes the offering. Lips close around my fingers. Suck.

Then.

That index finger on his left hand takes its own leisurely jog through the glaze, filching an inch of decorative trim along the top. He drags that sweet finger along my collarbone, gaze so blazing it strips me bare. Fiery.

I hold my breath, waiting.

Moan when his tongue hits my frosting-soiled skin, licking an unhurried line along my clavicle, lapping it up.

He takes another swipe at the cake, dragging his finger between the valley of my breasts. Busies his face between them, licking. Pushes up the undersides of my boobs, sucking the smooth globes above my neckline.

I want to rip my dress off and cover myself with frosting so he spends the rest of the night with his mouth on my skin.

"Take your shirt off," I utter quietly, head still tipped back from his ministrations, and I don't have to ask him twice; his shirt is ripped off within seconds, dragged up that shredded, firm body.

I push the cake plate to one side of the table, out of my way. Scoot forward so I'm in front of him, fingers drifting to the waistband of his jeans, unbuttoning the fly below his belly button.

Give a soft tug.

He's a quick study, and his ass rises so I can tow the denim down over his hips. Skim the pants down his thighs and onto the floor.

"Take your dress off," he utters quietly, the timbre and tone of his voice giving me goose bumps. Rhett watches me with hooded eyes; they're at half-mast, lust-filled. Full of yearning and desire when the cold metal zipper of my dress whirs down its track.

Rhett braces himself up by the arms, watching me, following my movements like a starving man waiting for his next meal. I follow the lines of his body, the way he positions himself on the table, starting at his calves, working my way up his legs as he sits cross-legged on the table top. Over the bulge in his boxers, across his defined, washboard abs. His rock-hard pecs. Those incredible unyielding shoulders.

Flared nostrils. Serious expression.

My mouth waters a little at the sight of him sitting next to a cake, knowing what is inevitably going to be done with it.

I shimmy the black dress up my ribcage; it moves like velvet over my skin, as slowly as I can tease, until the cool air from the dining room hits the naked flesh of my stomach. I shiver when I'm before him in nothing but my sheer panties—a thong, black and barely there.

Crawling across the table toward him, I straddle his lap so we're facing one another, my breasts brushing his chest. We both moan. Rhett's giant bear paw hands grapple for my ass, pulling me in while I tip to the side, whisking two fingers into the cake.

Smear frosting on my boobs and arch my back so he can lick it off. He squeezes my ass as he sucks my nipples clean with his flattened tongue. Tastes my necks. Licks my jaw.

Slowly his mouth moves over my bare flesh, the heat from his breath and the texture of his tongue creating premature waves of pleasure down below. It has my hips rotating in his lap, lining up my slit over his underwear, teeth dragging along my bottom lip from the pleasure.

"What do you like better?" I ask. "Cookies or cake?"

Rhett buries his nose in my cleavage, nuzzling, hands splayed on my back. "I'm always going to choose the cookies."

"What if I try to change your mind?"

"You can *try*."

I climb down off his lap. Dip my finger in the buttery white frosting, run it along his inner thigh. Lean down and lick it, lapping it up, brazen. Spread more on the head of his dick, bending to suck it off. Draw in the tip over and over until he's moaning, large hand brushing my hair out of the way so he can watch.

"Fuck...shit." His eyes are glassed over and distant, teeth raking his bottom lip. "Fuck you're sexy. God, don't stop."

I don't stop, not when his fingers find their way into my hair, tugging.

I gloat in the satisfaction—the power. The ability to drive him wild and make him beg. To bring this huge, powerful boy to his weakest point. Make him vulnerable.

"Laurel." He pants, gasping. "Oh *sshh*it—baby, l-let me...I have to be inside you."

Baby. Inside you.

Whatever you want, I'm tempted to say.

Whether he knows it or not, I'm completely in love with this guy. Head over heels, instalove, enamored—whatever you want to call it. I wipe icing on his abs, lapping it up as I crawl up his gorgeous torso.

Swipe a little on the corner of his mouth, our tongues rolling for a taste of the sweet sugar. He remains in a sitting position when I climb into his lap, align myself, and sink down onto his burgeoning erection.

Groans.

Moans.

Swiveling hips and labored thrusts upward, I'm perilously close to banging my head on the chandelier above the table as I ride him, up and down, head listed back, his nose buried in the crux of my neck.

Those hands hold me tight, grasping my hips, pulling me onto him, deep as he's ever been. Rhett's strangled moans in my hair send my eyes rolling to the back of my head. Intoxicating.

The table groans under our weight, under the thrusting and grinding from our loud, fervent lovemaking and impassioned kisses.

My body is not my own.

My soul?

His.

Rhett's expression is so raw, so real and exquisitely pained as he comes, it almost has me saying the words out loud.

"It was one of those
'since we're both naked anyway'
type of situations…"

Laurel

"We should probably talk about the fact that we didn't use a condom this weekend."

We're in the library on campus, alone in the back corner; I chose it because it's secluded, dimly lit, and private—the perfect spot for me to mention our *slipup*. Although when I say it like that, it sounds so trivial when in fact, it's not.

Rhett's entire demeanor changes, body ramrod straight, pen suspended above his paper, mouth drawn into a firm line.

"Is it somethin' we need to talk about? Are you…"

"Don't freak, I'm on birth control—you know, the pill—but we never talked about it before you, you know…went bareback, and we should have."

"I'm sorry." He plows a hand through his hair, frustrated. Blushing. "I wasn't thinkin'."

"This isn't on just you; it's on both of us. Now that we're talking about it, I wanted to, um…" The blinking cursor on my laptop blinks back at me, winking from the stalled Word document. "I think we can agree that we're exclusive?"

I prattle on, unable to control my mouth or my emotions. "I want you to feel me—and I thought since we're adults, we should have an honest talk about it."

He's staring at me, color still high on his cheeks.

"We're both safe, I assume? I haven't had sex with anyone in months, and he and I were a thing."

Though when I suspected Thad cheated on me, I went and got tested, despite his always wearing a condom. He'd never really trusted anyone not to trap him into a relationship with a pregnancy—not with him getting ready for the NFL Combine his senior year.

Still, I was tested, with clean results.

"I'm not dating anyone else and don't plan to." Rhett doesn't reply, so I prompt him. "Do you?"

He finally responds with a smirk. "The fact that you're even askin' makes me wonder about you sometimes, Laurel," he jokes.

"What do you mean?"

"Take a look around; there's no line at my door."

My brow creases. "Aren't you still getting random text messages?"

"Well, I mean, yeah, but it doesn't mean anything."

"How many?"

"I don't know, a few a day?"

A few *a day*? How did I not know this? My face gets hot at the thought of random, slutty girls messaging him. Girls who would willingly blow him off or let him screw them.

"There's nothing stopping you from responding to them, is there? I have to trust you."

"None of them *actually* want to fuck me, Laurel, and if they do, they're the type of girl that will fuck *any*one."

"How do you know?"

He actually looks impatient. "I just *do*."

"Come on," I push. "They can't all be easy. I bet a few of them are actually respectable, upstanding citizens."

His brown eyes roll toward the ceiling. "I still would have no interest in screwing any of them."

"Would you mind showing me?"

I'm dying of curiosity and it's the first time I've asked to see his phone. Consider it *personal*, but I want to prove a point—he has girls bombarding him with offers of sex, so why bother with me?

I never want to sound jealous, or possessive, but here we are. I am—have been this entire time, if I'm being honest with myself, just not recognizing the signs.

"You can see it."

He hands over his phone, messenger window open.

My keen blue eyes scan the screen.

Face flushes, hot.

Message after message appears on the small display, scrolling past as I move my thumb, each of them an unknown contact.

"I thought you said it was only a few."

There are *hundreds*. My finger swipes and swipes, sending each text flying past, one lewd phrase after the next. Photos. Memes.

He leans over, pointing to the screen by way of explanation. "These go back a few weeks. I only get like ten a day now."

"Just ten a day? *Lovely*," I deadpan.

"You seem upset."

"I'm not upset." I'm something else entirely.

I'm jealous—so jealous I wish I'd never brought up the subject or asked to see the stupid phone.

"Girls are throwing themselves at you."

"So?"

"*So?*"

"That's how *we* met, why do you care?"

"Because." I huff, exasperated. "That's how *we* met."

"I delete most of them." He studies my face. "Laurel, you sound…I don't know, jealous or somethin'."

"That's because I am!"

The poor thing looks so puzzled. So adorably clueless. "Why?"

"Are you being serious right now?"

"Are *you*?"

I flinch. I loathe sounding like one of those insecure, clingy girls I cannot stand to be around. All because he refuses to admit that he likes me. Hasn't told me how he feels. More importantly, he hasn't admitted to himself how *I* feel about *him*.

I crave those three little words, so starved to hear him say them I don't know what's come over me. It goes so much deeper than the lust I feel for him every day or how I long to see him when we're not together. Or how just the sight of his name on my phone or his car parked on the street makes me shiver.

The sound of his voice when he says my name.

The way he looks when he's excited or confused.

I'm falling in love with him.

And that has been our issue all along, hasn't it?

The realization dawns on me: I know how I feel, but does he? Rhett has convinced himself a girl like me—whatever that means—couldn't sincerely like him, let alone fall *deep*.

My hearts sinks.

"Rhett?" I hand his cell phone back.

"Hmm?"

"I…" I hesitate. Do I tell him? I shouldn't say it now—this isn't the right time or the right place—but I've always been a bit too impulsive for my own sake.

I want to call Lana for advice; she'd talk me down off the ledge. I do *not* know how to navigate a guy like Rhett, one who has his shit together. Who doesn't chase girls because he doesn't have the confidence.

Who knows what he wants but not how to take it.

I draw a deep breath into my lungs.

"I think I care because I'm…I think I might be, you know." My face is on fire, burning to the roots of my hair, praying he takes the hint. "I might be."

"You might be *what*?"

I can't gauge his reply, whether he's anxious or irritated or—

"You can tell me, Laurel. Whatever it is."

Rhett

" **J**ust spit it out—it's like ripping off a Band-Aid." Jesus, whatever it is, I wish she'd say it. Put me out of my damn misery.

She looks nervous. *Guilty.*

What the hell could be so hard to say? Is she seeing someone else? Is she dumping me? Fuck—that would kill me.

"Laurel?" I can barely get her name past my lips, the stretch of her silence making me want to fucking vomit.

When she opens her mouth, releasing a sigh, ten words I never expected her to say come pouring out: "I think I might be falling in love with you."

I blink.

Flushed, down to my boxers. Swallow down the lump that's formed in my throat. Repeat those ten words over and over in my mind until they're playing on a loop.

Did she seriously just say she's falling in love with me?

There's no fucking way.

"Just a little." She fidgets in her seat. "Aren't you going to say something?" Her eyes are bright, like the sky before it rains. Her voice? Timid and cracking and unusually small. A whisper. "Please say something."

I have no idea what to fucking say.

She *loves* me? This girl—this smoking hot, gorgeous, sexy, intelligent girl loves *me*?

It refuses to compute in my brain. Won't.

Can't.

"Oh my God." A sob escapes her. "You don't feel the same way." Her wide eyes take on a horrified gleam. Downcast.

No girl has ever told me they loved me before, if you don't include my mother.

I sit in stunned silence, processing, basically freaking the fuck out.

"That's not it," I finally croak out, my own words raspy. "I just don't know what to say."

"You don't have to say anything. I get it. I didn't tell you so you'd say it back. I just had to get it out, so you knew I was serious about you. So you'd know." She stands, almost knocking over the chair. "I should go."

"Jesus, Laurel, please—"

Her palm goes up to stop me, nose turning red. She's about to cry. "Please, just let me leave, okay? I want to go. I'll be fine."

But she won't be fine, and neither will I.

Not by a long shot.

I let her leave, actually sit and watch her pack up her things, fighting back tears as she shoves shit into her backpack, the whole time wishing my brain would work.

Fucking tell me the right thing to say for once.

23

#DOUCHEBAG

"Absence makes the
cock grow harder."

Rhett

"M om."

"Hey honey!"

"Hey." My unenthusiastic greeting has her proceeding with caution. Maybe she even assumes the worst—that someone on the team has pulled another stupid stunt.

"Everything okay? You never call."

"Everything is fine." After a few seconds, I clear my throat. "I need some advice."

"Is this about Laurel?"

I shift in my desk chair, turning to face the window. "Yeah."

"Did something happen?"

"No. Yes." I run a hand through my shaggy hair. Why haven't I fucking gotten it cut yet? "I don't know."

"All right," she says slowly, cautiously. "You know you can talk to me about anything."

"It's really not a big deal."

"Okay." She waits me out, patient. "Is it related to..." Her voice drops to a whisper. "S-E-X?"

"What? No!"

"Did you break up with her?"

"Huh?" Why would she phrase it like that: did *I* break up with *her*? "No, nothing like that."

"Because that young lady is sweet on you Rhett—those blue eyes sparkle when they look at you."

"They do?"

"Yes. Even your dad noticed."

"*Dad*?"

"Yes, your dad." Mom laughs. "We were young once too, you know. We remember what it's like to be jeune et amoureuse."

Young and in love.

"Is that it?" Her voice is quiet. "Does that have something to do with it? She's a sweetheart."

I don't know if *that*'s the word I'd use to classify Laurel, but I keep my mouth shut.

"And she likes you."

Loves me, actually.

Loves.

I roll the word around in my head, the concept foreign.

"Is that the problem? You don't think she likes you?"

My silence speaks for itself.

"Why do you think you're not worthy of her liking you?"

Leave it to Mom get to the root of the problem without even trying. The phone line is silent as I mentally catalogue the reasons why I'm not worthy of her liking me:

I'm not handsome.

I'm not outgoing.

I'm awkward with an embarrassing amount of inexperience.

My teammates treat me like shit though I'm now the team's winningest athlete.

Laurel is everything I'm not—beautiful, boisterous, and popular.

"Honey, are you still there?"

"Yeah."

"I want you to listen to me Rhett Clayton Rabideaux." Her tone is firm, her words encouraging. "You're smart, you're clever, and you're hardworkin'—not many young men your age can say that."

I roll my eyes.

"Handsome—"

I scoff, interrupting her monologue.

"Be quiet and listen to your mother," she snaps over the line.

I clamp my jaw shut.

"I've never seen anyone so young work hard as you do. It's all you've done since you were little. You'd set a goal and work toward it—we could never tell you no. I worry that I should have given you more limits, but you never wanted to settle."

She's quiet, considering her next words. "Practice, practice, practice. Helped take care of Nanan when she was alive. Worked every single summer, savin' every last dime to buy that Jeep."

She pauses again.

"I know you think Dad and I are upset you transferred, and that's probably my fault, but you couldn't be more wrong. Daddy and I are *selfish*. We didn't want you to transfer because we wanted to keep you close to home—it had nothin' to do with Iowa as a school. We're so proud of you, Rhett.

"You've always been a role model to your brothers, stayin' out of trouble, away from the alcohol and drugs. Don't you think it's time to let yourself have some fun? Get caught up in the love of an intelligent, pretty girl?"

Silence.

"Rhett honey, anyone with eyes can see that she loves you, even if she doesn't know it yet herself."

I give my head a shake she can't see. "She does know. She told me."

Mom's breath hitches. "When?"

"Today."

"Is that why you're callin'?"

"Yeah. She told me and I..."

Mom's voice lowers gently. "What did you say?"

"Nothing." Pause. "Is that bad?"

Mom's short intake of breath is *not* the reaction I was hoping for.

Shit.

"Oh sweetie. What did she do?"

"She got a little upset, got up and left me sittin' in the library."

"How do you feel about Laurel?"

"I like her."

"Is that all?"

Is it? "No."

"Do you love her?"

"Maybe." *Probably.*

"But you're not ready to say the words?"

I'm ready; I'm just fucking scared. "I don't know, Mom. I've never said it to anyone but you."

"I'm sorry honey, I wish it was easy. Wish I could give you an answer and tell you what to do, but I can't. This one you're going to have to figure out on your own—it's your heart." She pauses. "And Rhett honey?"

"Hmm?"

"Don't make her wait too long—don't make her wonder. She's probably already upset and embarrassed enough as it is. Go talk to her and tell her how you feel."

"Kay."

But I'm not sure if I will.

Because I'm not sure if I can.

24
#DOUCHEBAG

"If you're not my hair stylist,
or having sex with me,
don't touch my freaking hair."

Rhett

"**L**aurel, I've been givin' this a lot of thought, and last night when I talked to my mom, she told me I shouldn't make you wait for me to tell you how I feel."

Wait, *shit*. I can't tell Laurel I talked to my mom about her—I'll sound like a fucking idiot, a goddamn momma's boy.

I start my speech over, speaking into thin air—into Laurel's empty yard, where no one is around, leaving me no one to converse with but the squirrel eyeballing me skeptically from a big oak tree.

I give him the stink eye right back. "Stop judgin' me you little asshole, this is hard enough as it is. I'm tryin' to…I'm tryin'…"

Jesus, what the hell am I trying to do? I sound bat-shit crazy. *Look* crazier, pacing Laurel's yard, back and forth in front of her damn door, a light drizzle taking its cue from the dark clouds above, adding to my dark mood.

"Shit. What am I doing?"

A raindrop falls from the sky. Then another, until the sky opens up and I'm literally standing in the mothereffing rain.

Suddenly she appears in the driveway, barefoot, in a t-shirt and tight black leggings, running to her car on her tiptoes. Yanks the door open, ass sticking out of the cab when she leans in, swiping an unseen object from the center console. Slams the door and turns back toward the house.

She doesn't see me standing here.

"Laurel," I call her name in the rain, loud enough that she spins on the grass, brows raised, surprised to see me in her yard.

Shocked, actually.

"Rhett?" She steps toward me, clutching her phone charger. "Rhett, what are you doing here?"

She squints her blue eyes up at the sky as beads of water blanket her hair. Her skin is already dewy.

"I came to see you."

"Okay." She smiles, giving a hasty glance up at the sky. "Do you want to come inside?"

"No." My head shakes, adamant, the brim of my ball cap keeping only my face dry. "No, I need to say what I came to say."

Laurel nods slowly, hair now completely saturated, falling in limp sheets to her shoulders. She tightly winds her phone cord and tucks it into the back pocket of her jeans. "All right."

I take one step forward, then another, until I'm crossing the lawn. Until I'm not two feet in front of her. "I was goin' to come over with a sign—you know the green flyers they hung on campus? The Get Rett Laid ones? I was gonna make a new one, for *you*."

God I sound dumb.

"Oh yeah?" She closes the gap between us, blue eyes practically dancing they're so alive. "What would the poster have said?"

I brush the water off her forehead, eyebrows. "I had one all made up. It said"—I clear my throat, nervously gathering up my courage—"Rhett Gets Love." Pause. "Jesus Christ, did that sound as fuckin' dumb out loud as it sounded in my head?"

She laughs, tipping her head back, black mascara beginning to run a little. I swipe at the mess with my thumb, taking her face in my huge hands. Lean in close when Laurel cuffs my wrists with her hands, holding on to me tight.

"That doesn't sound dumb at all. It sounds romantic."

"Yeah?"

"Yes." Rain-drenched hair sticks to her lips. "Are you going to kiss me?" she asks.

"Not yet." Our foreheads touch. "I have somethin' to say first."

Patiently, she waits me out in the rain, breathing heavy, shirt soaked, nipples straining against the fabric. Bare feet in the water-drenched lawn.

"I'm sorry I let you walk out of the library. I was scared."

"I know," comes her murmur. "So was I."

"I don't want to fuck this up."

"You won't." Her lips steal a quick kiss to the tip of my nose. "I promise."

Then here goes nothing. "Je suis en train de tomber amoureux de toi." *I'm falling in love with you.* "Je t'aime, Laurel."

She tries pulling back so she can see my face. "What did you just say?"

"I said—"

"I know what je t'aime is, baby. I just can't believe you said it." Her hand brushes down the side of my jawline, sweeping at the rain. "Say it again—in English."

"I love you."

Her cheeks are flushed—whether it's from the cold or my declaration, I do not know. "You *love* me." She says it breathlessly. Giddy.

"I do." I cup her face, mouth hovering over her damp lips. "I fucking do."

"*Now* are you going to kiss me?"

"I thought you wanted to go inside?" I can't resist teasing her. "Get out of the rain?"

"No, I can't stand it anymore. I want your lips on me *now*."

"Then yeah, *now* I'm going to kiss you."

As if in time to the perfect beat, our mouths meet, breath and rain and tongues all in one effortlessly choreographed motion. Heads tilted, I lick the water off her lips, suck it off her tongue.

"You feel so warm. So good." Laurel's hands leave my wrists, straying down my ribcage. She presses her breasts against my chest. "Let's go inside. Get out of the cold."

My mouth drifts from her lips to her neck. "Want to get naked?" *Holy shit*, did those words just come out of my mouth?

Laurel moans against the column of my neck. "I like it when you're assertive. It gets me hot when you tell me what you want."

I back away, taking her hand, marching her to the entrance. "Let's get out of these wet clothes."

"I am definitely *so* wet." She giggles beside me, stumbling on the ground. I halt in my steps. When I sweep her up in one motion, she gasps. Wraps her arms around my neck and plants her lips on my mouth. "You are so sexy."

I manage to get her through the door without killing us both on the rickety wooden steps, kicking off my shoes in the kitchen and the door closed behind me.

Her roommate—Donovan, I think she said his name was—is sitting at the counter when we bust in while sucking face, his mouth slack-jawed at the sight of us, soaking and dripping from the rain.

"Um, hiii?"

"Donovan," Laurel says breathlessly, still flushed. "This is Rhett. Rhett, my roommate Donovan."

"Hey man." I give him a nod. "We're just going to..." My head jerks toward the hallway.

"I wouldn't *dream* of stopping you."

That's good, because I'm already halfway down the hall, walking down it sideways so I don't bang Laurel into the wall, still carrying this sexy, waterlogged wisp of a girl until I find the bathroom. She feels so fucking good in my arms I could carry her around all damn day and not get tired of it.

Setting her down, I bend to start the warm water in the shower.

Wordlessly, we start stripping once the door is closed, tearing off our clothes in tandem. I peel off my sweatshirt. T-shirt. Track pants and briefs, kicking them into a sodden pile.

Laurel stands in just a lace bra and black leggings, and though she hardly needs my help getting naked, I get down on my knees, pulling down the waistband of her pants, kissing her abs in the process. Kissing the tender flesh above her panty line.

Pull the black fabric down her hips. Thighs. She steps out of them, one foot at a time until they're lying in a heap on top of mine.

My mouth settles on the mound beneath her panties; they're damp too, but I'm determined to make them *wet*. Her hands grip the counter, bracing herself when I hike her leg over my shoulder. Bury my face between her thighs and suck through her underwear.

Her head tips back, moan throaty when I pull those down too. Tongue sinks into her pussy when her legs spread wider.

The sounds she makes are unintelligible. Indelicate. Desperate and quiet.

So fucking hot.

And she's all mine.

When she comes, I lift her effortlessly, setting her in the shower. Step in behind her, under the spray, unclasping her bra and tossing it onto the tile bathroom floor.

I take a pink bar of soap, lathering up my hands, palms gliding up her naked, damp flesh. Run them over her front, cupping her heavy breasts.

God, I've always wanted to do that.

And now I am.

My hands are on her tits and my hard dick is wedged between her ass cheeks where it's nice and tight and warm. It's like fucking heaven and I don't want to leave.

Laurel moans again, arm reaching around to grab me when my mouth hits the column of her neck and sucks her shoulder, my hips beginning a slow thrust against her crack.

We groan.

She turns.

Goes down on her knees, water sluicing off her back and my chest as she takes my cock in her mouth, head bobbing.

I brace my hands on the shower wall for support. Legs weak. Mind blank.

There's nothing I can do right now. Nothing.

I'm a useless bag of shit when my dick is in her mouth.

Fucking useless.

Quick, what's two plus one?

What the hell is a half nelson?

All I can think about is come and coming and the fact that I'm getting head in the shower.

I don't know if I'm being loud and I don't care.

It's not in me to give a fuck about anything but her mouth right now.

I'm so in love with her.

Shit, are my legs buckling?

"Oh f-fuck, baby, oh…f-fuckkk…"

Je l'aime. *God I love her.*

"I accepted my type is
not traditionally good-looking
when my friend asked me,
'Him? Are you sure?'
six times in front of him
at the bar last night."

Laurel

"**W**hy haven't we gone on a date sooner? This is fun."

Know what else is fun? Watching Rhett's amazing ass stick out when he palms the bowling ball before rolling it down the center lane, those white pins at the end falling like dominos.

Sleeves rolled to his elbows, I give his firm forearm a squeeze when he passes by, plopping down on the bench while I take my turn. God I love his arms.

I want to climb on top of him and make out with his face.

I love that face.

That flawed, scarred face.

I retrace my steps, planting a kiss on the bridge of his nose before returning to the hardwood bowling floor.

"We should have invited my roommates to come along. I don't think Donovan has ever been bowling, that diva."

"Donovan doesn't strike me as the athletic type."

Balancing the bowling ball, I squint over the top of it. "You're right, he's not. Plus, I don't think he'd purposely stick his fingers into *these* holes." I laugh at my own joke, giving my hips a little shimmy and shake to see if Rhett notices.

He does.

My arm pulls back, swings forward, ball sliding off my hand and onto the glossy wooden lane. Rolls *slightly* off-center, narrowly missing the gutter then slowly gliding past the right side of the pins.

Two fall.

"Darn it!"

"Want some help babe?"

I smile. "Sure."

I wait patiently for the ball, tapping impatiently on the return machine that automatically brings the balls back to the player. Rhett scoops it up for me when it swooshes out the contraption. Folds his arms around me from behind while I grip the pink ball. Kisses my neck. Places those mammoth paws on my hips, prompting me to bend my knees.

"Eye on the center pin the entire time," he croons in my ear. "And follow that swing all the way through after you let go of the ball."

I close my eyes, nodding, his southern voice doing that thing it does to my erogenous zones. "Mmm'kay."

He gently pats my ass before returning to his seat. "You got this."

Except now all I can think about is how soon we can get out of here and get naked.

Pull back my arm. Release the ball. Follow through on my swing, just like Rhett told me to. It flies higher than I intend it to, landing with a loud thump, rolling toward the middle pin. I tip left…then tip right, leg in the air, as if my movements will somehow, with some gravitational pull, control the movements of the ball.

I do not knock down the rest of the pins.

"Six isn't bad!" Rhett high-fives me when he rises. "You're gettin' better."

Gettin' better. Does his drawl ever get old?

"Thanks baby."

I stand, blue eyes scanning the bowling alley; it's a full house, the busiest I've ever seen in the few times I've come here with friends. I know it's a popular hangout since it's close to campus, and they often let campus organizations host their fundraisers here.

My smile falters when my gaze settles on a group that looks familiar: members of the football team, assembled near lanes one and two.

Giants among regular men.

Man-children, really, as immature as I've seen them behave.

I know it's the football team because I recognize Timothy Wilson, the linebacker and my ex-boyfriend's best friend—my ex-boyfriend, Thad, who raises his blond head in my direction the exact moment I notice him among the small crowd.

I mean, who wouldn't? The guy is *huge*, and he's wearing a pink shirt.

His tan face breaks into a toothy grin when he notices me accidentally noticing him, a grin I once considered charming and handsome that I now know was all for show.

Thad Davis is no gentleman.

He tussles his sandy blond hair with his fingers, dipping his head to speak to Wilson, eyes locked on mine. Hand goes out to part the crowd, beginning his slow saunter in my direction.

Ugh.

He's so obviously posturing with male bravado, I'd roll my eyes if I thought he was worth the time it would take.

Rhett palms his ball, throwing it as my eyes narrow, stalking the movements of my incredibly ridiculous ex-boyfriend.

I hear the telltale sound of a strike.

Turn to throw my arms around his neck, blocking out the looming figure that's hell bent on invading my first official date with my new boyfriend.

Maybe if I ignore him, he'll just go away.

"Hey Red," comes his voice. "Long time no see."

I stiffen at the sound of Thad's nickname for me, loosening my arms from Rhett's with a groan. Blush, aggravated. Turn to greet him.

"Thad...*hey*."

My eyes roam his chest, scanning the words screen-printed on the pocket of his gaudy pink shirt: *I'm not a gynecologist but I can take a look.*

Classy guy, my ex-boyfriend. Not a pig whatsoever.

He reaches me in a few more strides, arms enveloping my shoulders, pulling me in for a squeeze and spinning me around. Sniffs the top of my hair like he used to do in the brief time we were dating before setting me down.

"Mmm, mmm, mmm. Damn Laurel, you smell as good as I remember."

Over Thad's shoulder, I watch as Rhett takes a slow drag of his water bottle, eyes scanning and never leaving Thad's hands on my body. On the small of my back.

I cringe.

Give Thad a nudge out of my personal space, backing up three paces, putting distance between us. Slide my arm around Rhett's waist when he sets down his water bottle.

The guys take measure, sizing each other up.

"Hey man." Thad's chin tilts toward Rhett. "Do I know you?"

Rhett gives his head a curt shake. "Nope, don't think we've been introduced."

"No, I do know you." Thad studies him closer until it's uncomfortable, snaps his fingers when he places Rhett in his gray matter. "Rabideaux." He butchers the pronunciation: Rab-i-doo. "Didn't they just plaster your face on the side of the stadium? For wrestling or some shit."

Rhett nods. "Guess so. Marketing must be getting ready for the championships."

"What?" I turn to him, excited. "You're on a billboard? Rhett, that's amazing!" I kiss his lips, unable to stop myself. "Imagine that, *my* baby's face is on the side of the stadium?!"

Am I squealing? Bouncing up and down on the balls of my feet like a toddler on a sugar rush? I make a mental note to celebrate the special occasion with whipped cream and sprinkles on all his most delicious parts.

Thad's face contorts, affronted. "You never called *me* baby."

I can't stop the bubble of laughter welling up inside me. Is this guy for real?

"Anyway." He heaves a sigh, turning his attention back to me. Wiggles his brows suggestively, the big dope. "I came over to say hi, see what you've been up to. How long as it been?"

"I honestly have no idea."

"Well I must say, you look...*great*." He says it in a way that old, sleazy guys say it. It makes my skin crawl, and I sidle closer into the safety of Rhett's warm side.

"Um, thanks." My cheeks get as red as my hair, embarrassed that he's kind of a douchebag and I wasted my time dating him. I cough. Rest my hand on Rhett's forearm. "By the way Thad, this is my boyfriend Rhett."

"Her boyfriend. *Really*." Thad looks smug. "Thad Davis, her *ex*."

"Ah, okay, this makes sense now." Rhett, nonplussed, grins when my fingers tuck into one of his belt loops.

"Boyfriend huh?" My ex crosses his thick arms, hawk-like quarterback gaze studying my boyfriend. "So there's no chance of you and me, you know..." His eyebrows do that weird, inappropriate wriggling thing again.

Rhett replies before I can get any infuriated words out. "Dude, what the fuck?"

Thad's hands go up. "What? I'm just checking. Some couples are into that."

"Well we're not." I put on my lying face. "It was really good seeing you again, but we're heading out. Say hey to Wilson for me, would ya?"

"Why don't you come over and say hi for yourself?"

"Another time maybe."

"All right." He's so oblivious. "You should stop by the row sometime, stop in at the house."

Um, yeah...*no*. I'm not an underclassman anymore; his popularity doesn't lure me like it used to—like it does so many clueless girls, chasing the name and not the heart.

I snuggle into Rhett's side, content. "Good luck with your season."

"Yeah." Green eyes drift to the guy at my side. "Yours too, Rabideaux. It was good meeting you. Take good care of my girl here."

There's a long, tension-charged pause. Then,

"She's not *your* girl." Rhett's voice is low. Steely. "She's mine."

Whoa.

Whoa.

Whoa.

My mouth gapes, tuning them out, because *what the hell was that?*

She's mine.

And the way he says it? With conviction, in his sexy southern accent? The insides of my panties are melting. Rhett, drawing boundaries, letting my ex-boyfriend know he crossed a line? Yes *please.*

I tighten my hold around his waist when Thad finally saunters off, pressing myself and my breasts against him, "That. Was. *The* sexiest thing. Ever."

He rolls his gorgeous brown eyes. "What the hell were you doin' datin' that dickhole? I can't fuckin' believe you—"

I cut him off with a kiss. "Please don't remind me. It's not my finest moment."

"I know, but damn Laurel, what a fuckin'—"

"Honey, please. Stop. I know he's a dick. I get it." I brush at an imaginary piece of hair on his forehead. "Not all guys are as amazing as you, okay? You're a unicorn boyfriend."

This piques his interest. "What the hell is a unicorn boy-friend?"

"Rare and hard to find in the wild. And you're mine," I croon in his ear. "What should we do now that our date is over, Rhett?"

In the middle of the bowling alley, for everyone to see, my tongue traces his ear lobe. "Tell me, *baby.*"

"God that fucking word is my kryptonite," he mumbles. "I want...to..."

"What?"

"I want to take you home and..." He stalls, unable to get the words out; I know he's not accustomed to vocalizing what he wants—not just yet, but he's been trying.

He's getting there.

I'm patient, waiting him out.

"Je veux te baiser." He nuzzles my neck, mouth on my pulse. "I want to fuck you."

Holy shit, he did not just say that.

I have the biggest lady boner right now and do my best to nod my agreement without my legs giving out on me. "Yes."

"Really?" He pulls back to study my face. "Just like that, we get to leave and have *sex* because I asked for it?"

"Yes," I repeat, hands clasping around the back of his neck.

"Huh, how fucking cool is that?" he muses. "It's really that easy?"

My laugh is light, arms still around his neck. "I'm your girl-friend now—of course I want you to take me home and...you know..." I hope my voice sounds sultry and that it hits his cerebel-lum in just the right spot. "Fuck me."

"Jesus, now I'm hard."

"I know," I purr. "I can feel it."

"What if I can't wait 'til we get home?"

"You mean, like—do it in the Jeep?"

"Yeah."

"All right."

He grabs my hand, pulling. "Let's get the fuck out of here."

26

#DOUCHEBAG

"We ended up labeling
our relationship;
he is now officially my
designated butt-toucher."

Laurel

The last time I was in this bedroom, Rhett was leaving for a wrestling meet. Kissing my shoulder and telling me good-bye after a morning quickie.

The comforter is undone, a small pile of clothes at the foot of the bed. He kicks them to the closet so they're out of the way, slides his jacket off and hangs it on his desk chair. Pulls off his hat and runs a figure through his trimmed-up hair. Stands in his navy shirt, a blue button-down with a collar.

"I love that you dressed up for me tonight." I float across the room, immediately toying with the top button. Pluck it open. Then another, and another. "You look so handsome."

Three buttons.

Four more and my hands are skimming across his warm, bare skin, parting the shirt and slipping it down his biceps. Rhett's chocolate-colored eyes are a storm of desire, nostrils flaring. Lips parted, a small puff of pent-up air escapes when my palms breeze over his pecs. His beautiful, firm pecs.

I glide my fingers along his collarbone, rising to kiss his bare skin, sliding my hands around his neck. Our lips fuse in a perfect combination of desperation and calm, Rhett's hands tugging my shirt up my stomach, lifting. Dragging it up my torso until I'm raising my arms so he can lift it over my head. I shake my hair when he tosses it to his desk, shimmy out of my pants.

Fumble with the buckle on his jeans, unzip them and shove them down his hips. By the time he steps out of them and kicks them aside, I'm already on the bed, working the clasp of my bra.

He climbs up next to me, naked, palms drifting along my smooth legs. Tip of his nose caressing the inside of my thigh. Mouth kissing the apex of my legs. Sucking. Licking my belly button, ribcage, nipples.

I lie there, letting his mouth explore my body, watching as he goes, eyes drifting closed, each sensation greater than the last.

I stroke his hair while he suckles, hovering above me, braced by his bulging arms. Big, strong, and gentle, he murmurs to me when he threads his fingers through my red hair, mouth at my temple. My body stiffens at his words.

"Je t'aime."

We both gasp.

Gasp again when he moves his hips.

I cling to him as he begins a gentle thrust, rocking back and forth, braced on his elbows. Whispering into my ear. Rotating his hips, pelvis pressed into mine, deep as he can go.

In silence we make love, mattress and bed groaning under our weight in the sexiest possible way.

"I love you so much." I kiss his neck, the throbbing inside me swelling. "*Oh, Rhett.*"

He buries his face in my neck, short puffs of air as he pumps his hips into me. Slowly. Up and down. Lazy circles. Lips on the skin under my ear, latching on. Kissing me there. My shoulder. My jaw and the corner of my lips.

Sucking on my bottom lip, moaning into my mouth.

Up and down, up and down.

Lazy circles.

My head tips back when he goes deeper still, hands burying under my ass, lifting. Lips sucking. Tongues rolling. Twirling.

Tingles.

A spark.

Quivers.

My thighs begin to shake, head tipped back when he breathes my name. The tip of his dick finds my g-spot, penetrating in just the right—

"Uhhhhhhh, that feels g-goo-d," I moan, lips parted. Sweat dampens my brow as I gasp again. "G-God I love you."

"Je t'aime aussi," comes his guttural reply. "Je t'aime bébé."

His words are too much; I can't say anything else, it just all feels…way *t-too damn g-good.*

I-Indescribable.

Oh God, oh G-God…

His hips drive into me once. Twice. Jerk, glutes stiffening, pumping and pulsating into me. When I feel his warm come, my own orgasm hits home, long and hard and intense.

My toes curl.

Mouth opens.

Throat moans.

Hands pull at his ass, gripping it, pulling him in.

Rhett's still shaking, pelvis spasming every few seconds, our breathing labored.

We lie like this for I don't know how long, wrapped in each other's arms, my head against his chest, listening to the rhythm of his racing heart.

His beautiful heart belongs to me.

And mine belongs to him.

Rhett
Six months later

"**B**abe." Laurel's head sticks out of the kitchen, where she's been unpacking cooking utensils into the drawer next to the stove. "Gunderson and Oz are here with the couch—can you get the door?"

"On it."

Down in the yard, Oz Osborne and Rex Gunderson are in the process of backing into the yard with Oz's big black pickup truck, an oversized blue couch strapped down in the back.

My hands flag them in, directing them straight. To the left. Straight.

"Stop."

We make short order of jamming that fucker through the front door, settling it in the exact spot against the wall where Laurel told me she wants it. *"Let's not put it in front of the window,"* she reasoned. *"What if we have sex on it? I don't want anyone to see me riding you—we don't have curtains yet..."*

Fair enough.

"Babe." Her voice interrupts my musings, walking into the living room, flaming red hair parted into two French braids. She's holding a toaster box. "Where should we put this toaster your mom sent us? Now we have two."

"Give it to me," Gunderson responds, holding his arms out. "Me want."

"Get your own damn toaster." I smack his hand down. "We're not fucking givin' you ours."

Laurel laughs at our bickering. "Maybe I can take it back and exchange it?"

"Yeah, let's do that. I think I could use some stuff for the bedroom."

Bedroom.

I flush at the word and all the things we're going to do in there, night after night. Alone.

She grins. "Whatever you want, baby."

"Baby?" Oz snorts. "Jesus, even Jameson doesn't call me that."

Gunderson rolls his eyes. "That's because she calls you babe and sweetie. *Gag.*"

Oz shoves him so he falls backward onto the couch. "Shut up fuckwit, I love being called sweetie. It's my favorite."

Laurel interrupts their arguing. "Hey guys, I hate to intrude on your love fest, but is the couch the last of our stuff?"

"Yup, this is it," I say. "We don't have much."

"Maybe not." She sidles up to me, sliding an arm around my waist and hugging me. "But it's ours."

"Can I vomit now?" Gunderson snorts. "I can't fucking believe you're living together."

"Hey," Oz says. "Don't knock it 'til you've tried it. In case you fucking forgot, New Guy here gets to have sex twenty-four hours a day while you're at home waiting for your one-nighter-a-week to try to score."

"Is the bed already set up? I could use a nap," Gunderson huffs.

It is, and has already been broken in—twice. "You're not takin' a nap in our house. Get the fuck out."

He rises, smacking Oz on the way to the door. "Is this the thanks I get for moving you into your new place?"

"You moved one couch, and didn't even help load it."

"Fine, but I get some credit for moral support."

Oz nudges him in the stomach. "No you don't." Gives him a shove onto the porch. "Let's go, I have to pick Jameson up. We're going to dinner and I need a shower so I can trim my balls."

"Dude, that's way too much information."

"How? I'm telling you, it makes my dick look bigger when I trim my ball fro."

"Sorry about that." I shut the door behind them. Lean against it. "I don't know what Gunderson is going to do when Osborne and Daniels graduate at semester."

My girlfriend's russet eyebrow quirks. "I can tell you what he's going to do: he's going to follow you around like a puppy dog instead until you're the one graduating."

Two semesters that once seemed like they were taking an eternity to get here are now flying by too fast.

"God I hope not."

I flop down on the couch, exhausted, legs spread, hands on my thighs.

My dad might not have been thrilled when I announced I was moving in with my girlfriend after only dating her for six months, but my mother was—sent us a few hundred bucks cash so we could swing a new mattress and couch.

Laurel eyes me on that couch, tilting her head as she studies me, a blush creeping up her neck. Her cheeks get red.

"What?" I blurt out.

"I like looking at you in our living room. It's sexy to say that." She pauses. "We can do whatever we want, when we want."

My dick twitches when she lifts the hem of her sweatshirt and pulls it off.

She's not wearing a bra. "When do you have practice?"

I'm already working the button of my jeans. "Five o'clock."

It's three thirty.

Laurel's panties come off, a pink puddle on the hardwood floor, at the same time I shove my pants down. Kick them off and yank off my shirt just as she climbs on top, straddling me with her tits in my face.

Right where I fucking love them.

I suck in when she eases herself onto me, her head already tipped back, gripping the back of the couch as she lifts herself up and down on my shaft.

I slap her ass, palming it. Squeezing.

Slap it again to prompt her into action, get her to move faster.

"Like that?" She licks my ear. "You like that, baby?"

"Yes I fucking like that," I growl. Wrap my arms around her waist, pulling her down, impaling her.

"God I fuckin' love you." I'm pushing and pulling her along my cock now, wanting to draw the whole thing out but also wanting to dump my load inside her.

"I think I'm going to love having couch sex." She pants, eyes rolling to the back of her head. "Do you think we need more pretty pillows?"

"Fuck pillows." My core muscles work overtime, glutes clenching to thrust up. One more thrust and I rise, still inside her. Set her in the center of the sofa, drag her ass to the edge of the cushion. Hook my arms under her calves, hauling her up. Pound into her.

But.

Jesus, I can't stand not having my tongue in her mouth.

Pull her to the floor, leaning in, latching my lips on hers, kisses sloppy. Hump the shit out of her right there on the rug, just like I think about doing every second of every goddamn day.

"Oh God, I love you," she whines. "Yes, just like that, just like that, don't stop," she chants. Chants like she always does, every time we fuck. Have sex.

Make love.

"Shit baby, you're so beautiful," I croon, the telltale tightening of my balls sending a shockwave up my spine.

"I love you." She never gets tired of saying it, and I never get tired of hearing it. Her fantastic boobs bounce as I thrust into her hard, and I can't believe this is my new reality.

This pretty, intelligent woman loves me.

Wants to live with me.

Is *my* fucking girlfriend.

I'm going to pinch myself every day thanking my maker for those stupid fucking posters in the quad, because if not for that sign and those douchebags, I wouldn't be screwing Laurel on the floor of our shitty off-campus rental.

Our bodies.

Our breathing.

Notre maison. *Our house.*

I don't know what will happen after we both graduate next spring, if I'll move back to Louisiana or…someplace else, but we both know we want to be together.

And knowing that is enough.

The End

Coming Soon

JOCK ROW

Scarlett is always the sensible one: Always the sober driver. The planner. The one keeping her friends out of trouble.

Week-after-week, she hits Jock Row—the off-campus housing block for student athletes, and the universities hottest party scene—with her friends. *Week-after-week*, it's Scarlett's job to get her friends home safe, and guys out of their pants.

The job isn't easy, and gets her noticed for all the wrong reasons; gets her thrown out and banned from The Row.

No guy wants a girl around who keeps their jock friends from getting laid.

Sterling "Rowdy" Wade is the star short-stop for the university's baseball team—and the unlucky bastard who drew the short straw: keep Miss Goody Two Shoes out of the Baseball House. But week-after-week Scarlett returns, determined to get inside...

Releasing early 2018

Exclusive, unedited excerpt.

Scarlett

A tap hits my shoulder and I turn.

Turn to face one of the hottest guys I've ever seen in person, in my life; tall, tan, and ridiculously good-looking.

His full pouty lips—better suited for a male model—are moving, his words competing with the loud music and laughter.

"I'm sorry, what did you say?" I shout over the music.

He leans down, broad shoulders dipping and brushing mine as his exquisite mouth speaks slowly near my ear. "I said, sorry little cock-blocker, I'm going to have to ask you to leave."

His deep baritone sends a shiver down my spine and,

Wait. What? *"What* did you just call me?"

"I called you cock. Blocker." Without warning, he plucks the red plastic cup from my hand and tosses it to the floor, large hand wrapping to cuff my bicep, fingers wedged beneath my armpit.

I look down at his hand, shocked.

I look up, outraged. "Hey! What the hell is wrong with you? Why would you do that?"

"You're going to have to leave. I'm kicking your ass out."

Kicking me out? Is he serious?

I laugh, head tipped back. "Very funny asshole. Now let go of my arm, people are starting to stare."

"Sorry ma'am, but you've disturbing the peace. I've been sent to escort you from the premises."

Is this guy for real? My head tips back into a laugh. A nervous, giddy laugh usually reserved for moments when I don't know how to react. Like when I'm called on in a crowded lecture hall.

Like at funerals.

Moments like *this* one.

"What are you, an undercover cop?"

His mouth curves into a wry smile. "No—I drew the short straw."

The short straw? What the heck does that mean?

I hear him sigh. "It means I'm the unlucky bastard who has the privilege of kicking you out."

Holy shit. He's serious.

My eyes go down to his hand, still shackling my arm. I pull. "Let go of me you brute."

I'm strong, but he's stronger. "Sorry. The deal is, I have to get you outside."

I don't normally curse, but, "Fuck you!" Give my arm a yank, trying to get out of his grasp. Slowly begin to panic. "Get off me!"

"Christ, could you keep your voice down? Calm down, we can discuss this outside."

"I'm not going outside with you alone!"

"Trust me, I'm not going to try anything." He ushers me through the stifling crowd, toward the door, despite my protests. "I'll keep my hands to myself and there will be plenty of witnesses. Promise."

Two minutes later, I find myself on the covered porch, door slamming closed behind us with a bang, this big, bronze, hulk of a guy blocking my re-entry.

He changes his stance, spreads his legs and crosses his arms, my traitorous eyes fall on the sinewy muscles. Tan, toned and, "Look, I'm sure you're a really nice girl, but you can't keep coming into our house and getting in everyone's business."

The way he says *nice girl* makes it sound anything *but*.

"It's not my fault those guys inside are drunken slobs and won't keep their hands off my friends. I'm not letting them sleep with any of them—gross. I don't care if they're baseball players. I'm the sober driver—it's my job to make sure everyone gets home okay."

He shrugs. "Not my problem."

"Well can I at least go back inside and tell my friends I've been kicked out?"

"Nope. I'm under strict orders not to let you back in."

"*Whose* strict orders?"

"Mine." He smirks and *god* is he cute. So cute I have to glance into the yard to stop myself from staring directly at his white smile, chiseled jaw and sparkling eyes.

"Please?" Jeez, now it sounds like I'm begging.

"Hell no."

My arms cross definitely. "I'm not leaving this porch until you let me back in."

"That's fine; have a seat on the stairs." He leans against the wooden siding on the house, next to the door. Removes his cell from the back pocket of his jeans, its screen illuminates his stupidly handsome face. "Be my guest."

I eyeball him. "You're really not going to let me back in?"

"Nope."

"What if I promise to leave your friends alone?" I cross my fingers behind my back, putting on my most complacent smile. See? I can be agreeable!

His head gives a slow shake. Tsks. "It's going to be a *really* long night if you keep doing that."

"Doing what?"

"*Begging* to get back inside."

"I'm not begging. I'm *asking*."

His eyes leave the screen of his phone, raking me up and down with a dismissive brow. "It's begging—I know what the difference is and it's annoying."

The skin on my neck feels hot, the telltale signs of a blush brightening my face with desperation. "If you don't let me back inside, I'm…I'm calling the cops!"

"Again, be my guest." He takes a loud, slurping sip of his beer. "Tell them Rowdy sent you."

I stomp my foot, frustrated. "Ugh! Why do you have to be so stubborn?"

"Because you're a nag?" He mumbles the word Jesus under his breath, and it's on the tip of my tongue to lecture him on using the Lords name in vain, but I bit the words back instead. For once.

"I-I…I'm sorry. I just…" feel helpless out here on the porch.

His eyes narrow as he studies me. "Bet you were one of those girls in high school that used to raise your hand during class to ask for extra credit."

My, "So?" slips out before I can stop it. What's wrong with raising your hand and asking for extra credit?

"So. No one liked those girls."

I flush again, loosing count of how many times I've turned bright red in the amount of time we're been standing here.

Fake a scoff. "And you were one of those dumb jocks that barely passed their classes and cheated off girls like *me*."

He spreads his arms, wing-span wide. "Yet here I am with a full ride to college. Imagine those odds."

JOCK ROW

Releasing Early 2018

Acknowledgements

I was sad to see this book end; I have a soft spot in my heart for Rhett, and couldn't get the love story inside these pages off my mind for days after closing the last chapter. I am a sucker for the underdog, which is why, in all three of these novels, there is a little something socially awkward about each and every one of my characters.

Not unlike myself.

Thank you for loving these characters as much as I do because of their "flaws."

Thank you to my family, for tolerating my long hours of writing, the lack of dinner, and my lack of organization; I'm sorry I always forget milk.

To my assistant, Christine Kuttnauer, for always being honest, sometimes brutally so—I never know it's needed until everything falls into place. Isn't amazing how much we've grown in the past year? *Incredible*.

My publicist, Danielle Sanchez, and my agent, Kimberly Brower—thank you for taking a chance on me. I look forward to seeing what the future holds.

It's not easy finding people who are honest with their feedback, but I couldn't be more grateful for my Beta Readers: Author Amy Daws, Author SJ Sawyer, Laurie Darter, and Laurie Pepperling. Because of your input (and seventeen pages of notes), Rhett and Laurel's story is stronger.

Megan Brinkman, Merci beaucoup pour le Francais translations. Did I get that right? Don't answer that—I don't want to know how bad I botched that on my own. E suis vraiment désolé.

Caitlyn Nelson (Editing by C Marie), please stop correcting these acknowledgments. I wanted to surprise you by doing the acknowledgment edits myself. How did I do? You're more than an editor, you're a magician. And to my proofreaders, Melinda Lazar and Ellie McLove—I had no hesitation turning this manuscript over to the formatter after you combed through it. For every misplaced comma, period, and overused word—thank you.

Who are the people who make the book beautiful, inside and out? Look no further than Sarah Hansen with Okay Creations, who nails it every damn time, and Julie Titus with JT Formatting for her attention to detail. Books should all be this gorgeous.

"My crew" at the Starbucks in Germantown, WI—you guys are awesome. I appreciate every time you've taken care of me, brought me my breakfast, gotten my water, brewed my latte, added extra ice, and let me put my feet up on your chairs. Rearranged your furniture to get comfortable, and pulled down the shades. YOU ARE THE BEST.

Lastly, I want to thank the one person who will never see this. Miss Alina, who I think about every single day and thank god for every night—I have no words to express what you meant to us. We love you still. www.owlsforowies.com.

S ara Ney is the USA Today Bestselling Author of the How to Date a Douchebag series, and is best known for her sexy, laugh-out-loud New Adult romances. Among her favorite vices, she includes: iced latte's, historical architecture and well-placed sarcasm. She lives colorfully, collects vintage books, art, loves flea markets, and fancies herself British.

For more information about Sara Ney and her books, visit:

Facebook
https://www.facebook.com/saraneyauthor/

Twitter
https://twitter.com/saraney

Website
http://www.authorsaraney.com/

Instagram
https://www.instagram.com/saraneyauthor/?hl=en

Facebook Reader Group: **Ney's Little Liars**
https://www.facebook.com/groups/1065756456778840/

Other Titles by Sara

The Kiss and Make Up Series

Kissing in Cars
He Kissed Me First
A Kiss Like This

#ThreeLittleLies Series

Things Liars Say
Things Liars Hide
Things Liars Fake

How to Date a Douchebag Series

The Studying Hours
The Failing Hours

With M.E. Carter

FriendTrip
FriendTrip: WeddedBliss (a FriendTrip novella)
Kissmas Eve

Made in the USA
Columbia, SC
13 September 2017